WAKING NOAH'S VINES

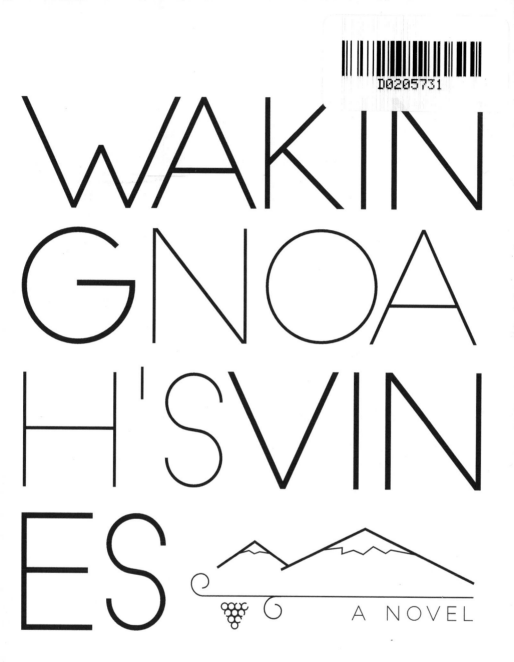

A NOVEL

VAHAN ZANOYAN

This book is a work of fiction. All names, organizations, events and places are the product of the author's imagination. Any resemblance of actual persons, places and events is coincidental.

Cover and Interior Design by: Sofya Khachatryan of OneArmenia
and Kerrie Robertson Illustration
Author photo by Charlotte Zanoyan.
Copyright© 2019 by Vahan Zanoyan

ISBN 13: 978-0-9983924-17
Library of Congress Control Number: 2019918939
gampr books

gampr
books

New Port Beach, CA

For Hera, Leda, Silva & Nora
Thanks for the earliest memories

Also by Vahan Zanoyan

A Place Far Away

The Doves of Ohanavank

The Sacred Sands

Drink the wine that moves you.
    —J. Rumi (1207-1273)

Then the ark rested in the seventh month, the seventeenth day of the month, on the mountains of Ararat.
—Genesis 8:4

And Noah began to be a man of the soil and planted a vineyard. He drank of the wine and became drunk, and lay uncovered in his tent.
—Genesis 9:20-21

WAKING NOAH'S VINES

A NOVEL

gampr
books

PROLOGUE

The first thing that Haig Koleyan noticed was the upper right central gold tooth and the matching heavy gold chain hanging over the pinkish, freckled, hairless chest of the Russian. The top three buttons of his black shirt were undone, and the tips of its wide, pointed collar swayed in the breeze like the flapping ears of a running puppy. He was a big man—six foot four, huge belly, abnormally large hands, clean shaven round head, small, brown eyes exuding a malevolent, mischievous smile.

"Finally, *ve* meet," he said extending a monstrous hand to Haig. "Honor to meet maker of famous Korah *vine*." The shining tooth flashed a bright ray at Haig, who somehow overcame his fear-infused revulsion and took the hand. To his surprise, it did not crush his fingers. The giant's handshake was soft and loose. "I decide to pick this order myself to meet the great *vine* maker Haig," continued the Russian. "I am Misha."

It was mid-afternoon, and the bright sunshine of the morning had already given in to the gathering clouds. The first few raindrops, although slow and reluctant as they started to hit the ground, augured the rain storm expected later in the day. Misha's driver stayed in the Mercedes SUV, while the local driver waited in the van parked behind them. The way they were parked, the two vehicles blocked the entrance to Haig's winery in the outskirts of Yerevan.

This was the encounter Haig had feared. The third order for Korah wine from the same heavily accented Russian caller in just a few weeks was for 75 cases, which he could not fill. There wasn't enough Korah in his warehouse. He scrambled among his distributers and retail outlets and gathered 30 cases, unleashing a barrage of angry protests, half in Russian and half in English, over the phone.

And now he was here, at his winery, the man he assumed was the person behind the voice over the telephone placing the orders, to pick up the 30 cases of Korah.

"Would you like to come in while they load the van?" asked Haig. There was no point in being overtly rude, now that the man was at his door. Misha smiled and nodded. He led him to the small reception area and immediately shut the internal door leading to the winery. There would be no tour, even if Misha asked for one.

"Load it fast," he told his warehouse manager.

"May I offer you a glass of water?" Haig turned his attention to Misha. "I'm afraid that's all we have here, aside from wine of course."

"No, thank you." Misha had occupied the better half of the black leather sofa. He looked vaguely disappointed as his eyes scanned the bare walls. There wasn't much to look at in the small reception room. Awkward moments of silence followed, as Misha shifted in his seat, as if trying to decide what to say next.

"May I ask what you do with all the Korah you buy?" asked Haig, genuinely curious.

"I buy for client. I am only buying agent. My client love *vine*."

"Can you tell me what he does?"

"Sorry. He very private man. He love *vine*." Misha's face turned stern. After a few moments of awkward silence, Misha added:

"Reason I come personally is *ve* disappointed this order not met fully. My client disappointed. I look bad *vhen* I not deliver."

"Our production of Korah is small," said Haig, resenting that he had to explain. "We can't always meet demand."

"I look bad *vhen* I not deliver," repeated Misha, as if stressing a point so a child could understand it better. Haig just stared at him, barely able to suppress and angry outburst.

"I *vant* to reserve part of this year's production. To be safe." Misha sat straight and leaned over to look directly at Haig.

"That won't be fair to our other clients." You will not intimidate me, he thought, even as his worst fears were being played out.

The warehouse manager rushed in to announce that the van was loaded.

"Not much," said Misha, dead serious, and stood up. "500 cases. We'll pick 50-100 cases at a time. As needed."

"I'll try," said Haig leading him outside. "I cannot promise, but I'll try."

Misha extended his hand again. "*Spasibo*. I appreciate. Glad *ve* not be disappointed again." He held Haig's hand for a moment while his stern gaze lingered on his eyes.

As they walked out, Misha's driver jumped out of the car and held the passenger door open for him. Then they drove away.

Sev Areni, Black Areni, Areni Noir: one of the oldest indigenous Armenian varieties, dating back more than 6,100 years. Widespread in the Vayots Dzor region. The tip of the young shoot is white gray. The mature leaf is medium, circular, and five lobed. The bunch is medium, conical, often winged, and dense. The berry is medium sized, ovate with a rounded top, and covered with a grayish-blue bloom. The skin is thick. The flesh is juicy and colorless. Its wine is a light- to medium-bodied red with a fresh and pleasant bouquet and intense color.

CHAPTER ONE

Early fall, 2013

Around 6 p.m. The Realm began to fill up, and both the noise levels and the scurrying of the wait staff escalated. Van Dorian finished his second cup of coffee and was about to take a sip of water when a woman in her early forties walked in and perched on a bar stool.

"I need a drink! I need love! God, how I need *love*! And Jack's sitting outside with a bunch of women!" she blurted, out of breath, barely able to stifle a slight sob as she uttered the last words.

"So, the usual, then?" asked the bartender with a chuckle, picking up a bottle of white wine from the cooler. "And a good evening to you too." Dorian had hired him four months earlier, largely because of his bartending demeanor—tranquil, relaxed, always smiling, often offering a friendly laugh to put a stressed and bothered patron at ease. He was in his mid-thirties, fit, with a short black beard and a crew cut. His signature look was a dark T-shirt with a light blue silk scarf wrapped around his neck, hanging down to his belt like a necktie.

"Yes, Arthur jan, the usual," she pouted. "And, by the way, it's not funny."

"Sorry I laughed, but you have to admit your entrance was quite dramatic."

Van Dorian studied the woman for a moment. She was flushed and agitated. She was conservatively dressed in a gray silk turtleneck and jeans; her long hair was tied in a ponytail. From her profile, which was all he could see, she looked pretty, with dark eyes, pleasantly arched eyebrows, and a cute nose. Arthur was about to pour her a glass of white wine, when Dorian put down his glass of water and stood up. Arthur noticed. It wasn't the first time that Dorian would intervene in a bar scene. Dorian made a barely noticeable gesture with his head for Arthur to join him in the kitchen.

"I'll be right back," he said, putting the bottle away and placing a bowl of peanuts and a glass of water in front of her. "I'll fetch a colder bottle from inside."

"Pour me a glass of what you have before you go," she demanded.

Arthur exhaled, poured her a glass of Voskehat, the most popular dry white wine grape variety in Armenia, and rushed to the kitchen.

"How well do you know her?" asked Dorian as soon as Arthur walked in.

"She's a family friend. I've known her since childhood. She's close to my older sister. Why?"

The Realm had outgrown its original kitchen, which was designed to handle fewer diners than it now served. Dorian stepped aside to get out of the way of the hectic movement of waiters carrying trays.

"She mentioned a Jack. Who's Jack?"

"Some guy she likes. As far as I know, nothing serious."

"What do you mean 'nothing serious'? Nothing serious is going on between them, or she doesn't like him seriously?"

Arthur thought for a few seconds. "Nothing serious is going on between them as far as I know. But I have no idea how seriously she likes him. Van, why does that matter?"

"The lady shouldn't drink white wine in the state she's in. Not Voskehat, not even a Montrachet, or any other type of Chardonnay or even a Sauvi."

Arthur gave him a puzzled look. "For as long as I've known her, she's only drunk white wine."

"Look," said Dorian, noting his hesitation, "she feels she's missing out. Missing out on chances, on life. She's getting older, and life's opportunities are passing her by. She suffers from a fear of the transient nature of life."

The baffled look on the young bartender's face drove Dorian to explain further. "This is a real thing," he insisted. "The Germans have a word for her condition: *Torschlusspanik*. It means, literally, 'Gate-closing-panic.' She feels opportunities are closing shut around her, and she panics. It makes her want to experience everything in life now, immediately, all at once. There's no time to lose; she'll be too old tomorrow. Voskehat is crisp, young and playful; it will only excite and agitate her and reinforce her angst. It just won't do."

"Then what?"

"She needs a calming, settled, mature red. What she needs right now, more than anything else, is *perspective*—a wine to meditate by, to reflect on life calmly. The VanDor Reserve would do. The Alma Areni Reserve would also do. Or a Coor red vintage 2010 or 2011. If she's into foreign wines, a full-bodied, mature Zin or a Petite Syrah would be fine, though not a recent vintage. Nothing playful. Offer her any one of those. If necessary, insist."

He returned to his small square wooden table sandwiched between the end of the bar and the kitchen door, and picked up the book he had left open, face down, at the corner. The yellow tassels hanging at either end of the brown runner draped over the table, embroidered with images of ripe pomegranates, swayed as a waiter passed. He was reading Samuel

Beckett's *Waiting for Godot*—driven to it some thirty years after he had first read it in college by his mounting obsession with 'disillusionment,' one of the more elusive human emotions which he found difficult to grasp in its depth and range of nuances. There were so many variations—disillusionment with love, with work, with friends, with a spouse, with country, with social justice—each different and complex in its own way.

Even though he had faith in the project, he hadn't imagined this level of success when he opened The Realm. It was the most popular wine bar in the city, and for good reason. Aside from a delightfully diverse wine list featuring wines from around the world, it boasted a rich menu of Intercontinental cuisine and a competent kitchen staff to back it up. Its stone and brick walls gave its spacious interior a rustic, cozy ambiance. Located half a block from the popular Cascade Square, lined with sculptures by Fernando Botero and Jaume Plensa, it was easily accessible to both tourists and the young professionals of the city. It was the first of the new generation of wine bars to open its doors fifteen years ago. Since then, over thirty trendy wine houses had come to life in Yerevan. They enlivened the nightlife and energized the sidewalks along Saryan and Isahakyan Streets. But The Realm was still viewed as the original classic.

A young waitress brought him a grilled vegetable salad and a glass of VanDor Reserve, an Areni and Syrah blend, from his own winery near Ashtarak. Now the place was in full swing, and Dorian's eyes wandered more frequently away from his book.

He finished Act I. The pace of the food service had picked up, with tray after tray being hauled out of the kitchen door next to his table, leaving in its trail the smell of risotto, mussels in Roquefort sauce, grilled octopus, boeuf bourguignon, French fries. At the beginning of Act II, he delved into Estragon's memory loss issues. The scene captured his imagination so much that he did not notice when a pot of steaming mussels arrived at another table, without a bowl for the shells. He realized the problem when the agitated patron complained that he had to ask for a bowl twice before it was finally brought.

He managed to read uninterrupted until Pozzo and Lucky returned to the stage, one having lost his eyesight and the other his hearing, when his concentration was broken again by a plate of risotto being served cold, or at least not hot enough—he could tell, because he did not notice any steam rising from the plate.

At the end of the evening, he'd spend time with the exhausted staff to carefully and patiently explain every detail that was not just right. For now, he was happy to notice that the lady at the bar had a glass of red wine in front of her. She was noticeably calmer. Arthur saw him looking and produced a bottle of Alma Areni reserve to top off her glass. Dorian gave him a barely noticeable nod of approval.

Around nine o'clock he finished the book. The place was now overflowing and noisy. Fortunately, customers preferred to sit at tables, not at the bar. The two dining sections, indoor with twenty tables and the outdoor section on the sidewalk with another twenty-five tables, were packed. The bar was usually empty, leaving Dorian in a small island of relative peace. The customers didn't like to have their backs to the room. After all, aside from the food and wine, the point of being at The Realm was to be seen and watch who else was there.

He started to make his rounds. He greeted old friends and longtime acquaintances. He was not in the habit of socializing with all the regulars at The Realm, even though the manager had often urged him to do just that. He was the owner and the founder, the philosopher and the intellectual force behind the institution, and he was not going to do the manager's job by schmoozing with the patrons.

In the outdoor section the tables and chairs were more rustic and rugged than those inside. It was early April, and the city was bursting with life after a long and harsh winter. It was still cold enough to turn on the outdoor heaters and to offer blankets, which were laid neatly over the backrests of the chairs. But the chill in the air had not stopped pedestrians from swarming Isahakyan Street and the entire Cascade Square. People were simply tired of being indoors.

The process of "making the rounds" at The Realm often reminded Dorian of his sleep pattern. Deep into the night, when all was supposed to be quiet, sounds filled his ears—a dense web of sounds, a mesh of unclear, indistinguishable noises—creating an overwhelming buzz in his brain. Then, out of nowhere, he could hear clear and distinct voices of people he knew—loud, pure, flawless, in clear focus compared to the amorphous web of voices, often full sentences, sometimes just words—they came suddenly like shooting stars and then quickly disappeared and died into the thick web of sounds.

He joined some old friends from Los Angeles at one table for a few minutes, unable to refuse their persistent requests for him to sit down; he heard their voices, then let them die in the web. The chemistry between him and them was different now, when he saw them again as tourists in Armenia, from when they all lived in LA. Some of his friends were still impressed by the "Armenianness" of Armenia—a Diaspora tourist's fascination with the hospitality, street signs, and street language in Yerevan. And they were quick to criticize the country's faults, whereas Dorian had started to take both qualities for granted soon after he settled here more than fifteen years ago. At each table, he scrutinized the wine people drank. Sapor was the most popular, basic, local red table wine. A blend of mostly Bordeaux grapes with a small percentage of indigenous Armenian grapes, it had become the default order.

He was cautiously gratified by the small but growing community of wine drinkers in the city who liked to experiment and who were eager to smell and taste what they were drinking. To focus on a wine's taste, deliberately and purposefully, was uncommon in this city a decade ago. But that was small progress compared to what Dorian would have liked to see. Why was it so difficult for people to choose the right wine for their emotional state? They cared about pairing wine with food, which, by comparison, was a simple exercise. As nourishment to the soul, wine spoke to one's essence, reached deep into one's psyche, and stirred up moods and emotions that would otherwise remain dormant. But the struggle was still at the basic level—to teach people to smell and taste what they were drinking, rather than gulp it down for the alcohol like they gulped down Russian vodka.

He returned to his seat and took a few bites of his salad, his eyes lingering on the book laying at the corner of the table.

Haig Koleyan was one of the few people who had tacit permission to join Van Dorian at his private table at The Realm. After all, he was a fellow vintner, pioneer, and dreamer. More important, he shared Dorian's passion for reviving the 6,000-year-old wine tradition of Armenia.

"It's almost ten o'clock, and I see an unfinished salad and an empty wine glass," said Haig as he joined him. "What's the problem this time, Van? This?" He picked up the book.

"I wish."

"I remember reading this years ago. Cultural Studies course at AUB. A thinner book than your usual, but kind of freaky."

"Yeah, well, I have to get to the bottom of this 'disillusionment' emotion. It is so rampant in this country."

"Why don't you read psychology books instead?"

"Art can explain what I'm after better than science."

"No wonder people mistake you for a crazy artist," said Haig and laughed.

"They do?"

"Sure they do. And it's not just because of your long hair, tall, skinny frame, collarless silk shirts and linen pants." As he rattled off the features, Haig's hand moved, pointing from Dorian's head to his feet. "It's because of the way you think."

"Well, the fact remains that one can reveal deeper truths through art—a poem, a painting, a story—than by gathering scientific facts. A clinical approach won't get to the essence of an emotion like this."

"And Beckett does?"

"This play has more interpretations than most other books I know. Religious, philosophical, psychoanalytical, war, hopelessness, you name it. But at the heart of it I sense a deep disillusionment that overwhelms the characters—disillusionment with their condition, with unfulfilled expectations, with each other, perhaps even with social justice, which is the nuance I'm most interested in."

The waitress approached. Haig ordered a bottle of VanDor and a plate of mushroom risotto.

"Would you like one too?" he asked. Dorian nodded.

"Make that two plates," he told the waitress.

"OK, if the book isn't the problem, then what?" asked Haig.

"We still have a long way to go with this wine culture thing."

Haig chuckled. "But you have to admit, we've come a long way."

"We have."

"I have news which may cheer you up," said Haig. It was not uncommon for him to resist getting sucked into Dorian's somber mood. "Do you remember the story I told you about Henry Cobb?"

Dorian nodded.

"I've been telling him about Armenia's potential as a wine-producing country. You know how he put Malbec and Argentina on the world wine map, right?"

"I do."

"Imagine what he could do here with our history and terroir."

"So what's the news that's supposed to cheer me up?"

"He's coming next week. He'll be in Europe and will stop by for a few days. We'll show him around. You never know; if what we know in our blood about the Armenian wine potential is true, maybe he'll get it too. In fact, I'm sure he will."

"Always the optimist," mumbled Dorian. "Good luck. Bring him around if there's time."

"I'll try."

"I heard you kicked out some young people last night," Haig said, changing the subject.

"They were here to get drunk and show off their wealth. Three spoiled brats, loud, disrespectful, laughing at their own vulgar jokes. They ordered two bottles of Korah at once. They had no appreciation whatsoever for the wine. They just knew it was expensive. If I had served them pomegranate juice mixed with rubbing alcohol, they wouldn't have known the difference."

"At least I'm glad someone's spending money on Korah," said Haig with a broad smile.

"Hate to disappoint you, but I refused to sell it to them."

"Why?"

"Just because they could afford it doesn't mean they deserved it. I told them if they wanted to get drunk to go somewhere else and drink vodka. Neither you nor I need clients like that."

"Van, I would have educated them instead of kicking them out. I would have given them a short, five-minute presentation on wine. Isn't that why we're here, after all?"

Maybe, he thought. At least that's part of why we're here.

He had risked everything he had worked for for twenty years in Los Angeles, left a successful practice as a CPA, sold everything he owned, and moved his young and growing family back to Armenia. All he had was a dream: he'd start a vineyard, produce quality wines, and open a wine bar where he could develop his theories about wine and human emotions.

"I didn't want my children and grandchildren to remember me as the man who took them out of their motherland and brought them to LA," he told a friend soon after they settled in Armenia. "From here, they can go anywhere in the world. For them, LA would have been a dead end."

"LA a dead end?" his friend had asked.

"For them, yes. We would have been entrenched in the Armenian community in the LA area, which could easily have turned into a dead end. Besides, their country was no longer part of the Soviet Union. It was independent. It made no sense to stay away. From here, they can explore the world—Europe, the Middle East, other former Soviet countries, and, if they want, they can return to LA. One always has more options if they start from a real home base rather than an adopted one."

But there was more to his being here, a lot more, just as there was a lot to every new vintner's return to Armenia in the last decade. Every case was an epic story. These were extraordinary people with a vision that covered more than love of wine. Their vision spanned history, culture, and the dream of returning to a homeland that had been out of reach for too long. It was a vision nurtured by a passion to uncover a lost tradition of winemaking, a drive akin to that of an archeologist determined to uncover and reconstruct a prehistoric civilization.

"I did not feel like educating this bunch," he said at last. "It would have been a useless exercise. We would have only managed to annoy each other."

Haig's boisterous belly laugh filled the room. "I grant you that," he said. "I just had a vision of you lecturing those kids about how Armenia should lead the global discourse on wine."

"You can laugh, but I risked everything I had for that vision."

Before Haig could respond, his sales manager, a young man in his mid-thirties named David who had moved to Armenia from Lebanon two years earlier, barged into the wine bar, pulled a chair and as he collapsed on it, blurted: "They called again. They want another fifty cases. Like, yesterday."

"Same guy who called last time?" asked Haig. David had not been at the winery when Misha had visited.

"I think so. Very rude. Started speaking Russian. I told him I didn't speak Russian. He got angry."

"Catch your breath," said Haig, pushing his untouched glass of water towards David. "How did he get angry? What did he do?"

"He yelled. '*Vhy* no speak Ruski?' he kept yelling while carrying on in Russian. I got mad too. 'This is not Moscow,' I said. 'This is Yerevan. Why no speak Armenian?'"

"Good for you," said Dorian, laughing, even though he had no idea what was going on.

"This is not funny," said Haig. A dark cloud had descended upon his eyes.

"OK, time you told me what this is all about," said Dorian.

"In a good year, we sell a total of five hundred cases of Korah in Russia. Around two months ago, someone from an obscure small wine shop demanded 70 cases. 'Urgent,' they said. Two weeks later, they wanted another 50 cases. A few weeks later came another 75 case order, which I could not fill. I gave them 30 cases instead. So in two months we have orders amounting to 40 percent of our entire annual sales? This is over and above the normal sales through the normal channels. Now they want another 50 cases?"

"But that's not necessarily bad, is it?"

"I was paid a visit from a nasty character a month ago, to complain that I could not meet his last order. A real cutie built like a guerilla. A thug anxious to see to it his wine orders were filled. What if it's a scam? What if they're using my Korah in some kind of wine fraud?"

"You think? How?"

"I don't know how, but we both know it happens. You remember the case when a couple of fraudsters were relabeling cheap French wine as exclusive Bordeaux and selling it for a fortune? If it's a scam, I'd bet anything the Russian mob is involved."

"Are we back to your Russophobia, Haig?"

"The guy on the phone sounded like a real thug," chimed in David, still agitated but calmer than when he first came in.

"No phobia. Just facts. The guy paid me an uninvited visit to threaten me. Now he chides David for not speaking Russian, as if this country is part of Russia. He demands 50 cases, as if it's his right, and yet he is rude and condescending, as if he's doing us a favor by buying our wine. I don't like it."

"Can't you track the shipments beyond the small wine shop, see where they eventually end up?"

"Very difficult to do. I don't have the resources for something like that."

"Don't you want to go to Moscow to investigate?"

"Who has the time for that? Or the patience? Besides, since we have no clue who we're dealing with, I want to keep a low profile in this. The less we tell the Russians the better. The less they know about how much I know or don't know, the better."

"So you'll just let it be. Not that that's a bad thing, by the way. Sometimes letting things be is good."

"When Isabelle heard about the first 70-case order, she wanted to go to Moscow right away and visit the wine shop. She's excited about investigating, but I wouldn't let her. She thinks she knows the Russians, but she's young and naïve like a clueless, overconfident lamb in a wolf's den."

"How do they pay?"

"Cash. Full retail price. There's been no bargaining. Their local driver comes with a pickup truck, loads, pays, and leaves."

"Maybe that's all that matters. You're not involved in any scam, even if they are."

"Yeah, but I'm being pushed around by the fucking Russian Mafia."

Voskehat, Golden Berry: a widespread variety in Armavir and Aragatsotn regions. The tip of the young shoot is greenish gray. The mature leaf is medium, circular and deeply five lobbed. The bunch is medium, short conical, winged by one or two lateral bunches, and very dense. The berry is medium, round, yellowish-white, or amber. The skin is thick and transparent. The flesh is juicy. Voskehat is also good for sparkling and fortified wines.

CHAPTER TWO

EARLY SUMMER, 2014

Isabelle Karayan couldn't make up her mind about requesting a leave of absence in order to enroll in a four-month course at Enotria, the famous wine school in Moscow. The main attraction of the course was the opportunity to meet one of the most revered wine authorities in the world, Professor Sandro Kashvili. While there, she could also investigate the spikes in demand for Korah, which had continued for over a year, even though Haig was opposed to her getting involved because he suspected that the Russian underground was involved. It would be exciting to uncover the mystery—especially if the Russian mob was involved.

But she wasn't sure how her boss, friend and mentor, Carla Almayan, the chief executive of Alma Wines, would take it. In her mid-thirties,

Carla was full of energy, charm, and charisma, and her passion for her winery was a legend in the city. She probably wouldn't take kindly to her leaving for four months.

So she was thrilled when Carla suggested that they take a day trip to Vayots Dzor to visit the vast Areni cave, where the oldest winery known to man was discovered a few years earlier.

"We'll leave late morning, get to Areni around one, in time for lunch, we'll check on some of the vineyards around Areni village which supply us, then we'll visit the cave." As usual, Carla had every detail planned.

It was past 2 p.m. when they arrived at the cave. It was an unusually hot, sunny, and breezeless day. It took a couple of minutes for Isabelle's eyes to adjust to the darkness, and a chill went through her body because the temperature inside the cave was some ten degrees lower than outside. Areni was not just one cave. It was a vast complex of interwoven caverns with a network of intricate narrow passageways leading to different chambers. The 6,100-year-old clay amphorae where the wine was made lay in neat rows along with clay basins where the grapes were crushed. They were surprisingly well preserved, and so were the chambers where human sacrifices were performed.

The history that Isabelle witnessed in the cave was exhilarating. Sharing the experience with Carla drew Isabelle closer to her with a force that was new to her. She stared at Carla, especially when their guide, an engaging young man called Armenak, was not looking. Carla smiled, but that didn't necessarily mean anything; to Isabelle's dismay, Carla had persistently shown that she knew where and how to draw the line to make sure she did not send any signal that could be construed as encouraging.

Yet here, as she walked in one of the dark passages that connected two caverns, as the cool air from the passageway roused the skin on her face, as the musky, acrid smell of millennia-old earth, bat and swallow droppings, and hundreds of swallows' nests that cluttered the rugged ceiling of the cave stirred her nostrils, and as the dark, porous walls of the passage came alive with sinister shadows created by the single light bulb hanging at its entrance, when the chilling question in her head was: *Who was here 6,000 years before us?* at that moment, Carla was not only more irresistible, but seemed more accessible than ever.

They walked through all the chambers that were open; a large number were not. They started at the entrance where the 5,000-year-old shoe was discovered, immaculately preserved leather with laces and packed with dried grass. They passed through the first main chamber inside, where the 6,100-year-old amphorae containing equally old grape seeds and stems lie in neat rows almost untouched by time, and the adjacent chambers where the sacrifices to the gods were made, and the space beyond, where no archeological shovel had yet struck the earth. Isabelle felt like she had just disembarked from a time machine. She could feel prehistoric activity surrounding her, with vague, gray, faceless forms scurrying around like ghosts, oblivious to their presence, focused on tending to whatever they were called upon to tend.

They left the cave with Isabelle feeling they'd had a communion of sorts, an eerie, yet elating connection with the past and a connection with each other, which she understood and interpreted differently than Carla. As they walked out, the bright sunlight almost blinded them. It was like returning to the present in that same time machine. It took her a while to find her bearings. They were covered with the fine, powdery dust of the cave. Their shoes, the hems of their pants, and up their legs to their knees had acquired the grayish-brown color of the dust. They stamped their feet, shaking part of the powder off, but much of it remained stubbornly imbedded. They laughed, as carefree as two children who'd soiled their clothes playing in a puddle.

They visited a few more vineyards and decided to spend that night at a country resort in Hermon, thirty minutes up the mountains from Areni. It boasted twenty-five individual chalets spread along a riverbank on the Yeghegis Valley in Vayots Dzor. It beat the 90-minute nighttime drive back to their apartments in the center of Yerevan. They took two rooms in one of the chalets, separated by a shared sitting area. Carla bid Isabelle good night and wanted to retire early. Isabelle went to her, arms open, hoping for a hug, or an embrace, or whatever warmth Carla was willing to allow. But Carla shook her head with a distant, forbidding half-smile, went to her room and shut the door. The old wine god would not answer Isabelle's prayers that night.

Isabelle went to her room barely able to hold back her tears. She lay on the bed for a long time, covered her face with her forearms, and tried to figure out whether it was the humiliating rejection that hurt her most or the embarrassment of her miscalculated move, which kept flashing in her head and, in retrospect, struck her as utterly inept and clumsy.

The next morning, in the large breakfast room of the resort, at a table by the wide window overlooking the swimming pool, as Carla took a sip of coffee while they waited for their omelets, Isabelle told her of her decision to enroll in the four-month course at Enotria school in Moscow.

FALL 2014

Isabelle could not take her eyes off the professor. He was a renowned wine superstar, fluent in several languages and, unlike the rest of the faculty, he was young, handsome, and confident. Legend had it he could name over a hundred different wines and their vintages from all over the world by his nose alone. He could have been a master sommelier if he had cared to take the exams.

But in his interviews he had often stressed how much he loved to teach. He knew every wine-producing region in the world and every grape variety. And if that weren't impressive enough, he knew the genetic ancestry of most grape varieties. Vines moved throughout history, he explained. The journey of the vine is the journey of peoples and civilizations. From the times of the Romans, of the Phoenicians, and earlier still, during the Babylonian era, both wine and vines traveled and, like people, adapted to new environments. Everyone at the school knew that if they wanted to find out where specific vines came from in the course of history, there was one authoritative source: Professor Sandro Kashvili.

He paused and scanned the classroom. His thick, black hair was combed straight back and his beard, by contrast, was light and meticulously trimmed. His black eyes were small but so piercing and focused that they commanded attention. He had loosened his dark blue tie and undone the top button of his white shirt, but he always kept his coat on when he lectured. He ran his fingers through his hair, combed the thick and unruly locks back, and scanned the room one more time. Isabelle willed him to take notice of her. She was sitting in the middle of the third row with no one on either side of her. She was wearing white pants and a bright red sweater, which should have made her easy to notice. But he was not looking in her direction.

It was not a large classroom, only around fifty students. The white desks, white chairs, and white walls reminded her of a hospital. Too clinical a setting for a discussion of wine, but Enotria was a wine school, not a wine bar.

After three lectures, it had become clear to her that history more than just mattered to Professor Kashvili. He was enamored by how old viticulture was. He loved the historical process of wine, the evolution of the tradition of viniculture interwoven with human history. He saw wine as an integral part of human lifestyles, traditions, cultures, and even religions as it evolved with man through history.

"As the recently discovered archeological finds tell us, wine was being produced not too far from here—in fact, exactly 2,335 kilometers away in a vast cave in Areni, Armenia—more than 6,000 years ago," he proclaimed. "Now, I want you to put aside all other thoughts for a moment and focus on that number. Can you fathom what 6,000 years is? Can you comprehend the distance that 6,000 years puts between them and us? I mean, the distance physically, culturally, spiritually, and religiously. Remember, that was 4,000 years before Christ.

"Who were these people? What did they look like? What language did they speak? How did they organize their life, their society? What god did they worship? We may never find out all the answers, but we do know something about that last question that I posed, what god did they worship?

"For them, the grape, saturated as it was with the sun, was divine. Several millennia later Galileo Galilei would say, 'wine is sunlight, held together by water.' These folks knew that some 5,500 years before Galileo. For them, grape juice was the blood of god. Drinking wine meant ingesting part of god, *becoming* part god. Then, 4,000 years later, Christianity would adopt the same concept and bring it into the practice of communion. 'This is my blood,' says Christ, passing a cup of wine to his disciples. But these folks went further. In their relentless quest for ways to bring man and god closer, they made human sacrifices, mixed human blood with divine blood, and drank the mixture. More than 6,000 years ago, wine was not just something you twirled, sniffed, tasted, and paired with food. It was a religion. It defined these people and their lives. It embodied the meaning of life. They had more faith in it than the vast majority of people today have faith in whatever god they choose to worship."

The scene sent a chill through Isabelle. She envisioned Kashvili as the all-knowing, all-powerful high priest—the tip of his long, pointed beard reached his waist, his black robes purposefully swayed with his movements, and his fiery eyes exuded such intense charisma and magnetism that his sacrificial subjects submitted their throats to him voluntarily.

She envisioned her high priest as he walked ceremoniously among the amphorae. His movement was smooth; with his feet covered by his long gown, he looked as if he was gliding. He looked nothing like the priests at church during Sunday mass—no colorful gowns, gold-laced garments, no clouds of incense to create mystique. All he needed was the power of his personal charisma. He dipped a dark brown clay cup into an urn and filled it with wine. She imagined some inscriptions on the cup with special religious meaning. She saw his lips move as he muttered incomprehensible words of prayer, more to himself than to anyone in the chamber. She saw him lift the cup of wine to his lips, then offer it to the young virgin about to be sacrificed, who gave him an intoxicated, distant glance.

Just as the girl swallowed the red nectar of the gods, he sliced her throat while several assistants held her up. Her blood gushed out and mixed with the wine, uniting the human and divine worlds and bonding man with nature, the earthly with the heavenly.

"But not all grape varieties have travelled," flowed Kashvili's lecture, bringing Isabelle out of her reverie. He had not yet noticed her. There had been no momentary eye contact either. Had he looked at other women in the class? "And, unfortunately, some old indigenous varieties have started to be neglected in their own countries, as the more popular European grapes make their commercial intrusion into old winemaking regions. There are some who take this argument to its extreme. They look at foreign varieties as a hostile assault. They make a case for 'authentic' versus 'inauthentic' wine, depending on whether the wine is produced from grape varieties indigenous to the country or not. Some are adamant about it. Others aren't."

Kashvili stopped and moved his gaze again from the right side of the classroom to the left, then from the back of the room to the front. For the briefest moment in that sweeping scan, his gaze met Isabelle's. It was at that precise moment that Isabelle's right arm went up. It was an involuntary reaction that both terrified her and sent her heart pounding with excitement.

"Please," she heard him say. "What's your name?"

"Isabelle, sir." She was relieved by the confidence in her voice. "And I have a question."

"Where are you from, Isabelle?" The question was not unusual given the multinational student body. There were at least a dozen different nationalities in the class, and Kashvili, given his interest in the various wine regions of the world, was curious about the country of origin of his students.

"Armenia," she replied and thought desperately of a question to ask.

"Ah, where that ancient winery sits intact in Areni. Have you seen it, Isabelle?"

He pronounced her name perfectly.

"Yes, I have," she said more proudly than she intended. She was aware that she was attracting the attention of her classmates. The students had been generally reserved, probably unsure how Kashvili would react to being interrupted by questions during his lecture. Almost all students at Enotria were from the former Soviet Union republics, where engaging a professor during his lecture was not commonplace.

"Perhaps you can share your impressions with the class one day. But now, please tell me, what's your question?"

"You said some are adamant about 'authentic wine' while others not so. How important is it to cultivate indigenous varieties? Is 'authentic wine' necessarily better than 'inauthentic wine?'"

"Ah, Isabelle, there you go with 'better' or 'worse' wines. I'll let you in on a little secret. It's a matter of personal taste. Yes, there are certain objective criteria: fruit, acidity, tannin, balance and so on. But even those tend to be personal preferences. Basically, if a wine does not taste like vinegar and if it can safely be classified as wine, its quality is in the palate of the drinker."

Could he see the disappointment on her face? That was not the answer Van Dorian would have given. Nor Haig. She had expected him to take her question more seriously.

Then she noticed some of the students turn and stare at her, a few with sarcastic sneers. Competition among classmates. Ridicule the one who tried to sound smart. Competition among women, too. Were all the women in the class trying to get his attention? And just as her embarrassment was beginning to turn into anger, he came to her rescue.

"But you put your finger on a critical issue," he said in all seriousness as he focused his gaze on her for a few seconds. "How important is it really to protect old indigenous grape varieties? I think it is extremely important, because those old indigenous varieties are a part of us, part of our history and culture. Their future should not depend on the superficial, whimsical, commercially nurtured taste of today's supposedly sophisticated wine drinkers."

Then his list of endangered grape varieties bombarded her unabated. There was no way to remember every name that he brought up. She barely kept up with him, taking frantic notes, unsure of the spelling of most of the names he was rattling off. She swore she'd learn and remember every grape variety in every country in the world.

He had a stack of pages scattered over the table, but he had not referred to them even once. Her gaze fell on Kashvili longingly. This degree of command of a subject was intoxicating, sexy, arousing, and it drove her to distraction.

Isabelle walked into the 'I Like Wine' wine bar on Pokrovka street around eight o'clock, just as she had done the previous two nights. Having asked a question in class, she felt an introduction of sorts had been made and hoped she'd find him there this time. "He loves that place," the young administrative assistant at the registrar's office who she had befriended when she registered at Enotria had told her when Isabelle had asked if she knew the Professor. "We run into him there all the time, often sitting alone, sipping and reading."

It took her a few minutes to find him, as the place was large and spread out. His choice of table was fitting. It was in the rustic section of the bar with exposed brick-and-stone interior walls and large oval lamps. He wore a plaid cashmere coat with an antique-yellow and green scarf wrapped around his neck and tucked inside his white shirt. A stack of papers lay neglected on the table. His eyes were intense and focused as he watched a waiter open a bottle of wine and pour him a few sips to taste. Isabelle watched, absorbed in Kashvili's graceful enactment of the tasting process—holding the glass between thumb and forefinger at the base of the stem, studying the color of the wine at various angles, deliberately and slowly sniffing first without twirling the wine, in order to capture the accumulated vapors in the glass, then twirling to release more of the aroma and smelling again, then taking a sip and chewing it, swishing back and front in the mouth, inhaling with the mouth open while the wine was still lingering on his tongue, and finally swallowing. Kashvili turned the process into an art form. He was to wine tasting what Mikhail Baryshnikov was to ballet.

She watched him for a few more minutes and took a deep breath. After two more deep breaths she walked to him.

"Good evening, Professor Kashvili."

He did not seem to recognize her—he looked confused, as much as surprised.

"Isabelle, from Enotria."

"Ah, Isabelle. Yes. What a surprise. Would you care to sit for a few minutes?" He stood up and drew her chair.

"I don't want to interrupt anything," she said pointing at the papers on the table, but took a seat.

"Don't worry about that. I was looking for a good excuse not to read them." Then, turning to the glass of wine in his hand, he said: "This is more interesting. It is a Goruli Mtsvane." She noted the pale, straw-yellow color with greenish hues. "It's a rare variety from south central Georgia. It's best if made in a *kvevri*, a clay amphora, which brings out its aromas of plums, lime, citrus, and nuts. Some detect wildflowers in it, but I don't. Let me know what you think."

He poured her a glass. She got straight to business, and without uttering a word, took the glass, smelled deeply, took a small sip, swirled it in her mouth, moved her eyes from the glass to him and finally swallowed.

"There's a faint hint of wildflowers," she said at last, "but only in the finish. It reminds me a bit of the wild jasmines that used to appear in our garden every spring. But the plum and lime dominate, no question about it. What I like most about it is its crisp, clean palate."

She put down her glass while staring straight into his eyes. Kashvili met her gaze, then his eyes moved from her eyes to her hair, to her red lipstick, and down to her white silk shirt and brown cardigan. He scanned her like he scanned the classroom.

As Kashvili's eyes returned to the wine glass, she noticed the red smear on the rim. The lipstick had been a major mistake. Who wore lipstick when she knew she'd be tasting wine? She knew the drill at professional wine tastings: no perfume, no scented soap or detergent, no mouthwash, no hot peppers or hot sauce, and for the true fanatics, no coffee, salt, sugar, or anything that could dull or confuse the two most critical senses, taste and smell. The only sensory input should be from the wine. She had managed to give up most of the items on that list except the occasional coffee, even when she wasn't tasting wine, because they did dull the senses when used regularly; but on an evening out in town, the urge for a little mascara and lipstick remained.

He took another sip, taking his time as before. At the end, he conceded, "Yes, I do get the wildflowers in the finish. Very good, Isabelle. I hope my taste buds don't get dull with age. Now, tell me, what's your ambition?"

Her ambition about what? Him? He scrutinized her face and waited. She knew what he was seeing—lily-white face, pitch-black eyes, crimson lips—but what was he feeling about what he saw?

"Professionally, it is to become the best winemaker in the entire region and eventually the world. And to know as much about grapes and wines as you do."

"And what's your story? How will you realize that?"

"Well, I've attended the Yerevan Wine Academy and lived in Germany for a few years..."

"Germany? What were you doing in Germany?"

"It's a long story. I was young, only fifteen. I graduated from high school in Germany. But I'm sure that does not interest you."

"It interests me. But most of all, I want to know what you were running from."

"Running from?"

"How many fifteen-year-olds do you know from Armenia who decide to pack up and go to Germany at fifteen and actually pull it off?"

"As I said, that is a long story, and honestly, it has nothing to do with wine."

"But it has to do with you." His eyes were trained on her like an unwelcome camera. She had so much she could have been running from.

Her mind went back home to her supportive mother, whom she adored, who had always shown boundless confidence in her and nurtured her adventurous spirit, and to her father, whom she despised for his alcoholism, selfishness, and the way he treated her mother. The image of her controlling paternal grandmother flashed in front of her eyes. She lived with them and ran their lives. Her mother had confided in her once about how grandma never allowed her relationship with her husband to flourish, to mature. She used to run away to stay with her maternal grandparents.

Had she been running the whole time?

"Why do you assume I ran from anything?" she asked. "Couldn't I have done it for adventure? Or ambition, as you'd probably put it?"

"A fully content person rarely seeks adventure or fosters ambitions. The lure of a new world is always enhanced by discontent with what we have. Don't you think?"

Isabelle had not thought about her life that way. For as long as she could remember, her quest for new experiences and for learning had been a constant, an integral part of who she was. Defending her personal freedom at any cost was paramount. There had been no point analyzing it.

"I believe there's always more than one reason that motivates us to do what we do," she said. "But regardless, can we dwell on wine instead?"

He smiled warmly. "Very well, Isabelle," he said gently. "I'll drop the personal part for now. But what got you interested in wine in the first place?"

She'd been waitressing at a Moroccan restaurant in London one summer when the CEO of a major US-based multinational corporation and his guest appeared at her table. They'd ordered some type of Moroccan white fish with a side of beautifully stacked and butter-soaked asparagus. The chef had told her to recommend a Chablis. By the time she got to the part of the story where they'd ordered a £500 bottle, Kashvili had interrupted her twice—first to express his surprise that she had been to the UK in addition to Germany, and second to ask why she'd been waitressing.

"Anyway," she said, having smiled at but otherwise ignored both interruptions, "they were absorbed in discussing a business deal. They barely ate half their food, and when they left, there were two good glasses of wine left in the bottle. That just doesn't happen. They must have been satisfied with their meeting because they also left a £60 tip."

She paused for a minute, wondering if she was boring him.

"Please go on," he said, as if he had read her mind.

"Well, I kept the bottle until my shift ended and took it to my small room at the International Students' House. Also, I bought an expensive piece of cheese and a baguette on my way home. I poured the wine into a water glass. I couldn't afford fancy stemware, and besides, back then I didn't know the difference. All I knew was that the bottle cost three times my monthly salary, so I had to try it. I raised my glass and toasted the American. I remember even toasting to the success of whatever deal they had struck at our restaurant. That ritual is an Armenian thing, by the way. We can't just drink without raising our glass to something, even when we're alone. When the wine first touched my tongue, I became an instant believer. I decided at that moment that in addition to my academic interests, I would pursue the intellectual, culinary and—why not?—sensual pursuits of the oenophile." She knew her smile had an effect on him because he blinked compulsively.

"So, a sip of Chablis," he said. "One expensive sip of Chablis did it for you."

"Yup. Love at first sip."

Would he even have known she was his student had she not raised her hand? She knew nothing about the man, other than his qualifications in his profession, which, having read everything published about him, as well as most of his academic papers and interviews, she knew better than most. Her comprehensive knowledge of his professional life had given her a sense of familiarity with him, which belied the fact that she knew nothing about his personal life. She did not even know if he were married.

"Then what?" he asked.

"Then, when I returned to Yerevan, I worked at Vinoma Consulting for a while, and then I did another year at Alma Wines..."

"Vinoma Consulting? With Haig Koleyan?"

"Do you know him?"

"Of course. Well, I know *of* him. He's a big name. Many believe he kick-started the new wine era in Armenia."

"There are some winemakers in Armenia who would disagree with that claim."

"Why did you leave to go to Alma Wines?"

"There were both personal and professional reasons. The main professional reason was that I wasn't involved in making wine. Haig had me do the administrative stuff: keeping books, making payments, procurement, etc. I want to be a winemaker. It didn't look like I'd do that at Vinoma."

"And at Alma? Did you get into winemaking there?"

"A little more than at Vinoma, but still not enough. That's when I realized I needed to be better qualified, hence the enrollment at Enotria, under the tutelage of the renowned Professor Sandro Kashvili." At this point, Isabelle still knew what she was doing—the crimson lips and black eyes flashed a synchronized smile, aimed with deadly precision at Kashvili's eyes. He blinked again.

She had drunk far too fast—three glasses of wine in the first thirty minutes. Though she knew better, meeting the revered Professor Kashvili in a wine bar alone had gotten the best of her nerves. Now crouched over her kitchen counter, desperately trying to drown her hangover in a large cup of black coffee, she couldn't even remember which of them had brought up the subject of the Russian wine tycoon.

They had finished the bottle of Goruli Mtsvane and moved on to a second bottle, and then a third and, she was fairly sure, fourth. The second had been an Alma Areni Reserve from Carla Almayan's winery, and the third a Russian Muscat Noir. She could not remember what the fourth was. They had discussed the Alma Areni in some detail—how the earthy aroma of the wine reflected the terroir where the grapes were grown, the balanced tannic make-up, and the overall harmony of the various flavors and aromas. He had talked at length about the various gradations in both the Areni grape and the wines.

She had enjoyed that discussion. It was like being in a private wine tasting class. She couldn't remember much of their discussion about the Russian Muscat Noir, except for a brief comparison with the Alma Areni Reserve, and how Muscat lacked some of the complexity of the Areni. They had also gone through a plate of charcuterie and a few appetizers. With the white wine, they had had the cheese mousse with salmon and iceberg lettuce salad. She remembered talking about how well the various flavors had fused with the dressing, and how well it paired with the Goruli Mtsvane. Then, when they had moved to Areni, he had ordered the beef tartare with potato cream and mushrooms. Although she was wary of eating raw meat, she had tried it and had been impressed by the freshness and the harmony of flavors.

Somewhere interspersed with the wine talk, possibly around midnight, Ludwig's name had popped up. He could have brought up the company's name—maybe something to the effect that one of the founding partners of Ludwig, the largest wine merchant company in Russia, was Sergei Petyan, an Armenian. She remembered his saying that now there was only one active partner—that two-and-a-half years earlier, Petyan's partner had been murdered in cold blood, shot in his car in the center of Moscow in broad daylight. The event had sent shockwaves through the community of wine merchants in Moscow, but the murder was never solved. The partner's widow inherited his shares in Ludwig, but Mrs. Stella was a silent partner and delegated the regular monitoring of her interests to a high-powered Russian attorney named Dmitri Markov. That detail seemed to matter to Kashvili, because she remembered his repeating it more than once.

She remembered their discussion about how strange it was that most large wine merchant companies in Russia, even the largest one, were started and owned by Armenians. She remembered their discussion that both making and trading in wine were engrained deep in Armenian history back to several centuries before Christ and that the historian Herodotus had described the wine trade between ancient Armenia and the Babylonian Empire in detail. So he could have brought up the name of Ludwig in that context.

The only interest she herself had in the wine merchant was the possibility of a clue to solving the mystery of the surges in Korah sales. Sometime after their discussion of wine merchants, he had picked up his phone and, although it was late, called Sergei Petyan, and explained that one of his excellent students had expressed an interest in meeting him. She also remembered how, after he mentioned her first name, he had hesitated for a minute and then cupped the phone with his palm and asked her what her last name was.

"Karayan," she answered.

Kashvili repeated her full name again into the phone. She recalled his telling her that Petyan liked to be called Mr. Sergei, not Mr. Petyan. For some reason, that remark stayed with her.

Her daring seductive moves of the early evening had all but fizzled and disappeared toward the end. Isabelle knew that she was different from most people; alcohol did not always reduce her inhibitions. Quite the contrary, after a certain level of intoxication, as she started feeling her control over the situation dwindle, her defensive instincts forced her to put on the brakes. It was not a deliberate, conscious act. It was an instinctive reflex of sorts that made her more withdrawn. By the fourth bottle her demeanor had changed from a daring, outgoing flirt, to a reserved and guarded companion.

Till the end, through her swinging moods, Kashvili had been the perfect gentleman. He had stopped a cab for her, opened the door, and waited until she gave the driver her address. Then to be absolutely certain, he had leaned over the driver's window and made sure he understood the address and knew how to get there. She had watched him as the cab pulled away from the curb and wondered what he thought of her. Her head was buzzing, and the moving traffic, light though it was at that hour, had made her dizzy and nauseous. She had closed her eyes.

But amid all the questions that kept piling up in her mind about the night, one thing was clear: she had an appointment with Mr. Sergei Petyan, the founding partner of Ludwig, at four in the afternoon on Thursday, two days after the wine bar meeting. That much she was certain of, because the date, time, and address were written in Kashvili's handwriting on a cocktail napkin and stuck in her purse.

Karmrahyut, Red-Juiced: a hybrid variety cultivated in the Armenian Scientific Research Institute of Viticulture and Winemaking in the mid-1970s. The tip of the young shoot is light green and bare, with red edges. The mature leaf is medium, round, and five lobbed. The bunch is medium to large, conical, and mostly dense. The berry is medium, roundish, and black. The skin is thick. The flesh is pulpy and juicy. The juice is red. The wine is a strong and velvety red.

CHAPTER THREE

When Isabelle walked into Kashvili's classroom she didn't look at the podium. She kept her head low and walked straight to her seat. Would he judge her harshly for last night? Even while he was acting as a perfect gentleman, was he being fatherly and protective or disdainful?

Kashvili entered the classroom in a black coat, a white shirt, and a red bow tie. His expressive eyes focused on everything within his line of vision.

"Who has been to any part of the California wine country?" he asked, facing the class, his notes discarded on the table. The lighting seemed brighter than usual, forming a halo above his head. "Any part of Northern or Central California at all?" He raised both arms as if trying to coax a response.

Several hands were up as he perused the room and paused briefly on Isabelle, sitting in the same seat as yesterday. Had she done that for easy detection? Not consciously, but probably. But the more worrying question was, had she told him about her trip to six small but exquisite wineries in Fair Play and Placerville? Not that the trip per se had anything sensitive about it, but she had made it with Haig, and she may have talked more about Haig and the Korah Areni Noir than Haig would have approved. What was it with Haig and his paranoid mistrust of Russians anyway?

Kashvili's gaze rested on her for another split second, but she did not raise her hand.

"Only six," he declared at last. "Too bad. You know how much I value the ancient wine world. But it is equally important to know where we are today. To understand the modern wine world, one has to visit California."

The lecture, augmented by a slide show, was touring the Santa Ynez Valley, some 370 miles south of Fair Play. He had chosen to walk the class through some of the stops depicted in the movie *Sideways*, which made Pinot Noir famous not only in California, but also around the world. He described the characteristics of the land's properties in and around Santa Maria where the Foxen and Kenneth Volk wineries were located. He then took them on a tour of various vineyards in Los Olivos and explained that these were much closer to the Burgundy-style Pinots than the heavier, bigger, Pinots of the Russian River valley in Sonoma.

Then in what seemed an abrupt shift, Kashvili said, "Who tells you which wine is good, bad, complex, deep, balanced, lacking structure, weak?" He paced with his right arm raised, as if declaring war. "Who articulates for you what you're supposed to be tasting when you taste wine? Sadly, a significant part of the demand for wine today is guided and directed by the pundits. The glitter of a light perspiration on his forehead reinforced the halo effect of the light pouring down from the ceiling above the podium. He brushed back a strand of hair that had fallen on his face, then using both hands, he pushed all his thick hair back into place.

The red bow tie gave him a half-aristocratic, half-comical look. It couldn't keep its horizontal position through his animated movements and had tilted to the left. Isabelle felt a momentary urge to walk up to him and straighten it.

"Don't misunderstand me," he continued. "Wine has been discussed as early as it has been made. How could it be otherwise, given the importance it had in people's lives? But it's only in the past few decades that it has been commercially rated, influencing not only a large number of wine drinkers' perceptions, but, apparently, also conditioning their taste buds.

"The modern-day numerical rating system of something as subjective as taste and smell and complexity started primarily in the US, possibly initially as a well-intended guide to the American masses who were beginning to discover the virtues of wine but were overwhelmed by the diversity and staggering number of choices that the world offered them. But the power of a credible rating became instantly apparent in the marketplace. Prices of highly rated wines went up. And commerce followed. Money smelled an opportunity to multiply and grabbed it."

Was he talking about fraud? Could this have any relevance for her in figuring out the Korah issue? Haig had always suspected some foul play. She had a burning desire to ask the question, but she did not want to raise her hand again. No one else had asked a question except her.

"And where's there's money, there's corruption," continued Kashvili, as if responding to her thoughts. "And a lot more than the rating system has been corrupted in the modern wine industry. Fraud in wine production is, well, I wouldn't say rampant, but certainly not uncommon. And in wine trade, probably even more. But that's the topic of another lecture."

She wished she had raised this issue with Kashvili the night before.

Thirteen months earlier.

Fall in Northern California was spectacular. To break the six-and-a-half-hour drive from LA to Fair Play, they spent one night in Visalia, a quaint town around mid-way. Early the next morning, they headed for Fair Play. The drive was uneventful, but once off the freeway, the scenery got a new life. The drive to Lucinda's Country Inn was a delight, with the road winding through thick pine forests and a landscape painted in the enchanting colors of fall. The occasional screech of a hawk filled the air as the narrow, curvy road came alive with the light-and-shadow play created by the afternoon sunrays that seeped through the pine trees.

"We'll focus on the small, boutique vineyards," Haig had told her near the end of their flight to Los Angeles, to which they'd traveled from Yerevan via Moscow. "They're much closer to what we have in Armenia. Unlike the big names in Napa and Sonoma, they're still competing for recognition, just as we are. Let's go see how they do it."

They checked in and went to have lunch at the Gold Vine Grill, a few minutes' ride from the inn up Mt. Aukum Road. The décor of both the inn and the restaurant—with displays of wine and wine posters—proclaimed that they catered largely to wine tasters.

"This place claims to have planted the first Syrah grapes in the US back in the early '70s," said Haig, pushing one of the many brochures that he had collected on California wine regions on the table toward Isabelle. It was opened to the page on the Eberle Winery in Paso Robles. "The '70s. They obviously mean the 1970s, not the 1870s or 1770s. Can you imagine how new this place is? And back home we measure time in millennia."

The first winery they visited after lunch was the Windwalker. It was a beautiful estate with an equally beautiful tasting room. The place was packed with signs celebrating the virtues of drinking wine. *Around here, we drink wine only on days that end with Y*, declared one sign. *Sometimes I drink a glass of water just to surprise my liver*, boasted another. The owner, a charming lady full of energy, was scurrying around attending to club members.

Haig waved his hand around the tasting room, buzzing with life and laughter, many club members hauling cases of wine to their cars, and a cheerful staff barely keeping up with the constant flow of tasters. The staff was friendly, talkative, eager to explain, and they even accommodated the patrons' wishes for a second tasting of specific wines.

"This is what we want to create," he said.

Isabelle remembered how difficult it had been to train the waitresses at The Realm to smile and be friendly to patrons they did not know. Smiling to a stranger was considered unbecoming for a young woman. Being friendly to a stranger, even while serving him, was undignified. That culture was already changing, but they were still a long way from the cheerful and welcoming demeanor of California girls.

"Don't listen to any of the wine jabber," said Haig. "Just taste the wine. Listen only to the wine." He and Van Dorian have been hammering that message for years.

"We'll learn the wine-jabber to sell wine," chimed in Isabelle, "but we won't listen to it when we buy it." She had heard the lecture many times; the best way to end it was to finish it herself.

They tasted some of the established varietals: Syrah, Zinfandel, and Barbera. Then the man behind the bar serving them brought out two bottles. One was called *Starry Night*, the other *Shady Lady*. These two were a notch above the rest in terms of smoothness and character. So was their price. *Starry Night* was a blend of Zinfandel, Petite Sirah, and Mourvedre. It had a velvety, inky feel, with strong vanilla and peach on the palate. Haig found it exceptional. Isabelle loved both but was taken by the *Starry Night*.

"This is 100 percent Primitivo," explained the man, proudly straightening his back. He looked sixtyish, clean shaven, with graying hair. He was wearing a purple T-shirt with the Windwalker logo on it. They mistakenly assumed he was the vintner. "Basically, Zin," he added. "This lady, shady or not, is our pride and joy."

Haig swirled his glass, sniffed, took a sip, swooshed it in his mouth and swallowed. This was too good to spit. He looked at the man and nodded his definite approval. "Do you know that the *Vitis Vinifera* species, to which the Primitivo belongs, was domesticated in the Caucasus about 8,000 years ago, 6,000 years before Christ?" asked Haig.

The man looked at Haig for a few seconds.

"You don't say!" he exclaimed. "Six thousand years before Christ!"

"Yep. The Vinifera was domesticated in what is today Georgia and Armenia, and then it eventually spread from today's Armenia through the Mediterranean into the rest of the world. But Croatia was home to several Zinfandel varieties, and so the Zin is thought to be indigenous to Croatia."

"When did it finally make it to the US?" asked the man.

"Oh, that didn't happen until the late 1820s," said Haig promptly. "It was introduced to the East Coast first, Boston, if I'm not mistaken. The Austrian Imperial Nursery is credited for having brought it over, but it is believed that the Zin vines that they brought were of Croatian stock. Croatia was part of the Austro-Hungarian Empire at the time."

"Are you a professor or somethin'?"

"Not even close." Haig laughed.

"I detect an accent. Where are you from?"

"That's a long story," said Haig so quickly that it was clear he had heard and answered that question far too many times in his life. "I've spent fifteen years in Italy. Maybe that's what you detect."

"The Shady Lady is delightful," said Isabelle. It wasn't often that she brought a conversation that Haig was having to an abrupt end, but she didn't like where the dialogue with the man behind the bar was going. "Can we please have a bottle?"

They bought two bottles of the Shady Lady and two bottles of the Starry Night and left.

"Do you realize that you were annoying that guy?" asked Isabelle jokingly when they drove out of the winery.

"I felt some irritation in his voice, but frankly I don't know why."

"I think he felt you were lecturing him. That's why he asked if you were a professor."

"So what if I was lecturing?"

"He's used to tourists and wine enthusiasts. For years, he's been the one explaining wine to the visitors to his bar. I don't think he appreciated you giving him a lecture."

"How did you become so observant all of a sudden?"

"Hey," said Isabelle and laughed out loud. "I wish I could be observant when I'm in the scene myself. I sense these things only when I'm watching from the sidelines. The tension was making me uncomfortable, but now that we're out of there, I think the whole thing was kind of funny."

"I bet I taught him a thing or two," said Haig with a chuckle.

"Sure you did, I also think he asked you that question about when the Zin made it to the US hoping that you'd not know the answer. And then you go ahead and rattle off the details like a walking encyclopedia! That was priceless."

On the way back to the inn, they stopped at the only store in the area, Holiday Market on Mt. Aukum Road, and bought a whole roasted chicken and some fresh vegetables. They gathered in Haig's room, where he carved the chicken, and Isabelle washed and cut the vegetables: tomatoes, cucumbers, lettuce, and green peppers. They opened a Shady Lady, filled their plates, and sat in the huge armchairs with their plates on their laps.

"Did you check that tasting room?" he asked, in work mode.

They were on this tour to learn. He wanted to launch the Food and Wine Society next fall and had it fully up and running by the following spring before the onslaught of the tourist season.

There was a lot to learn if she was going to meet Haig's perfectionist standards. He wanted the inaugural event of the society to top the best in the world. Several wineries had agreed to participate, but not all, and not yet Alma. She felt she had failed both Haig and Carla for not being able to mend the rift between them. She was the only one who stood a chance, being so close to both. They were both self-centered and stubborn advocates of excellence in everything they did.

And they couldn't stand each other.

Haig was critical of some of the grape variety choices made at Alma, which infuriated Carla. When Alma launched the Karmrahyut Rosé, a popular wine with a distinctively shaped and attractive bottle, it did not meet Haig's approval. Karmrahyut was a hybrid grape developed in Soviet times with the rare quality of having red rather than colorless juice.

"Karmrahyut" meant 'red-juiced' in Armenian. For Alma wines, it was a special variety, which was good both alone and in a blend and the market rewarded Alma by a surge in demand for the rosé.

But Haig did not consider Karmrahyut a worthwhile grape variety in general and deemed it especially unsuitable for rosé wine.

"I don't care for it," Haig had told his wine maker, Armen, with whom he had worked first in Lebanon, then many years in Tuscany, before he moved to Armenia with him. "It may be elitist on my part, and I know the wines seem to be popular, but so is pomegranate wine. Big deal. Popularity of the wine doesn't absolve the grape. As much as it being a hybrid, what bothers me is that it's a creation of the Soviet times. A waste of land. It's not a noble wine grape. Who in their right mind would want to perpetuate something from the days when Moscow ran this country?" Armen would nod sympathetically, but the issue that animated Haig did not seem to matter much to him.

For Haig, the grape mattered, but he was not fanatic about the use of indigenous varieties. His Vinoma Consulting advised several winemakers that imported many Bordeaux and other typical European vines. One such winery was Sapor, which blended a number of classic Bordeaux varieties and Khindeghni, which was the only Armenian variety in the mix, a grape indigenous to Karabagh. Haig had helped them start, and Sapor became one of the first post-Soviet wines produced in Armenia to enjoy widespread popularity both at home and internationally. Moderately priced at around $10 per bottle, it became the obvious wine of choice at wine bars, most restaurants, receptions, and parties in Yerevan.

But Sapor, and by association Vinoma Consulting and Haig personally, came under criticism for importing foreign varieties. Some even criticized Sapor for having brought in diseases along with the vines. The accusations were often harsh and added to the existing acrimony among the wineries.

"They were close to the president of the republic at the time," Carla told as many people in the wine producing community as she knew. "That's how they secured the import license, which, technically, was illegal. God knows what types of louse and fungus have come in with their vines, even phylloxera. It won't affect them, of course, because what they brought in has the phylloxera-resistant American rootstock. But it will affect much of the rest of the country, and possibly the region."

Success of the Food and Wine Society gala dinner was as strong an incentive as any for Isabelle to try to patch things up between Carla and Haig.

"Too bad we don't have Zinfandel in Armenia," said Haig, savoring the wine. "We should probably try to introduce it. It's a Vinifera, after all, and we domesticated the species when God was a baby! It'll be like repatriating a member of the species, just like I was." His belly laugh filled the room.

At that moment, through her tired, jet lagged eyes, Haig appeared as a larger than life figure. There seemed to be nothing that Haig didn't know about wine, from its history to the minute technical details of how it was made. The confidence that such knowledge brought had seduced her once. Even though she herself had done a fair amount of traveling, the different worlds in which Haig had worked were exotic—from the vineyards of the Bekaa valley in Lebanon to Tuscany, to the wine markets of Europe and Asia. She wanted to own all that. Their brief affair over two years ago had been relegated to memory, but at times like this the fire of his passion got the better of her. She looked at him longingly, wanting his strength, his passion, his seemingly infinite confidence. She wanted to cradle his head on her chest, aware that everything she adored about him resided in that skull. She found herself licking her lips and a tingling in her skin made her crave his intimacy and his warmth.

But she resisted the temptation to go to him. Claiming fatigue and jet lag, she left for her room. He gave her a quick peck on the cheek and wished her goodnight.

The next day brought new and more difficult challenges. Around noon they arrived at a winery in Fair Play called Mastroserio in the center of the local wine region. They had packed a few sandwiches for lunch. Isabelle had done her homework. She'd read about the owner, an Italian called Ruggero Mastroserio, a textbook Renaissance man with competencies spanning engineering, geology, music, finance, and of course, enology. She'd read about how he took pride in "crafting" wine. She'd gone down the list of all the wines offered by Mastroserio, representing some fifteen different grape varieties. She was looking forward to meeting him.

But all her advance research did not prepare her for the scene that unfolded when they pulled up to the winery. Ruggero rushed out of the front door and, while Haig was only half way out of the car, he grabbed him and gave him a passionate embrace. Then a barrage of musical Italian overflowed and filled the air between the two men, a symphony of nostalgic expression accentuated with wild but choreographed hand and arm gestures. Isabelle stood there, her jaw dropped, baffled. She had no idea Haig knew Ruggero.

"Didn't I tell you?" asked Haig, finally turning to her, flushed with excitement. "Ruggero and I worked together for many years in Tuscany."

The two men laughed, arms around each other's shoulders, and headed for the tasting room. No, she thought, still amazed at the chemistry between them. You didn't tell me. You didn't say a word.

Half the conversation during the tasting was in Italian, which Isabelle found irresistibly romantic. But Ruggero's American wife took pity on her and started to chat with her. They started with some of their main whites, Sauvignon Blanc and Chardonnay, then something he called Greco Dry. Isabelle was not impressed with the whites. But then Ruggero pulled out some of what he called his library wines: Private Reserve Barbera, a reserve Cabernet Franc, and a special reserve Zinfandel, which were in a different class altogether.

They moved out to the front terrace and spread their lunch on the round metal table. Ruggero brought out a bottle of his favorite 2010 Barbera and joined them. Haig took a sip, closed his eyes and turned his face toward the sky. "I'm in heaven," he murmured. "How can a wine be so rich, so plush, and yet so soft on the palate? I have a handful of dark chocolate covered cherries still lingering in my mouth." Isabelle was equally enthralled. She savored every drop of her second sip. "This warms me inside like a soft, cashmere sweater," she said.

Ruggero appeared both pleased and inspired by the praise, because he went inside and after a few minutes came out with his tenor saxophone. He played lovely, melodic tunes while they finished their lunch and the bottle of Barbera. The entire experience was charged with sensuality for Isabelle. The personalities of Ruggero and Haig, the surprise of their past association, the wine, the music, all were irresistible. She kept looking from one to the other, immersing herself in her own sexually charged mindset, wanting the moment and the feeling to last.

In the evening they had a nightcap in Haig's room. It was a bottle of Lidia, named after Mastroserio's ninety-year-old aunt.

"Isn't Ruggero something?" beamed Haig, handing her a glass.

"You're not half bad yourself," she whispered softly, and walked over to him. She knew she would succumb to all the accumulated urges of the day. When she had once confided to a close girlfriend that she was physically aroused by intelligent people, including, to her surprise, men, her friend had told her that sapiosexuality had no bounds and was gender blind. She was fascinated that a word existed that described her condition. She rested her hand on Haig's shoulder then sat in his lap, threw her arms around his neck and shut her eyes. No words were spoken. He wrapped his arms around her waist and rocked her in the armchair for several minutes, and then she stood up, took his hand, and they walked to his bed.

Kashvili's tour of Santa Ynez was over. But something was off. Isabelle did not feel the same magnetism as yesterday. It had nothing to do with the professor. He was as dynamic, animated, passionate of a walking encyclopedia as always. Somehow, her flashback to Lucinda's Country Inn had overshadowed his tour of Santa Ynez.

As she was getting ready to leave, he called, "Isabelle, if you have a moment, I have something for you."

She walked up to the podium and waited in silence. He handed her an unsealed envelope.

"Check it out," he said.

There was one sheet of paper inside with a hand-written note on top and a typed paragraph below it.

Isabelle, this is the account by Herodotus that I was telling you about last night. At first I thought of sending the link, but I think a written note is better, no? I hope you found last night's conversation informative. This is such a rich and ancient world. Always remember that when dealing with wine. It is not old, not even ancient. It is prehistoric. It predates most human intellectual endeavors, scientists, mathematicians, architects, even philosophers. It is the original human discovery on earth. And your small nation is right at the center of it.

Best, S. Kashvili

Herodotus, *The Histories*, Chapter 194.

I am going to indicate what seems to me to be the most marvelous thing in the country, next to the city itself. Their boats which ply the river and go to Babylon are all of skins, and round. They make these in Armenia, higher up the stream than Assyria. First they cut frames of willow, then they stretch hides over these for a covering, making as it were a hold; they neither broaden the stern nor narrow the prow, but the boat is round, like a shield. They then fill it with reeds and send it floating down the river with a cargo; and it is for the most part palm wood casks of wine that they carry down. Two men standing upright steer the boat, each with a paddle, one drawing it to him, the other thrusting it from him. These boats are of all sizes, some small, some very large; the largest of them are of as much as five thousand talents burden. There is a live ass in each boat, or more than one in the larger. So when they have floated down to Babylon and disposed of their cargo, they sell the framework of the boat and all the reeds; the hides are set on the backs of asses, which are then driven back to Armenia, for it is not by any means possible to go upstream by water, because of the swiftness of the current; it is for this reason that they make their boats of hides and not of wood. When they have driven their asses back into Armenia, they make more boats in the same way.

Haig Koleyan settled in the large teak armchair on the long terrace of his winery and stared at the neat rows of vines extending beyond the hills. He was tired but content. He had spent the day inspecting the vineyards and conferring with Armen, about the coming harvest. They had even paid a short visit to the Cobb vineyards some ten kilometers west of his in the outskirts of the village of Aghavnadzor. It was eighteen hectares of idyllic rolling hills 1,400 meters above sea level amidst the most spectacular mountains.

Haig described the mountain range in this part of Vayots Dzor as 'feminine peaks.' They rose in smooth, graceful slopes carpeted with green meadows, dotted with wild rosehip bushes and oak trees that burst into life every spring. The bright colors of yellow and purple wildflowers speckled the slopes, all the way up their mauve crowns in uninterrupted curves. The fluid elegance of these slopes and peaks was the most poetic, live beauty that Haig had experienced in nature. What he called the 'masculine peaks,' by contrast, were rugged, rocky, with huge vertical boulders forming their slopes; the silhouette of the elevation of these mountains from certain angles looked like the teeth of a giant saw. These ranges were more common north-west of Areni.

The masculine peaks reminded Haig of a short, six-line poem by Hovhannes Shiraz, a popular poet in Armenia:

> We were peaceful, like our mountains,
> You charged like ferocious storms.
> We stood defiant, like our mountains,
> You howled like senseless storms.
> But we're eternal, like our mountains,
> You'll perish like brutal storms.

The poem, written in 1941, went viral in the Armenian social media every time Azeri forces broke the ceasefire on the Azerbaijan-Karabagh border more than 70 years later, especially in 2010s.

The Cobb vineyard was ready for planting. The layout, rows, watering infrastructure, and canopy groundwork were ready. Aside from the classic indigenous Armenian varieties like Areni, Voskehat, and Khatun Kharji, they planned to plant several Bordeaux varieties as well as Syrah and Pinot Noir. The Koleyan-Cobb line of wines would be produced in four to five years. The first generation of wines would be from indigenous grapes, two reds both 100 percent Areni and a white blend. The other varieties would be tested, and new blends developed over time.

Haig fell asleep in his teak armchair on the terrace of his winery. Darkness had covered the vineyard, and the air had turned chilly. He pulled his blanket under his chin. As he fell into a peaceful sleep, he had a feeling that he and the vineyard were keeping watch over each other. He did not want to move inside quite yet.

His cellphone rang as a gust of wind made him stir in his seat. He had to reach under the blanket, pull the hem of the cardigan out of the way, and then coax the phone out of the tight front pocket of his jeans. He smiled at Isabelle's name on the screen.

"Hey," he said in a groggy voice. "How warm is Moscow these days?"

Isabelle laughed. "I can tell you're relaxed. You must be at Korah."

"I wish you were here. I opened a special bottle tonight."

"Any particular occasion?"

"No. Just for me and Armen."

"Good for you, but I think you'll be happy that I'm in Moscow instead."

"I'm all ears," he said, barely able to stifle a yawn.

"Tomorrow afternoon I'm meeting with Mr. Sergei, one of Ludwig's founders, at his office."

Haig did not react right away. This was significant, and potentially valuable, but he knew how impressionable Isabelle could be. When in control, she could handle anyone and any situation, probably better than he could. But he had seen Isabelle succumb to the pull of extraordinary people and to emotionally charged situations. He did not personally know the Ludwig partner. The Russian-Armenian diaspora remained an enigma to the rest of the diaspora from the Middle East, Europe, and the United States. They were as foreign as any "*odar.*"

Soon after settling in Armenia, Haig had realized the importance of the diaspora in Russia and started taking Russian language classes. He spoke English, Italian, French, Arabic, and Armenian fluently, so adding a sixth language was relatively easy. But that did not help him understand the mentality as much as he hoped it would. Both the establishment in Armenia and the Armenian diaspora in Russia were the product of a culture alien to him. It was the old Soviet-Russian mindset, impossible to penetrate by language alone.

By birth Isabelle was from that culture but not necessarily of it. She could talk the talk, but she was not a true insider. She did not think like them. Her situation could be more dangerous than his. At least he knew he was an outsider and could be on guard. She, on the other hand, had the illusion—and often the confidence—of being an insider, which could make her reckless.

"What's the matter?" he heard her say. "Don't you think it's a good idea?"

"Depends."

"Haig, my appointment is fixed, and I cannot break it. My professor fixed it. So I can either go and, as a student at Enotria studying enology, act like I'm so glad to meet the great man and leave it at that, or I can use the opportunity to bring up the Korah issue. I need your input on this, so don't give me this 'it depends' nonsense."

"What does your professor know about the Korah issue?"

"Absolutely nothing."

"Why did he make the appointment?"

"We were talking about the wine trade business, and he mentioned how the largest wine merchants in Russia were Armenian and offered to introduce me. That's all. He knows nothing else."

"Where were you talking about the wine merchants? In class?"

"Haig, c'mon, what difference does it make? He's Sandro Kashvili, the famous authority on wine. He knows about you." She stopped her sentence abruptly.

"OK, I admit it's an opportunity, but you have to be careful. The big question is whether Ludwig's partner is involved. If he is—which, by the way, would mean he's the main man behind it because I doubt he's the type who'd be involved from the sidelines in anything—you'd be inviting attention you don't want by just nosing around."

"I agree. How about if I start as 'the student glad and honored to meet him,' and then play it by ear, depending on how he conducts the meeting? If he asks me what I did in Armenia, I will mention Korah and see how he reacts. Haig, you must trust me on this. I will be able to tell from his reaction to the mention of Korah if he knows anything. Then I'll play it as it comes."

Despite his reservations, Haig agreed. There was no other way to manage the situation long distance. But how seriously would the big wine merchant tycoon take a young woman?

"Just be careful," he said. "Don't let your guard down even for a second. And try to stay clear of talking about me. I'll be happier if you don't bring up my name at all."

"Done. One day I'll try to understand why you mistrust the Russians so much. But for now, I want you to know that if he picks up on Korah, and we delve deeper, I must mention you. In the very least, I have to say that you are aware of the issue and are following it closely."

"If it comes to that, yes, I agree," said Haig so reluctantly that he knew Isabelle must have winced. But he felt both his agreement and his reluctance were necessary to achieve the balance in the message he wanted to convey to her.

The only person he had talked about his feeling about Russia had been his lawyer, long after he helped him set up his wineries in Armenia and they ended up becoming friends. Most of the legal structure and bureaucratic procedure in Armenia hailed from Soviet times.

His lawyer had invited him for a home cooked meal at his house one night. After dinner, they had retired to his study with a bottle of wine, which was mostly for Haig. All the lawyer wanted was to smoke. He took a glass and barely touched it.

"I don't trust the Russians," said Haig. "They've always been and always will be an imperial power vis-à-vis smaller countries like Armenia—whether Czarist or Soviet or Russian Federation, makes no difference."

He went quiet for a while, sipping his wine and staring at his lawyer's bookshelf, lined mostly by fat Russian volumes. The lawyer watched him and let him be.

"You know, my father refused to visit Armenia. He wouldn't consider it during Soviet times, even though my mother did come once to visit relatives. But my father died without seeing any of this."

"Why?"

"It was personal for him."

The lawyer waited.

"I've seen my father cry only once," continued Haig. "That's a big deal with us. Fathers don't cry, especially in front of their children. Only mothers do. But he could not stop the tears when he told me the story of my grandfather, who had somehow escaped the massacres of 1915 and ended up in Lebanon. That's another epic story..." Haig stared into his wine glass for a few seconds then downed it. The lawyer refilled his glass. "Then, sometime in the mid-1940s, at the height of Stalin's power, a delegation from Soviet Armenia visits the exiled Armenian communities in Lebanon, trying to convince people to migrate to Armenia. Fantastic promises were made of abundance and a fair social life. My grandfather decides to go. My father tries to talk him out of it—they're just getting settled in Lebanon, he has a good job as a teacher, they have a small plot of land they can cultivate, why take a chance on an iffy proposition?

"But my grandfather is determined. 'I've been in exile all my life,' he tells my father. 'My entire family was wiped out in Sepastia, I wandered throughout Turkey for months, then the Levant, Egypt for a while, then Musa Dagh and finally Lebanon. Throughout that forced journey, what I feared most was that I'd die in some foreign land. I'm tired. I want to go not because I believe their propaganda. I want to go so I can finally rest and take my last breath in the Motherland. I'll take this last journey so I can die in peace in Armenia.'"

Haig stopped again, took a sip of wine and stared out the window.

"What happened to him?"

"A year after he got to Armenia, they accused him of being a national-ist for returning to Armenia not out of devotion to Communist ideology, but for love of the motherland, and they exiled him to Siberia. He died there. That's when my father couldn't hold back his tears."

"Haig, I'm so sorry."

"The man came here to die. They wouldn't let him. I'm a descendent of a Genocide survivor *and* a descendent of a victim of Stalin's tyranny. It baffles me that there are people here who miss the Bolsheviks. Some even miss Stalin."

His lawyer filled his glass.

"But I never allowed my mistrust of Russia to taint Armenia for me, like my father did. To him, Soviet Armenia wasn't any better than Soviet Russia."

"Growing up here was different. Russia was a given. A Part of life. In some ways, it still is."

Karmir Koteni, Red Stemmed: a rare native variety spread in the old vineyards of Goris as single vines or vine groups. The tip of a young shoot is light green and hairless. The mature leaf is medium, circular, lightly five lobbed, with sub-lobes. The bunch is big, cylindrical-conical, dense, and medium-dense. The berry is medium, round, and black. The skin is medium thick. The flesh is juicy. The wine is good quality with a pleasant aroma and taste.

CHAPTER FOUR

Sergei Petyan watched as Isabelle approached and entered his office building. The security cameras at Ludwig's main office building were among the most sophisticated in Moscow, with five different cameras covering every inch from the sidewalk to the gates to the long hallway leading to his private office. He could zoom in on any point, and he could turn on the sound to listen to any conversation that could be going on in that stretch. As she approached the gigantic, polished brass gates of the stone building, his attention shifted briefly to the two armed guards who watched her closely, while a Ludwig employee met her at the entrance and escorted her inside. She was wearing a navy-blue pant suit with a white shirt. The four additional guards standing at regular intervals in the hallway seemed to focus on her even more intensely than those at the entrance, perhaps because of how loudly her black sling-back heels echoed in the elaborate hallway leading to his office. She either was not used to wearing high heels, or she liked putting on a show. He lowered the volume on his speakers. He was amused to see Isabelle's attention shift to the walls of the hallway, which were lined with Russian and European classical frescos in fading light pastel colors, where the blues, greens and gold dominated scenes of unnamed eighteenth and nineteenth century nobility in lavish clothes lounging in extravagant drawing rooms and manicured gardens in front of castles. All his visitors, with the possible exception of those who came to his office frequently, would be taken by the artwork. She briefly stopped in front of one the paintings for closer scrutiny.

Her escort knocked Petyan's door, opened it, and gestured her to go in.

Sergei Petyan stood up and leaned over his wide desk to shake her hand. He pointed to the chair across the desk. He sat back down behind his gigantic, immaculately polished mahogany desk, which, except for a couple of expensive-looking golden statues (a racing horse and a female figurine) and a large crystal ashtray, was bare. He liked to watch his first-time visitors check out the desk, often shifting their glance from him to the desk, as if unable to decide what to focus on.

Petyan liked to study people. He wasn't just the largest wine and spirits merchant in Russia, but a revered philanthropist in Karabagh and Armenia, who met with presidents and lesser political leaders at a whim and won public acknowledgments and accolades for his good deeds. He considered his powers of observation as one of his most important assets.

The philanthropist angle was real, in the sense that Petyan did donate to many worthwhile causes. But it was also a helpful façade that distracted attention from the bloody history of Ludwig. He was adamant about maintaining the façade and hiding the details. He had questioned Kashvili about every detail of his conversation with Isabelle concerning Ludwig and him personally. He needed to know what she knew, and, as importantly, he needed to confirm that Kashvili had not told her that there was more to Mrs. Stella's silent partner demeanor than met the eye, that she scrutinized the books that Dmitri brought her and demanded that he ask for regular updates of the Ludwig client list and employee roster. At first, she had been after clues about her husband's murder. She was convinced the murder was work-related. Work had been her husband's entire world. She became angrier and angrier as the police made no progress on the case and eventually—she thought too abruptly—dropped the investigation.

Over time, her anger shifted to Petyan. She thought he could have been more helpful in the investigation. But Petyan had kept arguing that her husband's murder must have been a case of mistaken identity. The man had no enemies, either among Ludwig clients or among the employees, he insisted. His dismissiveness and unwillingness to even consider the possibility threw him under Mrs. Stella's suspicion. She intensified her scrutiny of every detail of Ludwig's operations that she could get her hands on through Dmitri. And Petyan was accommodating. Given Mrs. Stella's thirty-five percent stake in the operation, he did not expect her to use the details to harm Ludwig.

Six months after her husband's murder, Dmitri had convinced Mrs. Stella to take a vacation. "Go to Europe," he said. "Maybe France. Check the French wine country. Take a tour of the Bordeaux region. You need to get out of Moscow for a few weeks." He made all the arrangements, including arranging of guides at every stop. After that, Mrs. Stella would return to France every few months. Once Dmitri accompanied her, and they stayed in Bordeaux for two weeks.

In Moscow, Ludwig was primarily known for its range of liquors and spirits: grappa, tequila, Armagnac, brandy, Calvados, vodka, Cognac, and whisky. In terms of wines, they were mostly known as a distributor of high-volume, low-quality wines, even though they featured a few high-end wines on their list of products, primarily rare Russian collections of vintage European wines, included as trophy exhibits with little or no significance to Ludwig's volume of trade. The scale of the operation was impressive: suppliers in over thirty countries, two dozen representative branches in Russia, and several awards won for quality and service.

"Thank you so much for agreeing to meet with me," Isabelle said demurely. "It's a pleasure to meet you."

"Sandro thinks highly of you," he said, which could have been either a compliment or a disclaimer.

"He's an amazing man. I doubt if there are many people in the world who know as much about wine as he does."

He had used Kashvili as a consultant on occasion, seeking his advice on how to handle niche markets of wine consumers with a more discerning taste than his normal clientele. Kashvili had always come through for him, narrowing down and customizing the wines for each group of potential clients and teaching him to talk the right talk for each grouping, saving him not only time and expense, but also possible embarrassment. But for Petyan, all that was just pixie dust, meant to add some class and glamour to his otherwise purely commercial operation. The real money was still made by selling hard liquor and cheap wine to the alcoholic masses in Russia.

Petyan studied her face. "Yes, he is," he said. "And you're lucky to be studying under him. And by the way, I was impressed that he called on your behalf. He does not call often to make appointments for his students. You must have impressed him."

"Professor Kashvili is kind and gracious, Mr. Sergei, as you are. And you're right, I am lucky."

"So, how can I help you?" he asked standing up and walking to the large mahogany cabinet set against the wall adjacent to his desk. "A drink? I don't keep wine here, I'm afraid, but I have practically everything else." The cabinet was lined with over two dozen heavy crystal bottles of liquors and brandies. He grabbed a flat, circular bottle and poured a golden-brown liquid into two crystal snifters.

"This is my favorite Armenian brandy. The Ararat Erebuni special edition. A toast with cognac is tradition." He handed her one of the snifters.

She stood up to accept the glass, a much heavier crystal snifter than she had held before.

"Here's to our meeting," he said. "*Barov ekar.*"

They drank. "To be frank, Mr. Sergei, I did not come here to seek your help in anything. I'm a student of wine, among other things. But wine is a passion. Professor Kashvili said that Armenians have not only been one of the earliest makers of wine, but also among the earliest merchants of wine. To be honest, that's how your name came up in the conversation. So, I'm here to meet the person who's perpetuating an age-old national tradition."

"'Tell me about the wine industry in Armenia," he said. "I understand you're quite familiar with it."

"Oh, I wouldn't say I'm familiar with everything that's going on, but I worked at two of the fastest growing operations, Vinoma Consulting and Alma Wines. And I can tell you with no hesitation that they're transforming the wine industry in Armenia. They have taken it upon themselves to help revive a 6,000-year-old tradition, and they're almost there."

"So I hear," he drawled. "But surely there is more to the new trend than just those two operations. We buy a lot of Sapor, for example, as well as Hayasa and about a dozen other wines. Hayasa is by far the largest exporter to Russia."

"Absolutely, Mr. Sergei. The wine industry in Armenia is booming. I can't keep up with the new appearances on the market every month. I just talked about the two places where I personally have some experience. As I'm sure you know, both the Korah and the Alma Areni Reserve are in a class of their own, not to be compared with Hayasa."

"Fair enough. I understand the class difference. And I have to admit, Korah has become quite popular in some circles in Moscow."

Petyan knew that Sapor was a good wine, but Hayasa was a low-quality mass producer. And while its low price made it popular, it was not considered to be part of the rebirth of the Armenian wine industry, despite being the largest winery in Armenia. He had even heard that Haig Koleyan had once referred to Hayasa as "the wine for the wino masses in Russia."

"We've noticed the popularity of Korah in Moscow. But to be honest, we don't fully understand it. Even Haig Koleyan wonders sometimes about how demand surged." She shrugged.

Petyan sensed that Isabelle wanted to talk about Korah. It was a fleeting realization which he did not dwell on but didn't dismiss entirely either.

"Didn't Korah win that award a few years ago? One of the best ten wines in the world, or something?"

"Yes, it did. It was part of a Bloomberg survey. One of the top ten in 4,000 bottles tasted. And there was an understandable surge in interest in the wine then, but we've seen a new trend in the past year—occasional one-time bursts in sales at irregular intervals, and then things return to normal until the next burst."

"What do you mean by one-time bursts?"

"Well, Korah production is small. Total around 4,000 cases per year. The Moscow market normally consumes 500 cases per year. Then, out of the blue, we get a few orders that add up to 100 additional cases in a matter of a few weeks. It happens at least three times a year. So we're talking about surges that amount to sixty percent of the normal Moscow market."

"He can't track the buyer?" Having noticed her eagerness to give details, Petyan had started to wonder if this was the reason for Isabelle's visit.

"It's difficult. They come from different wine shops, some so small and obscure that no one has heard of them. We've even heard about private sales of Korah by merchants, which Haig finds hard to believe, so he tends to dismiss the stories as baseless gossip."

"I'm not sure what you mean by private sales," said Petyan as he stirred in his seat. "Where? I mean, private among whom?"

He walked back to his cabinet to fetch two glasses of water.

"That's it, we don't know. But you know how it is with the wine rumor mill. People talk. It's probably nothing, as Haig keeps saying. But there surely are wine enthusiasts in Moscow who'd participate in unique offerings, aren't there?"

"Thank you," she said as he placed a glass of water on a coaster in front of her.

"Of course there are enthusiasts." He raised his hands. "And there are private sales of unique vintages—and not just for wines. Two weeks ago, we sold six bottles of rare, pre-independence Armenian Nayiri cognac. Forty-five years old. They just don't make it like that anymore. The bottles alone are priceless artifacts with wonderful grapevine carvings on the glass and the old Soviet plastic tops and tin covers. There's no way to sell that stuff other than approach a small group of customers who appreciate its value. A few weeks ago, I was approached regarding ten cases of a rare vintage Bordeaux by a close friend of mine who knows the region. I bought a case myself and helped him sell the rest. But Korah? Why would anyone want to put Korah in a closed sale?" His eyes narrowed as he leaned toward her.

"Well, if you haven't heard of private Korah sales, it means either they don't exist, or they're far too insignificant," she said calmly. "The surges in sales will remain a mystery."

Petyan was getting annoyed. Isabelle was being less than candid with him, and he had just realized that there was more to Korah, and her visit to him, than he had suspected. She was fishing for something.

But the tense mood didn't last more than a moment. He started to laugh. "A mystery, indeed," he said, raising his hands, palms turned up toward the ceiling. "Make sure to let me know if you ever solve that mystery. And let me know if I can be of any help to you while you're in Moscow."

"This town is in a perpetual avalanche of sensory overload," said Van Dorian. "Emotional sensory overload."

"What are you talking about?" Haig asked.

"Good luck figuring out every emotion that saturates the air, let alone identifying the right wine for it."

It was only 4 p.m. on a Friday afternoon and The Realm was already beginning to fill. Every table was reserved from 6 pm to midnight, and Dorian knew that even the bar would be filled before the end of the evening.

In the glass-enclosed, temperature-controlled room at the back of dining area which served as the wine cellar, Dorian was checking forty-six cases of wine he had just received from France against the packing list.

The room being too small to spread all the cases on the floor, they were stacked in four columns. The manager of the cellar helped move the boxes around for easy detection, while Dorian's eyes darted to the dining hall frequently as he checked off items on his list. Haig had popped in because he was curious about the new arrivals.

"Are you kidding?" Haig laughed. "Yerevan is a tiny village compared to New York or London. What are we talking about? A million people? That's not even a small borough in New York."

Then Haig's eye caught a case of wine. "You've splurged on this order, haven't you? 2000 Petit-Village Pomerol. Impressive."

"Yeah, that one's good, but there are a few more impressive cases somewhere in here," said Dorian in a dismissive tone. "But I've been to New York, and I've lived in Los Angeles. I'm telling you, there's more emotion here. This little village of one million people is not one city. It's many cities."

"Many cities," repeated Haig with a quizzical look and waited.

"The original *Yerevantsis*, with their Russian cultural heritage, are living the day but not the dream. You, and others like you from the Middle East, are living the dream, but not always the day. Some of you are trying to do both. The young professionals, who are regulars at The Realm, are living in their own world, strangers to the old city. They create the vibe that most tourists relate to, but they remain invisible to the locals. The distance between the haves and have-nots is vast. The haves come here to show off. The have-nots haven't heard of us. And then there are the Repats from Syria, versus those from Iran, Europe, Russia, US—wait, check this out," Dorian interrupted himself pointing to a case of wine as the manager of the cellar uncovered it from the middle of the piled column, "the 2005 Chateau Pichon Baron Pauillac. I have high hopes for this one—there's so much richness, density, substance, complexity in this bottle, that I expect to pair with many nuances of nostalgia, among other deep emotions. It's fruity but has a strong silky blackberry streak—suitable for contemplation, more than celebration."

"When can we try it?" Haig beamed.

Dorian scanned the dining hall, watching the arriving guests and the service, and once in a while his gaze lingered on a table for several seconds longer than others.

"And I haven't even mentioned the historical layers yet," he picked up his train of thought on Yerevan. "There are those who were moved to Yerevan from the provinces by the Soviet authorities to bring the population of the city to one million so they could build a metro system; and those who immigrated from abroad back in the 1940s, like your relatives, at the height of Stalin's repression, the original "Akhbars," who were frowned upon. There are many cities in this small village. Each has its unique emotional baggage. Each is on its own odyssey. Each requires its custom-made oenological prescription."

Haig had no words. He could not articulate it like Dorian, but he knew that was Dorian right. "What about the avalanche of emotions?" he said finally.

"That's a crowded, noisy field," said Dorian. He gestured to the manager of the cellar to open a bottle of the Pauillac. "This needs to breath a while," he said half to Haig and half to the manager of the cellar. "And it needs food. Get us some strong cheeses and some cold cuts." Then he turned to Haig. "You name it, we have it here. From extreme nostalgia—and we're talking about the most nuanced, complex nostalgia known to man, which is engrained in the Armenian DNA—to irrational euphoria, and on to hope. Hope has nuances too. And disillusionment comes in at least two dozen shades and colors, but I'm obsessed with disillusionment with social justice." His eyes kept moving to the dining hall. "I sense also fear of end of life, helplessness, chronic restlessness, and that's not even the tip of the mound. I bet there are emotions lurking in this city that have not been named yet. Sometimes, I feel I have to plug my ears and shut my eyes, or I'll go crazy. Look around you. Do you feel it?"

"Everyone seems to be having a good time," said Haig with a passing glance at the tables at The Realm. It was relatively early, but the place was already buzzing. "I see people laughing and cheering. What do you see? Can we taste the wine now?"

"Look at that couple at the corner," said Dorian as he picked up the glass of wine, checked it against the light then sniffed it. "Don't stare. Watch them for a few minutes. They seem calm and composed, and yes, they're smiling and even having a laugh here and there. But they cannot mask the pensive melancholy that weighs on their hearts—this needs a few more minutes," he said putting the glass back down. "There is a sadness around them, a sense of a pending loss, as if they both know that something beautiful is about to end and will never come back. Do you see it?"

"Not the way you do."

Dorian's eyes focused on the couple with a chilling intensity. "How can you not see it?" he said at last, almost whispering. "They're saying goodbye to something. I'm not sure to what. Maybe to each other, maybe to something else. But something is coming to an end at that table as we speak."

Haig, though anxious to try the wine, was now more absorbed in watching Dorian and the couple.

"There's a Danish word for their condition," continued Dorian. "*Vemod.* It describes them well. I have not been able to find it in either English or Armenian."

Haig watched the couple for a few minutes. Unlike many patrons at The Realm, who tended to get loud and animated after a few glasses of wine, they seemed collected and at peace. They had a charcuterie board and were drinking a rosé. He could not see the bottle; it was in an ice bucket.

The woman was in her early thirties. She seemed reserved, had a kind smile, and spoke with elegant, gracious hand movements. The man, whose back was to Haig, had the same reserved manners. Haig did notice a sense of resignation and acquiescence between them.

Suddenly Dorian's description of the couple came to life in Haig's mind: a revelation that would not have occurred to him had Dorian not pointed it out. He looked at Dorian and wondered how many times a day he noticed situations like this while the rest of the world just passed by.

"There's something spiritual about being able to detect all that," he said. "Van, we've known each other for years, and I'm still learning new things about you. Are you religious?"

"I prefer spiritual. I've come to despise organized religions, especially the church in Armenia."

"I can't stand them anywhere," said Haig. "Here's a piece of wisdom I picked up a long time ago: 'Don't trust a horse when you're standing behind it, or a bull when you're standing in front of it, or a man of religion no matter where you're standing.' It is supposed to be a joke, but I take it seriously."

"Did you know that my father was a priest? I think we can try the wine now."

Haig's eyes opened wide. "I'm sorry, Van jan, I didn't know, and I certainly didn't mean any disrespect to your father."

"Oh, don't worry about that." Dorian laughed. "Let's taste."

Tasting a wine is serious business. It requires total concentration, and all other thoughts and distractions have to be tuned out. They went through the motions in silence.

"It is everything you said it was," said Haig. "Definitely silky-smooth with depth. Reflection and contemplation." Dorian smiled.

"My father was a priest during the Soviet Union," he continued. "When the church was ridiculed and persecuted and when every priest was looked upon with suspicion. That couldn't have been easy for him. It wasn't for me either. Back in Soviet times, it was not cool for a kid to have a priest for a father."

"I can imagine," said Haig. He had heard the stories about the fate of the church in Armenia under Soviet rule.

"But that's the real test, you know: to be—and to remain—a Christian under persecution. It's been that way since the early days of Christianity. It took courage and conviction to be a priest back in the Soviet days. Today, the church has neither. My father was the most loving, honest, and believe it or not, happiest man I knew. He used to say that Christianity is a revolutionary religion. He genuinely rejoiced in his faith."

Haig could relate to what Dorian was saying; he had retained enough stories from his childhood about how Armenians on death marches during the Genocide had stuck to their faith. As villagers were being burned inside their churches, young women were being crucified for refusing to denounce their faith, priests were being beheaded in village squares, and piles of Bibles were being burnt, helpless women and children were on their knees praying. While that made many Armenians proud, it infuriated Haig. "Christianity turned us into a nation of sheep," he had told his mother decades ago. She was a devout woman who read the Bible every night and wanted Haig to pray with her. "We literally turned the other cheek while being brutally massacred," he had yelled, refusing to pray. "Can't you see that Christianity has taken a lot more from us than it has given us?" His mother had retreated to her room and shut the door without saying a word. But Haig had heard her sobs all night. He never argued about Christianity with her again.

"My father said Christ himself was a revolutionary," continued Dorian. "He went after the moneylenders at the temple with a whip; he loved telling that story. Christ spoke against corruption, materialism, and injustice, he'd say; he criticized those who had unfairly become rich; he was a rebel. Today's church is part of the very system that Christ criticized. If Christ were here today, he'd whip them all, he'd say and laugh!

"But enough of that. The short answer to your question is no, I'm not religious; I don't go to church, and I don't respect the religious establishment. But I do thank God for all the good that has come to me and my family."

Haig had not stopped checking the couple the whole time they were talking. "OK," he said. "Let's get back to that couple. What would you prescribe for them?"

"Now, that's the complicated part. Would you say they need to let their melancholic mood run its course and dissipate on its own, or would you suggest that they snap out of it as soon as possible?"

Haig waited.

"What I mean is, should they nurture the mood until they sort things out, until they come to terms with whatever it is that they're about to lose? Or should they opt for some relief now, like sticking a Band-Aid on a wound?"

"Van, how on earth would I know that? You tell me."

"If they snap out of it through a vibrant, perky Viognier or a Voskehat, the mood will return once the wine wears off. So, I think they should nurture their melancholy."

Haig waited for the implied prescription in vain. Dorian was still pondering the couple's condition.

"Van, no need to keep me in suspense," he said at a last.

"Oh, if we agree on what mood to nurture, the prescription is easy," he said in a tone that reminded Haig of Sherlock Holmes telling Watson 'that's elementary my dear.' "Obviously, they're drinking the wrong rosé. I can't see the bottle, but judging from the color in the glass, it is probably from the new Cub winery, which is light, refreshing, youthful. It doesn't match the mood. If they like rosé, they should be having the Alma Karmrahyut rosé, which is heavier, more serious, more complex, less playful, and certainly more versatile, or a light Pinot, preferably a Burgundy, not a California Russian River-style big Pinot."

"You know I don't care for Karmrahyut. Only Russians who miss the Soviet days would waste valuable land on a hybrid grape like that."

"Never mind that now. Almayan is not Russian, and you know it. And the Alma Rosé is pretty good, and you know that too. Stop being so stubborn about the small stuff. The Alma Rosé would work much better in this case."

Haig didn't want to get into an argument about noble grapes versus hybrids, or about the futility of perpetuating Soviet legacies. The condition of the couple seemed more interesting.

"So, what do you do in situations like this? Do you get up and walk over to them and say, 'Excuse me, I'm really sorry to intrude, but I notice that you are afflicted with a bad case of *vemod*, and therefore I believe you should be drinking a Pinot and not a Cub?'"

"I wish," said Dorian with a chuckle. "You may think that's funny, but if I knew them really well I might do just that. Sometimes I ask the staff if they know a customer well enough to propose a different wine, but it's not possible to explain the reason for suggesting something different. Who wants to be psychoanalyzed in a wine bar?"

Dmitri Markov placed two folders on the coffee table in Madame Stella's living room and sat on an armchair facing her. She looked more stern and drab than usual, skinnier than he had last seen her only two weeks earlier, and had the conceited air of someone who felt she was being forced to waste her time and resented it, even though she had insisted on seeing the Ludwig financials and personnel roster. He studied her for a moment—dark grey vest and jacket, black pants, small pearl earrings, a gold and emerald frog brooch on her chest, grey hair gathered in a bun, small, black eyes—and the one distinct sentiment that exuded from the matriarchic figure sitting in front of him was anger.

"Shall we start?" he asked as he opened the first folder and turned it around, so it was the right side up for her. "Here's the quarterly income statement, with comparison with the same period last year."

She stared at the page open in front of her for a moment, then grabbed it and held it closer in her bony fingers.

"The costs have soared," she said.

"Yes. They've expanded operations in three new cities in Russia and in China."

"Waste of money. Vladimir would never have allowed this." He wasn't sure if she was talking to him or just mumbling the words, as she did not look up from the sheet of paper she was holding, and her lips didn't seem to move. It sounded more like a hiss than a sentence.

"Look at the revenue line. Look at the net income. Both have increased as well. I'm not sure I'd call the expansions a waste of money."

A male servant, wearing black pants, a white dinner jacket and white gloves, walked in with a large silver tray loaded with a fine china tea-pot, two cups and saucers, and a plate of pastries, plates, silverware and napkins. The man was in his sixties and struggling to balance the heavy tray.

"On the table," said Stella, barely looking in his direction. The man put the tray on the table and started pouring the tea.

"That will be all, Igor."

The man hesitated for a second, then, having received an encouraging nod from Dmitri, left the room.

"You don't have to defend every decision Sergei makes, you know," she said as if reprimanding a child, shifting her wiry, skinny torso.

"I don't. But the expansions have paid off. I'll serve." Dmitri walked to the table. "That first page was just the summary," he said filling the two tea cups. "Check the rest of the folder for details. You'll see that the increased revenues are basically from the expanded operations—more offices, more staff, more distribution outlets." He placed a cup of tea in front of her and went back for his and the plate of pastries.

Madame Stella was quiet for a while, rapidly turning page after page, eyes focused with an ice-cold expression fixed on her face. She then picked the next folder, which included details of personnel.

"Twenty-two new employees in just three months! What's he trying to do, build an empire?"

It was as if she resented the success of Ludwig, even though she was a major shareholder. She resented Sergei Petyan and the fact that the company had grown and become more successful after her husband's death—as if deep inside she would have preferred if the company had faltered and shrank.

"Stella, I'm your lawyer and I watch for your interests, and yours alone. I will not stay silent if I see any type of waste or mismanagement at Ludwig. You'll hear about it and Sergei will certainly hear about it. But no matter what else you or I may think of him as an individual, he is a good businessman."

"Look at the travel expenses," she said dryly, as if he had not spoken. "Up twenty percent. What's he doing? Touring the world on company expense?"

Although Dmitri dealt with this type of feedback every quarter, it still intrigued him. Sometimes he thought responding to her comments and questions was useless. She never seemed to voice concerns genuinely hoping for clarification. She raised them seeking confrontation, but confrontation with who? She refused to go to the board meetings herself, having delegated that function to Dmitri, so she was not in contact with Sergei Petyan to fulfil her seemingly boundless desire to confront him directly.

Dmitri's dilemma was that he served as the surrogate for both Stella and for Sergei Petyan—for Stella at Ludwig board meetings, and for Petyan when he briefed her on Ludwig.

"Check the details," he said taking the last sip of his tea. Neither of them had touched the pastries. "Almost all travel is marketing related, done by the marketing staff, not Sergei. Sergei doesn't like to travel. He likes his office."

"Well, he used to like to fly to Armenia and even Karabagh."

"Those trips were personal. Not at company expense. And they are much less frequent than they used to be. He hasn't been to Armenia for well over a year."

Stella closed both folders and pushed them to the center of the coffee table.

"Has there been any further talk of bringing in new partners?"

"No. Anyway, that cannot happen without the unanimous consent of the three current shareholders. You don't have to worry about it."

"The same percentages?" She got up and walked over to the table to refill her tea cup.

"Yes. 35 percent yours, 45 percent Petyan, and 20 percent Isaksson. Isaksson's brother attends the board meeting on his behalf."

"And still only five board members," she said as she sat back down, her tone suggesting that it better be that way.

"Yes," said Dmitri and stood up. The question about the board was her last question at each quarterly briefing.

"Good," she said. "I won't allow any 'expansion' –here she made quotation marks with her two index fingers—either in the board or in the shareholders."

Khatoun Kharji, Lady Kharji: a rare variety scattered in vineyards in Vayots Dzor. The tip of a young shoot is light green with barely visible cobweb hairs. The mature leaf is medium and circular and lightly five lobbed. The bunch is medium, cylindrical-conical, and medium-dense. The berry is medium, round, yellowish-green, and turns yellow under direct sun. The skin is thick and tough. The flesh is juicy. The juice is colorless. The wine is good quality with a unique varietal bouquet and flavor.

CHAPTER FIVE

Isabelle was barely out of Ludwig's office building when Petyan summoned his assistant, Jack Hakobyan, who, after 5 years at Ludwig, and 3 years as the head of Moscow operations, was still trying to prove himself. He was in his late forties, a self-conscious, fit man who shaved his head, dressed in designer suites, didn't drink alcohol, and didn't smoke. He did his best to run eight kilometers most mornings, outdoors if the weather permitted, on a treadmill in his bedroom if it was snowing heavily.

Jack and his office staff of twenty managed the demands of all their distributors in and around the city. He knew about every major sales event that his distributors either attended or organized, and he had a list of thousands of retail outlets—bars, restaurants, hotels, casinos, nightclubs, liquor stores—in and around Moscow.

"What do we know about Korah private sales in Moscow?" asked Petyan as soon as Jack was seated. Jack recognized two Petyan signatures in that one sentence: "What do we know," not "What do you know?" Petyan believed any information that any employee of Ludwig had about the liquor and wine business belonged to Ludwig. "We" was his most commonly used pronoun. It was not that he treated the staff of Ludwig as members of one large family, as some had once naively hoped. "We" simply signified central ownership of all knowledge and market intelligence.

The second part of the sentence was equally a Petyan classic, but much more subtle; "about Korah private sales," suggested that such sales in fact took place. Otherwise, the question would not have been so definite. Anyone else would have asked, "Have you heard of any Korah private sales?" That would have been an easier question to tackle. Even a simple yes or no would do without the psychological pressure of confessing to some type of shortcoming. But the question, as posed, implied that "we" already knew that there were Korah private sales in Moscow. If Jack was not aware, that constituted a failure. If he was aware, but did not know all the details about them, that too constituted a failure. If he was aware and had failed to mention anything to the boss until now, that was the ultimate failure. He was happy that in this case he could choose the least damaging option without lying.

"Sorry, boss. I've never heard of Korah private sales."

"How often do you or your men attend private wine sales?"

"Not often. They have not been the norm in Moscow. They're beginning to pick up. Depending on the season, I'd say one a month or every two months, not more."

"I assume by invitation only?"

"Yes."

"Is it possible that there were sales you weren't invited to?"

"Possible, yes, but not likely."

"Could there have been some private sales of special Korah bottles?"

"Again, possible. But we haven't heard of them. In fact, I've never heard of there being special Korah bottles." Jack crossed his legs and slackened his shoulder. The questioning had taken a different turn.

"Boss," Jack said, with more confidence, "do you want me to investigate this?"

There was an oversized, intricately carved wooden coat of arms on the wall behind Petyan's desk. Jack had never understood what it represented. Ludwig did not have a coat of arms. It could have been a family crest, or just a decorative carving. Whatever it was, it provided a background frame around Petyan's head, which looked like a round moon floating between the desk's surface and the wooden carving. Jack had often wondered if Petyan had ever seen a photo of himself as he was now.

He had joined Ludwig after a nine-year career as an independent procurement agent for several casinos in Moscow, which had been a lucrative career, albeit wrought with intense competition and often foul play. But the good times had ended several years earlier when the Kremlin had decreed that all casinos had to move out of Moscow's city limits. In a matter of months, every casino in the city had been shut down. Some moved to the suburbs, while others just closed their doors.

That's when Jack decided to apply to Ludwig. Given his experience, it was a good match.

Now Petyan swiveled his chair to face the coat of arms, turning his back to Jack. He rubbed his temples, and his hands moved to the back of his head while he reclined in his chair and stared at the wooden carving, as if the solution he sought had to be deciphered from the wiggly shapes etched on the wooden plaque.

Jack stared at the gold-plated racehorse on the desk to avoid looking at the back of Petyan's head. Finally, his boss spun his chair back toward him.

"Here's what we need to do. Put out word that there is interest in special Korah wines. But listen carefully about how this must to be done. It cannot come from Ludwig. If we don't know about this so far, there must be a reason for keeping us out. You can pick one of our high-end nightclub clients, the Soho Rooms, Icon Club, or Gipsy—something of that level. You have to make the inquiry as if it's coming from the nightclub you pick, without their knowledge. Choose carefully. No one should suspect that it's you or Ludwig making the inquiry."

"Boss, forgive me, but can you tell me what this is about?"

"I'm not sure myself. There may be an operation involving Korah that we're not aware of. Or maybe it's all nonsense. We should find out."

"I'll talk to my men who handle the nightclubs. If there is an operation, we'll find out about it."

"It doesn't necessarily have to be a nightclub. I gave that as an example. But it must be a buyer who isn't directly in the liquor trade, someone who buys for retail. You don't want the buyer you use as a front to hear about their own alleged interest in Korah in the street and complicate your life."

Jack called in the man on his staff who handled the nightclubs, a chain-smoking blond Russian named Vitaly, and explained everything—well, almost everything. He relayed all that Petyan had said and the details of the task now entrusted to them. After making sure that everything was clear and understood, including the urgency of the assignment, he dismissed him.

But he didn't share with Vitaly the special significance this assignment had for him or tell him how hard he had struggled to stop himself from calling Aram Almayan right away. He would eventually call him, though, once he found out more and validated that there was, in fact, a Korah operation in Moscow.

Almayan had become as much of a mentor to him as it was possible to have mentors in that environment in Moscow in those days, by giving him his first break as an independent procurer for the several casinos that he owned. Jack owed him a professional debt of gratitude—which few people in that business in Moscow would ever take seriously, though Jack did. Without that first job, Jack would have been just another hopeless soul wandering the streets of Moscow during the great chaos of the transition from communism to capitalism that engulfed the nation.

Jack had seen Carla Almayan only a few times when she visited her father from Los Angeles and fallen desperately in love with her. It was one of those hopeless loves that poets write about, lived in solitude, unattainable, and unreachable. He had never dated Carla. In fact, they barely spoke more than a few words during chance meetings at her father's house where he'd gone to report on some business matter. He could not be sure if she even noticed him—just another employee of her revered, larger-than-life papa, here to receive his instructions and leave.

Before he knew it, she had returned to Los Angeles, like an apparition that came and went while leaving indelible marks in his mind and soul. He couldn't ask Almayan about her without a good reason, even though he was dying to know when she'd visit again, what she did in Los Angeles, and, most importantly, whether she had anyone special in her life.

That was over a decade ago. He had since married and had two children, but the memory of Carla never left him. Years later, when Aram sold his casinos and built the Alma Vineyard, he heard about Carla's move to Armenia, and Armenian wines acquired a whole new significance for him. He followed the progress of Alma wines in Moscow closely. Once in a while, he'd call his former mentor to report a relevant market detail, but contact was infrequent.

Jack had heard about the enmity between Alma Wines and Korah, but he did not understand it. Having been born and raised in Moscow, he had no real connections with Armenia. He had visited only once to attend the funeral of a second cousin, as was custom and had been dictated by his late mother, but there was little else to tie him to a distant, small country where his ancestors had their roots.

Out of the forty-six cases of wine on the packing list, only forty-one had made it to The Realm. Dorian checked his watch and turned to Haig.

"It's five o'clock. The warehouse at the cargo terminal at the airport will be open for another hour. If I leave now, I may be able to recover the remaining five cases."

"This really pisses me off," said Haig. "How could they miss five cases? When will this country get rid of all the damn Russians who run our customs services?"

"Calm down. They're not all Russians. We're still in the process of building the country. It is what it is. I know the drill after so many years. I even know exactly where to go. You want to come along?"

"Yeah, I'll come," said Haig a bit more calmly. "We can talk more about wine and emotions."

Aware of the time and Friday afternoon traffic, Dorian rushed to his car, parked right outside The Realm. The most straightforward route was to go down Mashtots Avenue. The traffic was bad, but at least moving, and Dorian was an unusually calm driver.

"Now tell me," said Haig once they had past Amirian street, and the traffic started to move a bit more easily, "how much of this wine-emotion thing is real, how much of it is BS?"

Dorian maneuvered around a taxi that was signaling to move to the curb to pick up a passenger. "No BS. There is a scientific basis to the link between wine and emotions. I hope you don't think I'm making it all up."

"I never thought you made it up. But what scientific basis?"

"There've been several experiments. They put a person in an MRI machine, squirt red wine into his mouth through a plastic tube and ask him to swish and swallow. The subject cannot see the wine or smell it. Then he's given white wine in the same way, and then water. Throughout this process, his brain is monitored. The tests show two things: first, the brains of sommeliers light up much more than those of novices. This shows how important training is when it comes to detecting flavors and smells. Second, the parts of the brain responsible for recognizing smell and taste aren't the only ones that light up. The insula does, too—the most anterior part of the insular cortex, to be exact. It's the part of the brain that makes us experience emotions—happiness, sorrow, anger, sadness, elation, excitement. The link is real."

Dorian was momentarily distracted as they passed the Blue Mosque on the left. It was an imposing, beautiful building. Haig was staring at it too.

"You know, I'm glad the mosque is here," said Haig. "I'm glad it's operating. Our problems with the Turks and the Azeris were not religious.

They used religion to fuel pogroms, but the real issues were territorial and ethnic. Armenians got along very well with Muslims all over the Middle East."

Dorian nodded. Unlike Haig, he had had no contact with Muslims anywhere, and was happy to defer to him. They were now crossing Victory bridge where the traffic was a bit lighter than downtown Yerevan.

"We should be there soon," he said. "We'll retrieve the missing cases and be back in time for the Friday crowd."

"Your scientific study results are interesting," said Haig, as if he had never let go of that train of thought. "But how do we move from that to wines for specific emotions?"

"That's where we come in. That comes with years of experience and our own experimentation. Our conclusions cannot be universal. Wine affects different people differently, after all."

"Doesn't the social setting matter too? Drinking with friends has a different emotional impact than drinking alone."

"Of course. But there are age-old correlations between wine and certain emotions, confirmed through poetry over the ages. Love and wine, for example, are a perfect pair. But I bet not every kind of wine pairs well with love."

Dorian instinctively stared at the long, fortified structure as they passed by the U.S. embassy on Admiral Isakov Avenue.

"Omar Khayyam: 'A loaf of bread, a jug of wine, and thou.'" Said Haig, once they had cleared the embassy.

"That's a good example. In those 10 words Khayyam says it all and sets the perfect mood. Wine and love, and wine and poetry are paired brilliantly. He doesn't even use the word love. But we know it's there. He paints romance in its purest form—no bells and whistles, no description of slender waists and almond eyes, no roses or violets—but you feel the love and the romance. That's because you recognize the emotion through the pairing of wine and love. Replace the word 'wine' in that line with any other word and you won't get the same effect."

A middle-aged woman, carrying a large bag, was crossing the street in the middle of the traffic. It was not an intersection, there was no traffic light nor a crosswalk. She moved slowly, oblivious to the honking horns of agitated drivers. Haig raised his hands, exasperated, while Dorian just smiled.

"I still ask, though," continued Dorian, "what kind of wine was Khayyam drinking when he wrote that line? I have no idea what kinds of wine they had in the eleventh and twelfth centuries when Khayyam lived. If this were today, I'd say he was drinking possibly a Burgundy, maybe a Sauternes or a Troika Reserve. I don't think it'd be Champagne or a German Grand Cru Riesling, for example, which, although compatible with romance, pair better with opulent, celebratory and lavish moods. There's no trace of opulence in that line."

"Van, that's deep," said Haig.

They were quiet for a while. They passed the Police Academy building.

"OK," said Haig. "Let me throw a different log in the fire:

It's all there is, no quarrel there, bring your glass
This too shall pass, just like a dream, bring your glass
Life is gliding, jingling its bells through the sky
Some are living, others waiting, bring your glass

"This is our own Tumanyan. He died seven months after writing this. He was only 54. I'd say he was drinking a different wine than Khayyam, wouldn't you? He was drinking a contemplative, reflective wine. His wine in this poem paired well with wisdom and perspective on life. It could have been a Brunello, an old vine Zin or a VanDor Areni reserve."

"You're getting the hang of it." Dorian felt he had a convert on his hands. "Let me bring another old sage here—the thirteenth century master of both verse and wine, Rumi: 'There are thousands of wines that can take over our minds. Don't think all ecstasies are the same.' Think about that. What did he mean by not all ecstasies being the same? Granted, he didn't mean 'thousands of wines' literally. For Rumi, one could get drunk on love or by delving into mystical thoughts. But, eight hundred years ago, this man had also realized that different wines stir different emotions in us. 'Drink the wine that moves you,' he said. He did not ask for a scientific basis for which wine to choose. He just knew."

Haig went quiet again, and Dorian realized that the wine-emotion pairing concept had finally hit him in a real way—it was no longer just something interesting to talk about.

"You should offer your expertise as a service," said Haig as they approached the Cargo Terminal.

"A service?"

"People don't like unsolicited advice, especially about their emotional state, remember? But if you make it formal, a service offered to the patrons of The Realm, they'd go for it. 'Pairing wine with your mood. A courtesy offering of the ever-so-perceptive Van Dorian! Let wine work with your emotional state, not against it.' Something like that."

Although Haig's broad, cheerful smile suggested that he was kidding, Dorian was intrigued.

"You're still thinking about that couple, aren't you?" he chuckled. "Believe it or not, you have a good point. What better way to teach this public how to drink wine? But forget one-on-one consultations. That gets far too personal. How about an occasional wine tasting with 'pairing with moods' as the tag line? We present and explain wines as we do at any wine tasting, but then we add an emotional dimension."

"You can prepare a matrix of moods with a choice of wines to go with each." Haig's tone softened and his volume grew louder. "You can have two wine choices for each mood: one that nurtures the mood, and one that blunts it."

"If we're going to do this, I have to tackle disillusionment with social justice," said Dorian.

"What does justice have to do with it?"

"After nostalgia, disillusionment with justice is probably the most common, hidden, subtle emotion lurking around here. And what a challenge it would be to find a wine for it. We can't have a service like this without tackling it. It is an entirely different feeling from disillusionment with love or with your job. It transcends you personally, and yet it is deeply personal. Think about that for a minute. It's overwhelming. I've read a lot about justice, practically every philosopher, and I'm disappointed. They tell you everything there is to know about justice but virtually nothing about the emotional state of a person who's disillusioned with justice. And yet that's a big deal. I'd say that's *the* big deal in this town. There should be a separate word for it. And definitely a wine."

"Maybe we should make one. A wine custom-made for disillusionment with justice."

Dorian's gaze lingered on Haig. "You're full of ideas today," he said.

Fourteen months earlier.

"The man is an artist," Haig told a somewhat skeptical-looking Dorian after he and Henry Cobb returned to Yerevan from a marathon three-day excursion that took them to three main wine-growing regions. He had gone to visit Dorian at his winery in Ashtarak. Dorian was busy checking the progress of the next generation of wines in the making, walking from one large steel tank to the other with his winemaker, tasting and scrutinizing the wine in progress. Haig tagged along.

"He doesn't just make wine. He composes wine like a composer composes music. Every note counts. Every pause between two notes counts even more. He checked the soil, I mean, he literally tasted the soil. He checked the drainage, the air flow, the sun, the rocks; he looked for the smell of sulfur in the rocks; he breathed the air with the same intensity of a wolf looking for the scent of prey."

"How do you know they weren't all gimmicks?"

"Van, gimmicks? To impress *me*? Why on earth would he want to impress me? He was so pressed for time. We drove 800 kilometers in three days! No breaks. First, we went to Armavir where the Sapor vineyards are and where I have some land. I was hoping he'd like it so we could avoid buying new land."

"And? The land of the Sapor vineyards wasn't good enough for him?"

"It's good for Sapor, but not for us. We're planning a higher-end wine. The summers there are too hot. It gets over 40 degrees. The fruit ripens too fast. It loses some of the necessary concentration for deeper wines with more complexity and character. It's perfect if you're producing large volumes of $10–20-a-bottle wines. But you cannot produce a $50–80-a-bottle wine in Armavir."

Dorian nodded, passing a glass of pre-wine of his Syrah Reserve to Haig.

"Then?"

Haig took a sip and raised his eyebrows, then gave Dorian a thumbs up.

"Then we took him to Tavush."

"That's much further north and east, and doesn't get too hot, right?"

"Cobb loved Tavush. Every note was right, especially for Pinot. He thought it would be perfect for Pinot."

"But?"

They dumped the glass of Syrah in a bucket and moved to the next tank, marked "Kangun." This was another hybrid grape created in Soviet times, and Haig didn't care for it.

"There isn't enough land for sale in Tavush. We could find a hectare here, a hectare there, but nothing large enough to turn into a worthwhile vineyard. And when the villagers learned who was asking, the prices shot up off the roof—too bad because I would have loved for him to produce his Pinot here."

Haig took a tasting shot of the Kangun dry white pre-wine.

"You'd do much better with a Voskehat or Garan Dmak or any of the indigenous Armenian grapes," he said.

"The next stop had to be Vayots Dzor, I presume," said Dorian, ignoring the comment.

"Right. And that's where the artist in Cobb woke up. It sprang from him like a force of nature, irresistible, unstoppable. He was transformed in Vayots Dzor. I could tell."

"What did he do?" Dorian asked, putting his tasting glass down on an overturned barrel.

"Nothing. That's the point. Absolutely nothing. He did not speak. He did not even listen. He was absorbed in the place. I have not seen anything like it. We went to Rind, Chiva, Aghavnadzor. Perfect climate everywhere, 300 days of sunshine. He crumbled handfuls of soil in his hands, tasted the dirt, hit two rocks together to get a sense of the volcanic nature, and everything was right.

"We went to the Areni cave. He spent hours not only in the cave, but just as long later in Yerevan with the archeologist involved in discovering it. He delved as deeply as he could into the history of wine in the region, asking questions that had not even crossed my mind. He told me he was intrigued by the purity of research that the archeologist had done. It reminded him of the expeditions that National Geographic used to organize around the world. Even the old churches and monasteries fascinated him; he commented on how seamlessly they fused with nature, with the peaks and cliffs over which our medieval churches are built. I don't know how religious the man is, but there's certainly something mystical about him. And there was something else, something much more important, something beyond all the wine needs."

Dorian stared at Haig but said nothing. Haig knew that Dorian would not discount his words as hyperbole.

"He told me there was only one other place on earth where he had had an out-of-body experience like that," Haig said. "The Perito Moreno glaciers in Argentina near El Calafate. He got the same feeling in Vayots Dzor. He mentioned the snowcapped mountains, vast meadows and valleys, rolling hills at over 4,000 feet above sea level, skies that seemed more boundless than anywhere else on earth, air more fertile and pregnant than anywhere else. You know how the region gets in the spring—full of life, brilliant colors everywhere, sensuality everywhere, every living thing, from insects to birds to animals to plants preoccupied by procreation. The magic of Vayots Dzor had struck him. I was shocked."

"The same magic has struck you too. Why be shocked?"

"I always thought I felt it because Vayots Dzor was mine. The history is mine. Remember our conversation years ago? But here is this *odar* on his first ever trip to Armenia, tired, jet-lagged, trying to get used to the local food and water, and he *gets it*. He is hit as if he were one of us. The artist in him rises and takes over, and he overcomes the formidable practical hurdles of starting a project in Armenia."

They went quiet for a while. Dorian resumed checking the wines, but he was distracted. Haig had often seen Dorian dive so deep into his own thoughts that he forgot where he was.

He knew Dorian's theories well enough to relate to the moment. Could the allure of Vayots Dzor provide a new clue to matching wines with human emotions? Was the secret in the land itself? Most of the names for the human emotions that he had heard Dorian talk about were German, Gaelic, Yiddish, and Japanese, but they all reigned in Yerevan. Nostalgia was universal, even if it acquired a unique meaning among Armenians. *Torschlusspanik* was a German word, but Dorian claimed he had seen it in play in Yerevan every night. What could Vayots Dzor provide as a terroir that no other region in Armenia or the world could?

"Did you take him to any of our old Soviet wineries?" asked Dorian. "Has he seen the ugly reality, aside from the boundless skies?"

"We sure did," said Haig with a broad smile. "He's seen the ugly, alright. The Avagian winery near Areni, to be more precise. Before we walked down the steps into the cellar, I warned Cobb. 'You'll be shocked,' I said. 'This is a relic from an era past, an era you have never known, an era even I have not known.' He laughed. 'I've been in the dungeons of Argentina in the 1980s,' he told me. 'Nothing can shock me. Let's go down.' And we go down.

"The place was cluttered with leaking barrels, amphorae covered with mold and tattered hoses and fittings. Rusty equipment was strewn around the wet floors. The whole place stank of mold and alcohol and fermenting fruit. Cobb turned to me and said: 'I grant you: I'm shocked.' But, to my surprise, he decides to take on the project."

Dorian gave him a perplexed look and waited.

"Avagian gave him a glass of wine from one of the amphorae. Cobb reluctantly took a sip, then another. He probably thought he was poisoning himself. Then he turned to me. 'If they can make this with *this*,' he said, pointing to the rusty, smelly cellar, 'imagine what *we* can do,' and that was that. We were partners. The Koleyan-Cobb winery was conceived right in that smelly, suffocating cellar."

Dorian was silent again. He probably was wondering about the land and about how many yet unnamed emotions he could nurture with the vines of Areni.

But Haig was past the wondering stage. He had formed a partnership, bought an expensive piece of land in Aghavnadzor, and was about to plant a vineyard as a joint venture with the world-famous Henry Cobb.

Henry Cobb arrived on time for his 2 p.m. appointment, but Gaspar Melkonian was not in yet. His office was quite large, but there was barely room to sit, or stand, for that matter. A ten-foot-long, wooden conference table was covered with countless archeological finds: stone, clay, iron, obsidian, bronze, and wood. Most of the pieces had been numbered and arranged into groups, but some were yet to be classified and lay scattered in a pile at the edge of the rectangular table. The only contemporary item squeezed against the relics at the edge of the table was a large, black plastic ashtray, which was empty, but the thick residue of solidified ashes at the bottom testified that the ashtray had more than fulfilled its mission.

The room was full of cardboard boxes, stacked from floor to ceiling, marked with several lines of inscriptions, containing, Cobb presumed, thousands of other relics. Only one long and narrow window was spared the wall of cardboard boxes, allowing some daylight into the cluttered and stuffy room. The smell of dust and mold dominated the air.

At first, he wasn't sure that he had the right office. It looked more like an abandoned warehouse, with an overwhelmingly chaotic clutter of archeological miscellanies. He was about to leave to check around the building, when, from behind a small desk buried behind a pile of boxes, emerged the head of a young man with long black hair, wearing thick eye-glasses and a loose white T-shirt.

"He's on his way," said the young man, briefly taking his eyes away from the computer screen. "He's driving from the provinces. Delayed by traffic." He offered Cobb a chair squeezed between two columns of boxes and turned back to his computer screen.

Cobb took the seat, wondering if he's made a mistake coming here. But Gaspar was a member of the Institute of Archeology and Ethnography of the National Academy of Sciences of the Republic of Armenia and had done pioneering work in both discovering and later studying the Areni 1 cave. He had authored and co-authored hundreds of scientific papers on various archeological finds throughout Armenia and was an expert in the history of the ancient world. Awkward or not, Cobb decided to wait.

Gaspar arrived some thirty minutes late, huffing and puffing, soaked in perspiration, his black pants and T-shirt covered with dust. He was a big man with an ample belly, gentle but focused black eyes, and his face, nose, and forehead were dotted with moles. He fetched a bottle of cold water from the small fridge buried behind a stack of boxes like everything else in the office and sat in the chair next to Cobb.

"Sorry," he said. He opened his leather shoulder bag and produced a small clay urn, no more than a few inches long, about two inches wide at the widest point at the middle, tapering off to less than an inch at the base and the neck, with a distinctive, blue-turquoise thin band neatly painted around its narrow neck. It was well preserved with only a small chip at the base. The blue-turquoise paint showed no signs of fading.

"This is from the Urartu period," he said and lit a cigarette. "We found it on an archeological site north of Yeghegnadzor. We have no clue as to its true origins yet or how it got to Yeghegnadzor."

Gaspar drank half the bottle of water in one go, oblivious to the loud slurping noises he made, and tried to catch his breath. He wiped his face and forehead with a brown handkerchief and took a few more swallows. Cobb was beyond feeling awkward by now; he was just intrigued. They had not even introduced themselves yet, but that seemed entirely irrelevant to Gaspar. He knew whom he was meeting, and so did Cobb.

The young man walked over and started inspecting the small urn.

"It was probably used as a perfume bottle," said Gaspar. "It had to have belonged to royalty or a wealthy merchant or maybe to a high-level military wife."

He drank the rest of the water, took a last deep drag on his cigarette and put it out in the black ashtray. He looked up to Cobb.

"So, you've been to Areni 1," he said. Then he turned to the young man.

"Ara jan, will you make us some coffee?"

"I should have visited the cave after talking to you, not before. I bet I would have had a much better idea of what I was looking at."

"We don't know much yet either." Gaspar frowned and lit up another cigarette. "We haven't excavated even one percent of the potential of that place. Even if we had all the resources we need, it would take decades to unearth all that's there. And we don't have the resources. I don't think we'll get to it in my lifetime. Budgets, priorities, you know." He frowned again.

"That's too bad. There's so much that's survived intact in that cave."

"There's thousands of years of history waiting to be excavated. Think about this: Between the 6,100-year-old winery inside and the 5,000-year-old shoe discovered at the entrance of the cave there's twenty-thirty meters. 1,100 years after the winery was built, there were people there with pretty advanced shoe making skills. One could spend a lifetime trying to figure out the history of those 1,100 years alone. Once you focus on that, it's hard to fathom what else may be buried in there."

"Any guesses as to who these people were?" Cobb's eyes were already feeling the effects of cigarette smoke in the already musky air of the room.

"We don't know for sure, but we know they were the indigenous people of the Vayots Dzor region. The center of that community was Yeghegnadzor, today's capital of the province, which I find fascinating. Imagine that type of continuity through 6,000 years, in spite of countless invasions and occupations. We also know that the Urartians, who were the largest grape and wine producers of the ancient world, settled in that part of Armenia sometime between the late Bronze Age and the early Iron Age, probably around 1,200 BC."

"But these folks were making wine much earlier."

"Oh yes. The Urartian Kingdom itself was established 3,000 years after the people of Vayots Dzor were making wine in the Areni 1 Cave."

"But not much is known about these original people?"

"Not yet. But we know that whoever they were wine was central to their identity and their daily life, as it was to the Urartians 3,000 years later. In fact, I believe that the Urartians settled in this region because they saw what an incredible grape and wine country it was. They would not have stayed otherwise."

"They came here looking for new wine country?"

"Absolutely," said Gaspar and stood up. "And the physical evidence that they settled because of the grape is irrefutable," he continued while walking to one of the long stacks of boxes. "Ara, help me with this," he said as he started going up a ladder. "Right up the road from Areni, in Aghavnadzor, the grape-growing landscape is unmistakably Urartian," he said, grabbing a box and handing it to Ara. He placed the box on his chair and started sifting through the contents. "If we do some more excavations, I am convinced we'll find a lot more, such as Urartian harvesting and crushing equipment. Just thirteen kilometers north of Areni in the village of Yelpin we've found Urartian religious monuments with their characteristic stone steps leading to a sacred platform where they performed religious rites," he said placing a black-and-white photo of the religious monuments he was talking about on the corner of table for Cobb to see. "They would not have built all that," he said pointing at the photo, "if they did not settle, and they would not have settled if they did not find a thriving grape country and wine culture."

Staring at the photo, Cobb had a vision of an army of prehistoric wine-maker-conquerors marching into the slopes of Vayots Dzor with their swords and lances and black beards and fiery eyes looking not for opportunities to loot and plunder and rape, but for new vine terroir. He thought about how the essential quest for new wine terroir had not changed much in several thousand years. The same happened today as winemakers look for new land fit for vineyards. He felt a bond with the prehistoric vintners of Urartu, who had been on the same single-minded, purposeful odyssey as he, some 3,200 years ago. It was like feeling the presence of their ghost on his skin.

"And the settling of the Urartians went beyond wine culture," continued Gaspar, replacing the photograph on the table with another one. "They adopted local deities, expanded their religious ceremonies to appease the locals, and even created mixed rituals. In the ancient burial grounds of Aghavnadzor there are graveyards that show an amalgam of Urartian and local burial rites. The Urartians favored cremation, but in the old tombs in Aghavnadzor you see the body of deceased buried, not cremated. On one side of the skull is a wine jug," he said pointing to the new photo at the corner of the table, "on the other a wine cup, and under the skull is a cup containing the jaw of another person. The jaw is a uniquely Urartian obsession which we still don't fully understand. The Urartians did not just conquer and impose their ways on the local population; they adopted many of their ways as well."

"I wonder how much of the ancient ways have survived," mused Cobb. He guessed that Gaspar's ashtray had over ten extinguished cigarettes and watched him light another one.

"Many," Gaspar responded with confidence. "To this day during funerals, especially in the villages of Vayots Dzor, after the village head gives his eulogy at the graveside, he raises a glass of wine, toasts the deceased, drinks half the glass, and pours the other half on the grave. It's an Urartian tradition that has survived for millennia. It celebrates life—life of the living at this end of the world and of the dead at the other end. They believed that the dead were resurrected somewhere else and celebrated their rebirth with wine. Hence, the sharing of the glass between this world and the other."

Gaspar was talking about these rituals as he would recount any every-day normal phenomenon, as a newscaster would give a traffic report or a weather forecast. Cobb, who was hearing about the sharing of a glass of wine between two worlds for the first time, was fascinated both by the tradition and by the fact that it had survived for millennia. He stared at Gaspar and realized that for him a ceremony practiced 3,000 years ago was as real, normal, timely and immediate as anything else that people practiced today. The archeologist in Gaspar was so dominant that it made him live the past as matter-of-factly as he lived the present.

"Wine was the bridge between the two worlds," said Cobb at last.

"The bridge and the common denominator."

Ara brought a tray with two small cups of Armenian coffee and lay it at the edge of the conference table. Gaspar offered Cobb a cup and took the other. It was a thick, black liquid of boiled, finely ground roasted coffee beans and sugar, served in a small demitasse on a saucer.

"Some irrigation methods have survived as well," said Gaspar taking a sip of coffee, and placed more black and white photos in front of Cobb. "The irrigation infrastructure, mostly tunnels dug through mountains, with intricate systems of water distribution, are more advanced in grape growing regions like Vayots Dzor than in other parts of Armenia, and I believe they are the legacy of the vintners of Urartu."

Cobb tried the coffee and returned the demitasse to the saucer. It is too sweet for him.

"Any idea as to what type of grape they cultivated?"

"Oh, yes. We gathered residues of seeds, stems, and grape skin. Interestingly, the skin residues survived better than the seeds and the stems. Their DNA is a perfect match with today's Sev Areni grape."

***Khindeghni**, Khndoghni. Old Medicine (according to legend, the grape has healing powers): a widespread variety in Nagorno Karabagh (Artsakh). The tip of the young shoot is light green and covered with light cobweb hairs. The mature leaf is medium, circular, and has five medium lobes. The bunch is large, conical, winged, and dense. The berry is medium to large sized, rounded, black, and blue-purple. The skin is elastic and covered with bloom. The flesh is juicy, sweet, yet lightly astringent. The wine is a deep colored, high quality red table wine.*

CHAPTER SIX

It took three weeks for the inquiries to generate a lead. Jack had finished an 8-kilometer run, showered, and ready to leave for his office when he received Vitaly's call.

"I have some news," he said. Jack could hear the muffled sound of early morning traffic in downtown Moscow and imagined Vitaly was cupping the phone mic with his hand. "We've caught the scent of something, but it's not within our reach."

Jack was not in the mood for riddles, but he did appreciate his employee's caution. Petyan had stressed to all Ludwig employees that cell phones were not safe. He knew his was monitored, and even though he couldn't be sure that the junior employees were being tapped as well, he preferred to err on the side of caution. This created a problem for quick communication, and some employees often ignored the rules to save time.

"See me at the office."

When Vitaly arrived, he was out of breath. Knowing his smoking habit, Jack pointed him to a chair and gave him a glass of water.

"What scent?" he asked.

"There's a small, closed sale, to be held in a private auction room in the center of town, but it's not an auction. We were told it is strictly for private wine collectors—no nightclubs, casinos, or any institutions. There'll be more than one type of wine sold, and one of them is from Armenia. The person looked surprised when I mentioned Korah, so I don't think it's a Korah. I'm not sure of the location but I could find out if we had someone to pose as a private collector. Someone new to them."

"How sure are you of this?"

"Pretty sure. It wasn't easy to come up with the information. It's well guarded. They wouldn't bother to be so discreet if it weren't real."

Jack took a sip of water.

"Do you know when?"

"They wouldn't tell us the exact date, but we were told in about a week."

"You keep saying 'we.' Who was with you?"

"Sorry. No one. Habit. That's how Mr. Sergei talks, so I've picked it up."

A private investor in wine would certainly pay a lot more than someone buying for a nightclub would be authorized to pay. Now he kicked himself for not pointing this out to Petyan when he first suggested the nightclub route. Petyan was thinking to use a faceless buyer for anonymity, but both he and Jack had missed this nuance.

"OK," he said, knowing Vitaly was anxious to get out so he could smoke. "Leave it with me for now. If I find a private investor, can you direct him to the same source?"

"Of course."

Jack's office was nowhere as large, nor as ornate, as Petyan's, but he had managed to turn it into his own space. On the credenza behind his burled walnut desk was a framed photograph of his wife and two young children. On the wall facing his desk hung a large, 4x4 foot, reproduction of one of

Wassily Kandinski's oil paintings entitled *Tableau* à *la Tache Rouge*, a complex abstract painted in 1914. Jack loved to stare at the painting every time he needed to focus. Neither the abstract shapes nor the colors seemed to have any rhyme or reason at first glance, but as Jack stared at the painting while contemplating a dilemma or a problem, things eventually moved and found their place, both in the painting and in whatever was on his mind.

It was not the private sales, per se, that were new, but the existence of a closed venture hidden from the eyes of the dominant merchants like Ludwig. It had significance for Ludwig beyond the initial inquiry about Korah. It wouldn't matter to Petyan if the wine were a Korah. What would matter to him was the event itself.

Petyan would probably say that such events would have been inconceivable a few years ago. The large merchants not only dominated the market, but they also knew everything. Times were sure changing, and as wine became more popular in this heavily vodka- and brandy-dominated culture, there were sure to emerge players to take advantage of the opportunities this presented. No one could tell how far this new interest in wine would go, but an outfit like Ludwig could not leave it to chance.

For Jack, it was the Korah that had special significance, more than a possible emerging trend. It could present him with a reason and an opportunity to brief Carla personally. The movements in Kandisnsky's painting helped him see this.

Turning back to the business at hand, he thought of the right "private investor" to unleash on the project. In the private sales he'd attended, three main nationalities bought expensive wines: Chinese, Russians, and occasionally Japanese. The Chinese and Japanese usually headed the Russian offices of large conglomerates based in their respective countries. Only once had he met a Chinese diplomat, attending a sales event as a private individual. He thought the safest choice for their front man would be a Chinese. The Chinese business community had been growing in Moscow much faster than the Japanese, which increased the plausibility of a new face appearing on the scene.

That afternoon, Jack went back to see Petyan. It was late, close to 6 p.m. Petyan looked tired; the bags under his eyes were puffier than usual. One of his usual gestures was to run his hand over his face, up and around his forehead and his eyes, as when drying it with a towel. Judging from how messy his bushy eyebrows were, Jack thought his face had undergone quite a lot of rubbing that day.

Petyan poured himself a cognac.

"You still don't drink?" he asked.

"No sir."

"Good for you. This is good stuff to buy and sell, but I'm not sure what it does to the body."

"In moderation, it's supposed to be good for you."

"In moderation!" Petyan laughed. "Don't say that on the street. Drinking in moderation can't be good for business. I prefer a quote from some other sage I heard the other day: 'There's nothing wrong with sobriety in moderation.' I forget who said it."

Jack laughed too and waited for Petyan to take his seat behind his pristine desk. Then he told him Vitaly's story and, without a pause, went on to ask, "Does Liu Li still work for us?"

Liu Li was the liaison between Ludwig and China and worked directly for Petyan. A portly, graying man in his late fifties, he handled all back-office administrative chores in both buying liquors from China and selling to distributors in Moscow—a small but highly profitable trade, catering almost exclusively to the expatriate Chinese community, concentrated in Moscow and the far east of Russia. Ludwig imported several top brands of Chinese liquors, including Maotai, Luzhou Laojiao, and the distinctive bottled Yanghe Daqu, and exported vodka and some brandies. The Chinese preferred to buy their wine directly from the producers in France, Italy, the US, and parts of Asia and Latin America. Jack had learned that Alma Wines was one of the first wineries in Armenia to start exporting to China and Japan.

But Li did not know much about wine. Wine was a different specialization—and different passion—than liquor.

"He does," answered Petyan, taking a gulp of his cognac. "And I think I know where you're going with this but tell me anyway."

"If he can act, even a little, he'd be perfect. He hasn't been visible on the street in Moscow, he looks like a rich Chinese connoisseur or I guess we could make him look like one with a little work, and we can think of one of the new Chinese companies established here which he works for. He's perfect."

So it was that Mr. Liu Li was groomed and trained for a role that Jack doubted he had ever played before. They had business cards printed with his personal information in addition to business cards presenting him as an official of the Shenergy Group of Companies managed by the Shanghai municipal government and specializing primarily in natural gas exploration and distribution. They spent two days teaching him the wine buyer's jargon and demeanor: how to taste, what questions to ask, and what to look for in a wine. He was coached to say as little as possible, to look serious, and to have minimal interaction with the other buyers.

"You'll play the role of a reclusive wine collector who cherishes his privacy. Do not volunteer cards to anyone. You have those cards to establish credibility with the organizers only if necessary." Petyan was giving instructions as if to a child, but Liu Li didn't seem to take offense. He nodded emphatically, like an eager student ready for new horizons.

They were in Petyan's office. Li, whose round, chubby face and squinting eyes made him look like the statue of Buddha in front of the Chinese restaurant that Jack frequented with his wife in downtown Moscow, was more animated than Jack had ever seen him before. He'd get up from his chair and pace the room, small spiral notebook and pencil in hand, taking notes as Petyan and Jack spoke.

"You'll have to pass two different tests," explained Jack. "First, you have to pass your interview with the recruiter, who, from what I understand, is a thug. Be careful with him. If he even suspects that you may be an imposter, he'd be inclined to harm you. I mean physically harm you. Do you understand?"

"Yes. He won't suspect."

"Second, you'll have to pass as a convincing wine collector at the event. You have a sizeable collection of French wines acquired over the years during trips to Bordeaux and Burgundy—Margaux, Pauillac, Pomerol, Pommard"—Jack waited while Li wrote down the names—"you're recently settled in Moscow, and now you're looking for some interesting regional varietals." Li scribbled frantically.

"But even that," jumped in Petyan, "is only to establish credibility at the initial meeting with the organizers. No need to elaborate. If they ask where in Bordeaux, etc., just brush them off. 'Long story, too many trips to remember,' something like that."

Li chuckled. "Don't elaborate. Long story. Too many trips." He kept writing.

"You're going to buy two to three cases of the Armenian wine. Play it by ear. Check how many cases are on offer, what others are buying, and decide on a volume that's meaningful, 5 to 10 percent of the total offer of one kind of wine would be meaningful. But don't exceed five cases. You won't be able to fit more than that in your car. So, let's say they have fifty cases of the wine from Armenia. You buy four cases. Clear?"

"Clear. Do I show any interest in the other wines?"

"Interest, yes, absolutely. There's supposed to be a French wine as well, but we're not sure exactly what. Taste it. Get the name. See if they'll let you take a picture of the label. Say you need to send it home to China to see if you have anything from the same chateau. Remember, 'so many trips, so many chateaus, so hard to remember.'"

Liu Li laughed again. "So many chateaus, so little time. Got it."

"It's important you ask about their next events," stressed Petyan. "But after you buy your cases and pay in cash; only then bring up the schedule."

"Yes, got it."

"And stress that you're interested in regional wines. Mention Georgian wines, for example, and other Armenian wines if what they're selling is Korah."

Li nodded.

Carla Almayan was keenly aware of the importance of impressing her guests, the US ambassador and the deputy minister of foreign affairs of Armenia, at a special wine-tasting event at Alma Wines. Her choice of timing—Saturday at 11 a.m.—was deliberate. In early fall, strong winds were common in the vineyard in the afternoons, which made the tour less pleasant. And she wanted it on a weekend to make sure the dignitaries were relaxed and to minimize the chances of work-related telephone interruptions of her presentation. During the visit of the French Ambassador a few weeks earlier, he had to apologize for having to take two calls during the tour, which disrupted the flow of her meticulously crafted performance. "No more diplomats during work days," she had told her PR team, who booked the special visits.

The winding road leading to the main building snaked through the vineyards that spread up and down the rolling hills on both sides. As they approached the entrance of the winery, the large metal gate opened, and the guard pointed them toward the main building. The ambassador's car stopped in front of the winery building, with the other two cars in tow. His bodyguard was first to get out. He scanned the surroundings for a few seconds, then opened the back door for the ambassador to step out.

Carla was waiting in front of the building to greet them, with several of her staff standing dutifully behind her.

"It's an honor, Mr. Ambassador. Welcome to Alma Wines." She took his hand in both of hers and shook it firmly. Joe Connors was a friendly, good-humored man in his early fifties. He had brown gentle eyes, brown hair, and a faint smile permanently glued to his face. Carla had met him and his wife Anna several times at embassy events, including a Christmas party at the ambassador's residence to which U.S. citizens living in Armenia were invited. "Too bad Mrs. Connors couldn't come."

"Please, call me Joe, Carla. Your assistant said this was an informal setting." He smiled back. "Anna sends her regards. Today is her monthly book club meeting. She did not want to miss it."

"That means we'll have to do this again." She gave Connors her warmest smile before moving on to greet the deputy minister of foreign affairs. He was relatively young given his position at the ministry, in his late thirties, thin, had thick black hair, small black eyes, and a pointed nose. Carla had not met him before and was surprised by his youth and overall appearance. High ranking government officials tended to be older, balder and portlier.

After a short reception of coffee and fresh fruit on the covered patio at the entrance of the building, she invited the ambassador, his bodyguard, and the deputy minister to join her in her SUV, while the rest of the group followed them in an Alma van. Security rules dictated that ambassadors ride only in their own cars, but since this was a private estate and the bodyguard was with him, Connors went along.

"Clearing the land alone took over two years," she explained as she drove her guests around the vineyards. She showed them a small section deliberately left untouched—massive boulders rested sunk deep into the earth with rocks scattered around. "This is how the entire 200 hectares were," she said and waved her hand over the rows of vines spread out for miles. "Every square inch of this land had to be cleared of boulders; the large ones had to be blown up before they could be moved. The fence you see around the property—she pointed to the long fence that ran along the edge of the vineyards and disappeared from sight behind the hills—is built entirely with the stones and rocks dug up from here."

"Why this particular location?" Joe Connors wanted to know.

"There's a great French word that I have not yet been able to find in English," explained Carla while maneuvering around a sharp turn on the narrow road. "'Terroir.' The word captures all environmental and natural factors that can affect a crop. It covers climate, days of sunshine, temperature, humidity, soil chemistry, soil structure, acidity, and mineral content. It even encompasses geographic location relative to the equator. This place has it all. Perfect terroir for growing grapes."

"But the rocks?"

"Once broken up and scattered into the soil, they're actually good. No good wine grape can be raised in rich, fertile soil. They say grapes are like people; they have to suffer and fight for their survival to build character. Otherwise, we'll get watered down, tasteless grapes, and the wine will be the same."

Both men laughed. "If suffering builds character," said the deputy minister, "we must have a lot of character in Armenia!" It was an unusual comment to make in the presence of a diplomat, but Connors chuckled nonetheless.

"Around thirty hectares is reserved for fruit trees: mostly apricots, peaches, apples, plums, and cherries," announced Carla as she drove by a row of peach trees. She then pointed to a cluster of machinery abandoned at the side of the path. "That's the graveyard of the heavy machinery that sacrificed their lives for this vineyard," she said, solemnly at first and then started to laugh. There were earth-moving machines, excavators, wheel-loaders, trucks; six gigantic rusting metal forms were laid to rest in a neat line at a corner. "They all broke down and fell in the line of duty here. They were repaired and put back to use until they couldn't be repaired any more. We've been offered good money for them as scrap metal, but I won't sell. They are part of the history of this place, a testimony of what it took to start the vineyard."

"That too is part of the Armenian character," chimed in the deputy minister to Connors. "Mr. Ambassador, I'm sure you've noticed that in Armenia we revere the dead more than the living. We have five Merelots days in our calendar to honor the dead. Carla, you should hold a Merelots service for these poor machines."

Carla laughed, but she wanted to stick to her "man against nature" story. She pointed to two long, narrow structures on the side of the road. "Keep those in mind," she said. "I'll tell you their story inside."

The tour moved inside to the winery. Carla went over the wine-making process and the equipment: a state-of-the-art distillery, fermentation units, huge stainless steel tanks, lines of oak barrels, filtration units, and sophisticated temperature control systems.

"The first year when we were finally ready to harvest our vineyard, we confronted yet another challenge from nature," she said with a smile. "In a matter of minutes, our entire crop was destroyed by a hailstorm. Eight hundred tons of grapes, gone! Imagine spending years to clear the land and waiting a few more years to see your first crop and then watching it brutally ruined within minutes. But we had an answer to that challenge from nature as well. Those structures I pointed out to you earlier are anti-hail rockets. When the weather forecast warns of hail, we shoot them, they explode in the air and scatter the hail-producing clouds. They were installed soon after we lost the first crop. We've successfully used them since."

She next led them into a room where hundreds of oak barrels lay on their sides, patiently cradling the wine aging in them. It was a large, fun room with the floors painted red and row after row of the light brown barrels sporting several hundred signatures of visitors over the years. Carla handed out red, black, and green magic markers, and the guests got busy trying to find a blank spot on the round lids of the barrels. She helped the ambassador and the deputy minister to a barrel on the sidewall, which had relatively few signatures. They all signed: We've been here.

Unlike the tasting rooms in other wineries where there was usually nothing to eat or where one could find a bowl of crackers once in a while and, even more rarely, some cheese, Carla insisted that wine tasting at Alma Wines should involve a feast. Wine couldn't be tasted and appraised with just a few stale crackers. It was important to create a fitting gastronomic setting for appreciating wine. When the guests returned from the tour, Carla escorted them to an elaborately set table, each place setting, aside from the standard plates and flatware, boasted a lineup of eight wine glasses. The food display was impressive, from rich cheese platters to various meat and vegetable appetizers to sumptuous main courses from traditional Armenian cousine.

Carla went through the sequence: Voskehat Dry White, Voskehat Reserve, Kangun Dry White, Karmrahyut Rosé, Karmrahyut Red, Areni Dry Red, Areni Reserve, and Kangun Semi-Sweet White. It was a ninety-minute presentation, interspersed with personal stories. It was also a tutorial covering the basics of wine tasting: how to hold the wine glass by the stem, how to whirl, look, smell, taste, and toast. The staff poured each wine as she signaled, and those who expressed a fondness for one particular kind got a refill without asking.

"Some wines can be consumed alone," she said. "These are wines that enhance the dignity of solitude. Our Areni reserve fits the bill. It doesn't mean you can't share it with friends; you can do that with all the wines. But you can also take a bottle of Areni Reserve and go to a secluded place, to a remote corner of this vineyard for example, read a book or listen to music, all by yourself, and return home only when the last drop of the bottle is consumed.

Other wines are best when shared. Our Voskehat Reserve is one. It reminds me of one of Ernest Hemingway's quotes: 'I drink to make other people more interesting,' he said. Isn't that ingenious? I can testify to that. I've seen our Voskehat Reserve make so many people so much more interesting over the years." She laughed as she said the last sentence, and, having learned over the years how to make her laugh contagious, the ambassador and the deputy minister couldn't help but join in.

A presentation like this couldn't just be about the wine, like some vintners tended to make it, primarily because that was all they knew. This had to be a presentation of love, as much as of wine. Carla was pleased with the day. Her delivery was impeccable. Her charisma was exhilerating. Her passion, contagious.

What made days like this even more gratifying was that it hadn't always been that good Carla. Her journey to reach this point in her life had been, to grossly understate the truth, rocky.

"This phenomenon we call *Karot* requires a pensive but not an overly reflective wine," Dorian explained to the vintners who had gathered in his

Ashtarak winery one Sunday afternoon to taste some of the new VanDor wines before their release. Afterwards, sitting by a fire, he shared with Haig and Carla and the makers of Troika Wines and Coor his prescriptions for emotions.

He had given up on the idea of prescribing wines to dull emotions. If emotions were real, deep, and worth considering, they couldn't be dulled, no matter how sad or unconstructive they were. Instead, he had been focusing on wines that would help a person live with the emotions that had taken hold of them, prescriptions that would allow the emotion to be accepted and internalized.

He had lumped *Nostalgia/Karot (Garod)* into one category. He also studied similar concepts from other cultures that applied in Armenia, such as the Japanese notion of *Natsukashii*—nostalgia for an idealized past that had never been. They formed the basic, age-old emotion of all Armenians. Centuries of living without a free homeland, families divided and spread all over the world, lost relatives whose stories had been passed from generation to generation with no hope of ever seeing them again, and the need to master foreign languages and cultures while trying to maintain their own in private had all embedded themselves into the Armenian DNA. This couldn't be dulled or denied.

And it *shouldn't* be. It had become too much of the average Armenian's reality. But it could be absorbed and turned into part of one's character, so it would no longer hurt.

"The balancing act is tough. You do need to dwell on an emotion in order to internalize it, but the problem with nostalgia is that as you dwell on it, it can suck you in like a black hole and bury you. That's how strong it can be. It can take us on a crazy, involuntary detour into depression. A measure of detachment is required to avoid that detour."

Dorian got up to stoke the fire and uncorked two more bottles. He didn't need to say more about the nature of the emotion. His audience knew it well.

"The same balancing act is required in choosing the wine," he continued. "The trick is to make the wine filter the emotion into you in manageable doses. This emotion rules out most light and overly fruity wines. This needs depth. It needs to inspire realism and perspective. Forget also the big, extravagant celebratory wines like Champagne and Sauternes. The wine should inspire—excuse the pun—emotional sobriety. Troika's 2010-2011 Reserve wines come to my mind. I have a feeling that the Koleyan-Cobb Areni would be pretty good for this in several years. From foreign wines, a 2010 Pauillac, or an old vine Zinfandel of 2008-2010 vintage."

"Some Barberas I've tried recently come pretty close to what you're after," Haig said.

"I can see that," said Dorian. "The Barbera can vary with vintage and winery a bit more than the Pauillac, but I can see how it could work. Notice we have not brought up any whites or rosés. There may be a rare exception buried somewhere deep in the cellars of Montrachet, but in general they are no match for this emotion."

The five winemakers went late into the night on this array of emotions alone. Fortunately, Dorian's cellar provided adequate diversity to test many theories.

Jerjeruk (Dzherdzheruk): an old Armenian variety. It matures in late September. The leaf is large, roundish, on the underside of the leaf the pubescence is dense spider veins. The flower is bisexual. The cluster is medium, cylindrical or cylindrical-conical, usually dense. The berry is medium sized, rounded, in the shade green, in the sun light amber, with a thick waxy coating. The pulp is juicy. The skin is thin, elastic, with brown dots, it is difficult to separate from the pulp. Jerjeruk is used for light table wines.

CHAPTER SEVEN

The gate to the imposing old mansion in the center of Moscow a few blocks from the Kremlin opened before Li had a chance to knock. An elderly man in a black suit bowed and pointed him toward the semicircular staircase.

"Second floor," he said. "To the right." He bowed again.

Rumor had it that the mansion once belonged to the late Armand Hammer, the one-time head of Occidental Petroleum, which he ran for well over thirty years. Hammer had close ties to the Soviet Union, having made deals with Vladimir Lenin personally, trading American wheat for Russian caviar and furs back in the 1920s when the Soviet Union was practically in famine. His dealings with Russia flourished during the early decades of the Soviet Union when he purportedly acquired several mansions in and around Moscow, which were sold over time by his heirs. Some were stately enough to be bought by foreign governments as ambassadorial residences. Others were grabbed by local entrepreneurs fortunate enough to be given an opportunity to bid on such estates.

The foyer was vast. The steps of the staircase were six-foot solid pieces of dark granite. The black cast iron railing was a piece of art in its own right, boasting the most intricate designs, polished to perfection. Li stopped halfway up the staircase to take a moment to stroke and admire the work of the blacksmiths who had probably devoted a lifetime to perfecting their art. He looked up. As far as he could make out, the building had only two floors, but above the landing of the second floor a massive dome soared at least a further twenty feet. It flaunted yet another intricate design, this time of colorful stained glass.

The building was undoubtedly a relic of pre-revolutionary Russia. Exquisite though it was, there was more to it than brick and mortar. On the wall around and up the staircase were a Cezanne, Matisse, and Aivazovski and also more modern paintings that Li did not recognize. Still others were only partially visible, hidden around the curve of the circular wall. He wished he could skip the wine tasting and take a personal tour of the artwork instead, but he was soon disabused of that notion at the top of the staircase by the emphatic welcome of a man with a heavy French accent, who stood at the top of the staircase.

"Monsieur Li, I presume," said the man. "*Enchanté*. Welcome to our exclusive community. I am Valerie Lefebvre."

The man was six-foot-two and sported a dark maroon cashmere coat, gray pants, white shirt, and a bright blue bow tie. His thick gray hair was neatly parted on the right side, and what stuck out on his face even more than his bushy eyebrows was his huge, eagle-hooked nose. Yet Lefebvre's manners were so courteous and gallant and his smile so warm that Li couldn't help but smile back. This was a long cry from the Russian who had interviewed him before giving him the address of the mansion and the time of the meeting. As Jack had warned, that man had looked and acted like a thug who, at the slightest provocation, would easily have shoved a blade between Li's ribs.

"Thank you," Li managed to utter, remembering his script. "I'm looking forward to this evening."

"I'm confident you won't be disappointed, Monsieur Li. This way, please."

Li realized he had made the first mistake of the novice by being on time. There was no one else in the large reception hall where Lefebvre led him and handed him over to a charming young lady whom he introduced as his assistant, Mademoiselle Dominique Martin. She greeted him in an elegant navy-blue suit with a knee-length tight skirt and perfectly tapered jacket, and a white silk shirt with shiny mother-of-pearl buttons. She kindly asked him to help himself to the refreshments laid on the table. Li watched with amazement as Mademoiselle Martin left the spacious room with her buttocks clearly outlined and the heels of her matching blue stilettos echoing on the marble floor.

He had no interest in the refreshments—Russian and European mineral waters and cookies. But fortunately the walls of the reception hall were lined with more paintings, and Li felt comfortable browsing through the artwork, happy to ignore any newcomers, who seemed equally happy to ignore him.

After thirty minutes or so, Monsieur Lefebvre reappeared in the reception hall. It seemed that all the guests had arrived. Li counted fourteen men, including himself, eleven of whom were Asian. From his perspective, the other three could have been Russian, European, or even American.

"Gentlemen," echoed Lefebvre's heavy French accent across the reception hall. "Once again, welcome. I'm happy to see some old friends and a couple of new faces. But whether old or new, you all know that this is neither an ordinary gathering nor an ordinary wine tasting. You will get to know two wines here this evening that you will not be able to experience anywhere else, not even in the countries where the wines are made, because the limited production of both has already been disposed of in China, the US, and Europe. Fortunately, we have managed to secure a small share for our friends in Moscow. After all, at the end of the day, that's the service that we provide to you. We choose these wines from thousands of bottles that we try every year."

All fourteen faces were turned toward Lefebvre, as if deliberately trying to avoid eye contact with each other. Li felt a sense of competition in the room. This was not an auction, so technically they would not be competing over the wines, but there was a sense of each man for himself, ruling out any urge to compare notes about the wines. Why wouldn't the fourteen wine collector-buyers want to discuss the wines with each other? Why wasn't this more like a buyer's club? He remembered Petyan's orders not to socialize with the other buyers, and while he understood the reason for reclusiveness in his case, he wondered why the others also kept to themselves. Regardless of the reason, the fact that the buyers tended to keep their distance from each other gave Lefebvre a distinct advantage in managing his audience. He was the center of attention and the maestro.

"Well then, gentlemen," said Lefebvre. "Shall we begin?" He waved his arm toward the side door, which led to another, smaller room. There were two bottles of wine on a large, square wooden table with over thirty wine glasses arranged in neat lines, rim-down. Mademoiselle Martin was standing behind the table, hair tied back in a bun and the middle button of her suit jacket barely able to hold her ample bosom, which looked like it could burst out of her shirt any minute.

"Dear friends," declared Lefebvre, as he straightened his bow tie and buttoned his cashmere jacket. "I'm afraid scarcity is a fact of life when it comes to exceptional wines. There are only 400 cases produced of one of the wines we will taste tonight, a rare Bordeaux from a tiny winery that rents a few hectares from a larger producer to cultivate its vineyard. And even less, only 320 cases of another remarkable wine from a less-known region. But trust me when I say, as a Frenchman, it tops some of the best Bordeaux."

He watched as Mademoiselle Martin started pouring small amounts from one of the bottles into fifteen wine glasses.

"I mentioned scarcity," continued Lefebvre. "What does it mean for us? Well, first, these wine tastings have to be exclusive, only for those who appreciate what's rare in life, and unfortunately, we can afford only a small sample for each worthy friend who is here tonight. Given the scarcity of what we're offering, I'm sure you can appreciate why this room is not full of everyday enthusiasts. On second thought, this may not be a problem after all because it gives me the opportunity to spend more quality time with each of you."

The men stirred and nodded.

"The second problem, I'm sorry to say, is that when something is so rare and unique, the price cannot be low. Yet I'm happy to report that these prices are nowhere near the bottle of 1945 Chateau Mouton Rothschild that was sold for well over $300,000 a few years ago."

Now that everyone had a point of reference, they turned their attention to Mademoiselle Martin. She finished pouring the last glass with meticulous care, in what seemed in slow motion, as if she was savoring the view of every drop that left the bottle.

"*Et viola!*" declared Lefebvre. "If you permit me a little bias, we shall start with the Bordeaux. As I said, only 400 cases were produced of which, alas, we have managed to secure only 42 cases. The rest are already destined for discriminating collectors in New York, Los Angeles, Shanghai, Beijing, and various European cities. The price per case is $42,000, a mere $3,500 per bottle." He then waved his arm and invited the buyers to approach the table and pick up their glasses.

Li followed his lead as Lefebvre held the base of his glass between his thumb and first two fingers, swirled, and held it up to the alabaster light hanging low from the ceiling over the table.

"My friends, do notice the darker depth than the average Bordeaux," he said in awe. "Notice the layers of velvet that make up this unique color." He was almost whispering, as if his voice could disturb the majesty of the color. Several concurring murmurs arose as fourteen additional glasses glittered under the mellow light of the alabaster.

"Let's move on, gentlemen," declared Lefebvre, satisfied that everyone in the room had in fact seen the layers of velvet glowing under the light. He then immersed his formidable nose into his glass. The expectant nostrils of the fourteen men followed suit, and the room was filled with a long *whoosh* as the men inhaled deeply.

This time Lefebvre waited, raised an eyebrow, and solicited opinions with a gesture of his hand. The buyers were too reserved to volunteer opinions at first, but Lefebvre patiently waited until someone stirred and uttered, "Plum."

Lefebvre smiled broadly and gestured to encourage him to continue. After a moment, the man murmured again, "Licorice."

Lefebvre smiled again and nodded. "Excellent nose, Mr. Chang, I congratulate you. It has both, but the licorice is not overpowering, which is why you noticed it after the plum. Superb detection. There are other scents lurking in the background, more fruity scents like black cherries, but the plum and licorice are the main actors."

Li stared at Mr. Chang for a moment, then back at Lefebvre. Could the performance have been staged? Was Mr. Chang a client like all the others?

The verbal calisthenics soared to new heights when the tasting began. The wine was chewed, rolled, sent to the back of the mouth and brought to the front again, and eventually swallowed. Now the chorus of impressions was more daring with more buyers venturing opinions under the constant encouragement and praise of Monsieur Lefebvre. Li had to double his efforts to memorize every word. Traces of chocolate, raspberries, vanilla, wood and earth were identified, which most participants noted either on small pads of paper or in their smart phones. He did his best to follow, but, hard as he tried, he could not detect chocolate, wood or earth.

There also was a discussion of complexity and depth, which one of the Asian participants described as having a "Zen quality" because of its "deep sense of stability." Even Monsieur Lefebvre looked surprised by that one and was delighted to confirm the observation with a shower of compliments to the proud author.

"A French wine blessed with a Zen quality," he declared. "Imagine that! The West finally meets the East in a legendary bottle of wine!"

Consenting hums and murmurs filled the room. Li noticed the momentary approving look that Mademoiselle Martin gave their host for his performance.

"Now, superb as this experience was," announced Lefebvre, still glowing in the West-meets-East-in-a-bottle masterstroke, "I have the pleasure of introducing, once again, a prized regional wine. Those of you who bought a few cases of the Areni Eagle last year must remember how its price rose by 50 percent after only a few months. This one promises even a steeper surge, and when I let you in on a little secret after the tasting, I'm sure you'll agree with me."

Mademoiselle Martin had already put away the first set of glasses and was pouring tasting portions in fifteen new glasses, as deliberately and carefully as before. That was fortuitous because Li, and, he presumed, the other men also, now had a legitimate reason to stare at her.

"This one is as exceptional as the Bordeaux that we just tasted, as rich and complex, but it has an added—oh, how shall I say? An added milieu. Or perhaps the better word would be an added mystique. This one, gentlemen, comes from the birthplace of wine. My French pride will not stand in the way when I say that Bordeaux is a child compared to the wine-making history of Areni."

The group then proceeded to go through the same ritual, examining color, smell, and taste, followed by a torrent of more intangible characteristics than even those cited in honor of the Bordeaux. In eastern cultures, 'older' connoted more venerable and esteemed. Aside from the Zen quality of depth and stability, which apparently the Areni Eagle also possessed in abundance, a certain "permanence of the ages" was detected in its earthy aftertaste. Lefebvre looked elated by the cooperative and responsive audience.

"Permanence of the ages," he repeated. "It is registered! This was bottled only four years ago. It is ready to drink now, but will also age beautifully. As I mentioned earlier, only 320 cases were produced, of which we managed to secure only thirty-five. The price per case is $30,000, only $2,500 per bottle. Now that you've tasted it, I will tell you the secret I mentioned earlier. I know that the famous wine rater, Mr. Bowker, is excited about the Areni grape. A reliable source tells me that a yet unnamed Areni wine will receive a rating of above 96, possibly as high as 98, from Mr. Bowker. Can you imagine what that will do the price of the Areni Eagle?"

Mademoiselle Martin had moved into an adjoining room. While the door was still open, Li could see her sitting behind an antique desk, laptop open, ready to record the orders. As Monsieur Lefebvre entertained the buyers with stories of how prices of various wines had soared in the recent years, he encouraged each one to go into the adjoining room and place his order. This arrangement was to protect the privacy of the orders. One by one, the buyers went in to see Mademoiselle Martin, closing the door behind them. The first five to go in were all Asians. Li decided it was time. He walked into the room and closed the door behind him.

"Monsieur Li," said Mademoiselle Martin in a low, seductive voice, and invited him to sit on the chair across the desk. "I'm so glad you have joined us. I hope you enjoyed today's wines."

"Thank you," said Li, nervous about the sexual aura in the room. "I enjoyed both very much. I hope you still have four cases of the Areni Eagle."

"You're not late, Monsieur Li. Twenty-five of the thirty-five cases are already gone, but we do have ten left. Would you like me to reserve four cases for you?"

Li nodded, his anxiety rising as Martin walked over to him to hand him a leather-bound notebook, pointing a perfectly manicured purple fingertip to a space where Li was supposed to sign. Her perfume, her physical closeness, and the proximity of her chest to his face as she leaned over to point out the signature line were all working their magic.

"Can you confirm this address?" she asked.

"If that is for delivery, may I have my driver pick up my cases from here instead?" asked Li. It was a line he had been instructed to use and had rehearsed.

"But of course, Monsieur, no problem at all. Just let me know when."

"If you have the wine on the premises, he's waiting for me outside, and he can pick them up now."

"I believe I can arrange that," she said, took the notebook, and moved slowly back to her chair. "Now, how would you like to settle payment? Monsieur Lefebvre does not accept personal checks, I'm afraid, but most major credit cards are acceptable."

"How about cash?" asked Li, as if he were proposing something naughty. "I can have my driver bring the $120,000 in cash now if that is acceptable and pick up the wine."

The expression on Mademoiselle Martin's face told Li that she had not had this kind of transaction before. Although transactions in cash were commonplace among Russians, this was a French operation with largely non-Russian clients. She hesitated for a moment, probably wondering if the monetary bills needed to be validated. But then she smiled.

"Of course it will be acceptable," she said. Having seen her initial hesitation about payment in cash, Li had thought that she may have to check it with Lefebvre. But she made the decision herself, with confidence. That struck Li as odd. "But I'll have to arrange for the four cases to be brought up from the cellar where they are stored. Would you mind waiting until I finish with the other guests?"

Li said he didn't mind. He was anxious to leave the room so he could breathe more freely away from Mademoiselle Martin's aura. In all his excitement, he had forgotten to ask about the Bordeaux or take a picture of the label. He didn't even remember what the label on the bottle that they tasted looked like. He also forgot to ask Martin about future events. He joined the others in the tasting room, moved to a corner, and called the driver that Petyan had assigned to him.

While he waited for the driver to arrive with a leather briefcase carrying the cash, he had a chance to chat with Lefebvre and remembered to ask about the schedule of future sales events.

Dominique Martin was still at the antique desk, pouring over some figures on her laptop, when Lefebvre, having bid goodbye to Li, returned to the room and threw himself on the armchair in the corner. He watched her as she worked on her bookkeeping.

"How did we do?" he asked.

She waved her hand telling him to be quiet.

She finally closed her notebook and looked at him. He half opened his eyes.

"All thirty-five cases of the Areni Eagle, gone; forty of the forty-five cases of the Bordeaux are gone. Total for tonight: $2.73 million."

"*Pas mal, n'est ce pas?*"

"You outdid yourself tonight, Valerie. Well done. I'll make sure your bonus reflects your excellent performance. But of course you realize that you've set a new record that I'll expect you to live up to." She smiled at him.

"*Merci, ma charmante patronne,*" he said, straightening his sprawling body in the armchair. "You make my job much easier by your unique energy."

"Now you know why I don't want to have women buyers. They'll see through the act right away."

"*Oui Madame.*"

"I have an early flight to Paris," she said shoving her notebook in a thin attaché case. "See you in a few weeks in St. Petersburg."

Haig estimated he'd reach his vineyard in ninety minutes. He had just exited the city limits of Yerevan on the newly constructed north-south highway, which was a marvel compared with the antiquated infrastructure in the rest of the country. A heavy cement construction with three lanes in each direction, it was smooth and flat, with no bumps or potholes. The maximum speed limit was set at 100 kilometers per hour but driving at 120–140 kph came so naturally on the flawless road that it became the de facto speed limit.

His vineyard extended over the hills south-east of the highway, four kilometers past the village of Areni, a few kilometers from the Areni cave complex. It occupied a hundred acres of rocky soil sprawling over a hilly terrain some 4,000 feet above sea level. At this winery, he produced one varietal: Areni Noir, branded as Korah.

He loved that drive, especially the segment that took him up the scenic mountain range after the town of Yeraskh, to the Vayots Dzor region, and then down into the villages of Chiva, Rind, Areni, Aghavnadzor, and Arpi. Beyond Areni, past the striking rock formations and monastery of Noravank, past the Areni 1 cave, he could drive into the heartland of medieval history through a string of other villages: Shatin, Yeghegis, Hermon, Vardahovit. It was a twenty-five-kilometer stretch saturated with archeological treasures, spanning the rich history of the region from the sixth to thirteenth centuries. It was where the Silk Road passed through, where international cultures and communities flourished, where some of the most beautiful medieval monasteries stood, some in ruins others in better shape, but either way oblivious to the malaise that reigned over modern-day village life. This was where Arab, Persian, and Jewish communities thrived in the middle of Armenian towns and where he could encounter vestiges from the Bronze and Iron Ages at practically every turn, not to mention the unexplored and undocumented traces of Urartian viticulture in every village on the way.

But there was more to this country. The land pulled him. The land— the only thing that had not betrayed its people throughout the ages. When kings, feudal lords, presidents, foreign occupiers, and even the church turned their back on the people, the land kept on giving. And the people bonded with the land seamlessly, timelessly. The abundance of the land had no measure. Mountain meadows and forests sustained a diverse, thriving animal and plant life so effortlessly that everything seemed to fit and belong together. Rivers, mountain creeks and lakes never ran dry, even in the height of summer, and river trout thrived in abundance even in the relatively small creeks. Magnificent mountain sheep and goats made the steep rock formations their home, and brown bears roamed in the oak forests. Red and black rosehip bushes grew wild in the mountainsides, and rosehip berries burst out of their skins in the fall. Wild sorrel and purslane and spinach returned every year as faithfully as spring. Wild thyme and mint erupted from the crevices of rocks. Hawthorn and cornel, with their hundreds of health benefits, took over the fields and mountain meadows with an abundance that took even the earth by surprise. No one cultivated or cared for these plants. They just appeared, as someone in love appears to meet their lover.

Here, spring was much more than a reprieve from a harsh winter; it was a renewal of vows between nature and man, a communion of sorts, a rite. Spring was when extended village families took to the mountain meadows to gather all those blessings and more. It was when the laughter of teenage girls in colorful sweaters and headscarves filled the air over green slopes and helped ripen the wild apples, pears, plums, and acorns that would feed the brown bears and the boars in the fall.

And of course, a land this generous could not possibly disappoint when it came to grapes. This was where the *Vitis Vinifera* was domesticated 8,000 years ago. This mountainous, volcanic land, with its scorching sun, high altitudes, warm to hot summers and cold winters, was created for the vine. Haig believed that all the other blessings, plentiful though they were, were mere fringe benefits.

As he approached Areni village, Haig decided to stop at his regular stand to stretch his legs. It belonged to a farmer called Ohannes, from whom he bought a few tons of grapes every fall to supplement his own production. He knew the family well—Ohannes, his wife, Arusyak, and three sons worked in their vineyards and orchards around the village. It was Arusyak, a chubby, bubbly woman in her early fifties, who manned the stand.

"*Bari or*, Arus jan," said Haig as he got out of his car and stretched his back. Good day. Arusyak was busy stacking a few cardboard fruit crates in the hut adjacent to the stand. She recognized Haig's voice and turned back, a broad smile on her sun burnt face.

"Haigo jan! *Barev, barev!*" She went to him and gave him a bear hug.

"How are Ohannes and the boys?" asked Haig.

"Great, thank you. Getting ready for the harvest. But we already have some of the early Majar from the pre-harvest a few weeks ago. Let me get you a bottle from inside. This stuff here is for tourists." She pointed at the wine in old Coke bottles lined up on the escalated wooden stand. Majar was newly made wine, just a few weeks old, usually light, and, with rare exceptions, generally bad.

"Wait," said Haig laughing as he usually did when he wanted to soften his approach. "I want to see what you're selling to the tourists."

"*De lav, eli*, Haigo jan. You fuss too much about this stuff. Who cares what a bunch of tourists think?"

"I do. What they think matters more than what I think, Arus jan. We're not trying to sell *me* on Armenian wines, are we?"

Arusyak chuckled nervously and brought him two bottles, one from inside the hut, and one from the stand. "There. Tell me if your tourists can even tell the difference."

Haig laughed with her, took the two bottles and walked back to his car.

"By the way," said Arusyak, "we're selling a lot of bulk wine. They come with these five-gallon glass jars and fill everything they can find in the village cellars."

"Who?"

"I have no idea. The driver is from Yerevan. He comes in a pickup truck, checks the wine directly from the clay urns in home cellars, loads, pays and leaves."

"What kind?"

"All Areni. From the villages here."

"Arus jan, how long has this been going on?"

"Ohannes just found out about it, but apparently it's been going on for a while. They started in Aghavnadzor, then, gradually, asking who else had home-made wines, spread to the other villages."

"Do you know how much wine they're buying?"

"Hard to tell. Some say they've seen more than twenty jugs lined up in the pickup truck."

What would his old professor from the University of Milan, Professor Attilio Scienza, say if he was here? He was a staunch believer that indigenous grape varieties should be protected. He called the globalization and universal acceptance of a handful of wine varietals viticide, meaning the extinction of unique indigenous varieties around the world. Haig had last seen him sixteen years ago in Milan, where he had gone to try to restructure his mounting debt with the banks. He'd had a successful business producing wine in Italy, in addition to selling Italian wines to international clients, particularly to large Swiss importers. But his enthusiasm had gotten the better of him, and he became overextended. He was on the verge of bankruptcy.

"Your ancestral homeland is the cradle of wine, Haig," Professor Scienza had said. "You have as many indigenous grape varieties in Armenia as we have in Italy. And you certainly have a much, much longer and richer history of winemaking. Why are you here? Go make a real difference."

What would the old Professor make of the surge in demand for Korah and home-made Areni wine? Haig wished he could bring him to Armenia for a few days and show him around.

What a revelation the Professor's advice had been. Armenia had gained independence after the collapse of the Soviet Union only years earlier. It had no worthy recent wine culture. The all-powerful and faceless Soviet central planning apparatus had decreed that Armenia would produce cognac, and Georgia, equally subject to the Soviet system, would produce wine.

Despite the gripes and protests of the French, who insisted that only wines produced in the Cognac region of France could be called cognac, the Soviet authorities labeled the brandy produced in Armenia cognac, and it became famous throughout the empire and beyond. One of its most famous devotees was Sir Winston Churchill, who was partial to the Dvin variety of Ararat Armenian Cognac. His World War II ally, General Secretary Joseph Stalin, used to airlift crates of Dvin to London to accommodate Churchill's one-bottle-a-night consumption pattern. Equally unlikely aficionados of Armenian cognac were Agatha Christie and Frank Sinatra.

The irony was that after the collapse of the Soviet Union, the Armenian government sold the famous Ararat brandy company to a French distiller called Pernod Ricard, and once under French control, the product was no longer called cognac, but simply brandy. Back then, most Armenians drank either Armenian cognac or Russian vodka. The collective attitude of villagers in wine-producing regions such as Areni sunk into a complacent, unchallenged routine, trapping them in a comfortable tradition of mediocrity. That was by far the worst part of the legacy of seventy years of Soviet mismanagement.

There were a few more sophisticated wine makers in Soviet times, the most notable being Harry Avagian, the man Haig sought to meet first. Harry was an old-school, Soviet-style vintner, set in his ways. He urged Haig to start a vineyard with an initial fifty hectares, and they went into a partnership where Avagian held a 40 percent share. But after they had completed all the paperwork and started operations, Haig discovered that Avagian had ended up with 60 percent of the operation. That was his first lesson in dealing with the old oligarchy of the former Soviet Republic.

Nevertheless, reviving the historic winemaking tradition of Armenia became a mission and an obsession.

"What the hell is going on?" Haig pronounced the words aloud as he approached Aghavnadzor. "Jugs of home-made wine?" he said aloud again, as if expecting the row of poplar trees by the roadside to know the answer. A large group of crows circled around one of the poplars and descended upon it, blackening the upper section of the tree. A five-gallon jug would hold over 25 bottles of wine. Twenty jugs are over forty cases. How often? Who? Why?

Sev Kakhet, *Black Kakhet, Kakhet Noir: a widespread variety in the Artashat region. The tip of the young shoot is white, due to cobweb hairs. The mature leaf is medium, circular, and deeply five lobbed. The bunch is small, cylindrical-conical, and dense. The berry is medium, roundish to elliptic, dark blue to black, and glossy. The skin is rough, elastic, and rich in tannins. The flesh is pulpy and juicy. The wine is strong and velvety red. The wine is also suitable for making brandy.*

CHAPTER EIGHT

Dorian had moved beyond nostalgia.

A larger group than usual had stormed into The Realm one night. A table for thirteen, reserved for 11 p.m. They were young, charged, boisterous, happy. Dorian put his book down, took a sip of wine, and watched. It was a mixed group—all in their mid-to-late-thirties, but he guessed that some were from California, a couple from Lebanon, a few repatriated Armenians and at least three from Armenia. He also suspected that at least two of them were American, probably friends of one of the California Diasporans.

"That was incredible," one of the ladies was saying. She looked flushed and elated, unable to sit still, her hand gestures leading her arms to fly around as she spoke. "What a show! What a concert! My parents used to play some of these songs when we were young, but I had never heard them at a live concert."

"Komitas is irresistible," said the young man hovering next to her, eager to impress the lady. "He gave us our popular music. Much of what followed, one way or another, stems from it."

"What a concert! It was *amazing*..." She did not seem interested in the young man's analysis.

At that moment, one word came to Dorian—*Duende*, a Spanish word that described a feeling of intense and overwhelming awe caused by viewing a piece of art, experiencing a musical performance, or reading a poem. The emotion suited Yerevan—one needed a forty-eight-hour day to catch all the art exhibits, concerts, and plays that filled the city's galleries, music halls, theaters, jazz clubs, and the opera house. And there was a large enough art-loving community in Yerevan to justify a *duende*-nurturing selection of wines.

He thought of wines for both before and after an art exhibit or a concert. One should go in emotionally prepared to live it and come out prepared to reflect on what they experienced. Of course, the occasion mattered. A classical concert would pose different requirements than a jazz concert or a folk festival. But one could still come up with generalized pre- and post- wines. The best pre-art wines were light and what Dorian liked to call 'happy' whites—wines that would lift one's spirit in such a way so as to make it to make it more receptive to artistic expression. The Coor white would make the cut. So would an aromatic, full bodied Viognier. The post-art wine had to have an added reflective element: A Sauvignon Blanc, either California or New Zealand, or a light Burgundy Pinot. That's what this group needed.

As the night progressed, Dorian realized that the group had a lot more to offer. His most significant discovery that night was an emotion that he knew existed in the city, but he had not yet encountered it as directly and strongly as he did when he turned his attention to the local youth from Yerevan and studied them as they watched their Diasporan compatriots. He saw the yearning in their faces for the adventures that they imagined the outsiders had, the travel that they had done, the places that they had seen. He saw their passion for adventure and their thirst for new experiences. The emotion was intense, and it was best captured by one word rooted in ancient Greek, *eleutheromania*, referring to an irresistible urge to be free. It afflicted younger individuals in Yerevan who could not afford to live alone and had to live with their parents even when they were in their thirties. It was also common among people who wanted to travel to see the world but couldn't. *Eleutheromania* was related also to *wanderlust*, a longing to break free, to be somewhere else, and was almost the opposite of nostalgia and homesickness.

Eleutheromania needed what Dorian called an 'explosive' wine—balanced, but full of fireworks; youthful, but rebellious rather that playful. The Armenian grapes did not offer many choices. Some Kangun-Voskehat blends came close, but what this needed was more of the Alsace style wines—Gewürztraminer or heavy German Grand Cru Rieslings. The common thread here was the feeling of what Dorian called of a 'grand finale' in the air.

By midafternoon, as Haig made the last turn on the curvy country road, the sight of the entrance to his winery brought a smile to his face. Two large granite columns held the twenty-foot high and thirty-five foot wide cast iron gate, which opened directly into the vineyards. He had debated whether to build a cast-iron sign announcing "Koleyan Vineyards" to place on top of the gate. He eventually decided against it. Although he did not shy away from being a show-off when it came to his achievements in the Armenian wine sector, somehow the idea of a sign screaming his name to the world seemed too immodest.

The narrow road inside the gate passed through the vineyards and reached the main winery building.

"We need another week or so," Armen said, greeting him. "Sugar was around 21 percent when I checked this morning. We can wait till we get 23–24 percent. Then we'll be ready."

Haig smiled. Beyond wine, there wasn't much worth talking about as far as Armen was concerned. He did not even bother to ask about the acidity levels, which had varied a bit beyond the normal range last year. Armen would be on top of that too.

It was early September, and pre-harvest preparations—which were as important as the harvest itself—were underway. A well-planned and implemented harvest meant that the grapes would be delivered to the winery in their prime condition. There was an excitement in the air. A new generation of wine was about to come to light. For dedicated vintners, it was like giving birth to a child. Reaching this point was the most unpredictable part of the winemaking cycle, because one never knew what nature would dish out. The weather during spring, summer, and fall dictated the quality of that year's grapes. Hot or mild summers, cold or mild falls, and the ultimate imponderable, hail in early spring which could destroy the entire crop in merely minutes, determined how nature had cast the die. Even without the dreaded hail in the spring, heavy rains in June could drop the flowers off the vines.

"Before we tour the vineyard, let's go look at the new land," said Haig. "It's practically next door. The owner will meet us there. I've decided to buy it."

The land was five minutes away by car, with only a narrow stretch of public forest separating it from the edge of the Korah vineyard. With a permit from the municipality of Aghavnadzor, he could extend the water supply from his vineyard to the new land directly through the public land. It needed some work—clearing rocks and wild fruit trees and straightening several sharp shifts in the topography for easier functioning of tractors, which required renting costly earth-moving equipment and hiring manual labor. But it was ideal.

Armen concurred.

Haig tried to haggle on price, but the owner, a sunbaked farmer with shrewd eyes, would not budge.

"The only concession I can make," he said, "is this: the area is slightly larger than 12 hectares. By precise cadastral measurements, it is 12.25

hectares. We won't count the 0.25 hectares. But the price cannot be below $25k per hectare—$300,000." They shook hands.

Haig called his bank and transferred 24 million drams to the owner's bank account, the equivalent of $50,000, as a down payment. They would close the deal and transfer title in a week.

As he walked down the rows of vines in his vineyard, seeing the ripe bunches hanging from the branches, Haig was reminded of a woman in the last week of her pregnancy: ripe, heavy, full of life and promise, and radiating a sensual brilliance so pure that it inspired only admiration. He saw pride in the posture of the branches—*look what we've got for you!* He remembered Alina's pregnancy. He could not stop his eyes from watering with pride and happiness, but could not stop worrying, too.

In this part of the country, birds and bears usually did most of the damage—aside from pests and wasps, of course. At the Korah winery not only was every bunch harvested by hand, but also every bunch was screened to remove unripe and rotten berries. That meant that the harvesters had to confront wasps and yellow jackets directly, in addition to removing the damaged berries caused by the voracious insects.

Birds devoured berries, but bears could uproot entire vines as they marched through the vineyard at night sampling the ripe bunches. The normal protections of netting and fences were not practiced. The necessary infrastructure would cost far too much for the capital strapped vintners.

Before one even started facing the challenges of making good wine, the challenges posed by nature had to be faced and overcome. As he'd heard Carla tell her visitors to Alma Wines, the vintner had to fight three battles: man against nature, which started way before the land was even planted; then man against man, which dealt with the bureaucratic hurdles of setting up the winery; and then man against the market, where, having survived the first two phases of the struggle, one had to prove themselves in the marketplace. Haig liked that characterization of their art, though he would never acknowledge it publicly. Carla hadn't earned the right to give that talk.

But that didn't matter now, on this spectacular fall evening in Vayots Dzor. Haig and Armen returned from their tour of the vineyard and sat on the terrace overlooking the sprawling hills of grapevines, drawn and submerged into the colors of the sunset and the myriad of shadows cast over the vines. Sarah, the jovial housekeeper of the vineyard who loved to tease Haig at every chance, brought out a bottle of the special reserve Korah that Haig had chosen earlier. The bottle had no label. He had taken it out of the vault where he kept his special vintages, accessible only to him. He marked the vintage of each bottle on small yellow sticky notes.

"This is a sad scene indeed," joked Sarah with a hearty chuckle. "Look at the two of you, sitting here in this most romantic setting without mates."

"It's quieter this way," said Haig.

"Bring that lovely wife of yours here, Haigo jan. Quiet is overrated. Someone has to keep an eye on you after all." She laughed out loud as she walked back in to get some food for them.

The special reserve differed from the regular Korah in several ways: It was produced only in years that the grape was exceptionally rich; not only had every bunch been handpicked, but every berry on every bunch had been hand-chosen, so that only the full, undamaged berries had been accepted for the vinification process; Haig would then add carefully measured volumes of stems to give a boost to the tannins and body of the wine. The reserve was aged a couple of years longer than the regular Korah. Because this process made the wine extremely expensive to produce, they did not even bother during years when nature had rendered the harvest less than optimal. But on good years Haig insisted on producing a limited volume of the special reserve, regardless of the cost. It was worth it. The wine had a deep, complex structure with strong spicy overtones on the palate which other Areni wines did not have.

Sarah brought out many small dishes of delicacies—a special stew of lamb, chickpea and eggplant with traditional Armenian spices, steamed fresh trout from the creeks next to the vineyard, and a few salads with the freshest ingredients in season—and another bottle of wine, this one from the common room, a regular Korah. Haig and Armen enjoyed the evening in silence.

After Armen and Sarah retired, Haig remained on the terrace. Darkness had fallen over the hills, and the temperature had dropped several degrees. He put on his thick wool cardigan, rested his feet up on the wooden railing, and threw a blanket over his legs. He could hear the familiar long calls from the nearby villagers as the last of the animals were brought into barns for the night. There were always a few difficult cattle or goats who'd fight bedtime, and the villagers had to chase them around the fields to herd them in.

Soon, that scene too would ebb into the night and leave nothing but darkness and absolute peace, at least until the nocturnal animals emerged to claim the night and start their watch. He would hear the fluttering of the owls and the bats, and in the distance the occasional howling of a wolf, which was always followed by the barking of the village dogs.

As a yellow half-moon emerged from the back of the eastern mountains, his mind drifted to his wife, Alina, and their two boys. One had been five months old and the other a year and a half when he and Alina had made the fateful decision to leave Lebanon and, instead of moving to Boston where she was from, settle in Italy where he could pursue his enological ambitions. He had been selling Italian wines for several years while in Lebanon and had visited Tuscany often. Having established excellent relationships with various Italian wine makers, he wanted to move there to establish himself both as a wine merchant and a producer.

Haig would never forget the day they landed at Leonardo de Vinci International Airport in Rome. It was the end of May, a hot day, and they had eleven pieces of luggage, two dogs, and the two boys. He had only $2,000 to his name and some good contacts and was headed to Figline Valdarno to start a new life and a new career.

The dogs had been caged in the cargo hold and at the airport for so long that they'd taken the biggest dump ever on the sidewalk right outside the airport. The kids were crying, and Alina needed to nurse, and he'd just felt like laughing. Which he did, out loud, right there outside the airport. And by the time they reached the farmhouse he'd rented a few kilometers outside the commune of Figline Valdarno in Tuscany, which normally was rented only in the summer to tourists, Alina was laughing too.

Sarah's words—bring that lovely wife of yours over—were still ringing in his ears when his mind drifted to the early days of his relationship with Alina, their meeting and courting in Beirut and their subsequent wedding in the early 1980s, which was widely questioned and critiqued in his social circle. She worked at the US embassy and taught English at the International College, not the kind of person Haig would have expected to meet at a high-end, presumptuous wine tasting event organized by a group of wine merchants at the Printania Palace Hotel in Brummana, a town around 10 miles east of Beirut. Before the civil war, such events were held at the Phoenicia Hotel in Beirut, but the Phoenicia was burned early in the war and remained closed for some twenty-five years.

And there was Alina, bubbly, happy, in the moment, and thoroughly absorbed in the "Wines of the World" event, a haughty title considering there were twelve wines from only four countries being featured. But that was the well-known Lebanese flare for overselling, and it did not raise even a single well-groomed eyebrow among the 150 patrons, largely members of Beirut's high society. Haig did not belong in that society. He was there for professional reasons as an up and coming international wine merchant. And she? "Oh, well," she said. "I wouldn't want to miss this, just for the thrill."

He found her adventurous spirit endearing. Lebanon was in a disastrous civil war that left the country in destruction and claimed hundreds of thousands of civilian victims. During ceasefires and lulls in the war, the country and the nation would lick their wounds and, as only the Lebanese could, resuscitate and jump-start the culture that catered to the bon vivant. It was in that environment that he took her to every newly opened or renovated trendy restaurant and bar, not only in Beirut but also up and down the main coastal cities along the Mediterranean.

His wedding proposal surprised him as much as her. "Why don't we just get married?" he asked as they were enjoying dinner at a seaside restaurant in Jounieh, a bustling city on the coast north of Beirut. It seemed like the most natural thing to say at the time, even though he hadn't thought it through.

That was a bold move, bolder than the decision to move the family to Italy, considering the taboo in the Armenian community in those days about marrying an *odar*. It was one thing to marry a non-Armenian after having lived in the US or Europe for a decade or so, which was bad enough. But to marry one while still in Lebanon, in the tight, close-knit community of the Armenian diaspora took either defiance or a good measure of indifference toward traditional norms. Haig may have had both in his younger days.

Over time, he realized that he did not have much of the latter. He was defiant, but certainly not indifferent toward his heritage and history, a trait that would play a major role in his moving to and settling in Armenia fifteen years later.

He also developed a deeper appreciation of something that he already knew: that the taboo about marrying a non-Armenian did not spring from blind nationalistic zeal. The Armenian community in Lebanon, as in most of the Middle East, was comprised of three generations of the survivors of the genocide. A major world power had tried to wipe out their nation. The survivors had arrived in the Middle East barely alive, with nothing to their name. They had lost all connection to their ancestral homeland; all that tied them to their roots was their language and culture. Protecting their national identity became more important than putting bread on the table. The first two generations of survivors, Haig's grandparents' and parents' generations, had devoted their lives to building schools, churches, and orphanages. Their survival would be a hollow victory if the next generation assimilated in exile. Mixed marriages were sneered at not because of patriotic fervor but because they were viewed as another genocide, albeit kinder and slower, that would eradicate their national identity.

Haig did not find the same attitude toward foreign spouses in Armenia, where the majority of the local population had not lived through the genocide. Foreign spouses would at most be curiosities, not threats to national identity. If anything, they would assimilate into the Armenian culture.

"It wasn't just the professor's advice," he had confided years later to Van Dorian. They were at Haig's third-floor apartment in Yerevan. After enjoying a great meal personally prepared by Haig, they sat on the balcony smoking cigars and drinking more wine. "I *had* to come to Armenia. It's not about nationalism or even pride. Being Armenian is a privilege and a challenge. We must build a modern nation, Van jan. There's no other option. Our mindset has to outgrow the genocide. The mindset of our historians and academics has to outgrow Urartu. First and foremost, we are survivors and humanists. That's an incredible combination, but now we need to build a modern nation."

"Is that what drove you move to Armenia?"

"I never even dreamt of buying land in Italy," said Haig with a distant melancholy in his voice. "I could have, you know. I have Italian citizenship, I speak the language as well as they do, and I was pretty much settled there. But you see, the problem was that Italy isn't mine. It couldn't be mine. I could live there like one of them, but I could never own their culture. If I cannot own the culture, how can I own the land?"

"And here? Do you own the culture here?"

Haig thought for a long time, staring past his friend at the back of Martiros Saryan's white marble statue shining under the light at the center of the park across the street.

"Not everything, but mostly yes. I don't get the mindset that still lingers here from the Soviet times. That mentality is so alien to me that anywhere else in the world would seem homier. We should have shaken that by now, but it persists, stuck on two generations like a stubborn leech. But that's just seventy years out of 4,000 years of recorded history. So, I'm happy to ignore the last seventy years, and own the remaining 3,930 years of history."

"And enough of the pre-Soviet culture has survived to make you feel like you belong?"

"Of course, my friend!" Haig lost his somber mood and reverted to his jovial self. "The history has survived; no foreign occupying empire could take our history from us, and I own the history. Traditions, the language, the music, the poetry, the stories have survived; I own them too. Especially the stories. The stubborn, unyielding survival instinct has survived, and I sure own that!"

Haig's laugh bellowed down the balcony and echoed into the park. "Let's not forget the big donkey in the stable; the all-important *terroir* has survived. The Soviets turned everyone's life upside down, but they couldn't change geography. Neither Marx nor Lenin nor Stalin could take away our terroir!" His roaring laugh returned to fill the night.

"Besides, there's something even more, umm, what's the word, let's say metaphysical, if you want. This is the only place where I can live both a dream and the hard reality of everyday life at the same time, every day. Do you remember, I told you once how we grew up dreaming of an independent Armenia? I'm not sure those who were living here at the time had the same dream. Maybe you dreamt it too. But for us, back then the Soviet Union seemed indestructible and the dream unattainable. Back then, for me, living in an independent Armenia would have been what fairy tales were made of. Well, here I'm living that dream, every day, even as I tackle the daunting challenges that the system throws at me."

Haig went quiet for a long time and then stirred as if he were about to add something.

"What?" asked Van.

"OK, let me get something else off my chest," mumbled Haig after a few moments of hesitation. "I love Alina. I love her dearly as my wife and the mother of my children. But I have often felt that I've failed as an Armenian for marrying an *odar*. I've always looked for ways to make up for that failure. Settling here helps me do that."

Now Alina lived and taught in Boston while he lived in Armenia. They would visit several times a year, and the boys would spend time in both places. The younger of the boys, Armand, was more enamored with Armenia than was his elder brother. He spent almost two years studying in Yerevan and returned to work in Haig's wineries. His brother, Piero, was more attached to the US and the Boston scene. So the family was divided, with Haig and Armand representing the Armenia "branch," as Haig liked to call it, while Alina and Piero represented the US branch. Haig had adapted to the arrangement, and, to his relief, everyone else in the family seemed content as well.

A sudden chorus of barking dogs from the village made Haig open his eyes for a moment. The half-moon had moved from the left corner of Haig's field of vision to the dead center of it. The rows of vines had come back into sight and cast long shadows over the half-lit, glittering hills. Once in a while, the frantic flight of a bat would disturb Haig's slumber, but the tranquility of the night would soon return to wrap around him and take him away.

Garan Dmak, Lamb's Tail: a late ripening variety widespread in the Armavir region. The tip of the young shoot is light green with a pale wine-red hue. The mature leaf is circular and lightly five lobbed. The bunch is medium, cylindrical, conical, and dense. The berry is medium, round, yellowish-green, and sometimes golden. The skin is rough. The flesh is juicy with a delicate pleasant flavor. The wine can be both light and a strong table white wine.

CHAPTER NINE

Dorian was still in his study at home going over his list of human emotions when Haig called.

"You won't believe what I heard yesterday."

"Tell me."

"They're buying large volumes of home-made Areni wine."

"Who?"

"I don't know. Some driver with a pickup truck comes, loads and leaves."

"Where? How much?"

"Truckloads of five-gallon jugs. The villages around Areni. Apparently it's been going on for a while. No one knows much about it. No one asks questions. The driver goes from home to home and buys their wine. They get paid cash, so they don't care to ask who or for what."

"It's worth finding out who's buying. Can you tell the villagers to ask next time the driver comes around?"

"I will. But chances are he won't know. Even my friendly Russian giant wouldn't tell me anything about the buyer, remember?"

"You think the two are related?"

"Can't see how they could be, but who knows? Korah is Areni too."

In a flash, Dorian recognized an emotion lurking behind the quality of Haig's voice. He had encountered it before among the young professionals who frequented The Realm. It was best described by an Inuit word, *iktsuarpok*, referring to a restless, eager anticipation of something about to happen or of someone about to arrive. In his observations, this was not a momentary restlessness while expecting a one-time incident like the arrival of a letter, but more of a constant state of mind while waiting for a consequential turning point in life.

"One day it will all be clear," he said, scribbling some notes in his thick black notebook. "Let me know what the villagers find out." The buying of bulk home-made Areni wine was intriguing, but at that moment he wanted to get back to his list of emotions.

He had made progress in identifying nuanced human emotions and pairing them with wines, but his quest to pin down "disillusionment with justice" had been fruitless. He had read enough philosophers to write a treatise on social justice himself. John Locke's version of justice as part of natural law, as an absolute and universal concept, attractive as it was as a theory, had little practical significance for Dorian's daily observations. Concepts of justice based on distributive equality were too reminiscent of the communist ideology to have any appeal.

Restorative justice, focused on reparations for victims and those treated unfairly, would be so corruptible in a post-Soviet society that it would not be worth even considering. Definitions of justice based on a social contract subscribed to by the majority of society had much more appeal in principle. It was the vast gulf between what the majority agreed to in principle and what was practiced in actuality that led to the disillusion he witnessed. There were crimes that went unpunished, and there was a class of fortunate oligarchs who did not pay taxes and who were openly granted monopolistic privileges. That was unfair.

But the irony that intrigued Dorian was that most of those who were not fortunate enough to belong to that class did not consider what the monopolists did was wrong. This was not about right or wrong. It was about fair or unfair, and unfair simply meant "Why does he have those privileges and I don't?"

Seventy years of Soviet rule had taught them that the individual couldn't question or challenge the system. The fact that the entire system was unjust did not bother most people—that was a fact of life, beyond their ability to alter, and therefore to be accepted as reality. To the majority of the public, justice did not mean eliminating corruption and monopolistic privilege; it meant joining the club. It was their exclusion from the looting elite that was unjust. No philosopher on Dorian's reading list had ever tackled this phenomenon. This was a Soviet code, void of the moral and ethical considerations that went into the definition of justice espoused by every thinker from Plato to John Stuart Mill to John Rawls.

"No one gets disillusioned in a just world," Haig had said once, which had impressed Dorian at the time. But how did one define a just world? What if a just world were a world where one was part of the prevailing injustice? Therein lay the problem. Should he even contemplate to produce a wine for aspiring oligarchs and monopolists? The dilemma drove Dorian to distraction.

"It will take a vast, grass-roots revolution to change this mindset," he told Haig one evening. "The entire system of governance has to change. Even more difficult, the way the average citizen thinks has to change. I don't think I'll see that kind of transformation in my lifetime."

"You never know, Van jan," responded Haig, ever optimistic about what he called 'the dream.' Revolutions like that don't come crawling; they *erupt*. Just because people seem to be used to the system doesn't mean they necessarily like it. An eruption may happen sooner than you think."

Jack Hakobian listened to Liu Li's account without uttering a word. It was past 8 pm. Li's driver had taken him straight from the mansion to Petyan's office. The driver and two guards had brought the four cases of Areni Eagle and placed them in the middle of the office.

Li could not control his fascination while recounting the story.

"They were *amazing*," he said, with a level of animation in his voice and manners which Jack thought was uncharacteristic of the otherwise calm and composed Mr. Li. "This man Monsieur Lefebvre is a sales magician. A *magician*! And the woman—oh, the woman, Mademoiselle Martin, what can I say? *What can I say?*" Li's cheeks were flushed, and his eyes were wide open darting between Petyan and Jack. "How I wish we could market our Chinese Maotai and Yanghe Daqu like these guys sold wine!"

Jack wondered if good old Mr. Li, being generally office bound and lacking experience in dealing with people, had been easy prey for two professional con artists. And yet the bottom-line facts remained: The Areni Eagle had sold for $2,500 a bottle.

Jack kept quiet because Petyan was doing a good job of asking the key questions: noting how many buyers, the description of the buyers and the wines, and every detail of the wording of Lefebvre's marketing pitch which Li kept repeating over and over again. The one question Jack had—how on earth had Petyan stumbled onto the initial clue—was not a question he could ask.

Petyan's first order of business was to learn about the scale of operations of Lefebvre both in and out of Russia.

"He can't pull off an operation like this without local help," he said, staring at the label of a bottle of Areni Eagle in his hand. "Import licenses, target clients, professional and logistical support to store, transport, and deliver the wine..."

"Everything was perfect. He and the lady. The buyers. The tasting, the Zen moment, *everything*..." Li didn't seem to have heard Petyan.

"Let's start with identifying the owner of the mansion," continued Petyan. "That may not necessarily give us a solid lead, but it's a start."

"We should alert the Ludwig office in St. Petersburg," said Jack. "I mean, if that's where the next event is."

Jack knew his boss well enough to know that Petyan needed to identify Lefebvre's local backers—that would decide whether he'd expose and destroy them or force them to take him in as a partner or, as the least acceptable option, leave them alone.

Later that week, Sandro Kashvili, responding to a call from Petyan, walked into his office. On the round, wooden table in the far corner of his office, Petyan had set two glasses of red wine on two cloth coasters labeled #1 and #2. The top of the table was padded with a beautiful green pebbled leather lining, with fine gold designs around the edge. He put his arm around Kashvili and led him to the table.

"I have a question for you, Sandro," he said.

He noticed the wine, but his eyes focused first on the table. He inspected the border gold design, running his index finger over it. "This is a beautiful piece, Sergei," he said. "I'd say the work of eighteenth-century Russian artisans; it most probably was made for card games. I'd guess poker. So maybe a glass of wine is not entirely out of place."

Kashvili detected a sense of anticipation in Petyan's manners. Or perhaps it was a restless impatience. His movements and his speech were a notch faster than usual. The history of the table did not seem to interest him.

"What can you tell me about these wines?" he asked.

Kashvili moved away from him and focused his attention on the wine.

"When did you open the bottles?" he asked. He was staring at the glasses without extending a hand toward them.

"I don't know. Maybe half an hour ago."

"And when did you pour these glasses?"

"Ten minutes ago. Why? Does it matter?"

Satisfied with the answers, Kashvili did not speak again. He lifted the glasses and held one in each hand against the light. He tilted and turned them, looking from one to the other, then returned them to their respective coasters. He produced a small notebook from his coat pocket and scribbled a few notes. He took the first glass and sniffed it without swirling at first because he did not want to disturb the air in the glass, which was saturated by the accumulated vapors and scents from the wine. Then he swirled to release more aromas and smelled again. He scribbled more notes. He followed the same process with the second glass. After he finished recording his notes, he turned to Petyan.

"I can tell you what I think, but you have to understand that this is not an exact science."

"Aren't you going to taste them?"

"I could, but I doubt that would change my conclusion. Do you have a bucket?"

"A bucket?"

"To spit the wine in."

Petyan rolled his eyes and fetched two large tumblers from his liquor cabinet.

"Here," he said as he placed the tumblers on the table at the opposite side from the two glasses of wine. "Spit in here."

Kashvili tasted both wines. He took his time, gave the process the full consideration due, and carefully spit two mouthfuls into the tumbler.

"OK, here's what I think," he said with so much confidence both in his voice and his demeanor that he expected Petyan to accept every word that came out of his mouth as the absolute truth. "Your #1 is a Korah. Pure Areni Noir. There can be no mistake about that. The #2 is trickier. It too is an Areni Noir, but not only Korah. It has *some* Korah in it—I'd guess 50 to 60 percent, but that is only a guess. Most of the balance is Areni, but different."

"Different how? Different better or different worse?"

"Different," said Kashvili sternly, as he would speak to a student. "There are subcategories of Areni. I detect different Areni grades in #2.

Also, there is an element of lower quality bulk wine. I tasted some a couple of years ago in Areni village in Armenia..."

As he made that statement, Kashvili remembered something and paused abruptly. His mind struggled to make a connection between a series of conversations he'd had in Moscow and the situation he was now facing with #2. But he didn't want Petyan to notice the break in his voice. "Homemade wines from mixed varieties of Areni have a peculiar taste, and #2 has some of that," he continued, pretending that his pause was nothing more than an effort to remember what he had tasted two years earlier. "And then there's something else. There's a small part of something entirely different from Areni in here. It could be a Bordeaux variety, possibly a Merlot, which gives it a softer, mellower aftertaste. I wouldn't put it at more than 5–10 percent. But there certainly is something."

"Can we confirm these findings in a lab test?" Petyan asked the question without looking at Kashvili. He walked over to the liquor cabinet, produced two bottles, and poured himself two glasses. One of the bottles was a Korah. The second had a homemade-looking label with an antique-yellow and light brown eagle soaring over snowcapped mountaintops. Sprawling green vineyards filled the lower half of the label. The crimson script that covered part of the vineyards at the bottom of the label proclaimed the wine to be 'Areni Eagle.' Kashvili grabbed the bottle and turned it around.

"Never heard of this one," he said. "Areni Eagle?"

"Private sale. Not on the market. It's the #2."

"It will be difficult to confirm what I said in a lab test. They may be able to confirm that most of it is Areni. But the technology isn't advanced enough to tell if the foreign ingredient is in fact a Merlot, and even less likely to tell you the exact percentage."

"Thank you, Sandro. This has been most instructive," said Petyan.

Although Kashvili was still struggling with the thought that had given him pause earlier, his interest was now piqued. He had seen a label for the first time.

"What's the story of the Areni Eagle?" he asked, as he invited himself to an armchair next to the round table and crossed his legs, not giving any indication that he was in a hurry to leave to make a phone call.

Petyan ignored his question. "Let's say the Areni Eagle is 50 percent Korah, 40 percent some cheap bulk Areni wine, and 10 percent a middle-of-the-road Merlot. Can they mix those three and rebottle it as a new wine?"

"Who's 'they'?"

"I have no idea, Sandro. What does it matter? Whoever they are, can they do it?"

"Well, it does matter who 'they' is because, if they have someone with the nose and taste buds of a blood hound, they can do anything. And in case you're wondering, there are people like that. They can experiment with various proportions and different wines until they get something that leaves a good first impression in a tasting. They may let the mixture sit in a cask for a while and blend. They may even use chemical additives, which would be hard to detect by smell and taste alone but may be revealed in a chemical analysis or when you get a severe headache after drinking a couple of glasses. The kind of mixing and rebottling we're talking about takes some resources. But the short answer to your question is yes, it can be done."

"And they can dress up a mediocre wine enough to pass it as something unique? These collectors may not be experts like you, but they know wine."

"These days, a lot can be fixed. If your wine is not tannic enough, drop in a few drops of liquid oak tannin; you can even choose a flavor to go with it. If it doesn't have enough body, fix it with a little gum Arabic. You can increase or decrease the alcohol level. You can boost specific aromas and tastes by various yeasts. And as a last resort, you can add a little grape juice concentrate, which will give it a richer color and add more body and character to the wine. So yes, if they know the tricks and have some experience, they can do a lot to contrive a wine that the collectors will fall for."

Petyan was quiet for several minutes as he stared at the two glasses that he had just poured. He picked the Areni Eagle.

"The market value of those ingredients would be around $35–45 per bottle, depending where they are getting the Korah, wouldn't you say?"

"Yes, and if they buy the Korah wholesale, possibly even lower. Closer to $25."

As he probed deeper into his memory, the connection between his tasting of home-made Areni wines and his conversations in Moscow became clearer in Kashvili's mind. He had to make a phone call as soon as he got a chance. But he also wanted to find out more about the Areni Eagle before leaving Petyan's office. So he stayed in his chair.

Leaving Kashvili in the maroon brocade-covered armchair at the end of his large office, Petyan took the glass of Areni Eagle and went to sit behind his desk. Even if a bottle of Areni Eagle had cost the Frenchman $50, factoring in the cost of mixing and bottling, his profits from the thirty-five cases alone were well over $1 million. If he did this four times a year, say twice in Moscow and twice in St. Petersburg, he could net over $4 million from Areni alone. God only knows what he made on his velvety Bordeaux, whatever concoction that was, he thought, part in admiration and part in anger.

How could Ludwig have missed an operation like this going on right under their noses? Could Haig Koleyan be in on it? If he were, the profits would be even larger because his cost of Korah would be insignificant. But if he were, why would he wonder out loud about the newfound popularity of Korah? Unless, of course, all the talk about the Korah mystery was a ploy to throw off Isabelle and whoever else was in the know about the surge in the Korah sales. Petyan himself would easily do something like that to mislead his employees.

Kashvili had moved to the chair by the desk, where Isabelle had sat not too long ago, and was studying Petyan's face as he thought.

"Are you going to tell me what this is all about?" he asked.

Petyan looked at Kashvili as if he had just noticed he was in the room. The paid consultant had talked back. Suddenly, Kashvili became a presence, a person, no longer a mere machine there to answer his questions.

"We recently found out that there are closed, private sales of premiere and rare wines to unsuspecting wine collectors," he said casually. "The Areni Eagle is one of them, along with a Bordeaux or two." He waved his hand in a dismissive gesture, as if the 'Bordeaux or two' were unworthy components in the mix. Petyan was holding his glass of Areni Eagle with his thumb and forefinger at the base of the wine glass, as he'd seen Kashvili hold his glass, and staring at it while he spoke.

"Premiere and rare? The Areni Eagle?"

"Well, yes," said Petyan, putting the glass down on the desk and looking at Kashvili. "Limited production. Tops Bordeaux qualities. Intense velvety color. Nuanced aromas of wildflowers and ripe melon. Complex yet simple. Stability reminiscent of Zen quality, exuding permanence of the ages." He paused for a moment and raised his arm for emphasis before adding, "And as an extra bonus, straight from the birthplace of wine."

He enjoyed watching Kashvili's jaw drop. After giving him a moment to absorb the flowery description, which he had made Li repeat a few times until he memorized the details, he lifted his glass again and added, "Sandro, don't tell me you failed to detect all that in this unique wine!"

Petyan was so serious that for a moment Kashvili's shock returned to his face. But then he burst out in a roaring laugh.

"Yes, how on earth did I miss all that?" But the expression of incredulity did not leave his face.

"Why would they bother with Korah for a scam like this? Why not just focus on the higher priced Bordeaux or Burgundies?"

"We come back to who 'they' is," said Kashvili, looking like a man trying to solve a riddle. "There have been several wine scams involving French wines. The gullible wine collectors have learned a lesson or two and become more careful. They're getting better at recognizing Bordeaux and Burgundy. To do a good con job on a French wine, they have to start with expensive wines. Yes, they will slap on a large markup, but they cannot fool people unless they include in their mix old Bordeaux. So, to concoct a bottle of counterfeit Bordeaux may cost them $500–600, instead of $25 for the Areni Eagle. No matter how much they mark it up, the Bordeaux is a much larger risk in terms of initial outlay. What if it doesn't fly?"

Petyan had swiveled his chair to face the wall behind his desk. He was trying to get into the heads of the swindlers. Would they find it easier to risk $25 rather than $600, even if the markup on the latter were higher? How did the economics of fraud work?

"So, cost is one factor," continued Kashvili. "Chances of getting caught is another because, as I said earlier, the French wines are better known and under stricter scrutiny. But there is a third factor," he said, eyes wide open as in a eureka moment. "The exotic factor. Collectors are offered rare and exceptional Bordeaux and Burgundies all the time. They probably have cellars full of them. I bet the men who bought the Areni Eagle already have at least one rare Bordeaux displayed in a glass case in their living rooms. So, once in a while, a more exotic, less known varietal can command a premium just for being rare and unusual."

Kashvili stopped talking and sat back down in the chair by the desk. After a few moments, he turned to Petyan.

"May I ask what price the Areni Eagle was sold for?"

Petyan was expecting the question. His first instinct was not to give a lot of details. But he found Kashvili's thought process interesting. Who knows what the professor could deduce from the price of a bottle of Areni Eagle?

"A lot. Big number. Do you need to know the exact price?"

"It wouldn't hurt."

"$2,500."

Kashvili did not show any immediate reaction.

"And how about the Bordeaux?"

"A bit higher. $1,000 more, to be exact."

"Well, there's your answer as to why bother with Areni. They risked $25 to make $2,500, which is a much higher return than risking $600 to make $3,500. Their return on risk ratio in the case of the Areni is 100-fold, versus a mere 6-fold on the Bordeaux.

Petyan smiled. He had already figured that out.

"And there's nothing you can tell me about who 'they' is?" asked Kashvili. "Nationality, background, assets and resources in Russia?"

"French. At least the front man is, the man doing the selling. No idea who's behind him."

"Times have sure changed, haven't they, Sergei? Who would have thought this type of thing would happen in Moscow?"

"What are the chances that Haig Koleyan is involved?" asked Petyan and noticed that Kashvili was surprised by the question—he looked like the thought had not even occurred to him.

"I need to know for sure if he is involved," he said. "How close are you to that student of yours?"

Taking a break from the pre-harvest chores, Haig focused on the preparations for the inaugural gala of The Armenian Food and Wine Society. The lack of consensus among the winemakers was exasperating. Yet this had to be a joint undertaking. He wanted every winery in Armenia to be represented. Of course, the one exception was Hayasa, which he had not invited.

But there were too many egos, too many opinions, too many voices. Some argued that an eight-course dinner was too much. Others wanted their wines featured prominently in every course. Most objected to the vintages proposed by Haig. And there were his personal problems with Alma Wines and Carla Almayan.

"The Food and Wine Society is a cornerstone," he told Dorian over the phone, having called him for the second time that day. "Eventually, it will be the face of Armenian wine to the world. It will bring all the wineries together and coordinate joint 'Wines of Armenia' campaigns. It will educate; it will promote; it will present and represent. Imagine doing that without everyone on board."

"If we start, they will join," said Dorian in his typical detached tone. "All we need is the initial core. We'll grow from there."

Haig knew that Dorian was more interested in educating people about wine than in creating a platform to promote local wines globally. Dorian understood the importance of the platform, but he believed it would come gradually, through word of mouth and tourism.

"To understand any country," he told Haig, "one has to taste its food and drink its wine. History and geography alone are not enough. Let's get the wine culture established here; the rest will follow."

But Haig wanted to start with a bang: all in, a lot of traction, high visibility. After all, they had an incredible story to tell and some exceptional wines to back the story.

He put the phone down and went out into his vineyard. It was a very hot day. It was past noon, and the heat rose from the earth in waves that one could not only feel, but actually see. Translucent airwaves ascended from the rocky, gray earth like ghosts, blurring everything in their wake. The leaves on the vines looked like they had fainted in the heat. A deafening paralysis had descended over the vineyard.

That was when he noticed something strange in the giant walnut tree at the far end of the row of vines. It stood majestically towering over the vineyard as always. Judging from the circumference of its trunk, which was a whopping 6.5 meters, Haig had estimated that the tree was 365 years old. In late summer, the walnuts were still small, and the leaves were dark and plush green. He had seen the tree close up countless times before, and noticed the old, rough, rugged and cracked bark, discolored into a dead grey, against the fresh, pale green leaves of early spring, and he had thought 'this is renewal in action.' The tree knows how to renew itself—that's how it has lived for almost four-hundred years.

But at that moment, from a distance, he sensed something mysterious about the way the branches and leaves of the walnut tree were swaying. The wind didn't seem to have anything to do with their movement. None of the vines around the tree was moving. It seemed it was a force within the tree itself—from within the trunk, the branches, and the leaves—causing the fluttering. Could a tree muster and direct so much inner energy? It was a living thing, after all. And it had been there for a third of a millennium. Who was to say what the tree was capable of?

The branches of the walnut tree were waving, and its leaves were fluttering, as if winking at him in the otherwise total stillness of the midday heat. It had done this for 365 years. Nothing had interfered with it. It had produced walnuts and emitted its own energy, oblivious to centuries of statelessness, seventy years of Soviet rule, and independence. The branches were waving at him, as if in agreement. His hand waved back while his eyes remained fixated on the tree, unable to look away.

He told himself to become like that tree—to do what he felt he was meant to do without worrying. He'd start the process of organizing the gala while deliberately remaining blind to the problems. The conventional wisdom that one had to understand hurdles to overcome them was, in this case, nonsense. Analyzing the problems was a distraction. Just delving into the project was a surer way: become the process, become the event.

Over the next several days, he secured the participation of a dozen vintners and ten restaurants and wine bars. He outlined a program, a work in progress, as he listened to and often accepted suggestions from the other vintners. The inaugural gala of the Food and Wine Society would be a seven-course dinner with twelve different wines featured with short, five-minute introductions to each course and accompanying wines. It would start with an introductory presentation about the history of wine in Armenia, and it would end with a couple of short presentations by different producers. He would plan for at least 300 guests and charge them basically at cost. They would include vintners from around the world, all the hotel and restaurant managers in Yerevan, most ambassadors, a few famous sommeliers, and the patrons of the major wine bars.

Sev Tozot. Tozot Noir, Dusty: a late ripening variety. It is rare, found as single vines in old vineyards of Goris. The tip of young shoots is light green and hairless. The mature leaf is medium sized, circular, lightly five lobbed, and hairless. The bunch is medium, conical, and dense. The berry is medium sized, oval or reverse-oval, and black. The skin is medium thick and covered with thick bloom. The flesh is juicy with a pleasant and harmonious flavor. The wines are rare, high-quality wines.

CHAPTER TEN

"You never told me how your meeting with Sergei Petyan went," Kashvili told Isabelle when she approached him.

"I'm so sorry, Professor Kashvili," she said with genuine regret. "I hope you'll forgive my lapse. I just have been—"

Kashvili waved his hand. "No need to feel bad. It's OK. Just tell me how it went. Were you happy with the meeting?"

Kashvili had devoted an entire lecture to fraud in the wine business. That was more than a week before he learned about the Areni Eagle phenomenon, a story that could have added a whole new level of relevance and timeliness to his lectures. A crucial side note, which Petyan did not seem to take seriously, was the mention of an upcoming high rating of an Areni wine by Mr. Bowker. That was more than a clever marketing tactic. The involvement of a respected, professional rater in the scam was significant.

But he did need to talk to Isabelle. He waited two days, hoping that she'd ask to see him after class, but she kept her distance. He noticed that she was not as engaged in class as she had been during the first few weeks. She'd been leaving the classroom as soon as the lecture was over. She had thanked him for the Herodotus story. She had also thanked him for the introduction to Petyan. But she had said nothing about her meeting with him. So, reluctantly, on the third day after his visit to Petyan, he asked her if he could see her for a moment after class.

"It wasn't anything to be happy or unhappy about. For me, just meeting the largest wine and spirits merchant in Russia was an achievement, thanks to you. But wine did not seem to be his main passion."

"It's not." Kashvili laughed to lighten the mood. "More than anything else, Sergei is a merchant. But, given your passion for wine, I trust that you brought it up, no?"

"Sure I brought it up. I told him he was keeping alive an age-old national tradition and mentioned Herodotus's story of the Armenian merchants selling wine to Babylon."

Kashvili laughed again. "I'm glad that story came in handy. And that was it? There was no talk of wine in more modern times?"

The conversation led nowhere. Kashvili confirmed what he already knew, that his mission, which was to find out from Isabelle if she suspected Haig Koleyan was involved in the Areni Eagle con without telling her anything about Lefebvre's operation, was ridiculous in the first place.

Isabelle left the classroom with a mixture of emotions: guilt, for lying to Kashvili; regret, for disappointing him; but most of all, concern that Kashvili and Petyan had spoken and that they knew a lot more than she did; that she was left out, and therefore not likely to be coached or mentored by either of them. In a flash, she saw a secretive world out there, a world beyond her grasp and reach, a world that her revered professor and the shrewd wine merchant shared, from which she would remain excluded.

Aram Almayan was in a good mood. They were celebrating his grand-daughter's birthday. Magnolia had turned eight. The lower hall of the winery reception area was overrun with children. In addition to Magnolia and her sister, Sophie, there were about a dozen other children at the birthday party.

There was entertainment for the kids: magicians, musicians, and games. Aram had made his appearance, kissed his granddaughter, and walked out as a surge in the shrill screams of the children, prompted by the entrance of a magician wearing a long, black wizard's hat, filled the room. He loved his family, but the noise and chaos of the children's party was no place for him.

Before leaving the lower level hall, he stood at the doorway and watched his daughter play mother. He was happy with his family and proud of Magnolia and Sophie. His Carla had come a long way since her days in Los Angeles. She was a single parent of two young children and the CEO of a major winery, but for him, she remained the young, crazy, unpredictable adolescent whom he had loved and worried about ever since she was born.

He walked up the stairs to the second level banquet hall and tasting room, and then out onto the terrace. He needed a smoke. As he sat in his favorite armchair and lit a cigarette, his phone rang.

"Good day, Mr. Almayan," said the cheerful voice of Jack. "It's Jack from Ludwig who's inconveniencing you."

"Hello, Jack, how are you?"

"Thank you, Mr. Almayan. Is this a convenient moment for a quick chat?"

He put his feet up on a stool and took a deep drag. "It's the perfect moment," he said, "as long as you don't have bad news." The image of the kids partying downstairs was fresh in his mind, but, on the terrace over-looking the vineyards, he was removed from it all. It was the best of all worlds.

For a short moment, Jack hesitated.

"What I have is *interesting* news, Mr. Almayan. But I can't tell you yet if it's bad or good."

"So tell me," he said. "Interesting is good, even if the news isn't."

After another moment of hesitation, Jack started to talk.

Almayan listened without interrupting. He had chain smoked four cigarettes before he asked his first question to confirm the prices of the two wines sold. Jack also told him about what Petyan was trying to figure out: Lefebvre's backers, the full scale of his operation in Russia, the owner of the mansion, and whether Haig Koleyan was in on it.

"Has Petyan contacted the police?" he asked when Jack was done.

"I don't think so. He has contacted the mayor's office, I believe only about the mansion, not the operation."

"Good," mumbled Almayan more to himself than to Jack. "The mayor's office wouldn't know much about the operation. The police commissioner might."

Jack remembered how close Almayan was to the police. No one could own and run several casinos in Moscow without cultivating a symbiotic relationship with the police. Back in the days when casinos were allowed in Moscow, Almayan had often entertained the police commissioner and the top officers of the department in his casinos. Jack recalled the extravagant evenings where nothing was spared to make the police commissioner feel like a czar. Private entertainment, exquisite food and drinks, and generous gifts were the norm.

Almayan was right. The municipality might help them ascertain the identity of the owner of the mansion, but they'd be of no help in figuring out who was behind the wine scam.

"Thank you for bringing this to me, Jack," said Almayan after a long pause. "I appreciate it more than you know. Give me a few days to think about it."

"Sure," said Jack. "I thought it might be important to Alma Wines." After a moment's hesitation, he added, "I'd be happy to tell Carla more about any Korah activity in the Moscow market."

"I'm sure it will come to that. But I need a couple of days to think. And I'll fly to Moscow soon to talk to some people."

That was more than Jack had hoped for. The possibility of sitting face-to-face with Carla to tell her about one of her competitors and winning her trust and gratitude had been inconceivable only a few days ago.

"Of course, Mr. Almayan. But may I ask one favor of you?"

"Sure. Anything."

"As you know, I've broken some rules by telling you about this. I ask that you let me know what you find out before you tell anyone else. I'm sorry to ask this, but I hope you appreciate my position."

"Jack, I thank you again for bringing this to my attention. I won't say a word about it to Sergei, and you'll be the first to know when I find out something."

The son of a genocide survivor from a small town called Shar Keshla in eastern Turkey, Aram Almayan was born in Moscow in the late 1940s. His father had been a teenager when, with the few survivors in his family, they had made it to Russia. While his parents lived through and remembered the harshest days of authoritarianism during Stalin and his immediate successors, by the time Aram became an adult the system had started to unravel. Privileged insider entrepreneurship, which had always been practiced in the Soviet Union to varying degrees, became accessible to a larger group of ambitious, business-minded young men. That environment fit Aram's personality and drive perfectly.

He started trading in timber and construction materials when he was in his twenties and within a few years made a small fortune and a name in the circle of local entrepreneurs. He handed the management of the trading business to a cousin and moved into construction, which drained much of his resources with no redeeming results. He could not break into the established oligarchy of construction contractors. He decided to go back to trading and expanded his business into textiles and carpets. But his true interest remained in construction and real estate.

He was in his early-forties when the Soviet Union collapsed and a wave of privatizations opened such vast new opportunities for the likes of Almayan that they didn't know how to begin to fully exploit them. Overnight, almost everything the state owned was up for grabs. Real estate, factories, mines, oil fields, and production facilities: the vast riches of the all-powerful Soviet state had been made available to a select group. Although he was at the far fringes of that circle, a few crumbs would fall his way if he knew how to act fast and smart. He could smell the possibilities.

The problem was that there were far too many. The old Russian saying, "He who chases two rabbits catches neither," had acquired a whole new meaning; there weren't just two rabbits, but hundreds. He had to focus.

The rabbit that he eventually caught came in the form of several lucrative casinos in Moscow. By then, his lovely Carla had just turned fifteen. She was adorable with fair, almost blond hair, even though he and his wife had dark hair. Carla had his dark brown eyes, a perky personality, and an innate charm that burst out effortlessly with her every movement and sound. That's when he decided to move his family to the United States while maintaining his business interests in Moscow. Even though his wife, Arax, also the child of genocide survivors from Marash, was a competent and intelligent woman and Aram trusted her to care for Carla, he did not have the peace of mind that his daughter was growing up in the right environment. He had one of the longest commutes on the planet for many years. He did the round-trip Moscow–Los Angeles flight every two to three weeks for over ten years.

Almayan had reason to be concerned about Carla. He was a protective, conservative father who hated the distance that he had put between his family and himself. He had seen the fear with which his parents lived during the Stalin years. He had had his share of setbacks in business and realized early on that in the business world there were no friendships, only interests. He had made and lost fortunes and rebuilt businesses after losing them. He had seen his younger brother die at an early age, and he had sworn off alcohol and strived to live a healthy life. That too was protectionism.

As much as his own circumstances, the misfortunes endured by his wife's family shaped his outlook. Arax had seen her father, charged with 'having contacts' abroad, go to jail for seven years when she was a young girl. While her father served his time, her brother went into a deep depression and passed away under questionable circumstances when he was only twenty. Her mother passed away at the young age of fifty from heart failure, or so the official hospital report had said at the time. All that conditioned her outlook and reinforced her husband's take on life: the world was a perilous place. All they had was each other, and their little Carla had to be protected and sheltered at all costs.

So when Carla won a full scholarship to study art in Vienna, they refused to let her go. She was livid. She had lived in the US for five years and Aram did not expect her to be able to reconcile her ultra-traditional and protective home with the open and relaxed society of LA. But he was determined to protect her daughter.

Then a close family friend, Azad Sahakyan, another Russian-Armenian resettled in Los Angeles, entered her life. Azad ended up practically living in their house. He was twenty-eight, a lawyer who had just passed his bar exams and started working in a boutique LA law firm. Carla had just turned twenty-one. He was personable, polite, and domestic. Arax trusted him. She'd let Carla go out as long as he was chaperoning. Over time, he simply became an integral part of the family, and no one questioned his presence.

What they were not prepared for was that he was falling in love with Carla. To win her trust, he gave her unconditional support in her rebellion and anger. The strategy worked. Soon, they were dating. As far as Almayan was concerned, marrying Carla off to Azad was by far the safest route. Only forming a family could contain her and protect her like they wanted her protected.

It was an extravagant wedding. Almayan did not spare a thing. He flew in some of the best entertainers from Moscow and lavished the newlyweds with generous gifts, including a house and a car. Carla was finally settled and happy. And she was pregnant. Azad had been a considerate and caring husband during her pregnancy. Their daughter, Magnolia, was born nine months later.

That was a turning point for Almayan. When he first saw and held his granddaughter in his arms, he knew that it was time to make another move. Los Angeles was no place for his granddaughter any more than it had been for his daughter. And if Moscow was also out of the question, what options did he have?

"Back to our roots," he told himself. And he did not mean his geographic roots, which were now in modern-day Turkey. He meant the roots of the traditional preoccupation of his great-grandfather as a winemaker in their village in Sepastia. Legend had it that his ancestors were the prime wine makers in the nineteenth century in Sepastia, with a history in winemaking predating Christianity.

"Let's go back to where we belong," he told Arax. "We'll build something that we can proudly leave for Carla and Magnolia."

He returned to Moscow and put everything he owned up for sale: three commercial buildings, a trading company, and several lucrative casinos in Moscow. He went on a wild selling spree, often leaving money on the table, and moved to Armenia. He bought 200 hectares of land in the Aragadzotn region, cleared the boulders and the rocks, and planted a vineyard.

In the four years that it took for Aram to complete all that, Carla had had a second daughter, Sophie, and she had divorced Azad. He had become too indifferent to her needs. The initial infatuation that had bound them was gone. Carla knew how to love and to give, but she also demanded the same. He got tired. She noticed and resented him.

Her loneliness overwhelmed her. Her life had been reduced to spending every evening at home alone with her daughters as she was reluctant to impose on her mother to look after them. Her father had not visited for over a year. The hyperactive, creative Carla felt like a trapped wild animal circling in its cage.

Almayan completed planting the vineyard and constructing the main building of the winery. Everything was ready for the equipment to be imported and installed. He stood on the terrace and, surveying the vineyards and the estate, realized how much more needed to be done. He needed his family.

He flew to Los Angeles and explained the project to Arax and Carla in detail. In all their years, neither of them had heard so much about his business from him. He never considered his business dealings in Moscow a fit subject for family conversation. But now, having described what he had built and having shown them dozens of photographs of the sprawling vineyards and the beautiful stone buildings of the winery, including a banquet hall, tasting room, kitchen, vast rooms with forty-foot ceilings where winery equipment and storage would be housed, and several guest bedrooms, and while the two women looked on in silence with their jaws dropped at the scale of the endeavor, he nonchalantly asked Carla if she'd come and take over the management of Alma Wines as the CEO of the company.

While Carla was busy drying her tears, he explained that he did not have the energy to complete the project to its end. He said the project needed young blood, young and ambitious blood. He explained how important this project was for the family, both financially and in terms of the mission to return to their roots.

"My accountant warned me against the project," he said. "'You know, they say to make a small fortune in wine, you have to start with a large fortune,' and he laughed. But his joke didn't discourage me. I took it to heart and started with a very large fortune. So now we're at least set to make a small fortune," he added, smiling.

He then explained that he knew nothing about wine. As the family knew very well, he said, he didn't drink alcohol and since Carla was a major consumer of the product, she was better qualified to run the business than he was. At that, a new gush of tears emerged, even as she laughed amid sobs and threw her arms around her father and held on to him. He had come to rescue her from a life she was more than prepared to leave. She was ready to say goodbye to her ex-husband in Los Angeles, take her two daughters and move to Armenia to assume the management of Alma Wines.

Over the years, Carla had heard it all. "Her father started it." "Her father put the money." "Her father built the place." In a conservative, gender-conscious society, the attitude echoed louder than it would have had Alma Wines been a traditional father-and son venture.

She was not fazed. The prevailing mindset did bother her sometimes, but she had developed a thick skin. She was the CEO of the winery, and she ran it, period. She was proud of her wines. Her wines had won several international awards. Many dignitaries—politicians, diplomats, famous artists, actors, and actresses from around the world—had visited her winery and left impressed. Not only did she make good wines, but she put on an excellent show for the visitors by going over the history of the winery in conjunction with the history of wine and Armenia's role in it. She had opened markets in the US, Europe, and Asia without her father's help. She had promoted Alma Wines in difficult niche communities single handedly. She was winning the "man against the market" battle alone as a woman against the market.

"Yes, the initial capital is important," she'd tell friends and adversaries alike. "But what matters most is what you do with it. The initial capital could have come from a bank, a relative, a silent partner, or your father. What difference does it really make in the end if you blow it all away? What's important is what you do with an opportunity, regardless of how it came to you. And I'm proud of what I've done with mine."

But while the idyllic, emotional handover of the business from father to daughter remained true to the letter of the arrangement, in the sense that her father left her fully in charge of Alma Wines, he made no secret of his disapproval of her personal life: her divorce and raising her daughters as a single parent.

Carla's feminism was not an ideology that she adopted because she thought it sounded good. She lived it in every aspect of her life. That drove her to take the gender discrimination issue public and turned it into a crusade to educate a younger generation of girls. It started with talks to her own staff, which included about a dozen young women in their mid-twenties, and then spread to public talks at schools and community centers.

"Just remember this," she'd say to the young faces looking at her with admiration and hope. "No one, and I really mean *no one*, has the right to run your life just because they were born with a penis."

The girls would blush and giggle at first, but the image was powerful. She had stripped the omnipotent male authority figure down from its traditional, unchallenged stature to a simple, comical biological phenomenon, and she knew that the impact of the image would keep working and growing way after the talk. It would stay with the girls and reappear every time some male relative barked orders at them.

"And I want you to think about this," she'd continue. "Who guides you as you go through life? Do you allow your gender to determine how you live, how much you achieve, how far you go? Do you let your parents guide you? Your husband? Your older brother? Have you ever thought that you, and only you, can be the true navigator of your life? Girls, let me add this: being your own navigator is not just your right. It is your responsibility. It is your duty toward yourself. Every time you give that job to someone else, you betray yourself!"

Chilar, Chilar Blanc: *an uncommon wine grape variety found in vinicultural areas of the Ararat Plateau. The tip of its young shoot is pink. The mature leaf is medium sized, oblong-ovate, five lobbed, sometimes three lobbed. The bunch is medium, oblong-cylindrical, and foxtail-like. The berry is medium, oval or roundish-oval, and greenish. The skin is firm and elastic and covered with thin bloom. The flesh is juicy with a special harmonious aroma. The wine is high-quality, good for strong desert wines and lighter table wines especially from the Kotayk region.*

CHAPTER ELEVEN

Sergei Petyan stared at the photograph for a long time. It was a large, 8 x 10-inch, black-and-white printout. Li's body lay in the back seat of his white car, slumped over the dark brown leather interior. He was on his back with his right arm hanging down to the floor and the left arm squeezed between his side and the backrest. His head was pushed all the way against the back door, tilted slightly to the right. The right side of his coat was also hanging down the seat like his arm, exposing his soiled white shirt; there were large patches of dirty gray stains around the chest. Similar gray stains appeared on his black trousers around the waist and down his right leg.

Only one of the two bullet wounds mentioned in the police report was visible in the photo, a small, barely one-centimeter in diameter hole in the middle of his forehead, right above the bridge of his nose. There was a thin trickle of blood running down from the wound to the side of his head. Petyan covered the hole with his index finger and studied the picture again. Without the wound, Li looked calm, almost at peace. His eyes were shut, his facial muscles relaxed. Petyan could not discern any angst or emotion on his face or on his mouth and lips. Without the bullet hole, Li looked like he had died peacefully in his sleep.

The other bullet, presumed by the police to have been the first one shot, had entered his body through the lower back, but there was no exit wound visible in the photograph. The police figured that he was shot in the street in front of his apartment building around 8 p.m. the evening before.

"He most probably fell to the ground face down," the police officer explained to Petyan. They stood side by side in front of Petyan's large desk. The officer was in his mid-forties and heavyset. His thinning blond hair accentuated the redness of his face. His calm, almost bored manner of speaking made Petyan think that he did not have much interest in the case, and possibly even in his job. He seemed to be going through the motions so he could return and file his report. "The first bullet in all likelihood paralyzed him because it had shattered his vertebrae," he explained as if he were giving directions to a lost driver. "Then his assailant or assailants turned his body around, possibly to confirm the identity of their victim, and shot him one more time in the forehead before throwing him into the back seat of his car and walking away."

The police had no explanation for why the body had been thrown in the car rather than left in the street. "There's no question that Liu Li was shot outside the car," said the officer. "The blood on the street and his position in the car lead to that conclusion without any reasonable doubt." He then explained that the hit from the back followed by a shot through the head were standard execution-style operations used by the Russian underground. But throwing the body back into the car was not standard. Normally, they'd leave the victim where he fell.

The note left on Li's chest was an even bigger puzzle for the police. Handwritten with a thick permanent marker on a white sheet of paper were two Russian words: Держись подальше! *Keep Out!*

Mr. Li had no police record, said the officer, and the papers found in his wallet, identity, residency, and work permit, were all in order.

"Any guesses as to what he was supposed to keep out of?" he asked, staring at Petyan, seeming for the first time to be focused on the case. Petyan pretended to be too shocked to come up with any guesses. Keeping his gaze on the photograph, he shook his head.

"He was a quiet back-office employee," he mumbled. "Kept pretty much to himself. He handled the paperwork of shipments to and from China. Never got into any trouble at Ludwig, or anywhere else, as far as I know."

"Was there anything in his job that could have caused anyone to want to get rid of him? Was he stepping on anyone's toes handling your trade with China?"

"I strongly doubt it," said Petyan as he finally put the photograph on his desk and looked at the officer.

"How can you be sure?"

"He was just handling the paperwork. The Chinese clients and suppliers are long-time business associates of Ludwig. We've been doing business with them for years, long before Li started working here. He was processing orders from the same old clients and sending invoices like we've always done."

The officer seemed to be satisfied, for he left the photo with Petyan, asked him to call him if he remembered anything, and left.

Petyan shut his office door. "No calls," he told his assistant. He sat at his desk staring at the photograph and pondering all the imponderables. He had made no progress in figuring out who Lefebvre's backers were in Moscow. The official owner of the mansion had turned out to be a corporate entity, and the mansion had been rented for over a dozen different corporate and cultural events in the past several months. The agent managing the house had never met Lefebvre and did not know or care what the mansion was used for. A Russian representative of the client had paid the rent in advance and was given the key. That's all that the manager knew.

He called Jack Hakobyan, whom the police had already questioned, to his office and asked him to close the door.

"Aside from your man Vitaly, who knew about Li's mission?"

"No one."

"How much did Vitaly know?"

"If you mean did he know Li worked for Ludwig, the answer is yes. Aside from that, not much. He knows nothing about the operation that Li discovered."

"But he put Li in touch with them?"

"Right."

"Do you know how? I mean, how did he find them?"

"Sorry, boss. I never asked. It did not matter at the time."

Petyan pushed the photo across his desk toward Jack.

"It matters now," he said. "Find out if his sources contacted him again to ask about Li."

Even though Jack had seen the photograph before, his gaze froze on it. He looked almost paralyzed. Petyan couldn't decide whether with fear or shock, but he quickly pulled the picture out of his sight.

"We need to keep a cool head. No point in panicking. No one should know about Li's involvement in the Lefebvre operation. I did not tell anything to the police. You shouldn't either; at least, do not volunteer. If asked directly, do not lie, but minimize its importance. Now, see if you can find out if Vitaly was contacted."

Petyan didn't really expect Vitaly to know much. He handled Ludwig's nightclub clients in Moscow, essentially as a glorified deliveryman. He was obsessed, and often stressed, about doing his job right, but he did not cultivate new client relationships. And although he knew a lot of people in the trade, he was not taken for player; he was just a reliable person who filled orders on time.

Something told Petyan that Li was discovered at a different level from where he was recruited. Even if they had contacted Vitaly, they must have had a lead, a reason for suspicion.

Nonetheless, he wanted Jack to check.

Jack met with Vitaly that same afternoon in a small coffee shop near the office so Vitaly could smoke. As Petyan had suspected, Vitaly knew nothing. No one had contacted him since he put Li in touch with his leads. He was not even aware of Li's murder. He believed that the people he dealt with were intermediaries who did not know details of the operation themselves. Lefebvre's operation was well camouflaged.

Aram Almayan stood for a couple of minutes in front of the light-brown, U-shaped stone building on Petrovka Street with a black cast iron fence across the open part of the U that created an enclosed front courtyard. Service-friendly manners, which had finally started to seep into the retail and service industries in Moscow, were as alien in the police department as they had been during the worst years of the Soviet Union. President Dmitri Medvedev's reforms of 2011, which changed the name of the department from *Militsiya* to *Politsiya*, relieved several high-ranking officers from their jobs and claimed to have improved the efficiency of the police, had not changed the grim and unfriendly culture of the place.

But Almayan was not one to be intimidated by the stern and uninviting front of the guards. He had hard-earned good will and political capital in this establishment. He had spent more time with their bosses than they had, and he had done more favors for them than they could even imagine. He walked into the building with the confidence of the police commissioner himself, and his demeanor and body language did not go unnoticed by the officers manning the entrance.

He was there to meet with a young officer named Feodor Shulgin. With his light blue-gray eyes, well-groomed mustache, blond fine hair combed neatly with a right-side part, and his straight, almost arrogant posture, Shulgin often reminded Almayan of the early 1900s Russian aristocracy. He was in his early forties, devoted to the police profession, and proud to be part of it.

He had been a regular contact of Almayan's for several years when he owned and operated his casinos in Moscow, but he had risen up the ranks several levels since Almayan had sold those enterprises. Importantly for Almayan, he had since moved from the Directorate for Public Order to the Criminal Investigations Department. Feodor had always been a police officer with a sense of restored self-esteem after the collapse of the Soviet Union and the reforms of Medvedev because he came from a long line of police professionals, going back to the nineteenth-century Tsarist Russia. He had once proudly told Almayan that his great, great grandfather, Dmitri Shulgin, was the police commissioner of Moscow during the time of Tsar Nicholas I in the late 1820s.

While at the Directorate for Public Order, Shulgin had been a regular presence at Almayan's casinos, as the main liaison between Almayan and the police commissioner. He always gave Almayan and his handling of his casinos credit for his promotions, and Almayan, who also dealt with higher-ranking police officers, always treated him with more respect than his rank called for. With Shulgin, Almayan was a goodwill creditor.

Shulgin clearly had gone out of his way to receive Almayan with style. He had cleared his schedule, his office was far cleaner than could be expected from someone in the Criminal Investigations Department, a bouquet of flowers graced a shelf near his desk, a selection of exclusive French pastries was displayed on a scratched-up side table, and, as an added gesture, a bottle of Nayiri Armenian cognac with two snifters was set beside it.

The gesture was appreciated, as Almayan did not expect Shulgin to remember that he did not drink. Besides, the reception was as much, if not more, to show off Shulgin's power as it was to honor Almayan. Not every officer had the clout to stage such a welcome for an old friend. He embraced Shulgin as an old comrade.

They toasted each other with a shot of Nayiri, which Almayan barely touched to his lips, and briefly reminisced about the old days before moving on to business.

"Feodor Ivanovich," said Almayan, referring to him in the formal style of addressing someone by both his first name and father's name. "I have a specific question for you—an unusual one having to do with wine fraud."

"Go ahead," said Shulgin, "but be prepared to be disappointed, I don't know much about wine fraud."

Almayan recounted the story of the Areni Eagle without mentioning the role of Ludwig or the Chinese employee who had attended the private sale. He explained the scale of the operation: the volumes sold, the prices charged, the nature of the fraud including the likely composition of Areni Eagle. He also gave the location where the sale event took place and described what he knew about the mansion, and whatever Jack had told him about Lefebvre and some of the clients, including the fact that most of them were Asians, and specifically Chinese.

Feodor Shulgin's eyes opened wider and his gaze intensified at the mention of the word "Chinese." He went quiet for a while, staring at his snifter of cognac. His blue-gray eyes seemed to turn almost entirely gray as he gazed into the liquid. He took a sip and met Almayan's eyes.

"I should not be discussing an open murder case with anyone outside the department, but this may be a rare, justified exception. The victim is a Chinese man of fifty-two, shot in the street in front of his apartment building, execution style. As for a possible connection with wine, he worked for Ludwig. I don't have to tell you what Ludwig is."

For a few minutes, both men were silent.

"There was a message left on his body. A handwritten note."

Almayan waited.

"Obviously, it was not meant for the dead Chinese," added Shulgin after a short pause. "But we had no idea who the addressee was. The note said: 'Держись подальше!' Thanks to you, we now may have a clue what the note could be referring to."

"Did you tell Ludwig about the note?"

"Of course. We showed it to Sergei Petyan personally. We asked him if he had any guesses as to what the note might mean. 'Keep out of what?' we asked."

"And?"

"He had no guesses."

"No reaction at all?"

"Just shock at the picture of his employee with a bullet hole in his forehead."

"I doubt someone like Sergei would be so shocked as not to have a guess," said Almayan.

"Aram Sarkisovich," he said, using the same formal address of first name followed by father's name, while looking at Almayan with appreciative eyes, "to be totally frank, I never thought we'd solve the murder of the Chinese, and we still may not. We have several cases like this every week. Most go unsolved. And frankly, we don't bother much. We usually spend more time on a case if it is related to narcotics because we want to catch the source, but petty quibbles among local businessmen do not have priority—even if they lead to murder."

Almayan nodded.

"But the victim in this case being a foreign national creates different problems. And you've now given me a potentially interesting lead. Your wine fraud story and this murder may not be related, but my gut tells me to check it anyway. I will take this straight to the commissioner. I will tell him the source, with your permission. You can come with me if you want."

"Please give the commissioner my best regards," said Almayan. "But there's no need for me to be there. I've taken enough of your time already. Of course, you can call me anytime, and I'll be back as necessary to assist in any way. But, Feodor Ivanovich, may I ask that you keep me informed of any new developments? The wine scam has special significance for me, and if it leads to your solving the murder, so much the better."

"Of course," said Shulgin, standing up. "I'll be in touch."

Almayan rushed into his car and instructed his driver to head toward Riyabinovaya Street, where Ludwig's main Moscow offices were located. He buttoned his suit jacket and dialed Jack Hakobyan's cell phone number.

It was five in the afternoon, and Moscow was getting dark and cold. Early fall in Moscow had the same temperament as late fall in Yerevan;

it was reminiscent of the approaching winter. They agreed to meet at a coffee shop near the Ludwig offices just in case Petyan needed to see Jack at short notice. They met at an espresso bar two blocks away, a kind of Starbucks substitute—with a similar menu, except for the patrons' orders were taken at their table, not at the counter—a perfect place for two men who did not drink alcohol.

"I just learned about your Chinese," said Almayan, skipping the usual pleasantries. "And the note that was left on his body."

Jack told him why Li had been chosen and how the organizers had scrutinized him before he was allowed in.

"Sorry I didn't have a chance to call you to tell you about his murder."

"Don't worry about that."

"We still don't know how they found out about Li," said Jack, genuine remorse stamped all over his face. "Sergei is convinced it's personal. Personal against him, not Li. Otherwise, why the warning, he says."

"It's obvious that the warning is directed to him; the question is why bother to warn him? If they discovered Li and killed him, they can handle the next intruder the same way. Why warn Sergei and risk leaving clues?"

"Mr. Almayan, I never thought it would come to this. I mean, I never thought we were risking Liu Li's life when we asked him to play that role. The whole thing was my idea. I suggested to Sergei to send Li. He seemed perfect for the role. He *was* perfect. Who could have thought wine fraudsters would go so far as committing murder?" Jack's voice had turned brittle and wobbly.

"Jack, you cannot blame yourself," said Almayan. "He obviously was the perfect candidate, or he wouldn't have passed their strict scrutiny. How he got discovered is an entirely different mystery. It has nothing to do with you."

"I put him in that spot," Jack said.

"Let's focus only on how he got discovered. That is the only thing worth spending time on."

Jack stared at Almayan for a long time without saying anything. It was not the look of someone deep in thought. It was the look of someone numb with shock.

"Sergei is right about one thing," Almayan was saying as Jack stared. "The message is personal, and crazy as this may sound, so is the murder. There can be no other explanation of why they'd leave stupid clues. They wanted Sergei to take notice."

Isabelle left the Enotria school building and turned right onto 4th Main Street, headed to Polezhaevskaya Metro station. She was familiar with the area—having done the 15-minute walk from school to the metro station on her way back to her small apartment six metro stops away almost every day. On Wednesdays the last class ended at eight p.m.—pedestrian traffic was lighter, and it was darker and colder than other days when she left at four p.m.

As she crossed the first block, she had an uneasy feeling that she was being followed. She turned back and noticed a dark shadowy figure, light on its feet, walking close to the buildings by the sidewalk. She picked up her pace and almost ran to the next cross street. On her right was a long, light-brown brick building with decorative darker brown diamond-shaped bricks sticking out of the wall at regular intervals. To get to the metro station, she had to cross the street. Usually she walked straight until the large supermarket and crossed right before she reached the entrance of the station. She turned back again and saw the figure vanished in a doorway. Her heart started to race. If she could make it to the supermarket, the street would be lit better and there'd be more people. But she wasn't sure she'd make it that far safely. She decided to cross the street.

On the opposite side was a long white stone fence, around two meters high, with barbed wire over it. She walked close to the wall. She couldn't resist one more look back and just then someone grabbed her neck from behind and rammed her face with great force into the wall. She had only a split-second flash of awareness of her aggressor—much bigger than the dark figure who she thought was following her, wearing what she imagined to be a knit wool hat drawn down over his ears. Her last conscious sensation was his enormous size, then, less than a second later, a shocking pain shot through her nose and forehead and she passed out.

Sveni, Sveni Noir: a rare variety distributed in single vines in old vineyards in the Goris district. The tip of the young shoot is light green, with barely visible hairs. The mature leaf is medium sized, seldom large, circular, and lightly five lobbed. The bunch varies widely, small to large, cylindrical-conical, and dense to less dense. The berry is medium sized, round, and black. The skin is firm. The flesh is juicy, with a special harmonious and unique aroma. The wine is high-quality with a unique and pleasant taste.

CHAPTER TWELVE

When Anatoly Likhachev found Isabelle lying on the sidewalk, he could not make out her face—it was dark, her face was covered by clotted blood, her nose was indistinguishable, her eyes hidden under a layer of almost black blood with just the outer surface of the closed eyelids noticeable. She was lying on her right side, her arm and purse crunched under her, the strap of the purse still around her shoulder. Her dark brown pants were covered with a fine dust, and there was blood on the wide collar of her black leather jacket. A large, almost oval blood stain on the wall right above where she lay had several thin, red stains dripping from it like strings. For a few seconds his impulse was to walk away, like he presumed other passersby had done before him. He then turned on the flashlight on his cell phone and approached her for a closer look. She was breathing, but the light did not reveal much more about her face.

As he stood there staring at her, he knew he wouldn't be able to walk away, but a firm decision to help the girl was yet to take shape in his head. He looked up and down the street hoping that someone might join him in helping the girl. The closest hospital, the Number 2 Drug Dispenser on Kuusinena Street, closed at eight p.m. It was 8:45. Having decided he would not abandon the girl, he called his sister, Dr. Larisa Likhacheva, and described as best he could the condition of the what he called 'the victim.' He then stopped a taxi and with the driver's help carried Isabelle to the back seat. They drove to Medionika hospital, where Dr. Likhacheva, a surgeon specializing in head and neck injuries who treated mostly athletes, was waiting for them. Isabelle opened her eyes briefly when they moved her onto a stretcher, and made a feeble, impulsive attempt to sit up, but collapsed back a second later.

"Call the police," Dr. Likhacheva told the receptionist, then had Isabelle moved to the examining room. Anatoly decided to wait. He had the unfamiliar and peculiar feeling of being invested in a total stranger's fate. It was good that his sister was a medical doctor; otherwise, he wouldn't have known what to do. He went to the waiting room and started browsing through the magazines.

By the time two police officers, looking bored and annoyed, arrived at the hospital, Dr. Likhacheva had examined Isabelle, washed and treated her wounds, given her a sedative and left her to rest. The receptionist called both her and Anatoly to come to the front.

"Who found her?" asked one of the officers.

"I did," said Anatoly. The officers looked young, probably in their early thirties, only a few years older than Anatoly.

"Wait here a while. I will need you to take us to where you found her." Then he turned to Dr. Likhacheva:

"What's her condition?"

"Not as bad as I suspected when I first saw her. Nose shattered, forehead badly bruised and torn in one corner, but no fractures. She needed a few stiches and may carry a small scar. Chin and jaw were relatively unharmed. Back of the neck, at the base of the skull was bruised, but no bleeding there. Her cervical vertebrae, C1 through C5, were thrown off alignment. Our chiropractor adjusted them, but she needs to be careful for a week or so or she may throw them off again. No other physical injuries on her body, and we haven't detected any signs of brain damage. The nose will take the longest to heal—probably two weeks in bandages and a few months until it fully heals. The physical damage is not serious. But she is a shock. The trauma will last longer than the physical injuries."

The officer listened without any reaction.

"Did she have a handbag?"

Dr. Likhacheva produced it from behind the receptionist's desk.

They inspected the purse and its contents.

"It doesn't look like a robbery," said the officer who had been doing all the talking. Anatoly, who had checked the purse earlier and seen that her identity cards, cell phone, and cash seemed untouched, rolled his eyes but said nothing.

"When can we talk to her?"

"You can talk now if you want, but I prefer if we let her rest today. She does not remember much. Judging from the bruises at the back of her neck, someone must have grabbed her from behind and crashed hear face into the wall. Whoever he was, he had enormous physical strength. She is on pain killers now but not too sedated to talk, if you want to talk now."

"Aside from any details of the assault which she may remember, we need to know who she knows in Moscow. We need to inform someone."

"My nurse asked her that, and she gave two names." Dr. Likhacheva handed the officer a folded piece of paper, with two names on it—Prof. Sandro Kashvili, Enotria school; next line, Haig Koleyan, followed by a Yerevan number. There was no phone number next to Kashvili.

"She's already talked to her friend in Yerevan," added Likhacheva when the officer had read and refolded the piece of paper. "I understand he's on his way here. The Professor has not been contacted yet."

Even though it was past midnight in Yerevan, Haig called Carla and Van Dorian before getting ready to head for the airport to catch the 02:55 Aeroflot flight to Moscow. The hardest part of both calls was to fend off the barrage of questions which he could not answer.

"All I know is that she was assaulted and is in the hospital. She could not speak much. The nurse helped her text me the address. I'll be there early in the morning. When I know more, I'll let you know."

That, after a while, was good enough for Dorian, but not Carla.

"My dad is in Moscow," she said, speaking twice as fast as her normal pace. "I'll call him right now and let him know, and I'll text you his number. He's very well connected. He can help."

Haig felt hopelessly scattered by the various scenarios rushing through his mind. His every fear and every suspicion of anything having to do with Russians, which most of his friends in Armenia had repeatedly and nonchalantly dismissed as his phobia, often having a laugh or two at his expense, now invaded his imagination with a vengeance. Although he had nothing to do with Isabelle's move to Moscow, in fact, she knew he'd disapprove if asked, he still felt responsible.

His flight landed at Sheremetyevo airport around five am. With no checked-in luggage, he was out and in a taxi and at Medionika hospital on Khodynski Blvd by 06:20. It took longer than the taxi ride to convince the night attendant to allow him to visit Isabelle. It was not until the morning nurse came to make her rounds around seven o'clock and saw the notes from the night before with Haig's name on it, that the attendant agreed to let Haig into her room.

His first thought when he saw Isabelle was that he was looking at a Mummy. Except for her eyes and mouth, her entire head and face were wrapped in bandages. Propped up over two pillows, her eyes closed, she looked peaceful—breathing slow and steady. He rolled his carry-on bag to the corner of the room and sat on the chair by her bed. He'd wait until she opened her eyes on her own before saying anything. As he sat down, the image of Isabelle in Mummy wraps gradually gave way to the dim light and the quiet hum of the equipment in the room and the physical and emotional exhaustion of the day consumed him. He closed his eyes.

"We gave her a sedative early this morning," said the nurse. Haig opened his eyes and straightened his back. "She was in pain, and she needs her sleep." She checked her vitals on the monitor. "No fever. Pulse normal." She said as she scribbled some notes.

"How serious is her condition?" asked Haig in his broken Russian and stood up.

"She's fine. Just a broken nose and a few stiches on her forehead." Much of what Haig disliked and mistrusted about Russians was captured in the nurse's detached, almost dismissive, authoritative tone. It gave him a chill.

"The doctor thinks she can be released tomorrow morning. Maybe even later today. Will you be taking her home?"

As Haig struggled to understand what the nurse was saying and formulate a response, his phone rang.

"No calls in the room. You can take it outside."

Seeing that Isabelle's eyes were still closed, he walked out with the nurse and answered the phone.

"Koleyan?"

"Yes."

"Aram Almayan here. Carla called me. Are you already at the hospital?"

"Yes."

"Give me the address."

Haig had not imagined any scenario where he'd be thrilled to hear from Aram Almayan. He had met him only once at the sixtieth birthday party of a mutual friend in Yerevan, the introduction being made by Carla herself, and, given the background of disagreements between the two wineries, they had both acted like they'd had a 'so I finally meet the man...' moment. But here, in this microcosm of Russian dominion, where he felt as estranged and endangered as he would if air-dropped into a massive snake pit, Almayan's call and the few words spoken in Armenian gave Haig the most comforting and secure sensation he had experienced.

He went back in. The Mummy opened her eyes and moved her right hand, which Haig took as a sign of recognition. His smile beamed as he approached Isabelle and took her hand.

"Everyone here tells me you're fine," he said. "How do you feel?"

"My face hurts," Isabelle said. The tight bandage on her face restricted her facial muscle and jaw movements, and her voice came out muffled and coarse.

"I bet it does. I'm going to take a few pictures, so one day we can laugh about this." He chuckled.

"You can laugh about it now if you want, but don't try to make me laugh," she muttered.

"I won't ask you what happened yet," said Haig more seriously. "There'll be time for that later. For now, just tell me: when the hospital discharges you, do you want to return to Yerevan, or stay and continue to study here?"

Isabelle closed her eyes. Her right hand started a slow tapping over the mattress. The tapping stopped, but she did not open her eyes. Several minutes passed.

"I need to know what arrangements to make," said Haig.

Isabelle opened her eyes for a moment and then shut them again. "I want to talk to Professor Kashvili first."

"Do you have a student called Isabelle Karayan?" asked the policeman as soon as he and his partner had introduced themselves to Kashvili. They had been escorted to his office by Enotria school administrative staff.

"Yes," he said, walking toward them from behind his cluttered desk. "Is there a problem?"

"She was assaulted last night. She is in the hospital."

"Assaulted? How?"

"Someone smashed her face against a wall. She's fine. She gave your name as a contact in Moscow. How well do you know her?"

"Well, she's in my class. Is she OK? Which hospital?"

"Medionika on Khodynski. I said she's fine. Now, let me ask again, how well do you know her?"

"As I said, she's in my class."

"Do you know all your students equally well? Would they all have given your name if they got in trouble, or just her?"

"She's not from Moscow. Maybe she knows no one else here."

"She must know others at the school—other professors, administration, classmates."

"I guess."

"Any idea why she picked you?"

"I don't know. Maybe because I did her a favor once."

"A favor?"

"Yes, she wanted to meet the head of Ludwig, I arranged it."

"Ludwig?"

"A liquor and wine trading company."

"What's the name of the head of Ludwig?"

"Sergei Petyan."

"When was this?"

"Not sure exactly. Several weeks ago."

"Any idea why she wanted to meet this man, Petyan?"

"She's studying about wine. He's the largest wine and spirits merchant in Russia. And they're both Armenian. I know of no other basis for her interest."

"Do you know if she had enemies at the school?"

"No. She kept mostly to herself. I've been here for over a decade and I've never heard of a case where students used violence against each other."

"And the teachers?"

"What about the teachers?"

"Have they ever used violence against a student?"

"Of course not!"

"How well do you know Petyan?"

"I've known him for years."

"Is he prone to violence?"

"Not as far as I know. Certainly not against an innocent student."

The policeman gave Kashvili a skeptical look. "Innocent?"

"As far as I know, yes."

"Would he be prone to violence if the student was not innocent?"

Kashvili was getting annoyed.

"Why don't you check his police record," he said with a dismissive hand gesture, not hiding his irritation. "Now, if you don't mind, I'd like to go and see my student."

When the police officers left, Kashvili called Petyan.

"My student, the one who came to see you, was attacked last night," he said. "The police may come to question you."

"Is she dead?" asked Petyan instantly. The suddenness of the question surprised Kashvili.

"No, why would you ask that?"

"Never mind. Why would the police want to question me?"

"I told them I arranged her to meet you. Can you think of anything that happened during your meeting that could have led to this?"

"Nothing at all," said Petyan, then, with some hesitation, added: "When can you come over so we can talk here?"

Aware of Petyan's aversion to saying anything sensitive over the phone, Kashvili knew right away that there was more to the story.

Almayan was still at Medionika hospital when Kashvili arrived in the afternoon with a bouquet of bright red roses. Almayan gave him a look over—his red bowtie matched the roses, his dark grey blazer freshly pressed, hair combed back. Isabelle's reaction to his entrance was interesting—she could not smile, of course, or if she tried, it wouldn't be noticed under the bandages, but Almayan noticed her stir and her hand gestures became more animated. Kashvili went straight to her soon after briefly greeting Haig and Almayan, neither of whom he had met before.

"So, what kind of mischief did you get into?" he asked, putting the flowers on the side table.

"The mischief found me," she said. "I have no idea why. Haig, Mr. Almayan, this is Professor Kashvili. Professor, I think you've heard of Haig Koleyan and Aram Almayan."

"It's a pleasure, gentlemen," said Kashvili shaking their hands in turn. The conversation had turned into Russian, so Haig just smiled and deferred to Almayan.

"Good to meet you," said Almayan, in a businesslike tone. "We've been talking with Isabelle whether she should return to Armenia for a while or stay and finish the trimester."

"Oh, I see." Kashvili seemed to be surprised by the question. "But first, let me ask, what do we know about the incident? Was this one freak event or you suspect a more serious danger facing Isabelle?"

"At this point, we should not rule out anything. It was not a robbery; nothing was stolen from her purse and she was not assaulted sexually. So what could have been the motive of the attack?"

Almayan noticed that Haig, who could understand the general gist of the conversation, was getting jittery. He moved closer to Isabelle and said in Armenian: "Let's not say too much to him." He was loud enough for Almayan to hear.

"Oh, I don't have a clue what the motive might have been. In fact, I know nothing about what happened other than what the police told me, which wasn't much. Do you have a theory as to the motive?"

"We don't know," jumped in Haig, giving a stern look to Almayan.

"Isabelle, what do you remember?" Kashvili asked.

"Not much. It was dark. Someone was following me. When I turned back to check, someone else grabbed my neck and slammed my face against the wall."

"Where?"

"On my way to the Polezhaevskaya metro station. I had just crossed the street. I have a split-second memory of the wall—it was white with square reliefs. It was a fence, not a building. And then, in a fraction of a second, my face went straight into it. Then everything went blank."

This was a detail which Almayan had not heard before, even after about an hour of questioning. Either Isabelle's memory was gradually coming back on its own, or the Professor was helping trigger details of images.

"Anything else? Don't you remember anything about the aggressor?"

"I never had a direct look at him; I had a vague and very brief peripheral view. I *felt* his presence more than I saw him. He was huge, maybe more than two meters tall. I'm pretty sure he used only his right hand to grab my neck, but his grip covered the back on my neck and the base of my skull. He appeared next to me like a flash, like a massive, dark shadow, like a ghost."

The size of the attacker seemed to mean something to Kashvili, but Almayan couldn't decipher his reaction accurately. For a brief moment, a vague look of recognition swept over his eyes, as if Isabelle's description had reminded him of someone.

Kashvili went quiet for a while, then started pacing the room, walking from Isabelle's bed to the door and back, eyes down on the floor, right hand combing his hair back.

"I need to leave now," he said at last, to no one in particular. "And I think it may be best if Isabelle were to return to Armenia until the police figure out what this is all about." Then, turning to Isabelle, "You can always return later and re-enroll."

He rushed out of the room.

"You told him too much," said Haig with a frown as soon as Kashvili was out of the door.

"What do you think he's going to do with any of this? I told him about the wall and the size of my attacker. They know where the wall is, and I've told everyone about the attacker."

"That doesn't matter," said Almayan. "I agree with the Professor. Isabelle, it's your decision, of course, but it's best if you return for now. I'll stay for a while and check around."

"You think I'm still in danger?"

"The only explanation for the attack—given that it was not a robbery or sexual assault—is that it was meant to scare you. Someone somewhere in this town seems to have reason to frighten you away. If you stay, they'll try it again, and next time they'll be more assertive. Is it worth it?"

Isabelle closed her eyes.

After a minute, Haig repeated Almayan's question more impatiently. "Isabelle, is it worth it?"

Isabelle opened her eyes and looked at him.

"No," she said. "Not anymore."

Arevik, Little Sun, from the Arevik village in Meghri: a widely cultivated variety in the Syunik region. It has large to medium sized, conical, dense bunches, and big round berries. The skin is thick and covered by a layer of epicuticuar wax. The flesh is dense, juicy, and sweet. The bunches grown in the shade have a greenish color, and those grown in the sun acquire a light amber color. It is a highly productive, late-ripening variety. The Arevik wine is used to make white table wines as well as strong fortified wines.

CHAPTER THIRTEEN

"Everyone will think I came to Moscow to have a nose job," said Isabelle in a croaky voice, the effect of the pain killer she had taken a couple of hours earlier. She sank in the business class seat next to Haig on the Aeroflot flight back to Yerevan, and stirred her gin and tonic in slow, deliberate movements. Six days after the incident, the bandages from her head and face were removed, but not from her nose. Black and blue marks poked from under the edges of the bandage over her nose and under her eyes. Haig had secured their tickets, and, once on board, had told her there wasn't a worthwhile wine to drink on board, so they may as well go with gin or vodka for once.

"You'll fit right in," said Haig with a chuckle. "So many young women with bandages on their noses in Yerevan these days."

"Except for my nose did not need fixing."

"Forgive me if I disagree. Your nose has a bigger problem than any other nose in Yerevan."

Isabelle watched Haig smirk, waiting for her to react. But she kept quiet.

"Your nose, dear Isabelle, may not need surgery on account of its physical shape, but it certainly needs *fixing*. You see, it has a tendency to get into places it doesn't belong."

Isabelle took a big sip of her gin and tonic, reclined in her seat and shut her eyes. Her head was feeling lighter, but her groggy mind could not let go of some of the images from Moscow. Sergei Petyan's chubby, round face, with its thick eyebrows that were almost connected in the center—just a few hairs short of a unibrow, she had thought when she first saw him—kept appearing and fading away. The man seemed averse to sideburns, as his were shaved to the top of his ears, accentuating the roundness of his face. His black pin striped suit, which he wore with a collarless black shirt, would have been a fashion clothier's nightmare. His hair was cut short and he was balding. He had a warm smile, but, in her memory, the smile was only as a fuzzy background to the cold and merciless eyes that lurked behind them.

Her last chat with Kashvili weighed on her. Something had been different in his demeanor when he was questioning her about her meeting with Petyan. She saw flashes of Petyan and Kashvili sitting together, whispering, speculating, and sharing secrets. She realized, once again, with a tightening knot in her stomach that she was in way over her head when interacting with people like them.

She looked at Haig. He was flipping through the pages of the airline magazine.

"We don't know for sure if it was poking my nose where it doesn't belong that got me in trouble," she said. "All I did is ask Petyan if he knew of any private sales of Korah. That's all. So someone smashes my face for that?"

Haig finished his drink, shrugged his shoulders and turned back to his magazine.

She had thanked Anatoly Likhachev for bringing her to the hospital—'my good Samaritan'—she had said, even though she wasn't sure he'd understand the reference. She had felt an unspoken yet distinct connection with him, partly because she sensed he felt the same way. He had visited her only once, on her second day at the hospital. When she was discharged, she asked Dr. Likhacheva to convey her goodbye and regards to Anatoly.

What did she expect to achieve with this four-month course anyway? That type of doubt was not new to her, but this bout was more crippling than anything she had felt in the past. There was a more existential consequence to this doubt. It was a doubt that could upset her passion for the wine industry. It was a misgiving born out of disillusionment, not mere self-doubt: disillusionment with two titans whom she once felt lucky to know. She saw especially Kashvili fallen from the pedestal she had always imagined him on as the incorruptible, almost infallible, upholder and bottomless vessel of both the knowledge and the morality of the finest human discovery, wine. If someone like Kashvili could take that fall, what was she doing at Enotria?

Only Haig could reassure her. Only his dogged resolve could reignite her own passion and love for the industry. She imagined Haig had gone through worse periods of trials and doubts and had vanquished them. How could he not? She had some idea of what it took to start everything that he had started in Armenia as an expatriate. There was an almost mystical force driving him that she did not fully understand.

His main philosophy of why he was in Armenia, "We are survivors and humanists, and we have to build a modern nation," had nothing to do with wine per se. And yet it somehow drove him to overcome every obstacle and disenchantment with people, bureaucracy, corruption, and resentment directed at him personally, along with the occasional malice and envy. The disillusionment she was feeling seemed like a minor ego bruise, a mere hiccup, compared to what Haig had gone through.

When she opened her eyes, Haig was reading a newspaper.

"It wasn't just the threat, you know," she told him.

"What?"

"I'm not leaving Moscow because of the threat. I'm not that afraid."

"Oh?"

Isabelle took the last sip of her drink, which by now was diluted by the molten ice.

"Too many fallen angels," she said.

"The Professor?"

She nodded. "And Sergei Petyan."

"You think they're involved?" Haig's jaw dropped and his eyes opened wide.

"No, no, not involved in the attack on me. But involved. With each other. You've been right, by the way. Neither you nor I can penetrate that world."

Isabelle realized then that she cherished and needed mentors because they made her feel safe. She sought their acceptance of who she was, not their validation of her capabilities. She wanted them to like her and *include* her. Inclusion was important. There was safety in the knowledge that she had the best in the field paying attention to her.

Kashvili had played that role for a while, in her mind, even before she met him. Having read most of his published papers and watched several videos of his interviews and public presentations, she had recast him in her imagination as her mentor. At first, she had thought that even Sergei Petyan could grow into that role. He was a man of immense power and influence, even if he lacked the intellectual power and attraction of Sandro Kashvili. Petyan couldn't possibly have achieved all that he had if he were not exceptionally intelligent. Intelligence manifested itself in different ways, and aside from being physically attracted to it, Isabelle was always intrigued with what intelligent people did with their gift. The accumulation of vast knowledge was one overwhelming outcome. Sharp, penetrating perception was even more erotic, especially when it was focused on her.

But what turned intelligence absolutely irresistible was when it was revealed through power and influence, when one word from them instantly led to consequential action. In her mind, Kashvili could have moved mountains by just saying so. So could Petyan. But now both had been deflated and downgraded to mere mortals.

"I think they know more about the Korah issue than we do," she said. "And I know they've talked about it behind my back. And I thought they could coach me. How naïve ..."

"I never understood why you need coaches. You're smart and generally confident. Why do you seek these men? Why do you need to always idolize someone?"

"Can we get another drink?" she asked and closed her eyes again.

Why indeed. Why did she idolize Haig? He—her original conquest in the wine world—had always been in the pantheon. Aside from his intelligence, knowledge, and his contagious enthusiasm, Haig still had the uncanny ability to surprise her, such as that time with Ruggero Mastroserio in Fair Play, California, or by being amazingly supportive when she had expected him to be angry with her for the way she had handled Sergei Petyan. If he could still surprise her after so many years, it meant that their relationship was still evolving and that she had not yet gotten to the bottom of the phenomenon called Haig Koleyan.

The flight attendant refreshed their drinks.

On his way to see Sergei Petyan, Professor Sandro Kashvili called Madame Stella for the second time that week. The first time was immediately upon leaving Sergei Petyan's office after tasting the Areni Eagle.

"She just left for France," her housekeeper had told him when he first called.

"When will she be back?"

"This trip is relatively short. A few days."

Her lawyer, Dmitri, had not returned his call.

"She's not back yet," the housekeeper said apologetically when he called from the car. "But any day now."

"And Mr. Dmitri?"

"He went with her this time."

When he arrived at Petyan's office, Petyan turned off his phone. "Turn yours off too."

Then he called his assistant. "Lock these in the safe in the boardroom," he said.

"Do you want a drink?"

"I could use one."

Petyan walked to the cabinet and filled two snifters with brandy.

"A couple of days ago," he said taking a sip, "one of my employees was gunned down in the street. Execution style."

"Who?" It took Kashvili a moment to recover from the surprise.

"The guy we sent to the wine sale."

Petyan sat behind his desk and leaned over to get closer to Kashvili.

"And now an attack on Isabelle—do you think the two events are related?"

"If you're asking me, you must already have a theory."

"It was Isabelle who alerted me about the scam. She thought there were private sales of Korah in Moscow. Of course, she was wrong about that. But I got suspicious and ended up finding out about the Areni Eagle sale event."

"I didn't know that. I asked her if you two discussed wine, but she never told me about that." Petyan was staring at him with his penetrating gaze. Kashvili suddenly realized that he may have sounded almost hurt, as if Isabelle had cheated on him by not telling him, and quickly tried to recover his composure. "Oh well," he said, "God knows where her mind was at the time. She has been distracted a lot lately."

"What do you know about the murder?" asked Kashvili.

"I think it has to do with the wine sale. The police don't know that, because, as far as I know, they don't know about the wine scam." Petyan took another sip of his brandy and swiveled his chair toward the wood carving, and the back to face Kashvili. "We were warned to stay away," he said banging his fist on his desk. "A nice note on Li Liu's corpse..."

"Wait a minute, you didn't tell the police about Li going to the wine sale?"

"No."

"Sergei, that's crazy. Why not?"

"The less they know the better. Then they'll ask me why I didn't report the scam right away."

"What if they find out on their own?"

"How would they? They barely have time to investigate murders."

It was difficult to process all that Petyan was saying. It was one of those rare moments when he could not focus on the issue at hand. He didn't know who Li Liu was and didn't understand what Petyan meant by being warned and didn't feel like probing; normally, he would sit back in his chair, sip his brandy, and ask for clarification from the haughty position of the Professor. But a nagging feeling was disrupting his ability to think calmly. Every self-centered and paranoid hot shot in Moscow had a bodyguard who fit the description that Isabelle gave of her aggressor. Petyan certainly had more than one...

"Let me ask you something Sandro. What exactly made you call me late that night to ask me to meet your student?"

Kashvili looked at Petyan stare at him, dead serious, his gaze so focused and sharp that he could almost feel it penetrating his brain like an X-ray.

"I don't know what *exactly*," he said. "*We both had drank quite a bit, she said she wanted to meet the great man—the great merchant of spirits. So, I called you. Aren't you happy you saw her? You probably never would have found out about the scam if you hadn't.*"

"*She was not being honest with me. She was fishing for information.*"

Kashvili wondered if Petyan had seen through him also, because he was not being honest with him either.

Haig was surprised to see 326 acceptances three weeks after the 527 invitations were sent. Even more surprising was that 108 of them were from overseas—producers and enthusiasts from Burgundy, Boudreaux, Loire, Champagne, Tuscany, Puglia, Lombardy, Rioja, Napa, Sonoma, and Moscow. Indeed, they not only had accepted, but most of them had asked for suggestions for hotels, as many of the foreign guests had not been to Armenia before. Apparently, the word was already out about the emergence of Armenian wines. He knew the majority of the invitees, but not all. He had solicited names from his contacts and, after checking their backgrounds, included them. It was an impressive mix: restaurateurs, winemakers, wine merchants, sommeliers, food and wine critics, diplomats, *bon vivants*, and even several poets, writers, and musicians.

"I don't want to jinx anything," he told Dorian, "but we may be pushing on an open door here. They're dying to know what we're up to."

"Of course they'd be," said Dorian and lifted his nose from the book he was reading. "Why are you surprised?" Then, without missing a beat and the book still open in his hands, he asked, "Did you know that the Welsh have a word for a feeling that is innately Armenian? Even the English don't have a translation for it. We don't have a word for it either, at least not a precise translation, but we know exactly what the feeling is. The Welsh and us, go figure."

Haig waited for a few minutes, but Dorian's attention had already shifted back to his book, a hefty volume that seemed to concern social justice, even though Dorian had already moved on from the classical philosophers on justice to existential philosophy.

"So, are you going to tell me what's this Welsh feeling that's also so incredibly Armenian?" Haig demanded finally.

"Sit down," said Dorian. "Why are you so rushed and bothered? I told you once we start they will come, didn't I? Now you have more acceptances than you thought you'd get, and we still have a couple of months to go. That's great news. Why are you so restless?"

"You sound like you're about to recommend a wine for my condition." Haig laughed as he realized that Dorian was right. "Is there a wine for 'the nervous organizer of an event which may go better than expected'? Not that we're all there yet. I still don't have Alma Wines and a few others on board."

"They'll come aboard," said Dorian with such certainty that Haig wondered if Dorian knew something he did not. "Your problem with this gala is not going to be attendance. That's all you seem to be focused on, but you're focused on the wrong problem." He turned back to his book.

How could Dorian just tell him that and not complete the thought?

"Van, put that book down for a minute, will you? What's the right problem then?"

Dorian put a page marker in his book, closed it, and put it down. But he kept his hand firmly over it. He had the look of a man determined to make this apparently necessary interruption a short one.

"The right problems are logistics, menus, wines, and organization. How many waiters will you need for, say, 400 people? How will you serve a seven-course dinner with the right wines without a glitch? How will you present the evening: each course, each wine, and each break between courses? Where will you hold the event if you have 400 people? Will there be a few live musical interludes while people eat, maybe a string quartet in the corner somewhere? That'd be a nice touch. Have you thought about these details?"

Dorian stopped, picked up his book, looked back at Haig. "OK?"

"OK," said Haig and was about to let him open his book again, but he stopped and put out his hand.

"What about that Welsh feeling?"

"They call it *hiraeth*. I'm not sure how to pronounce it exactly, but that's probably close. The meaning comes close to our '*karot*.' You'd pronounce it '*garod*,' but regardless, not quite the same thing as *hiraeth*. It is nostalgia, but it includes a kind of homesickness mixed with grief over something that has been lost. In *hiraeth* there is longing, yearning, melancholy, and a burning, intense desire for something that has been lost and cannot be recovered. It is *karot* plus. For some of us, *karot* encompasses all of it, especially when it refers to the fatherland and its past glory. But *karot* also has more mundane uses. We can feel *karot* for something that we expect to have or see again such as a loved one we haven't seen for a while, but who could still visit us. *Hiraeth* is more hopeless; the loss is more permanent. At any rate, I can't believe the Welsh had reason to feel something that intense, but they obviously do, otherwise why would they have a word for it?"

"And? Do we have a wine to go with *hiraeth*?"

"We have many, Haig. You know that. We have to lump this in the same category as nostalgia/karot. But there are so many nuances to *hiraeth*, so many shades, depending on what loss or object of desire is causing the feeling. It becomes difficult to diagnose the exact version."

"OK, this hiraeth thing seems to be in good hands with you," said Haig with a chuckle. "By the way, I've decided to gamble on tripling the Korah capacity. Maybe I'm just feeling lucky right now, but I think demand for Korah will soar. So I'll plant nothing but Sev Areni in the 12 hectares. I've already made a preliminary commitment to buy more than 24,000 vines. I figure, in a crunch, I could divert some of the grapes to Kole bubbly. But I'd forgo more Voskehat, which we also need for our whites, and some other reds, like Syrah."

"So you're talking about a $700,000 gamble, in addition to the cost of the land."

"More like $800,000. I'm not sure which is growing faster, our grape production or the costs."

"Maybe you should drink on it first."

"Drink on it?"

"The ancient Persians would reconsider any decision or deal they made while drunk and finalize them only if they agreed with them again when sober. What's fascinating is that the converse was also true—any decision made while sober was not considered final unless it also made sense while drunk. The idea is that you are more honest with yourself when drunk. It's not enough for a decision to be logical—it also has to 'feel' right, has to be more in line with you."

"Now that's a first," said Haig laughing. "We agree that I'm about to make a huge gamble, and now I'm supposed to reduce the risk by confirming it drunk!"

"He has the nerve," Carla burst out at The Diplomat as soon as Isabelle brought up the Food and Wine Society Gala. Isabelle had invited her to the bookstore-turned-wine bar on Saryan Street, one of her own favorite places, to follow through on a promise to Haig that she'd broach the subject. She still had the bandages on her nose, but the swelling was down and the black and blue marks poking from the edges were gone.

It was a cozy place, with several interconnected rooms furnished with comfortable couches and coffee tables and lined with bookshelves. Book sales had improved since the wine bar and the kitchen had been added. Patrons would walk in for lunch or supper and, wine glass in hand, browse through the books, and even attend book dedications and poetry reading evenings, which Isabelle did as often as she could.

"The 'Wines of Armenia' was my idea. I talked to him about it months ago. 'Let's do it together,' I said. 'It will take a major drive to get us where we want to go.' He listened, smiled, and never got back to me. Now he's launching this thing on his own?"

Isabelle watched her for a few seconds and topped up Carla's glass. She'd ordered a bottle of Sancerre, hoping that by diverging from their regular routine of an Alma Voskehat, she'd set the mood for something different and a new way of thinking. No such luck.

"Well, that's just it," she said. "He's *not* launching it alone. He wants everyone in, including you. Especially you."

"But it was my idea from the beginning! He stole it! Now he wants me to join him as if he conceived the concept?"

"If it was your idea to start with, jump at it. Why don't you?"

"Fuck you."

"I understand your frustration. Fine, let's say he stole your idea. Isn't that the ultimate compliment?"

"Fuck you and your Haig."

"He's not my Haig, but you must admit he's smart enough to steal your idea. A lot of people wouldn't have recognized its value."

"*Of course* he's smart. And *of course* it's a great idea. After all, it was mine! And he stole it."

And so it went.

She wouldn't be able to resolve this in one session, but it was hard to believe that there was no way of doing so eventually. Both Haig and Carla understood the importance of the event. As Carla was struggling to swallow her pride and join his campaign, he was struggling to swallow his and lure her over. That was the knot that Isabelle had to untangle.

Colonel Feodor Shulgin expected to receive a pretty large folder when he asked for the police file on Ludwig. After all, it was the largest liquor merchant in Russia, with many offices all over the country, and had been in business for a few decades. He expected to spend the better part of the day reading, since he had had no reason to look into Ludwig's operations since his move to the Criminal Investigations Division.

"Is that all?" he asked when his aide, the sergeant who had visited Sergei Petyan after Li Liu's murder, came back with a thin folder containing no more than thirty pages.

"Yes sir. And that includes my last report on the murder."

"Is there anything in the electronic archives that is not here?"

"No sir—at least not anything having directly to do with Ludwig's operations."

Shulgin went through the folder in less than an hour. Until Li's murder, it covered standard updates on Ludwig's commercial operations, with practically nothing on the founding partner, Sergei Petyan, who seemed to have stayed out of police scrutiny.

But on the page right before the new entry on Li's murder, the bottom ten lines were blacked out. There was a space between the last legible paragraph and the blacked-out section, which Shulgin assumed signified that the black-out was at the start of a new section. He had a distinct impression that the balance of the new section had been removed from the file altogether.

Shulgin reclined in his chair and stared at the file lying on his desk. He was surprised that his aide had not noticed the blacked-out segment. He probably had just written his report and appended it to the file, without bothering to look at what was there before. His first impulse was to check the electronic archives, but he quickly changed his mind. He grabbed the file and headed to the police Commissioners office.

"I'm sorry to come without prior appointment," he told the staff sergeant outside the commissioner's office. "But it is important. And I won't take too much of his time."

After a few minutes, the staff sergeant let him in.

"Good day, Chief Bogadov. Sorry for disturbing you. This is what prompted me to come." He presented the folder to him, opened to the page which had the blacked-out section.

The Chief, who liked and respected Shulgin and had promoted him to Colonel a few months earlier, looked at the open page, briefly went to the beginning of the file, then back to the end which covered Li's murder.

"Sit down, Feodor Ivanovich."

Shulgin took the seat across his desk and waited.

"Let me start by saying that the clerk who handled this report was clumsy to leave it like this—it's an embarrassment to the department. Now to the substance: Part of what's missing here is, or has been in the past, public knowledge. Another part is not and is not fully known even to us. But I can assure you that this has nothing to do with the murder you're investigating."

"Excuse me, Chief. But there is a part that is public knowledge?"

"Yes. A few years ago, one of the two founding partners of Ludwig was murdered. I don't remember his name. That much is public knowledge.

The murder remains unsolved to this day. Now, what I will tell you next cannot leave this room, do you understand, Feodor Ivanovich?"

"Of course."

"We had come to the conclusion that it was a case of mistaken identity—the man had no enemies. As we dug deeper, we discovered who we believe was the intended target of the hit." Chief Bogadov hesitated for a moment, then continued. "He was Mikhail Edorov, an Oligarch who, as he got rich on privatized oil and gas assets, violated the most important rule of Oligarchy in Russia—he did not stay out of politics. And, to boot, he did not pay the right share to his masters. The confusion arose because he happened to drive an identical car as the Ludwig partner, and even looked like him. We started investigating him and thought we were getting close to where the orders for his murder came. That's when I received the call from the Minister of Internal Affairs. Close the case, he said—orders from the top. So the case was closed."

"You were getting close to where the orders came from?"

"Well, the trail led all the way to the top. Hence the orders to close the case."

"What happened to Edorov?"

"Last I heard he's in a jail in Siberia. No one cares or asks."

On his way out, Shulgin stopped for a moment at the door. "Chief, thank you as always for your confidence. As you said, this may have nothing to do with the murder I'm investigating, but I'm pretty sure Sergei Petyan has lied to us."

Karmir Kteni, Red Kteni: *an uncommon variety found in the old vineyards of Vayots Dzor and Goris. The tip of the young shoot is light green and hairless. The first young distal leaves have a light pink hue. The mature leaf is medium, circular and five lobbed. The bunch is medium, conical cylindrical-conical, and medium-dense. The berry is medium, slightly ovate, and a dark red-violet. The skin is medium thick and not very firm. The flesh is slightly juicy. The wine is used largely for blends with other varieties.*

CHAPTER FOURTEEN

"Good day, Feodor Ivanovich."

"Good day, Aram Sarkisovich. Please come in."

"I've just learned something which may be relevant to the murder case," said Almayan.

Shulgin offered him a chair and sat down next to him.

"Can I offer you a cup of coffee or tea?"

"No, thank you."

"Tell me what you've learned."

"A week ago, a student from Armenia studying at the wine school Enotria was attacked. I found out that her teacher, Professor Sandro Kashvili, had introduced her to Sergei Petyan of Ludwig. Apparently, the wine scam I told you about happened around four weeks after the student and Petyan met. A week after the scam, the Chinese was killed. A day later, the student was attacked. The police have questioned both the student and Professor Kashvili."

"That report hasn't reached me yet, which makes me assume that the student was not killed."

"That's right. She was discharged after two days at the hospital and flew back to Yerevan yesterday. If the Chinese victim was involved in the wine scam, then the two events could be related."

"And it means that Sergei Petyan lied to us. What do you know about the student?"

"She used to work for my daughter at our winery in Yerevan. I don't know why she went to see Petyan. She was in no shape for detailed questions. But I met the Professor, who came to see her. He said she was just curious because he's the largest wine merchant in Russia."

"So much here doesn't add up. What's the student's name?"

Almayan told him. Shulgin walked to his desk, called his aide and asked for the file on Isabelle Karayan.

"Sergei Petyan is smart enough to run his business empire and stay out of police attention. We have virtually nothing on him. He either is clean, or he managed to stay below our radar by lying."

"Maybe it's time for questioning him again?"

A few days after Haig returned with Isabelle from Moscow, Dorian arranged a meeting with him and Carla. He wished to facilitate a reconciliation, not through a direct approach, but by launching a discussion of the higher purpose of developing the wine industry in Armenia, hoping that it will make both sides forget their peeves and focus on what united them. He chose Golden Tapas as the venue, one of the rustic wine bars on Saryan Street that he liked for its wide variety of wines and good kitchen. When he walked in, almost every table both inside and outside of Golden Tapas, as well as along the row of seven adjacent wine bars that formed one continuous line of small, square tables that extended several blocks, was full. He had reserved the last table on the sidewalk, before the tables of the next wine bar began. Haig was to arrive some forty-five minutes after Carla, as Dorian had insisted on that time alone with Carla.

He ordered a bottle of 2010 Domaine Dujac Charmes-Chambertin, one of his favorite Pinots from Burgundy. He loved the exotic spice, pepper and herbs in the nose. By contrast, the palate was reminiscent of berries—an expensive and elegant wine.

He smiled when he noticed Carla's approach. Carla didn't just arrive at a wine bar. She made an appearance. As she walked into the sidewalk in her tan pantsuit and favorite purple silk scarf depicting the colorful images of the Armenian alphabet, her determined, confident gait was noticed by all, including those who did not know who she was. He stood up, the warm hug followed, then the quick peck on each cheek.

"Who would have imagined this ten years ago?" Dorian asked and pointed at the long line of occupied tables down the street, each boasting a bottle of wine.

"I did," said Carla and flashed a brilliant smile. "This was one of my early visions."

"I too had many early visions, some of which are being realized as we speak. I hope you like this wine." He filled her glass.

She checked the bottle. "If I didn't know you better, I'd think you're spoiling me because you want something."

Dorian laughed.

"Isn't that great, though?" she said. "Wanting something badly, imagining it before we're even close, and then, over time, seeing it unfold in front of your eyes?"

"It's great. But Carla jan, what has been achieved so far in the wine industry, impressive though it is in such a short period of time, was the easiest part. The far more difficult part is yet to come."

"I know. We're producing the wines, but we're not there yet."

"We're not there yet in many ways."

"Yes, but we're particularly not there yet in terms of global recognition. It's a pretty tall fence to jump."

"That it is. But I'm not worried about that, because it will come in time. The wines will speak for themselves, and of course a little marketing doesn't hurt. But is that all that we want, to produce good wines and have the world recognize them?"

Carla looked intrigued. "If we produce not just good, but excellent wines, and get the attention of the world, haven't we arrived?"

"Let me ask you this. It all started here, right? No one can argue with science when it comes to that. This country, Georgia, and, if I may add, the western part of this historical country, currently the eastern part of Turkey, is the cradle of wine. Fine. Then how come we have no say in the wine narrative of today? How many master sommeliers do we have who talk the talk on the global stage? Most Armenians still drink vodka and beer. Wine appreciation is just beginning."

He waited a few seconds to let the idea sink in as he refilled their glasses.

"We say we have the ideal terroir," he continued. "Which is true. We have all the prerequisites for producing excellent wines. Then is it really such a great achievement that we do produce them? We can't have it both ways: brag about our terroir and history, and then brag about how great our wine is. One dictates the other. The big, nagging question for me is, what have we really added to our and the world's wine culture since the people in those caves 6,100 years ago?"

Carla looked at him, clearly at a loss for words, which was not usual for her.

"Our biggest challenge is not how to produce excellent wine. It is to educate the best in class of consumers of wine. I've been to your tours, Carla jan, and I know you try to do some of that. You show your guests how to hold a wine glass, how to smell, how to taste, even how to toast with a glass of wine. That's good. It makes an impact. Haig, in his way, and I in mine, try to do the same." Carla half-frowned at the mention of Haig. "But imagine this: just like we have excelled, as a nation, at chess, computer programming or at certain sports, imagine if every Armenian knew how to truly appreciate wine. Imagine if the Mecca of wine lovers from around the world was Areni village." He paused for a moment and laughed. "OK, that was the wrong image, I guess the one thing you cannot have a Mecca for is wine. The point is, this should be the center of learning, not just producing.

"Wine is traceable. I mean, by taking one sip from a glass, we can trace back the process that the wine has gone through and decrypt, through its flavor, the grape from bud break all the way to harvest. Through the vinification process we can feel and understand the blood, sweat, and hopes the farmers, vintners, and winemakers have poured into that glass. Now imagine almost everyone in this country is trained to decipher that code. And it does take training to get there. People have to be aware of what they're smelling and tasting. They have to have a reference point. They have to know what 'earthy' means or what tannins are if they're to detect them in a wine. Most wine drinkers have no idea. Imagine if we taught students about wine starting, say, in the last year in high school and certainly as a required course during the first two years at all universities. Why not? Wine is much more of an Armenian legacy than chess or computer programming. Why shouldn't we finally, after more than 6,000 years, stake our claim as the original producers of this wonder, which the whole world seems to be suddenly enamored with?"

Carla was staring at him. Dorian took a sip, savoring the wine. He knew that he had thrown a lot on the table, and was uncomfortably aware that he was lecturing, but as long as he had her attention, he didn't care.

"I had never thought of it that way," said Carla. "I've put all my energy and passion into making the best wine I can. You've taken this to a whole new level."

That was all the encouragement Dorian needed to charge on.

"Imagine, Carla jan, aspiring sommeliers coming here to study wine, just as many countries are now sending their promising chess players here to study chess. And they come here not just to visit a cave and witness the history, but also to learn something of immense relevance to them today. Imagine the global standards for wine quality being set here, as much, if not more, than in Bordeaux or Napa or Tuscany. This is important because we cannot make an impact by wine production alone. Even if we turn every square inch of the entire surface of Armenia into vineyards, we wouldn't make a noticeable difference in the total volume of world wine production.

"So, I asked myself countless times, how then do we make an impact as the heirs of the founders of this industry? It comes back to the same answer as in every other field: it is by our intellectual input, not by volume or even quality of the product. By being standard bearers and thought leaders, innovators, teachers, leaders, advocates, arbiters of impeccable credibility in a complex and subjective arena. That is our legitimate inheritance, which we have squandered for millennia and which we now need to reclaim."

"Thank you for thinking beyond the daily pressures of our business. It's refreshing."

"It's this vision that gives meaning to my daily pressures."

"You just reminded me of a verse by Pablo Neruda," said Carla.

I like on the table, when we're speaking, the light of a bottle of intelligent wine.

"I've often thought of conversations with a bottle of intelligent wine. They'd be different."

"And that reminds me of another quote," said Dorian. "'The difference between wine and children is that you can sit down and reason with a bottle of Cabernet.' A winemaker in Paso Robles named Gary Eberle is supposed to have come up with it."

Dorian could tell Haig was on the premises before he could see him because there was a commotion around every table as he approached down Saryan Street. With people standing up, greeting, embracing, slapping backs, his approach was a moving hubbub down the sidewalk. Then he heard his roaring laugh and smiled.

Finally, there appeared the bulky torso and cheerful smile of Haig Koleyan, his white shirt untucked, hanging over his jeans a few inches below the hem of his black jacket. He struggled to maneuver through the dense obstacle course of tables, trying to avoid bumping into diners and their chairs. He finally made it through, leaned down to kiss Carla—a brief and formal peck on the cheek—and gave Dorian a high five.

"OK, what have you two been conspiring about?" he said and sat down. He reached for the bottle before Dorian could pour him a glass and checked the label. "Impressive," he said raising an eyebrow.

"Well, it's a good wine to conspire with," said Dorian. "The spice does it."

He was glad he had picked a French wine—it would make it easier to avoid a potentially controversial discussion of local grape varieties.

"We've been conspiring to turn Armenia into the intellectual hub of wine," said Carla.

"So, we're done with making it, then?"

"We've barely started making it, but we're not going to be satisfied by just making it."

Haig laughed. "Well said. I'm all for moving to higher ground."

"For starters, we should have no nattering wine BS," said Dorian. "Let's make that a requirement in the small community of wine makers in Armenia. Let the pundits around the world outdo each other with their verbal acrobatics if they must, but let's reject it here."

"It's a marketing style, more than anything else," said Carla. "I was watching this wine show the other day, and oh my God, you wouldn't believe all the flavors a couple of sommeliers were ranting about. They went way past the fruits and herbs, way past honey and chocolate, and toward the end, they were detecting sweat, stale beer, freshly tilled compost, wet autumn leaves, and leather. One of them identified the smell of soiled horse saddles!"

"I bet those who couldn't detect any one of those flavors would never admit it. That would be like admitting failure," said Haig. "The peer pressure and herd mentality are out of control. If you are an aspiring snob, you have to mimic the well-known snobs.

"And it sells," said Carla.

"For now," said Dorian. "And only within a small group of self-proclaimed gurus and their trusting followers. The problem is they lead the discourse. The wine-drinking world needs a breath of fresh air. We can be that breath of fresh air."

"What does one need to describe a good wine?" asked Haig. "I personally don't think it is specific tastes or smells that matter because, first, not everyone tastes the exact same flavor, and, second, not everyone likes the exact same flavor or smell. And just because one expert detects—what did you say, soiled horse saddles? Just because one expert detects something bizarre like that, it doesn't make the wine unique or better. What if I hate the smell of soiled horse saddles?"

"Yeah, right. Assuming you even knew what soiled horse saddles smell like in the first place," said Carla. "How many people go around smelling horse saddles, let alone soiled ones? Soiled how?"

"Exactly," said Haig. "A saddle can get soiled from the sweaty pants of a farmer or when a woman rides butt-naked on it for an hour. I bet the smell would be entirely different."

"Ha, ha, ha," said Carla and rolled her eyes. "You've heard the joke about the difference between wine and men, right?" She waited for a second. "Wine matures," she said.

Haig's robust laugh and Dorian's gentle smile were true to their characters. "OK, that deserves a counter punch," said Haig. "You know the similarity between wine and women, right? They both have an uncanny ability to give pleasure at night, and a severe headache in the morning."

Carla laughed. "But seriously, how would you describe a good wine?"

"I hope you don't mind, but I've asked Isabelle to join us," said Haig. "She should be here soon. Why don't we ask her that question? She's learned both from you and me. And by the way, she's not going back to Moscow."

"Good. She had no business going to that school in the first place. By the way, my dad is working hard in Moscow. He won't tell me much now, but he says he has several leads and suspicions about why Isabelle was attacked."

"Do you have any details?" asked Dorian.

"He doesn't like to talk until he has something. But he said he's been in touch with Ludwig as well as the police. That's all I know. But I know he'll get some answers—he never gives up, you know."

"He was a godsend in Moscow," said Haig. "I was suffocating in that place. I don't think I'll ever get used to Russia. I would have been back here the same day had it not been for Isabelle's condition. He's the only one who could somehow put me at ease, mostly because he was so confident, so strong, so in control."

"That's my dad." Carla's smile could have lit the street.

"All I want is for the bastards to leave me alone. I wish they'd leave *us* alone too. I don't even want them to buy my wines."

"*De lav eli*," chimed in Dorian. Enough already... Haig's anti-Russian rants could sound like a personal attack on Russian-Armenians. This was not the time for it.

"OK, fine, I'll lay off the Russians." There was a moment of tense silence. Dorian filled their glasses and raised his. "Here's to the incredible diversity of our Diaspora," he said. "Having thriving communities everywhere in the world is one of the greatest strengths of our nation." He knew that overcoming the cultural differences among some of these communities was a long-term challenge, but, in the meantime, why not celebrate their diversity?

"By the way, on a more practical level, Isabelle will need a job," said Haig. "I'm willing to offer her one, but since she last worked for you, you get first right of refusal. Let me know if you could use her."

"I'd be happy to take her back," said Carla without a second's hesitation. "That is, assuming you'd be willing to let me have her."

Dorian watched the dynamics between them with some amusement.

"You have first call, so she's yours. Besides, I think she'd be happier with you. She wants to get into making wine, and with Armen running my wineries, I could not give her much of an opportunity to do that." Haig raised his arms and laughed.

"She'll be a great winemaker," said Carla. "All she needs is self-confidence and maturity. It's funny; sometimes she tells me that I need to grow up when she herself is yet so unformed. But I guess we all grow up differently, at different paces, and in different areas. Isabelle is unique. She's a kid when it comes to handling strong personalities, but she's probably more evolved than I am when it comes to managing basic human relationships. It sounds like a contradiction, but it's not. That's who Isabelle is."

Dorian didn't know Isabelle as well as Haig and Carla but thought that was an interesting description. It made him wonder what had remained undeveloped in his own character.

He walked up and down the sidewalk until he found an empty chair he could bring to their table. He also ordered another bottle of the Burgundy and a plate of charcuteries.

Isabelle arrived smiling broadly, looking genuinely happy to see them. No one commented on the bandages on her nose.

"Tell us," said Haig, as she sat down, and Dorian filled her glass. "How would you describe a good wine?"

Isabelle looked suspiciously around the table.

"Is this an interview?"

"Not an interview," Haig said. "Carla has already told me she wants you back. But seriously, we're curious; how would you describe a good wine?"

Isabelle still looked suspicious.

"It's not an interview, not a test, not a trick question, right?"

"No. Will you tell us already?"

"OK, then. It's much easier for me to tell when a wine is bad. A bad wine can't find cover. But a good wine, well, that's more complicated. The goodness of a wine is more nuanced than the badness. To qualify as 'good,' I'd put balance at the top of the list of prerequisites. I don't like wines where a single flavor dominates. It's about the harmony between flavors, about how seamlessly everything has blended within the wine. Without balance, I feel I'm at a symphony orchestra where one instrument is screeching much louder than all the others. If citrus, green apples, vanilla, strawberry, even alcohol, or whatever dominates, something isn't right even if I happen to like the predominant flavor."

"Wonderful," said Haig nodding. "Then?"

"Given balance, I'd look for complexity next," said Isabelle, relaxing into the act. "A wine has to hit me in waves, not in one shot. It has to delight me through layers of nuance. Sorry, I know this may sound like wine jabber"—she smiled at Haig—"but honestly it's not. Complexity is a real hurdle a wine has to cross to go from just OK to good. There was a time when I thought one achieved complexity through blending many different grapes. But frankly, what I have discovered lately in Armenia is that you can achieve complexity with a single grape variety, like our Areni, or with a blend of two varieties, like Van's Areni-Syrah blend. By the way, Van jan, it is superb, both on the balance front and the complexity front."

Dorian nodded and smiled. Isabelle was clearly warming up to the topic and to her own performance. Haig seemed impressed also, as he kept nodding.

"This is the problem with the so-called engineered wines," continued Isabelle. "You can get everything right by engineering wine: color, tannins, acidity, alcohol, even balance, but then you end up with a perfect specimen with no soul, no life in it, even though every box on the checklist is ticked. What's missing? Complexity, character, soul, life, movement, progression of sensations, structure. You take a sip and feel that the engineered wine is talking the talk, but it all stops there at that first sip. There's no 'follow-up,' no 'let me see what else you've got' moment. Complexity is about that follow-up. And even more follow-up after the first follow up. Complexity is what keeps your curiosity going about the wine because it keeps gratifying you in stages."

Isabelle was so carried away with her own train of thought that she did not notice how the three people at the table were staring at her.

"That's impressive," said Dorian. He looked like he was noticing Isabelle for the first time. "You're spot on about balance and complexity. Would you stop there?"

"Pretty much. You can always add an attribute or two, but if a wine has those two, I'd be happy to call it a good wine."

"I'd add finish to your list," said Haig with a nod. "Although I admit it's impossible to get a good finish from a wine with no balance or complexity, but the finish goes a step further. It's the lure that continues rousing your taste buds and seducing you after you've swallowed that first sip. It makes you want to take a second sip, and a third, and a second glass. It goes hand-in-hand with complexity, as you described it so well, but *personalizes* it, at least for me. It's the lingering aftertaste, the exquisite sensation that, in its irresistibility, leaves you dissatisfied, urging you to take another taste, and then it still keeps you dissatisfied, so you'll need one more, and then one more."

"That is so sensual." The sentence popped out of Isabelle's mouth like a reflex. She noticed Carla staring at her with wide open eyes in surprise, and a light blush colored her cheeks.

"It sure is," said Carla. "And poetic too. 'Wine is poetry in a bottle,' as Stevenson said. Haig, you just described the poetry that sometimes blooms between a wine and its drinker, and the way you said it made me want to take another sip."

"All that's good," Dorian chimed in, momentarily breaking the spell around the table. "And it's great because you managed to define a good wine without mentioning a single specific taste or smell. So I congratulate you. "But all that is still based on what wine does for you physically, about how it works with your physical senses. Now, let's move on to wine as nourishment to the soul, which was its original use here in Armenia. How did the original winemakers nourish their souls several millennia ago? That's the little treasure we're after. That's the secret we need to unlock in order to give an entirely new meaning to the concept of good wine.

"It is a wine that speaks to you beyond taste, smell, balance, complexity, and finish. A wine that speaks to your sorrow and your joy, to your aspirations and frustrations, to your moods and to your hopes, and to the love in your heart. A good wine enriches your being and inspires you. It makes you feel how Rumi and Omar Khayyam felt when they came up with their best lines about wine and love. It often goes even beyond that and helps you bond with your fellow humans. It bonds friendships.

And don't think that it's the alcohol that does that. We make the mistake of attributing wine's effects to alcohol far too often. People gathered together drinking vodka or whiskey or even beer are more likely to end up in a brawl than in bonding. These are uniquely wine characteristics."

Carla had heard of Dorian's theory of pairing wine with emotions, but she looked almost mesmerized.

"Did they teach you anything like this at Enotria?" she asked Isabelle.

Haig was smiling, and Isabelle was staring at Dorian.

"No," she said. "This is way above their heads."

"Van jan," asked Carla, "where is your family from? Are you originally from Yerevan?"

"Oh no," said Dorian, smiling. "It's not a coincidence that my father named me Van. I was born in Yerevan, but my ancestors are from Van, in Western Armenia. I'm a proud *Vanetsi*. When we were in the US, I was actively involved in the Vaspurakan Compatriotic Society. I even served as its chairman for two years. I'm fascinated by the story of Van, especially the Kingdom of Van and Urartu. They were the best and largest wine producers of the ancient world. They elevated both the production and consumption of wine to culture and intellect. They saw wine beyond its influence on the physical senses; they recognized it as nourishment to the soul. I think they were the first to see wine in that light.

"And by the way, Carla jan, your ancestors from Sepastia also hail from that ancient world and from a long tradition of excellence in wine. The Kingdom of Van was the most sought-after wine supplier to the elite of the Assyrian empire and to Babylon. We still have a ways to go to live up to that legacy."

"I didn't know your ancestors are from Sepastia," said Haig. "So are mine. A small village called Gemerek."

"Mine come from a village that sounds like Sarkisla. The only reason I remember that is because it sounds like Sarkis, my grandfather's name. But I don't know much else."

"I don't either, unfortunately. My father wouldn't talk much about Gemerek. All his great uncles were hacked to death by Turkish mobs in 1915. That's all I know."

"My dad says his ancestors were wine makers and wine traders," said Carla. "That's why he calls Alma Wines his 'Back to Our Roots' project. Apparently they had pretty substantial vineyards going back a few hundred years. Like in your case, it all ended in 1915."

"When I was young, it didn't seem important," said Haig. "Now I'd give anything to find out how they lived and what they did in Sepastia. Along with all the lives, we've lost too much history."

***Kangun**, Durable, Erect: a complex hybrid developed in the late 1970s at the Armenian Viticultural Research Center outside of Yerevan. It is cultivated mainly in the Ararat Valley. The bunch is large, conical cylindrical, and dense. The berry is medium to large and round green or yellowish-green. The skin has medium thickness and is firm. The flesh is juicy. Kangun wines tend to be medium to full bodied with buttery characters, yet with fruity and flowery aromas. They're also used to make fortified brandies.*

CHAPTER FIFTEEN

Professor Sandro Kashvili tried to reach Madame Stella several times, with no success. Her housekeeper confirmed that she had returned from France, but she was unavailable "at the moment."

"It is important that I speak with her," said Kashvili dryly. "Have you been telling her that I'm trying to reach her?"

"Of course, Professor. But she's tired from the trip and has had many engagements."

When finally Dmitri called him, he couldn't hide his frustration.

"You've been playing hard to get lately," he said.

"How can I help you, Professor?" Dmitri's tone infuriated him more.

"You may remember that around ten days ago, I told you about one of my students, the one I introduced to Sergei Petyan."

"Yes, so?"

"She was attacked soon thereafter."

"I'm sorry about your student, but is that supposed to mean something to me?"

"Who did you tell that she met Petyan?"

"I don't know. Why? What does it matter who I told?"

"Did you tell Madame Stella?"

"I might have mentioned it. Again, why does it matter?"

"Dmitri, it would be a good idea to arrange a face-to-face meeting with Madame Stella and me. You can be present if she wants. But it is important that I talk to her in person."

"Does this have to do with your student?"

"Not really. It has to do with wine."

"Wine?"

"Has she been dealing with wine at all?"

"I don't understand your question. What do you mean by 'dealing'? Madame Stella doesn't deal."

"Are you aware of all of her activities?"

"Professor, I am getting weary of this inquiry. You know that she has two other lawyers. I handle only her affairs related to Ludwig. That's all. I don't know what she uses the other lawyers for, or how she uses her other staff."

"That's why a face-to-face meeting is necessary."

"To discuss what, exactly? I need to give her a reason if I'm going to suggest a meeting with you."

"Remind her that around two years ago we met in her living room to talk about Areni wines. I have some questions about that."

Carla Almayan knew right away that Isabelle, who delivered her the invitation to attend the small celebration at the Korah winery, had worked extra hard to secure it. This was not a call for a drink at a public wine bar such as the Golden Tapas, where Dorian had gathered them. This was a private party, on a private estate, to celebrate the planting of the

Koleyan-Cobb vineyard, and to honor Henry Cobb and his commitment to Armenian wine making. Why on earth would Haig Koleyan include her, if not for Isabelle's forceful arguments? And when Carla had shown her reluctance to accept the invitation, Isabelle had been quite forceful in explaining that she'd be a fool to decline, that this was a big deal, that eighteen hectares of meticulously designed rows had been planted in accordance with Cobb's demanding precision. 36,270 vines, she had exclaimed, as if the precision of providing that number carried special significance.

It was also the end of the harvest at the Korah vineyard, Isabelle had explained, so this was a double celebration. Carla jan, she had said firmly, stop fussing and just accept gracefully.

The long stone terrace overlooking the vineyards had been turned into a dining room. The weathered wooden dining table was set for six. It was a small group: Dorian and Isabelle were there, as well as Haig's winemaker, Armen, and, as the most unlikely guest, Carla Almayan.

"Henry has an insatiable curiosity about local customs," said Haig. "So we'll start with one of his favorite appetizers."

A huge, round aluminum tray, almost four feet in diameter, piled with fresh greens came out first—cress, mint, basil, parsley, cilantro, scallions, dill—followed by an assortment of cheeses and finally the hot lavash straight from the winery *toneer*, the underground oven used for baking bread. Cobb's eyes lit up as he started to pile a pinch of each of the greens and several cheeses into a piece of the thin, warm lavash and roll.

"Don't get full on this, there's a feast coming," said Haig pouring everyone a glass of the Alma Areni Reserve. Carla had brought six bottles of Alma wines. Two were Areni Reserve, two Karmrahyut Rosé, and two Voskehat Reserve. As a courtesy, Haig had opened the Areni Reserve and served it, but he put the Karmrahyut away.

Haig raised his glass. "Henry, this occasion calls for a special toast. And I know that over time you'll get to know how extravagant and complex Armenian toasts can be. It is a profession, here. I'm not kidding," he said when Cobb chuckled. "At traditional dinner tables there's always a head, a master toaster, and they follow rigid rules. We won't put you through that tonight. But I wanted to say that way before the custom of clinking glasses started, which is probably no more than several centuries old, the ritual of taking a drink as an expression of goodwill, hope and respect existed. To this day, the verbal expression of the ritual is far more elaborate in Armenia than just clinking glasses.

"So, with this first toast, I want to drink to your being here. *Barov yekar.* I know a lot will follow. I want to drink to the success of the vineyard we've planted, and to the success of the Koleyan-Cobb wines. So, Henry jan, we welcome you to Vayots Dzor. May your involvement here be blessed."

The resonating chime of crystal against crystal filled the terrace, with everyone repeating the welcome while toasting Cobb. Carla, still feeling out of place, found herself liking Haig's toast and resenting it at the same time. But what exactly did she resent? The fact that Haig was, in fact, an excellent host, or the fact that she was beginning to enjoy the evening?

The feast that Haig had promised started to arrive: the famous Armenian khorovadz, stuffed cabbage, lamb Khashlama cooked in beer and spices, eggplant with spiced minced beef, and a variety of salads. Haig had picked seven different wines for the evening, four from Armenia and three from abroad. More toasts were made as they went through the courses.

"Speaking of toasting," said Cobb, "clinking of glasses may have originated in medieval times, some say to ward off evil spirits. Another theory is that people used to get poisoned a lot in those days, so they clicked their glasses with enough gusto to make sure some of their drink spilled in the other guy's glass—clearly, not in line with the spirit of toasting here. Of course, in more modern times, we started justifying the clinking as a sensory additive to color, smell and taste—the pleasing ring of two crystal glasses meeting each other."

The temperature had dropped a few degrees, and a short gust of wind sent a chill around the table. Haig stood up and turned on the two outdoor heaters. His housekeeper must have seen him from inside, for she came out with a pile of folded blankets. While she passed them around, Haig picked one and spread it over Carla's shoulders. Whatever else she thought of Haig, she couldn't deny that he was a gracious host.

"My father had a theory about how different cultures came up with their toasts," said Dorian. "He said people drink to what they've lost, or what they feel they have the least of. No one drinks to something they take for granted, he'd say. For example, the British say 'Cheers.' Have you ever seen a really cheerful Brit, he'd ask? Just check the weather in London—cheer and the British don't go together. The French say '*Sante.*' Health. Notice how the wine drinking Frenchman is always complaining about his liver? *Crise de foie* is a big thing for the French. Sooner or later, a liver attack will come between a Frenchman and his wine. They have a health issue. The Armenians and the Jews drink to life. We say *Genats*, they say *Lekhayem*. Same thing. What have we both lost the most in our recent history? Millions of lives during our respective Genocides. We drink to what we've lost. *Genats*, Henry jan. And he'd go on with several other cultures which I can't remember now. Wait, I just remembered the Japanese. They say *Kampai*, which, literally, means 'dry cup,' or bottoms up. Interpretation? My father would say the Japanese don't feel they've lost anything—no regrets, no shortcomings or deficits to drink to, so they just say, 'dry cup.'

"At the end, he'd bring up Turkey. To get the context for this, you have to remember that my father was a priest who had nightmares about the killings during the Genocide. And what do the Turks drink to, he'd ask? *Sharafena.* To your honor. Any wonder? By the way, he'd add, the origin of the word *Sharaf* is Arabic. There is no word for honor in Turkish. That's how desperate they are with their deficit in this area."

As they laughed, speculation started about other toasts around the world. What did the Italians' *Cin Cin* mean? Perhaps the same as the Japanese—the Italians have been there, done that, had an empire, ruled the world, reached the peak of culture, no regrets, no losses. So, just Cin Cin.

If Carla was to make any meaningful contribution, she had to come up with something unique, smart and amusing to add to the conversation. Normally, that wouldn't be a problem for her—in fact, normally, she'd be leading the entire event. But she was in Haig's domain, and she found it difficult to adapt.

They were half way through dinner and after three bottles of Armenian wines, Haig had opened a 2000 Saint Émilion Grand Cru magnum, which had cost him the equivalent of two cases of Korah. He filled everyone's glass.

"It's time I told you a story," started Henry Cobb after one of the interminable toasts to the success of their new vineyard. "It happened more than ten years ago, and, in retrospect, it looks like some type of stroke of fate. In a strange way, what I'm about to tell you may have augured my being here today, even though I had no way of knowing that at the time. I had spent years cultivating my vineyards in Sonoma, and I was finally about to release some of my first wines, but I was lucky to be invited to this incredible party given by a great winemaker to honor and celebrate the wine making tradition in California. Those of you who were around in the mid-1970s may remember how a blind tasting organized by a British wine merchant, Steven Spurrier, changed the wine world forever. That's when California wines beat French wines in every category, with nine out of the eleven judges being French. And the wine that turned the French fiercely apoplectic about California was Stags Leap. Its red came first in two separate tests, beating the top Bordeaux, even the legendary Chateau Mouton Rothschild."

The initial tension that Carla felt vis-à-vis Haig started to dissipate somewhat. She was now focused on Cobb's story, and, it seemed that he was too. Egos, insurmountable though they seemed, were put aside, albeit for a moment, while Cobb continued his story. "The founder of Stags Leap, a venerable man called Warren Winiarski, who, I should add, was inspired to get into winemaking in Italy, like a few of you here tonight, presented each of his guests with a unique gift."

He then removed a small silver vial from the side pocket of his vest and held it up for all to see. "This was the gift. We were all curious as to what it was. 'Open it,' Winiarski told us. I opened the vial and saw two grape seeds inside. Two dry, dark, almost black, small grape seeds. 'Those, my friends, are two seeds from the birthplace of wine,' said Winiarski. 'They are seeds of the Areni grape. That's where and how it all started.' To be frank, that didn't mean much to me back then. It was a curious historical trivia, but not much more. But here we are today, more than ten years later, and we have planted a vineyard of the same grape in the same town. A stroke of fate? Destiny? Who knows?"

Carla had not heard the story before, and, as far as she could make out, neither had any of the others. The silver vial, a small vessel the size of a child's Tooth Fairy box, was passed from hand to hand, inspected, and admired in awe. Some opened it and looked at the two seeds nestled inside; others stroked the exterior and passed it on. But even more powerful than the vial was that story.

Carla warmed up to Cobb.

"Tell us, Henry," she said, aware of the effect her sensuality was having on the men at the table. "Are you feeling the history now? And does it really matter in the end, or does the wine have to speak for itself?"

"It's impossible not to feel the history here. It is everywhere, still alive and well even as it hails from millennia away. And it matters. But the wine has always to speak for itself, Carla jan," he added, and everyone chuckled at the use of the endearing moniker. "You cannot save a bad wine by history, but you sure can boost a good wine by it. Here you have everything: the history, the legends, the grapes, the all-important terroir, and the wines. In Vayots Dzor, you also have something else, something I cannot describe. It's not just the history and the terroir. Here the land speaks to you. It draws you. I can't say if that could affect the wine, though"—he chuckled—"But all you need here are the techniques, simple things like how to prune and harvest and ferment."

"How to prune, harvest and ferment," repeated Carla, looking at him, as if Cobb were the only person in the room. "I wonder how they did it 6,000 years ago."

"That's the problem with history," said Cobb, now looking at Haig and Armen. "Farmers here insist on doing it like it's always been done. How can you train them in the modern ways? Their grandfathers and great-grandfathers have done it this way. It has worked. Why change? Why indeed? And I normally am not comfortable going to a country and insisting that they change their ways. Except now we're trying to produce a different wine. Granted, a wine from the same grape, but a different wine from what has been produced for millennia. So the method has to change."

"Method matters," agreed Carla, aware that she now was monopolizing the conversation. "It's one explanation for the big difference in the quality of different wines produced from the same grape from the same region."

"Given the grape, the rest is mostly in the method. No question about it. Of course, the grape matters most—grape, season, vintage—but you can destroy a great grape by bad harvesting, and you can cripple a good vine by improper pruning and maintenance. They have no concept of canopy management in these villages, nor of shoot positioning and shoot selection while pruning. You look at a vine, and you see total chaos. Branches grow in every direction; some bunches tucked under branches, others are exposed to sun, others are covered by leaves, each ripening at different times."

Dorian, who had been quiet most of the evening, said, "That's the case here in the old grape-producing regions, but not in the new vineyards. I agree we can produce different wines from the same grape." He looked first at Cobb and then at Haig. "But do you think we can master a process so refined that, allowing for variations in individual sensitivities, we could create wines that pair well with specific human emotions? I mean, in its simplest form, can we make a wine that inspires art, poetry, music;

one that cherishes and celebrates love; one that dulls sorrow; or one that inspires melancholy, or contemplation and reflection?"

Cobb was silent for a few minutes. Haig quietly filled his glass.

"I guess the operating phrase is 'allowing for variations in individual sensitivities,'" said Cobb after a while. "A wine cannot inspire exactly the same emotion in everyone. But generally, I guess that is like Paulo Coelho's legendary journey in *The Alchemist*. How does the alchemist turn lead into gold in the end? If one can make gold from anything, we surely can make the wine we want from the original grape."

The *original* grape, thought Carla. What were the possibilities? This was a wine country with many microclimates. Areni in Armavir was different from Areni in Ashtarak, or Aghavnadzor, or Rind and Chiva, and in Areni itself. Each was different, even though some of these towns were no more than a few miles apart. But that was not all. Kharji, Voskehat, Koteni, Khindeghni, Tozot, Garan Dmak—who knew how far one could go with these grapes?

Carla, having witnessed Dorian's passion for matching wines with human emotions, watched him listen to Cobb and wondered if he was wishing for something like the alchemist's secret so he could craft any wine to match even the most difficult human emotions, like the elusive "disillusionment with social justice." Like in the alchemist, the task would require a secret ingredient, a sliver of the Philosopher's Stone, a blend of grapes, so nuanced, so balanced, yet so simple. It had to be simple.

"I don't think we should think in terms of turning lead into gold," said Haig, rolling up the sleeves of his dark blue denim shirt. He turned to Cobb. "You called it the original grape. In Coelho's *Alchemist*, where does the young shepherd boy find his treasure in the end? After crossing a continent and traveling a long time and looking everywhere, after making and losing fortunes, after falling in love, after risking his life more than once, he finally finds his treasure back where he first started. And here we are. We are where it first started."

Haig turned to each person around the table. "Carla jan, you roamed like that shepherd boy, in your case mostly between Moscow and LA, and ended up here. Van jan, you started here, made a life in LA, and ended up back here. Henry, you've been all over the world, from the US West Coast to Latin America, and now you're here. Armen and I spent decades in Italy, and now we're here. Coincidence? I don't think so. As the seeds in your silver vial testify, this is the birthplace; this is where it all began. The prize is right here where we sit."

Carla had not seen this side of Haig. Or maybe she had not wanted to see it. But now, in this serene fall evening in the mountains of Vayots Dzor, under the spell of Cobb's story of the silver vial containing the two seeds, through the passion-soaked words of Haig, she saw it. She saw his dream, his enthusiasm, and she felt his drive. She saw not only a side of Haig, but also the vision they shared, regardless of their personal peeves.

Dorian put his book down, not hiding his irritation at being disturbed, and picked up the sheet of paper that Haig placed on his private table at The Realm.

"This is still work in progress," Haig said. "Let me know what you think."

Food and Wine Society of Yerevan
Inaugural 'Wines of Armenia' Harvest Dinner

Menu

Chilled Duo of caviar: Beluga and wild Ishkhan trout—Buttered brioche
2013 Kole, Brut Extreme, Khachik 1750m, Vayots Dzor, Magnums
~~~
Seared filet of Karmrakhayt on grilled eggplant, cilantro pesto
2012 Alma Wines, Voskehat, Barrel Fermented, Alma vineyards

2013 Coor, Voskehat, Khamer vineyards
~~~~

Toasted Mante of beef confit, roast tomato and yoghurt coulis
2012 Sapor, Tchilar, Ashtarak vineyards
2013 Van Dor, Garan Dmak, Ashtarak vineyards
~~~~

Artsakh morel mushroom stuffed quail, crispy citron herb salad
2010 Korah Reserve, Areni Noir, Vayots Dzor
2011 Alma Wines, Areni Reserve, Alma vineyards
~~~~

Leg of lamb tagliata, on caramelized onion pancakes
Mushroom risotto with black truffles
2011 Van Dor, Areni-Syrah Reserve, Ashatarak
2011 Troika, Areni-Sireni Reserve, Canyon vineyards, Vayots Dzor
~~~~

Roast saddle of pork with charred potato dominos and seared foraged field
greens
2010 Sapor Reserve, Armavir
2012 Kole Khindeghni Reserve, Koleyan vineyards
~~~~

Saffron laced tonir gata with white cherry marmelate glaze
Toasted walnut ice cream
2013 Vardahovit Ice Wine, Hints of Rosé, Vayots Dzor
~~~~

Mountain herb tea infusion
Assorted preserves of hon, mulberry, and pumpkin
~~~~

Armenian coffee
Candied fruit truffles
Ararat, Erebuni thirty-year-old brandy

"This is not a dinner," said Dorian as he put the menu down. "It's an orgy, a bacchanalia. You want to bring the ancient Roman tradition here?"

"How do you know the Romans didn't copy it from here?" Haig laughed. "People were making wine and probably having orgies in Areni 3,000 years before Rome was even founded! They worshiped wine millennia before Romans would erect the first temple of Bacchus."

"Your problem, as always, is that you have no patience. You want to do everything all at once, now. You want to show as many wines worth showing as you can squeeze in one dinner. Is this the first inaugural dinner as the menu claims? If it is, why the rush? Why pour everything in? It sounds more like the grand finale to me. I'd do something this crazy for the last dinner, not the first, to end it with a huge bang."

Haig picked up the menu and went down the list of courses and the wines. Dorian watched his eyes dart from course to course, amused by his struggle to see what he could cut.

"Why on earth would I even think of the last dinner?" he said at last. "There will be no last dinner. What we're starting here will go on forever. It is the first dinner that has to start with a bang, a huge bang. We're bringing people from all over the world to show them what we can do with wine. Food is secondary for this event, but absolutely necessary. We need to amaze everyone. We'll never get another chance to make that unforgettable first impression. It has to be good."

"Even at the cost of displaying an appalling knack for excess?"

"Van, we're trying to impress gourmands, sommeliers, connoisseurs, restaurateurs, wine makers, aficionados. Excess? They *invented* gastronomic excess. They thrive on it! Of course, I want to display my knack for excess."

"Let me look at that again," said Dorian, taking the sheet of paper from Haig. He had not considered the context of this dinner.

"If you're trying to match, or outdo, the habits of the society of gastronomic surfeit, I guess this would do," he conceded.

"Don't worry about showing off too much at the first dinner and not having anything new for the next," Haig said. "There are so many new wines yet to come, not the least of which is the Koleyan-Cobb line, which, I assure you, will be a milestone. But there are others: Isabelle, Clear, the entire 'Amarone-style' line that Coor is planning, Allure's extra dark reds, Troika has a new Kangun-Voskehat blend in the works, your new Areni-Syrah blend will be spectacular next year, and new ice wines from Vayots Dzor from much higher altitudes than ever attempted before. We have enough for many orgies, Van jan."

Haig's enthusiasm could be, and often was, contagious. Dorian felt it.

"Have you calculated the cost?" he asked.

"All the wine will be donated by the participating wineries. The food is entirely local, except for the Beluga, which I have arranged to get at highly discounted dealer prices. This may come as a shock to you, but I can manage this entire menu with the wines and the service and rent for under $100 per person. Try that in New York or Paris."

"What do you know about the murder of your partner, Vladimir Konstantinovich Fedorov?"

The question surprised Petyan. When he was summoned to police headquarters for questioning, he had expected to face more questions about Li's murder, and possibly about the wine scam—assuming they knew anything about the wine scam in the first place. They had kept him in the interrogation room alone for half an hour before Colonel Feodor Ivanovich Shulgin had entered the room with an aide, introduced himself, and sat across from him. He was formal, businesslike and stern, both in his posture and his voice.

"Very little," said Petyan as he watched Shulgin sift through some notes. "To my knowledge, the case remains unsolved."

"Who inherited his shares in Ludwig?" Shulgin didn't look up from his papers while asking the question.

"His wife, Madame Stella Fedorov."

"And how are her shares managed and protected?"

Petyan was not sure how to understand the question.

"Her share is managed as the whole of Ludwig is, and protected as the whole of Ludwig is. I'm not sure I understand what you mean."

"Does she really get her fair share of Ludwig profits?" Shulgin, dead serious yet detached and almost mechanical, stared straight into Petyan's eyes.

"Of course. Ludwig is audited and the financial reports are made available to shareholders. There has never been any question of financial impropriety."

"Does Madame Fedorov have any say in the day-by-day management of the company?"

"No."

"Why not?"

"She has never asked for such a role. Her lawyer, Mr. Dmitri Markov, attends all board meetings and has access to company financials."

"We understand that at one point she blamed you for being involved in her husband's murder. Were you?" The cold, light-blue eyes lingered on Petyan.

"Of course not!"

"Did you in any way benefit from his murder?"

"Of course not. His entire interest in Ludwig was transferred to his wife. I did not seek, nor get, any of it."

Shulgin's aide whispered something in his ear.

"You and Mr. Fedorov had many disagreements on how to run the business. We understand that he was opposed to several major investments which you wanted to make. Is that true?"

"There were only two cases of disagreement. And he admitted to me that in both cases it was his wife, not him, who opposed the investments. One was establishing a presence in China, because she did not like the Chinese."

"And the second?"

"The purchase of our office building."

"So Ludwig made both investments in spite of Mr. Fedorov's opposition to them?"

"As I said, he was being forced by his wife to argue against the investments. Madame Stella is a strong woman, but she doesn't understand the business. Both investments have been profitable, by the way, and she's now reaping their benefits."

Petyan regretted his last statement—he thought it may have sounded spiteful.

"Has she voiced opinions about other Ludwig investments or decisions since her husband's murder?"

"As I said, she is not involved personally, and her lawyer has not voiced any opinions on her behalf, like Fedorov used to do."

"She gets her share, thirty-five percent, of the net profits. But she has no say in the expenses of the company, nor in how revenues are generated. Can't expenses be manipulated to minimize net profits and therefor her share?"

"Colonel Shulgin, you are welcome to examine Ludwig books anytime you want. There is no manipulation of any sort."

"When you make an investment to expand operations, or buy some expensive wines, it obviously affects your bottom line. Do you consult with Mrs. Fedorov before incurring such expenses?"

"No."

"Why not?"

"Those types of decisions are discussed and approved by the board. And she is represented on the board."

"Do all expenditure decisions have to be approved by the board?"

"No. Only major investments. As in most companies, the executive has authority to make certain expenditures without board approval."

"We understand that two days after Mr. Fedorov's murder you left Russia for four days. Is that true?"

"Yes, I had a business trip to several cities in China, arranged months earlier. It would have been awkward, not to mention extremely disadvantageous for Ludwig, if I had tried to reschedule a trip like that."

"Did Mr. Fedorov know Mr. Li Liu?"

"No. Li started working for us after Fedorov was killed."

"Does Mr. Markov know Li?"

"Yes."

An aide walked in and handed Shulgin a folder.

Shulgin took his time going over the contents of the folder—deliberate, methodic, determined, serious. Petyan, who was used to intimidating others and making them feel nervous and uncomfortable, found himself in an awkward reversed role.

"Let's talk about Li," said Shulgin, as he continued to read. After a moment, he put the folder down and looked at Petyan as a strict school principal would look at a student caught breaking a rule.

"You were asked a question after Li's murder, and you gave an answer. Now I will give you a second chance to answer the same question: Do you have any guesses as to what the note that was left on his body might have meant?"

"I presume you mean the note that said, 'keep out?'"

Shulgin just stared at him and waited. He didn't even bat his eyelashes. He was good—I'd love to meet him in more peaceful times, thought Petyan.

"I couldn't think of anything at the time, when I was staring at the photo of my murdered employee," said Petyan, returning Shulgin's gaze. "But I've had an opportunity to reflect on this a lot more since then. Now I do have a guess. But it is only a guess."

Neither Shulgin's posture nor his disapproving glance budged one bit.

"Li participated in a private wine sale," continued Petyan as matter-of-factly as he could make his voice sound. "Once in a while, we participate in private sales, so I didn't think much of it at the beginning. But by the time I discovered it was a con job, Li was already murdered."

"Back to the note," said Shulgin, his voice cold and mechanical. He was the ultimate interrogator, his blue-grey eyes displaying no emotion whatsoever, other than total detachment. 'Keep out.' Keep out of what?"

"I don't know. But if I had to guess, it was meant as a warning to keep out of the special wine sales."

"Meant to warn you?"

"I believe so, yes."

"Why you?"

"I have no idea."

"How many buyers were there at the private sale?"

"Fourteen, according to Li."

"And none of the others were warned or murdered."

"If you say so. I wouldn't know."

"None of them were. So, the question remains, why you?"

"I don't know."

"Mr. Petyan, I advise you not to lie to the police."

"If you want me to offer you guesses, I can do that. But I do not *know*. I never met the organizers of the wine sale. I don't know who they are, and certainly don't know their motives."

"What's your guess?"

"Li went to the event under a false pretense. He posed as a private wine collector, but he was there to find out about the operation."

"So he was spying on them."

"I guess you could say that, yes."

"On your orders."

"No, but at my request."

"Do you think that's why they murdered him?"

"I guess."

"How did they discover him?"

"I'd love to know that. I have no idea."

"Do you know someone by the name of Isabelle Karayan?"

"Yes. One of Prof. Kashvili's students."

"How is she involved in all this?"

"Is she involved?"

"Let me rephrase: did she play any role at all in your involvement in the wine scam?"

"She asked me if I knew of any private wine sales of an Armenian wine. I got curious and started checking. That's how we stumbled on the wine sale that Li went to."

"Do you have any reason to want her harmed?"

"Of course not."

"Or to go away?"

"Go away?"

"Do you have any reason to want her leave Moscow."

"None whatsoever. I met her only once, and I liked her."

Another aide walked in and handed Shulgin a piece of paper.

"That will be all for now, Mr. Petyan," said Shulgin and stood up. "Until further notice, do not leave Moscow."

Salli: a late ripening, uncommon variety spread as single vines in old vineyards of Vayots Dzor. The tip of the young shoot is light green with cobwebby hairs. The mature leaf is medium sized, almost circular, and slightly five lobbed. The bunch is medium, cylindrical-conical, and dense to dense. The berry is medium, round, and black. The skin is thick, firm, and covered with moderate bloom. The flesh is juicy with an astringent flavor. The wine is used largely for blends with other varieties to make red table wine.

CHAPTER SIXTEEN

When Aram Almayan walked into the coffee shop near the Ludwig offices five minutes early, Jack was already there. He looked less stressed and distracted than the last time they met at the same place, and, as always, impeccably dressed, in his navy-blue wool suit, light pink shirt and blue tie.

"They questioned Petyan," said Jack after the brief pleasantries.

"How did he say it went?"

"He told me some details, which surprised me. He usually keeps these things to himself."

"He probably wants you to know, in case they cross check things with you. They don't trust him."

"He even told me about a student called Isabelle Karayan. I always wondered what made him suspect that there could be private wine sales. Now I know."

"Did he tell you she was attacked?"

"Yes. He thinks the police suspect he was behind the attack, or at least they pretended to be."

"She's a former employee of Carla."

"Really? He didn't tell me that. Does Carla know?"

"She knows she was attacked. But not about the wine scam. No one in Yerevan knows about the wine scam yet."

"At least this solves the famous 'Korah Issue' mystery," he said. "I'm still traumatized that poor Li had to pay with his life for it, but we have an answer for Haig."

"He won't be having more surges in sales," said Almayan, "so I'm not sure how he'll take the news. And, Jack, I have an idea about that."

"I'm listening."

"I know you brought me the solution to the Korah riddle, but I'd like it to be Carla who breaks the news to Haig. It will be good for them both if she did."

"Absolutely, Mr. Almayan. If you recall, from the beginning I've been thinking how we can make this information useful for Carla. If it helps her, she should take it to Koleyan." Jack struggled with what he wanted to say next. "But may I request something in return?"

"Sure."

"I would like to explain all this to Carla personally, if that's OK with you. I'll describe to her the scam and the story behind the Areni Eagle, and I'll even take a few bottles with me for good measure. We have four cases of it. That is, if you don't mind."

"I don't mind." Almayan laughed. "In fact, I have no patience to explain all those details and answer a thousand questions that I know Carla will ask."

However, the protective instincts of the father were roused for a minute. He wondered why on earth would Jack want to connect with Carla.

They were quiet for a long time.

"Petyan says there's nothing definitive tying the wine scam to Li's murder or the attack on the student." Said Jack.

"No, nothing definitive. If it hadn't been for the note on Li's body, I wouldn't even consider it highly likely."

Almayan finished the last sip of his espresso and stared out the window, thinking of every conceivable scenario of how Li could have been discovered as the imposter.

"The police were wondering why they threw the body into the car," Jack blurted out.

"I'm sorry?"

"I said the police were wondering why they threw the body into the car."

"They did what?"

"They shot poor Li in the street from the back. He fell face down on the ground. They turned him around, shot him again in the forehead, and then threw his body into the back seat of his car. The police thought that was unusual. 'They normally leave the body right there in the street,' they said."

As Jack spoke, Almayan's mind drifted somewhere else. The information was new to him. Jack spoke the words without assigning any significance to them—as if to fill the silence. But Almayan had just had a revelation. He stared past Jack for a few more seconds and stood up.

"I have to go," he said. "I'll call you later."

He got into his car and told his driver to drive to police headquarters. Then he called Shulgin.

"Sorry to bother you again, Feodor Ivanovich." He was barely able to hide his excitement. "I know it's late, but I'm afraid I'll need to see you again."

Next, he called his wife.

"He really wants a face-to-face meeting with you," said Dmitri to Madame Stella, who happened to be in an exceptionally unaccommodating mood, even by her standards.

"What about?"

She was sifting through a wine magazine in her living room, sitting in an armchair with her back straight like a board. She gave only a passing glance to Dmitri.

"Something that happened two years ago, a meeting about Areni wines."

"What the hell are you talking about?"

"That's what he said. He said it took place here, in your living room. A meeting where you talked about Areni wines."

"And?"

"And he has some questions for you."

"Tell the Professor to go back to his classroom," said Madame Stella and stood up, dropping the magazine on the seat. "I'm sure his students will find his questions much more interesting than I do." She then walked out of the living room.

Two days after the celebration in Vayots Dzor, Carla was in her second-floor office when she heard a car pull in front of the Alma winery. She checked from her window and was surprised that Isabelle had taken the trouble to drive forty-five minutes out of Yerevan to visit. It was a Saturday afternoon, and Magnolia and Sophie were playing in the front yard. The children screamed and threw themselves at her, hugging her with such force that she almost fell to the ground. Carla smiled.

"I missed you girls so much," said Isabelle laughing at the top of her lungs and holding them in her arms. "How have you been?"

"Where were you?" asked Magnolia. "We missed you too."

"Well, I had to go out of town for a while. But I'm here now."

"What happened to your nose? Are you hurt?"

"No, just a little accident."

"Will you work with Mommy again?"

"We'll see," said Isabelle holding Magnolia tight. "But I'll see you often, regardless."

"Mommy's inside. In her office."

"OK, ladies. I'll see you two later."

Isabelle looked up and saw Carla waving. She walked up.

"Good to see you." Carla gave her a hug. "What made you drive all the way here?"

"Haven't been here for a while. It was great seeing the girls. They look great."

"They're growing up, sometimes I feel faster than I'd like, other times it doesn't feel fast enough." Carla chuckled. "Your face looks much better."

"Yeah, the swelling is gone. I can even wash my face without flinching."

"Very good. Tell me, what's on your mind?"

"Carla jan, I need to talk to you as a friend. May I?" Isabelle looked and sounded a bit more unsure of herself than usual.

"Of course, Isabelle jan. What's bothering you?"

"I appreciate so much that you want me back," Isabelle said. "It honestly means the world to me. But please, don't get mad...I want to work for Van Dorian for a while, but only with your blessing. I know I disappointed you when I left Alma Wines to go to Enotria, and I don't want to disappoint you again. But the man is fascinating, with his 'wine as nourishment for the soul' stuff. I don't know if he'll even consider giving me a job, but I won't approach him without your OK."

Carla's first instinctive reaction was not pleasant. A momentary sense of rejection swelled in her, even though not having Isabelle on her staff would not make a big difference for her operation. It was not about her needing Isabelle. It was about Isabelle needing Dorian more than she needed her and about her finding Dorian more interesting than she found her. Just when the attention that Haig and Dorian had started showering on her was working its charm on her ego, this hurt.

But she had been doing some deep soul searching lately, and not just about Haig. She, who had been working so hard to empower young women, could not now stand in the way of one who wanted to move on.

And Isabelle's approach was tactful and flawless. Carla looked at her young face, her shining, pitch-black eyes, and saw her thirst, her ambition, her delirious craving for new experiences, and she decided to let it go. She got up from behind her desk and sat on the chair next to Isabelle.

"I'll put in a good word for you, Isabelle jan," she said. She reached out and held her hand, a gesture she would normally avoid, given Isabelle's physical attraction to her. "Van will be a great coach to you. And you know what else?"

"What else?" asked Isabelle, eyes watering and holding on to Carla's hand.

"I think you'll be a great coach to him too."

Carla pulled her hand away. Given the green light to approach Dorian, Isabelle didn't mind. She pulled her hand away as well and tucked it in her lap. She already had a plan for how to approach Dorian.

Aram Almayan looked restless and anxious when he returned to the police headquarters. "Feodor Ivanovich, once again, sorry to bother you this late," he said as he shook Shulgin's extended hand and followed him into his office, "but I have a hunch about something."

"Please sit down, Aram Sarkisovich. It is not late. I've spent many late nights in this office. Tell me what's on your mind."

"Around two-and-a-half years ago," Almayan began, "maybe three, Sergei Petyan's partner was shot not far from the main Ludwig office here in Moscow. Unlike Sergei, who used drivers and bodyguards even back then, his partner had loved to drive himself. And he'd loved cars. That evening as he left his office, he was driving his brand-new Mercedes 600 sedan: black exterior, tan leather interior, top of the line, and loaded with the latest gadgets. He had just bought the car, and knowing him, he probably was in love with it and with its new smell and feel. He was shot while stopped at a red light two blocks from his office building. Twice in the head. Blood was all over. He died on the spot, and the car rolled and came to a stop against the high curb."

"Yes, I just found out about this," said Shulgin. "Apparently the murder was never solved."

"Like you said earlier, cases of personal vendettas are not a priority for Moscow police. There was a lot of speculation, of course. I remember one rumor that it was his debtors who shot him; apparently, he used to lend money to gamblers. There even was a rumor that he was shot by mistake, that the assassin had hit the wrong target. At any rate, I knew the partner. And I knew his wife, who was friends with my wife. Not close friends, mind you, but friends in the social circles, almost allies, getting together often to gossip about the same women."

Unsure of where Almayan was going with his story, Shulgin gave him a quizzical look.

"But I'm digressing. Here's what matters. What impressed me most about the night of the incident was his wife's reaction. She was hysterical, as is to be expected, but she seemed strangely obsessed by the fact that the murder happened in his car. 'They shot him in his car!' she screamed at the top of her lungs. '*In his car!*' That seemed to have a special meaning for her. I didn't understand exactly what, and to this day I don't, but it meant something to her. There's no question about that in my mind. It was as if shooting him in his car, rather than anywhere else, was the cruelest thing anyone could have done to him."

Shulgin was still unsure of what was the point Almayan was trying to make. The police had no patience for such emotional details in murder cases. The frantic reactions of a newly widowed wife would be the last thing they'd consider and the first to dismiss.

"All this would have meant nothing to me if I had not just learned that they threw the body of the victim back into the car," Almayan told him, and finally Shulgin's eyes lit up.

"Let's search the archives," he said and stood up.

"One more thing," said Almayan. "On the way over here, I called my wife. I asked her what she remembered about the widow. She told me the lady was incapable of being happy. Happiness bothered her, she said. She was uncomfortable when she had to laugh or smile out of social necessity. And she had a vindictive streak in her that came out every time they talked about someone she did not like."

"Anything else?" asked Shulgin. Why attach so much importance to one woman's opinion of another?

"This may not be significant at all, but my wife reminded me that more than ten years ago the partner's wife had a brief affair with one of Sergei Petyan's nephews. He was at least fifteen years younger than her. The affair lasted less than a month. He left her for a much younger woman. Apparently that's when her occasional temper tantrums turned chronic."

"Let's see what we can find in the archives," Shulgin said.

Making several right and left turns, he led Almayan down a long and unusually wide hallway. The walls were bare, white and shiny, almost like those in a hospital, but the floor was dusty, with large patches of stains around, and looked like it had been a long time since it was last mopped. He entered a room protected by a security code and went straight to a computer screen on one of the many desks lined up against the back wall of the room. He entered a password quickly, then turned to Almayan:

"Name?"

"Whose name?"

"The widow."

"Stella. I honestly can't remember her last name."

"Stella, Vladimir Fedorov," mumbled Shulgin and entered the three words.

There were textual reports, accounts of testimonies of witnesses, around forty photographs, and a few short video clips. Shulgin quickly scanned the written reports and moved on to the photos. The crime scene was pretty much as Almayan had described. The photos showed the blood-soaked victim lying in his car, toppled slightly toward the passenger seat, resting on the steering wheel and partially over the dashboard. There were also a few photos of the frantic widow. There were five different video accounts associated with the murder: a 75-second video showing the police discovering the body in the car, a close-up of the body with its focus on the head wounds, three twenty-five-second clips of the exterior of the car resting against the sidewalk, two showing the bloody upper torso of Vladimir Fedorov sprawled over the steering wheel, and a twenty-second video of Stella, screaming at the top of her lungs while the police tried to restrain her. She was right there in the middle of the street at the scene of the crime, screaming about how they shot her husband in his car. Shulgin replayed that segment for Almayan's benefit.

Shulgin went over some of the videos and several photographs one more time, but no new clue popped up. He checked the available information on Stella and found nothing other than her performance at the crime scene and her contact details. Her lawyer, Dmitri Markov, had a relatively thin file as well. He had a boutique law firm with a small number of special clients and looked after her interests at Ludwig. At the end of the search, they had nothing definitive.

But Shulgin's head was buzzing with scenarios too unusual to fit in an ordinary police murder investigation.

"I'd like you to try this," said Isabelle, placing a bottle of wine with a black label on Dorian's table at The Realm.

Dorian studied the label, curious but skeptical: black background, blue and silver stars scattered around, and the words *Starry Night* running across the top in ornate silver calligraphy.

"I picked it up at a small vineyard in Fair Play," she explained. "It's an interesting blend. I think we can learn from it."

"I hope they don't think they're emulating Van Gogh with this label," he mumbled. "And it makes no sense to name the wine after one of the most famous paintings in the world. It raises unreal expectations."

Isabelle agreed with him. "Both the name and the label are distractions from an otherwise superb wine. We won't be learning from their labeling skills," she said, laughing. "But the wine is something else."

Dorian turned to the back of the label: 50 percent Zinfandel, 25 percent Petit Syrah, 25 percent Mourvedre. He kept looking at the label, both front and back.

"There's no vintage," he said.

"Exactly. They don't give a year because it is mixed vintages. The Zin is a year older than the Syrah and Mourvedre. So instead, they number the vintage. This is number 10, the tenth generation of Starry Night."

He went back to the label.

"In the back," said Isabelle, "in small script, at the bottom. I have an idea about wines for special emotions, possibly including disillusionment with justice. But first, let's try this."

He looked at her pointedly then signaled to the bartender who came over with a corkscrew and opened the bottle. They let it breathe for a few minutes.

"I was amazed by this when I first tried it in California. That was a while back, and since then I've saved the bottle for a special occasion."

He gave her a puzzled look.

"I know." She laughed again. "You're wondering if this qualifies as a special occasion. Well, I too at first thought it would be a celebration of some sort or a romantic evening with someone, but that would be a one-time indulgence. I plan on making a much more lasting impact with this wine."

Dorian waited for more clarification, but Isabelle got busy serving them each a glass and said: "Let's check this out."

They were quiet for several minutes as they thoroughly scrutinized the wine. Isabelle couldn't repress a smile when Dorian reached for a second sip.

"This has everything we talked about the other day, don't you think? Balance, complexity and a seductive finish. The fruit is there, but it is so smooth and silky that you don't notice it at first. It creeps up on you as you swallow. But I also think this wine has a lot more to offer. I don't know how to describe it exactly, except that it makes you feel good. To use your own words, it's a wine that speaks to your soul."

Dorian took another sip.

The lure of the perfect finish, Haig had said. The exquisite, lingering aftertaste that leaves you dissatisfied and makes you want more.

"I agree," he said. "It is what you say it is."

"I think we can do wonders with Zinfandel in Armenia. Haig would probably like the idea more if I called it Primitivo. Same grape, but we both know he's partial to the Italian version of most things. So let's call it Primitivo."

"First tell me what this wine does for you aside from making you feel good," said Dorian.

"At first it was the subtleties of the taste that grabbed me," she explained. "The smoothness of the fruit, as I mentioned before, the balance, the complexity. But I soon realized that it affected my mood in a strange way, as if it had taken me somewhere safe. I had a distinct feeling of being sheltered when I had my first glass."

"Sheltered how? From what?" Dorian's interest was piqued, but he remained somewhat skeptical.

"The main ingredient in this bottle," said Isabelle holding the neck of the bottle, "is neither the 15 percent alcohol, nor the black cherries or berries or what have you. The active ingredient in here is an invitation for friendship."

Dorian raised an eyebrow and waited.

"You know how sometimes you meet someone for the first time and you know right away that you want to befriend them? Something clicks and says: 'Safe. Friend.' That's how it was. I could befriend this wine. And that matters to me, Van jan. I don't have many friends to whom I can confide some of my personal issues. Disillusionment with love, for example. I will go out on a limb here. I have made no secret of my sexuality. Everyone in Armenia who knows me knows that I'm a lesbian. Those who know me really well also know that I'm a gender-blind sapiosexual, which has led a couple of my close friend think that I am bisexual, but I'm not. Anyway, I came out of the closet early partly to punish my parents, and partly to be free. No one can be free hiding in a closet. Maybe you can recommend a wine that encourages more people to come out and be free."

"That's a common emotion in Yerevan. And yes, I can recommend wines for it. But tell me about the friendship part."

"The bottom line is this: befriending this wine helped me cope with the disillusionment with love. It really did. Although the feeling was strong, I didn't dwell on it much until I heard you talk about wine as nourishment to the soul. Then it all fell into place. Have I totally lost you already?"

"Not at all. Please go on."

"Good, because there's more. Don't laugh, but I had a dream the other night. I don't want to bore you, but it's kind of important."

"Go ahead." Dorian looked amused.

"I dreamt that we were experimenting with a marriage of our Areni and Primitivo. We were in this cellar with dark brown brick walls, thousands of bottles of wine almost buried in thick layers of dust on the shelves, oak barrels and clay amphorae all over. We tried different combinations: 80 percent Areni, 20 percent Primitivo; 60–40; we even tried 50 percent Areni, 25 Primitivo and 25 Syrah. Then we experimented with mixed vintages like this Starry Night. I saw us full of anticipation and excitement returning to the cellar and tasting our creations. And we came up with some spectacular blends for wines that spoke to our emotions. We then concluded that the Primitivo was the missing link, the secret ingredient that will help us work the magic."

"Who's we?"

"You and I, of course. You and I did all those experiments in my dream. And we had a lot fun doing them." She smiled. "We were a great team. And we got great results. So I propose I join VanDor and work for you and pursue this, in addition to anything else you want me to do in your vineyard and winery. I strongly believe in dreams, Van jan. They haven't failed me so far. The dream made me realize that the special occasion I was saving this bottle for was exactly what I'm doing now—showing you its potential."

"I'll admit that this is the most original job application I have ever received." Dorian finished his glass and poured himself another. Isabelle's was still half full. He topped it up. "I know you worked at Vinoma and at Alma Wines," he said. "Tell me a little more about you."

But he already knew that he'd give her the job.

Three weeks had passed since Haig returned to Yerevan, but his brief sojourn in Moscow still haunted him. Images of Isabelle in the hospital flashed in his mind, and her description of her aggressor kept reminding him of his encounter with Misha, the Russian thug who had paid him a visit to express his disappointment with unfilled orders of Korah. Often, what appeared to be, actually was. Of course, having proof was an entirely different matter. Isabelle never really saw the man who attacked her—just 'felt' him, as she kept saying. It would probably be impossible to prove, but if Isabelle's attacker was Misha, then there could be no question that she had her face smashed because of the Korah issue.

And, in spite of her best efforts to act normal, he could tell that Isabelle was not over the experience either—she tuned out her immediate surrounding more often and looked like she was transported into a different space, staring in the distance at nothing in particular. Haig had never known her to do that before the Moscow incident. The combination of the physical assault and disappointments she described as 'fallen angels' had certainly taken their toll.

Fortunately, Haig had the gala dinner to occupy his time and mind and energy. He offered that as a happy distraction to Isabelle as well, by involving her in every aspect of the planning of the details.

Almayan returned to Yerevan once, met with Haig and Isabelle briefly, and returned to Moscow. Haig gave him as detailed a description of Misha as he could reconstruct. "There are several interesting trails," Almayan said, "but one stands out, and, believe it or not, it doesn't appear to be Petyan."

"I think he's guilty of *something*," Haig retorted.

"Oh, fine, guilty of *something*..." said Almayan and laughed. "Maybe guilty of many things, but I don't think he was involved in the wine scam or Li's murder or the attack on Isabelle. The police considered him as a suspect at one point, not so much in Li's murder but in the attack on Isabelle."

Stella Fedorov did her best to look calm and composed as she sat in her living room armchair, her back straight as a board, hands neatly folded in her lap, and watched her bodyguard grab the first of three extra-large suitcases effortlessly, as if lifting a small lunchbox, even though the suitcase weighed a notch above the allowed 32 kgs. and head out the door. Her gray hair was pulled into a bun as usual, but she did not have her designer clothes on, nor any expensive jewelry. But her comfortable, loose-fitting pants and a sweater had not eased her stern and tense demeanor. Being unsure how long she would be abroad, it had taken her over a week to decide what to pack, changing her mind often and driving her maid, who did the packing and repacking based on her direction, to the brink of frustration.

Her lawyer had advised her to take the trip over three weeks earlier, but she had refused. His urgings had persisted and become more pressing over time. What finally made her change her mind was the lawyer's announcement that he himself had decided to leave Russia for a while. The bodyguard returned for the next suitcase, and the maid rolled in her two carry-ons from the bedroom, one of which contained her jewelry. It was almost time to leave, and she had not yet informed Dmitri Avakov of her trip. She thought it might be best to call him from overseas.

The van was loaded. Stella stood up and did one last tour of the apartment, her expression somber and resentful, eyes stern and angry. She checked the closets in her bedroom, now half-empty, and snapped a photo with her phone. She did the same with the drawers in her nightstand, make-up table and bathroom. There was no surer way to remember what she was leaving behind. This was not one of her regular visits to Europe; this time, she was being pressured to leave.

They reached Sheremetyevo airport around five p.m., two hours before her scheduled flight to London. She felt the airport was unusually crowded—very long lines of passengers checking in in economy class, families with children hauling luggage were noisy, chaotic. Her bodyguard hired a porter with a cart, approached the check-in desk for business class, and handed her passport to the attendant. She was allowed only two suitcases of 32 kgs. Each, so he had to pay for the extra luggage. She stood behind him, straight and stiff, bored and annoyed by the process. The first suitcase was placed on the scale, processed and put on the conveyer belt. She watched her bodyguard help the porter place the second suitcase on the scale and rolled her eyes.

That's when she noticed the bodyguard's gaze freeze on something behind her. She did not want to turn back but watched his face more carefully. Something seemed to bother him, possibly even alarm him. He left the bags to the porter and approached her, just as four plainclothes policemen moved in and surrounded them—one moved behind the bodyguard, two stood behind Stella, and the fourth approached her.

"Mrs. Fedorov?"

"Yes?"

"Sargent Kuznetsov with internal security," he said flashing an ID. "Please follow me." Before she could respond he signaled for one of his colleagues standing behind her to go to the check in counter. "We'll retrieve your bags," he added coldly.

She stood there, motionless, staring defiantly at the officer. The bodyguard approached the officer, but before he could say a word, the officer addressed him.

"Are you Misha? Mikhail Vasiliev?"

"Yes. What's this all about?"

"You'll have to come with us as well."

"You have to tell me what this is about," said Stella, staring at the officer with such anger and malice that he flinched for a split second.

"No Madam, I don't." he said, recovering. "I have orders, and authorization, to accompany you and Mr. Vasiliev to headquarters. That is all."

Vanki, Monastic: *a rare variety found spread as single vines in old vineyards of Vayots Dzor. The tip of the young shoot is light green, almost white, with light hairs. The mature leaf is medium to large sized, almost circular, and slightly three to five lobbed. The bunch is medium, conical cylindrical, and dense. The berry is medium, round, green or yellowish-green, with a violet hue. The skin is thin, soft, and covered with bloom. The flesh is juicy with a pleasant taste. The wine is a high quality table wine.*

CHAPTER SEVENTEEN

"You may be interested to know that I spent the last three weeks practically entirely with the police," said Almayan as he and Jack Hakobyan settled in their seats on the flight to Yerevan.

Jack looked alarmed. "I hope you weren't in some kind of trouble, Mr. Almayan."

Almayan laughed.

"Around six weeks ago, I gave the police what I thought at the time to be a far-fetched clue. They latched on to it and eventually solved the case."

Jack's eyes lit up. "They solved the murder? In six weeks? That must be a record for the police."

"It is, mostly because the whole thing intrigued Colonel Shulgin. It's an unusual case. Nothing here is standard, least of all motive. He went all out to figure this one out."

"And?" Jack sat up straight and unbuckled his seat belt so he could turn to face Almayan.

"I guess you're anxious to know what they found out," said Almayan with a smirk. Jack waited.

"The clue I gave them was triggered by something you said, and it involved Madame Stella." Almayan was amused by the suspense he had created.

"Something I said?"

"About throwing Li's body in the car."

Jack thought for a few seconds.

"But what about Madame Stella?"

"She's behind all of it—the scam, the murder, the attack on Isabelle."

"Madame Stella?"

"To be honest, when I went to them with the story of her obsession about the murder being in the car, I myself was skeptical. It made no sense."

"It still makes no sense. She has been quiet, absent from Ludwig's business since Fedorov's murder. Petyan insists on treating her right."

"Well, apparently, that's not how she saw things." Almayan waved the flight attendant offering them drinks away. "They believe she got deeper and deeper into her resentment during the past two years. She funded the wine scam and made a lot of money while it lasted. By the way, it was not Lefebvre's scam; it was Dominique Martin's. She was the mastermind and head of the operation. Lefebvre worked for her. Apparently, Madame Stella met Martin eighteen months ago in Bordeaux. They hit it off. The police thought they made a very odd couple—Stella old, thin, stern, and Martin young, sexy, charming. But I think they had something in common: in different ways, they both could make grown men cry—Stella by her venom, Martin by her charm. Martin already had an ongoing operation of selling fake wines but had never been to Russia. The potential size of the Russian market intrigued her, given the rising popularity of wine in the country. Stella provided support through her lawyers, who bought protection and contacts in the Mayor's office. She followed each sale campaign closely. She insisted on receiving the names and photographs of all the buyers. She had a small army of private investigators working for her. She also had a file on every key staff member at Ludwig through her lawyer. That's how she recognized Li."

Having met Stella only once, before Fedorov was killed, and having found her unremarkable, Jack could hardly follow all the details Almayan was throwing at him.

"But why kill Li?"

"She assumed Petyan had deliberately penetrated her operation and was livid. A message to keep out had to be sent. She has not yet forgiven Petyan for being dismissive about the investigation of her husband's murder. You see, the whole thing was personal for her. Her husband loved his cars and was shot in his car. She took that personally. She wanted Petyan to cooperate with the police and help solve the murder, but he didn't. That was personal too. She wanted to make money behind Ludwig's back in the wine business, and that was personal also out of spite for Petyan, not because she needed more money. When she recognized Li's picture at Lefebvre's sales event, she took it as a personal attack by Petyan on her. She had given instructions to shoot Li in his car, a kind of symbolic revenge for her husband's murder, but Li got out of the car before they could shoot him, so they threw the body back in to satisfy her demand. Everything about this case, from the wine scam to Li's murder, is directly tied to Fedorov's murder two years ago."

"We had no clue," mumbled Jack. "She was always in the background. Her lawyer was satisfied with every audit. At board meetings, he was supportive. We had no clue."

The flight attendant returned. Jack asked for a tomato juice with lemon. Almayan took a glass of water.

"Well, Dmitri didn't know about the scam or Li's murder. I personally think he would have talked her out of it if she had consulted him. It's like a mafia boss having a peacetime consigliere and a separate wartime consigliere. Dmitri was peacetime. She had other lawyers. But he did play a role, even if unknowingly—Isabelle's professor told Dmitri about arranging the meeting between her and Petyan, and Dmitri told Stella, just as a matter of record, since it had to do with Ludwig. When she found out that Isabelle had worked for Koleyan, she thought she was a spy too. I was right about the motive for the attack—what she wanted was to scare her, and, in her thinking, Haig Koleyan, away."

"I'm still shocked. Madame Stella?"

"Jack, no one can figure out a person who takes everything in life personally. When Shulgin saw the videos of her at her husband's murder scene, he hired a psychiatrist to run a profile on her—and they've been studying her personality for over a month now. They used to do that years ago during Soviet times, largely to analyze the personalities of potential national security threats. But when they realized how easily they could have identified Stella as a suspect, they decided to bring back psychiatry as part of murder investigations. It turns out that for Stella, everything happens exclusively to her. Even Fedorov's death happened to her. She never saw Petyan's kindness for what it was. She probably interpreted every gesture by Petyan as a con, an attempt to deceive her or cover up something."

"That still makes no sense to me. I have seen nothing that would suggest that Petyan ever tried to hurt her."

"The police psychiatric report says that Madame Stella thrived on anger. Think about that, Jack. She *needed* to be angry. Anger for her was not a negative state of mind. It was an activity, an occupation. She'd keep busy getting angry. She justified doing nothing all day by being 'busy' being angry. She pursued anger like normal people pursue happiness. And if life didn't give her a good reason to be angry, she got angry at life for depriving her. Then she used her imagination to invent something to be angry about. That's where her husband's murder and Petyan come in, even though the two may not be related. Her suspicions evolved as she invented new reasons to act angry. There are people like that, Jack, men and women. And a woman like that, especially one with the means of Stella, can be dangerous. Beware of a woman who takes everything personally, who lives in constant suspicion, and who thrives on anger. It is said that 'hell hath no fury like a woman scorned.' But a woman scorned is an angel compared to a woman who has the ego of an ancient god, who believes that the world turns for her and second-guesses and suspects the motives of everyone. That is the real monster."

Jack looked stunned. This was way over his head.

"Imagine being married to someone like that," Almayan was saying. "Imagine living with a chronically suspicious person who needed wrath to sustain herself. I now shudder to think what good old Fedorov had to put up with."

"You think she may have had something to do with his murder too?" Jack asked. The question was spontaneous, but it lingered in the air.

Almayan was staring at him in wonder, which shook Jack even more. But after a second Almayan waved his hand dismissively.

"So what happens now?" Jack asked.

"They have arrested Stella, the assassin, and two others who were accessory to Li's murder. Stella put up a fight at first, but eventually confessed. She'll have to pay a huge penalty—I was told the prosecution was considering a sum larger than they made during the last wine sale. The police were surprised she confessed relatively quickly, and without remorse. She probably thinks since she'll be forced to pay a huge penalty and, as she was not the one who pulled the trigger, she'll find a way to get off easy. And she may actually pull it off, given her wealth and lawyers."

"And the French?"

"My guess is Martin and Lefebvre will be deported, after paying a substantial penalty as well. I doubt they'll be allowed to return to Russia anytime soon."

They arrived in the early afternoon and Jack was invited to stay at the Alma Wines guesthouse that Friday evening and spend the weekend there if he wished. Carla would also be there over the weekend with her two daughters.

"You've met him a few times at our house in Moscow," Almayan had told her over the phone. "He remembers you and has asked me about you a few times over the years. Anyway, it will be well worth your while to hear the story directly from him. Then you can decide how to break it to Haig. It's big, by the way."

"Of course, Papa jan. I'll show him around and hear him out. But I honestly don't remember any Jack."

"I'm a bit surprised," said Almayan with a smirk. "He was young, always impeccably dressed, in perfect shape, and to this day runs a few miles a day, and, most important, like me, he doesn't drink alcohol. Don't bother to organize a wine tasting for him."

"I don't trust anyone who doesn't drink wine, except, of course, the man who built the best vineyard and winery in Armenia."

They arrived at the winery at four in the afternoon. Jack was shown to his room and left to settle in. Carla had to wait to collect the children from school before heading off from Yerevan. They were to meet later that evening for dinner.

Jack felt awkward sitting alone in the guesthouse. It was a large room but so cluttered that it appeared smaller than it was. A king-sized bed with four carved wooden posts and a thick mattress was the main attraction. There was a small sitting area on the opposite side of the bed, with a loveseat and a chair on either side, and a small but heavy wooden coffee table in their midst. Smaller round wooden tables carrying large crystal vases occupied three corners of the room, and thick, colorful curtains enclosed the space like a cocoon. The in-suite bathroom was also cluttered, with more towels of all sizes and boxes of tissue paper than one person could use in a week. The room was quiet and peaceful, but unfamiliar and oddly unsettling at the same time.

He stepped out and walked around the front yard, up to the edge of the vineyards, and back to his room, trying to make himself feel less strange being there. Then one of the staff appeared and said Carla had called to inquire if he'd like a tour of the vineyard. Jack took the offer. Like most visitors, he was in awe at the scale of the operation. Even without Carla's inspired presentation, he could see the magnitude of the "man against nature" phase of the project.

Dinner could not come soon enough. Jack had already showered and brushed his teeth after the tour. He put on his best Canali suit, a deep navy-blue wool with barely noticeable dark gray stripes, an off-white cotton shirt, and green-, gray-, and antique-yellow-striped necktie. He checked himself in the mirror and followed his guide to the dining area on the second floor.

The meticulously planned attire backfired when Almayan appeared in his jeans and a sweater, and even more when Carla finally showed up, also in jeans tattered at the knees and a bright red sweater. Jack sheepishly removed his tie and stuffed it in his coat pocket.

"The man desperately needs a glass of wine," Jack overheard Carla whisper to her dad, but he didn't mind. He felt her warmth as she looked at him—she was happy, bubbly, warm. Jack automatically assumed all that was directed to him.

"I know you can't imagine a dinner without wine," said Almayan with a chuckle, and here you are dining with two men who don't drink. Don't let us stop you."

Carla didn't look like she was about to—she opened a bottle of Alma Karmrahyut, and she felt perfectly comfortable serving herself and raising her glass in the direction of each of the men, in lieu of a real toast, before taking a sip. Jack acknowledged her toast by nodding awkwardly, and the uneven dining began.

It was a long night. Almayan ate quickly and left early. Being a non-drinker, he had little appreciation of the joy of long, leisurely dinners. Jack sat with Carla at the table set on the terrace of the main building of the winery for a long time. He did his best to focus on the Korah and Areni Eagle story, which was not easy given his renewed infatuation with her, but her interest in the story helped. He recreated, as well as he could, the performances of Valerie Lefebvre and Dominique Martin.

"She was the boss?" she asked unable to hide her fascination.

"Yup. And she played the sensuous assistant so masterfully that no one ever suspected."

"So she and Madame Stella conned fourteen men."

Jack watched her process the scene and kept quiet.

"$2,500 per bottle?" she asked after a few minutes, eyes open wide.

"And we bought four cases of it."

"And we're struggling here to sell a bottle of our Areni reserve for $35."

"But does yours have that Zen quality of depth and stability?" he asked. "Does it convey a sense of permanence of the ages?"

It was a free-flowing, unrestrained, natural laugh. It rose from her chest, passed her lungs, reached her face, took the form of a smile, and poured out of her eyes and mouth like a cascade. It engulfed not only the table and the terrace, but also the night. It lit up the evening like lightning in the sky. Jack couldn't imagine anything more beautiful in the world.

"A sense of permanence of the ages, eh? I have to hand it to them. That is good, really good bullshit."

"Well, that bullshit, with a little help from the sensual magnetism of Mademoiselle Martin, sold thirty-five cases of Areni Eagle in one evening, at $30,000 a case. Call it what you want, but they almost got away with it. It was only a set of coincidences that got them caught. And the initial trigger that unleashed the entire chain reaction came from right here, from one of your former employees."

"What are you talking about?"

"I was in the dark about that part of the story at first. I was dying to know what made Petyan first suspect that there were private Korah sales." He then patiently explained the initial hint of private sales Isabelle had given Petyan, and went on to how they had discovered the sales event and sent their man, and how the rest was history. He did not dwell much on Li's murder but explained the critical role that her father had played in helping the police solve the murder case.

"Imagine if Isabelle had never come to visit Sergei. The scam might have continued unnoticed, and Haig Koleyan would have wondered for years who was buying his famous Korah wine. Or, why not? You never know; they may have come up with a scam using Alma Wines. The same stories that they dished out about the Areni Eagle could easily have been told about some blend involving Alma Karmrahyut or Alma Areni Reserve. Then *you* would have been baffled by inexplicable surges in sales."

It was getting chilly on the terrace, so they moved to a table in the dining hall. She brought out fruits and pastries and made Jack a cup of tea. She stuck with the wine as they continued to rehash details of the story. She loved to hear about her father's role in solving the mysteries of the murder and the scam.

It was quite late when David arrived. He gave Carla a kiss on the lips and introduced himself in the understated fashion customary in Armenia by just giving his first name.

"David is my friend," said Carla. "He's a diplomat, both by profession and personally." She smiled sweetly at David.

As far as Jack was concerned, that ended the personal side of his meeting with Carla, a side that Carla had given no indication of even acknowledging. The irony was that he felt relieved. He had no idea what he could dare to expect in the first place, and in an instant a nagging pressure seemed to uncoil in his chest. A clear "off-limits" verdict was better than uncertainty, false hopes, or even worse, clumsy moves.

There was one glass of wine left in the bottle, which David split between Carla and himself.

"I'm going to need more of this," he said and rubbed Carla's arm.

"Are you hungry?"

"Not really. Munched on a lot of crap at the reception at the ministry. But they were serving Hayasa wine. I was embarrassed, to say the least. The reception was for a high-level delegation from Norway here for an event at the Nansen Foundation. Nansen is a big deal. He helped many survivors of the Armenian Genocide. And we were serving them Hayasa. Can you imagine?"

"One day, David jan, hopefully soon, they'll realize that wine is the ultimate Ambassador of Armenia. They don't understand the significance of wine yet. For them, wine is wine, right? If they can gain a favor with the producers of Hayasa, why not?"

"It was embarrassing," repeated David. "Norway is not a wine producer, but these guys knew their wine. They've done every diplomatic tour in Europe you can think of, and believe me, the wining and dining at those events is something else. So it came as no surprise to me that they were not impressed. And to add insult to injury, one of our young diplomats explained that Hayasa meant "Armenia," and that this was the beacon of the new generation of Armenian wines! Whatever it takes, I will have the guy fired this week. He was way out of line."

"Wine is the ultimate Ambassador of Armenia," said Jack. "That's a great line, Carla. You should use it in presenting Armenian wines to the world."

"You think so?" Carla smiled.

"Absolutely. Would you two like to try a truly unique Armenian wine called Areni Eagle? I have brought three bottles. I thought you'd be interested and maybe share one bottle with Haig."

"Truly unique, eh?" Carla laughed. "In fact, I'm dying to see what the whole fuss is about. I'd love to try it, if you don't mind."

Jack excused himself and walked down the stairs to the main level guest quarters to fetch the bottle from his room. He needed to get out, to clear his head and to come to terms with David's presence. He took his time, walked slowly, and breathed the fresh evening air. She has two children and a boyfriend. And don't forget, you're married too. This is a dead end on all counts. Dead end.

He grabbed a bottle of Areni Eagle from his suitcase and went back up. As he walked into the dining hall, he saw David and Carla kissing passionately. He hesitated for a minute, then cleared his throat and walked in.

"This, my friends, is a $2,500 bottle of wine," he announced. "I hope you appreciate all that it has to offer." He did not take his seat and looked like he was about to leave them alone.

"Wait," said Carla, "aren't you even a little bit curious about this? Those who bought this wine tasted it first, didn't they? Aren't you curious what they tasted that convinced them to pay $2,500 for the bottle?"

Jack was touched that Carla did not want him to leave, hollow as that gesture sounded to him under the circumstances. He sat down, looked Carla in the eye for a moment, and then, bewildered, turned and looked at David as if seeing him for the first time.

"Carla jan," he said so affectionately that even he was surprised by the tone of his voice. "It wasn't what they tasted that convinced them to pay the price. It was what they heard. The pitch was not just perfect, it was intoxicating. It was the talk, not the wine, that sold the wine."

"That's brilliant, Jack," said Carla. "'It was the talk, not the wine, that sold the wine.' Isn't that great, David?"

"Sure is," said David and stood up to open the bottle of Areni Eagle.

"It happens to be true, in this case," said Jack. "Mind you, a good talk doesn't always sell a bad wine. But it does often enough."

David fetched three new wine glasses.

"You're sure you won't change your mind?" he asked Jack.

"No, but thanks. I'll let you tell me what it's like."

David poured two glasses.

Carla went through the motions: scrutinize the color, smell, swirl, smell again, swirl some more, and taste.

"You can't miss the Areni base," she said. "But frankly, Korah is much better. So is our Areni reserve. Something is off in the balance here. It's like an annoying background noise while listening to music, like static or something. Both the Korah and the Areni reserve are far more refined than this."

"According to one of our expert consultants, that background noise is mostly cheap bulk Areni, with a small amount of Merlot thrown in to 'soften the edges,' as I believe he put it."

"Well, I don't think it has softened the edges enough," Carla said with a laugh. "David, what do you think?"

"I don't have your nose," he said winking at her, "I can tell if a wine is really bad or if it is really delicious. But I couldn't tell any wines in the middle apart. This certainly is not horrible, but I wouldn't pay more than $10 a bottle for it."

"A $10 bottle plus a good salesman talking the perfect talk equals $2,500, at least to a bunch of enthusiastic collectors," said Jack and stood up again. "Carla, thank you for a wonderful dinner. David, it was great meeting you. I need to retire. If you have any questions about the famous Korah scam, I'll be happy to spend more time with you tomorrow."

As Jack started to head toward the guest quarters, Carla stood up to accompany him. "I'll be right back," she told David and took Jack's arm. They walked down the stairs and into the long front yard of the Alma estate. The air had turned colder, and Carla held on tighter to Jack's arm. They walked down the beautiful stone pavement, passed by the benches and tables placed at regular intervals against the long outer wall of the guest quarters, and finally stood in front of the door of his room.

"This was one of the most informative and fun evenings I've had for a long time," said Carla. "I cannot thank you enough. You opened my eyes to a part of this business I know very little about."

Under any other circumstance, the situation would have been perfect for Jack. It was as romantic a night as he could have hoped for: crisp, quiet, in the middle of a 200-hectare vineyard, with enough of a chill in the air to make him feel the warmth of her body against his arm, to smell her breath and her hair. Here was the woman he had fantasized about, standing next to him, holding on to him, and they were alone in front of his room. He looked at her face, her eyes shining in the dim light hanging from the overhang covering the pavement, and for a fleeting moment Carla fused into the night, into the rolling hills of the vineyards, into the cacophony of the chirping crickets, and, eventually, into David's arms.

And what exactly were you thinking?

"I've thought a lot about you over the years, Carla jan." His voice was brittle. His words surprised him more than they surprised Carla, who simply smiled. He could barely resist the urge to kiss her. That was when she gave him a warm peck on his cheek and let go of his arm.

"*Bari Gisher*," she said. "I'll see you in the morning." And she walked back to the dining hall where David was waiting for her.

How to break the news to Haig Koleyan?

Carla went through various scenarios. She wanted to recount the story as effectively as Jack had done—his description of Lefebvre's operation was hilarious, especially his portrayal of the guests at the mansion, the tasting ceremony, and particularly his imitation of Lefebvre's French accent. The surprise of Mademoiselle Martin being the boss immensely amused and entertained Carla, but she wasn't sure how interesting it would be for Haig.

Of course, Jack had not seen any part of it firsthand. He was recreating what he had heard from Liu Li. She wondered how a native Chinese speaker would imitate the English accent of a Frenchman, which then a native Russian speaker would reproduce half in English and half in a quasi-Armenian translation. The format of the story had undergone quite a transformation through this process. And now it would pass through the filter of her own impressions and be colored by highlights that enthralled her most. But the essence of the story, the main events and outcomes, would remain the same.

Aside from the nuances of style in storytelling, she thought about what type of reaction she wanted to arouse in Haig. This would be big news for him. The Korah issue had intrigued and beguiled him for well over a year, and, just as it was finally resolved, it would end. Should the phenomenon of the scam itself be the main focus of the story? Should she highlight the power of presentation as a marketing force, which she had thought about at length? How much importance should she give to Isabelle's role in starting the chain of events that eventually led to uncovering the scam? Should she seek to instill in Haig new respect for the formidable influence that her father wielded in Moscow? In the end, was she looking for his gratitude or some type of recognition?

What was wrong with all of the above? After all, wasn't she the master multitasker?

When they finally met at one of the wine bars on Saryan Street, these deliberations were rendered irrelevant as the conversation took on a life of its own. This time he had a bottle of Puligny Montrachet to melt the ice. She came straight to the point and started with the explanation for the mystery sales and then wove in the details. Haig said he had expected foul play all along, but still found the story hard to believe. How was it possible for experienced wine collectors to be that gullible, he asked? He had heard of similar stories, but those seemed distant and far away from his reality. This was about his wine.

Carla enjoyed watching the shock on his face.

"It's actually a compliment to you," she said as she removed a bottle of Areni Eagle from a brown shopping bag she had brought with her and placed it on the table. "They chose Korah as the main ingredient in this remarkable story because they believed they could sell it for such an exorbitant price. And they got away with it!"

Haig picked up the bottle, the look of disbelief still on his face. He looked at it for a long time and scrutinized both sides of the label.

"Half of this is Korah," he said.

"Precisely."

Haig kept repeating all the key facts, as she had done when Jack was recounting the story to her, just so she could process them. Were they that much alike?

"I wonder if the other thirteen victims have found out what happened to the Chinese. I wonder what they've done with their Areni Eagle."

Carla realized with some amusement that the many dimensions and implications of the story had overwhelmed him. He's blinking like a frog in a hailstorm, she thought recalling a phrase she had learned years ago in the US.

"And your dad, my God! It's amazing how he handled the case with the police. The police didn't know about the scam, right?"

"Right." Her eyes were beaming with pride.

"And they had no clue as to how to solve Li's murder."

"Right again."

"Carla jan, that is amazing. Really. How he put all that together for the police. Please thank him for me."

"I will," said Carla, flushed with filial pride.

Haig did not seem to be interested in the main players: Lefebvre, Mlle. Martin, Petyan, Liu Li, and Madam Stella. Central though they were, he did not ask any further questions about them. The two actors in the story who seemed to matter most to him were Isabelle and Aram Almayan.

"And this whole thing was eventually exposed because of Isabelle's visit to Petyan."

"Yes."

"I'm going to enjoy recounting the whole chain of events to her," said Haig with a broad smile. "She felt so helpless when she returned from Moscow."

"She'll be happy to find out her efforts weren't wasted. I just wish she hadn't been hurt."

"One thing I was wondering about is whether the person who attacked Isabelle was the same guy who paid me a visit. A big Russian, with a gold tooth. I described him to your dad in Moscow and again here in Yerevan."

"One and the same. He's Stella's main henchman. He was sent here to scare you, but you won't be seeing him again anytime soon."

They went quiet for a while and sipped their wine.

"How do you think we can use this?" asked Haig.

"Well, as I said, it's a compliment to you and Korah. You've lost your windfall sales, but you have a great marketing story. If told correctly, it can create more curiosity about Korah than ever."

"By the way, you may not know this, but you just saved me from making a very costly investment decision. Betting on this being real, I was about to triple the Korah production capacity. I was going to plant 24,000

Sev Areni vines. Fortunately, it's not too late for me to revise the deal and reconfigure things. Now I'll divide the land between Areni, Voskehat and Syrah."

"I'm glad. You're right, I didn't know."

"But, Carla jan, I don't want to use it just to promote Korah. This is also an Armenian wine story. They could have used a Georgian wine to do the same thing. It has the same mystique, equally old history, etc., but they chose an Armenian wine."

Carla hadn't yet accepted Haig's invitation for Alma Wines to join the Food and Wine Society gala. That too was about promoting wines of Armenia.

"Let's use this to promote Armenian wines," he said. "We have to take Armenia to the global stage. Making one wine more famous is not effective. How can we use this to rouse curiosity in all Armenian wines? And in the country?"

"It happened to Korah," said Carla. "This is a Korah story. I'm not sure generalizing it would work. It's a specific case about a specific scam."

"It is, but the fact remains that the master fraudsters chose an Armenian wine to weave their web. 'Straight from the birthplace of wine,' they said. If they can say that about a fake wine so effectively, why can't we say it effectively for the real thing? Let's not waste this story on just Korah, Carla jan. Let's go all out."

"What do you have in mind?" she asked.

Haig took out a sheet of paper from his pocket and placed it in front of her on the table. It was the menu of the inaugural Wines of Armenia Harvest Dinner. She studied the menu, noted the two featured Alma wines, scrutinized the courses, and finally looked up and stared at him.

"Join me in this," he said. "Let's turn a new page. This could serve as a great stage to also mention the scam."

"Wines of Armenia was my idea," she said. "You're taking the credit for it."

"I don't want the credit for it, Carla jan. All I'm doing is launching the inaugural dinner. Join me. Let's share the credit. Let's be co-hosts. You'd give a speech, the first speech if you want. You give great speeches and presentations. Your passion for wine comes through in your every word. Let's introduce Armenian wines to the world. That's all that matters."

She was touched. But for Carla it wasn't just a matter of participating in the inaugural dinner. Joining Haig in the event would also require forgetting all past hurts, forgetting every insult that she had endured about her wines and grapes and every dismissive gesture that she had stomached. As far as she was concerned, Haig had not given her due recognition as an equal member of the wine producers in Armenia. She had felt an attitude from him marked by superiority, characteristic of the way in which some repatriated diaspora Armenians sometimes looked upon the local population, which she resented. She had to bury all that before she could join him.

"It's going to be a huge success," he said. "We already have almost 350 acceptances from all over the world. Everyone who's anyone in the wine business will be there from Europe, California, Latin America, Australia, New Zealand, Russia, and Armenia. Check that menu again, and if you have suggestions, we can fine-tune it."

"The menu is fine." Carla was at a loss for words beyond that. It looked like Haig had already secured the success of the event: guests, menu, logistics, program. Did he really need her?

"Yeah, the menu is great, isn't it? Van called it an orgy." He laughed. It was not the usual roaring, free-flowing, Haig Koleyan laugh. It sounded more like a grunt, like the kind of sound an agitated piglet would make but accompanied by Haig's laughing face.

There was a pause in the conversation. It was not as awkward a pause as it might have been because Carla needed it; she felt they were both combating the formidable current of their pride, and the pressure was mounting so fast that conversation could not possibly diffuse it. If anything, talking would have made it worse.

The pause helped. In their silence, she saw clearly that there could be only one meaningful outcome. It was now a matter of getting there.

His phone buzzed again. He glanced at it and this time picked it up.

"Well, well," he said with a broad smile. "Speaking of the devil! Guess who just accepted. Gerard Boudot, owner of Domaine Etienne Sauzet. He makes this superb Puligny Montrachet we're drinking. He's coming with one of his winemakers."

Carla watched him but said nothing.

"Another wine celebrity who's coming is Henry Cobb. He's flying in the evening of the Gala and leaving early the next morning. 'I wouldn't miss it for the world,' he told me."

Carla's phone rang. "Sorry," she said. "I need to take this. It's Magnolia." Haig watched her chat with her daughter and filled their glasses.

"Carla jan, it makes no sense for you, or for me, or for Armenia, to have Alma Wines be absent from this gala," he said when Carla put the phone down. "Let me ask you again, come and share the stage with me. Let's do this together."

Carla had come to the same conclusion, for her hand came up and was extended across the table toward Haig. For a moment, all he looked at was the extended hand, beautiful, with slender fingers, dark maroon, almost brown, fingernails, sturdy knuckles that conjured strong character and power; a hand that could work miracles and that could at once provide comfort or cause pain. His eyes moved from the fingertips to Carla's smiling face, and his hand grabbed the sturdy knuckles, and in total silence a thousand words were exchanged and the deal was sealed.

A few days later Haig told about his meeting with Carla to Dorian.

"Before we met, I had a clear script in my mind," he told him. "I was going to tell her, this is happening and will be a huge success, with or without you. I was not ready to share the stage with her, or make her co-host, or ask her nicely to participate. Your decision, I was going to say. If you think it would be good for Alma Wines and for the image of Armenian wines, come. If not, don't. But then she tells me this incredible story about the scam in Moscow. She gives me a blow-by-blow account from Isabelle's first meeting with Petyan to uncovering the scam. She even stresses how the whole thing is a compliment to me and to Korah. She just hands me the entire scoop without any expectations. And, to boot, her info helped me avoid a costly mistake with the new vineyard. There was no way I could be curt with her after that."

Jack Hakobian flew back to Moscow with a knot in his stomach. Seeing Carla had reawakened his infatuation with her and, at the same time, convinced him that he should forget about her for good. This was possibly the worst combination. How could he accept an inevitability so contradictory to his longings? Carla had been sweeter and more hospitable than he had dared to expect. But there was no question that the sweetness was directed to a guest, a special guest perhaps with an important message, but a guest nonetheless. Not even for a brief moment had she given him the impression of a personal connection beyond the perfect hostess. And of course David was there, front and center, toward whom all her affections gravitated. He knew that he would never return to Armenia, at least not to see Carla. He had come, seen, and confirmed, and now it was time for the final farewell.

Had Jack known Van Dorian, he would have learned about the exact nature of his affliction. Dorian would even have told him that his condition had a name. "*Pikit Mata*," he would have said, without any hesitation. "Philippines. Literally, it means eyes closed," he would have explained patiently but dispassionately. "What it really refers to is the need to accept that something against your yearnings must be done. There is no way to reconcile the two with both eyes open, and hence the reference to eyes closed."

And Dorian would certainly have gone further and, not knowing that Jack did not drink, recommended at least three wines for *Pikit Mata*. If you're into Armenian wines, he would have said, I recommend the 2012 VanDor Areni-Syrah reserve. If you prefer California wines, I recommend a wine that I was recently introduced to called Starry Night. If you're into French wines, it would be a St. Estephe, preferably a 2011 or 2012 vintage. Any one of the three will help you cope with the *Pikit Mata* syndrome.

But Jack did not know Van Dorian. As he boarded the plane, he had no idea that there were people who would understand the pain he was feeling, let alone give it a name. He settled in his seat with the knot throbbing in his stomach and a bursting restlessness in his chest, thinking he was the only man on earth to ever experience these emotions.

Lalvari, Glglan, an indigenous Armenian variety common in Tavush Province. The name derives from Lalvar Mountain. The bunches are large, dense and conical, sometimes with wings on both sides. The berry is large and ovate. In the shade, the berries are greenish, under the sun a light amber color. The skin is of medium thickness with small dark spots, covered by bloom, the flesh is soft and juicy, the juice is colorless. Ripe berries have low sweetness and high acidity. Lalvari is used to make sparkling wines and light table wines, well-balanced and tart.

CHAPTER EIGHTEEN

A week after their meeting, Carla called Haig again. "I have something to show you," she said. She sounded like she was trying to suppress her excitement. "I'm at Alma until around six but can meet in Yerevan around seven if you're free."

"Sure," said Haig, curious. "Do you want to meet at my winery? I'd like your opinion on some of the new wines in the making."

Carla had not been to Haig's winery before. It was a bit out of the way, at the edge of town, but she found it without much difficulty. When she appeared at the entrance, Haig was tasting his pre-bubbly brew.

"Hey Carla," he beamed when he saw her. "You have to try this."

Carla walked in, unable to refuse the offer to taste. Armen filled her a tasting glass from a small spigot at the bottom of the stainless-steel tank marked *"Kole Brut Extreme."* It was a greyish-yellow opaque liquid, still some ways to go to become sparkling wine. When she tasted it, her eyes lit up.

"You have a winner here," she said taking another sip.

"Isn't it? It beats last year's vintage lying down."

"I couldn't detect any strong aroma even though it has a refreshing, clean scent. It's very dry and yet subtle overtones of fruit lurk in the finish. Definitely a winner."

"This deserves the name *Brut Extreme*," chimed in Armen.

"Can we sit somewhere for a minute?" asked Carla. "I do have something to show you."

Haig wanted to have her taste a few other wines but was curious to find out what she had. They moved to his study. Carla removed an old, black and white photograph from her purse and placed it on the coffee table. It was medium-sized, approximately 6x9 inches, had a quarter inch white margin around its edge, faded and cracked in some corners. At the bottom-right corner, inside the white margin, "1901" was handwritten by what appeared to be a fountain pen, the ink possibly originally a dark blue but discolored into a lighter, greyish blue.

"Do you recognize anyone here?" asked Carla, trying her best to suppress an ecstatic chuckle.

The photo was taken outdoors, in front of an orchard or a vineyard—the background was too fuzzy and out of focus to tell. There were two rows of people pictured. First row, seated on chairs with wooden frames, were three men, in vested suits, white shirts and dark ties, legs crossed in the same direction, right leg over the left, all wearing the Ottoman fez, and boasting well-groomed mustaches. Leaning against the knee of the man seated on the left, staring into the camera with unusually intense and stern eyes for his age, was a young boy, no more than four or five years old. In the second row, standing behind the men, were three women. The first from the left had her right hand on the shoulder of the man sitting in front of her. The one in the middle was holding a toddler in her arms. All three had headscarves. No one was smiling.

Haig stared at the photo for several minutes. He looked at each face staring back at him, but his gaze kept returning to the little boy. He finally looked up to Carla. Her eyes were shining with excitement.

"Check the back," she said barely able to sit still.

Haig flipped the photo. There were two lines of names, also handwritten in fountain pen, in elegant, cursive handwriting that only the old generation—Haig's father's and grandfather's—had.

First Row, L to R: Standing, Vanés Koleyan. Seated: Hagop Koleyan, Sarkis Almayan, Garabed Almayan

Second Row, L to R: Arpi, Shushan (with Sarkis), Makruhi

His heart now racing, Haig flipped back to the photo. He knew his grandfather's name was Vanés, born in 1896. If this picture was taken in 1901, he was five years old. Hagop then must be his great grandfather, and Arpi his great grandmother.

"That intense little boy is my grandpa," he mumbled. "The one who came to Armenia to die but wasn't allowed to."

"And the baby in the arms of that lady is my grandpa, Sarkis, about nine months old, according to my father. This tough-looking gentleman here is my great grandfather," she said pointing at the man seated in the middle, "and this old man," she added laughing, "with the bushiest mustache of all, is my great great grandfather, Sarkis Almayan."

"Our folks knew each other," mumbled Haig, more to himself than to her, looking dazed and a bit stupefied.

"Oh, they more than knew each other. Are you ready for this? They had vineyards and made wine together. They were close friends and partners. The Almayans were from a village called Shar Keshla. I had once seen it written as Sarkisla somewhere, and always thought it had something to do with Sarkis, my grandfather's name. But that's not the real pronunciation. The Koleyans were from Gemerek, just twenty miles south-west. They also had apricot orchards."

Haig stared at her.

"It gets better," said Carla. "Apparently Shar Keshla had a fanatic nationalist Turkish population base, with only around 300 Armenian families, who lived in miserable conditions as second class citizens. Its Armenian schools were also dismal. Gemerek, on the other hand, was a town with a majority Armenian population, with much better schools. Now get this—she said barely able to sit still—in 1910, when my grandfather Sarkis was around nine years old, they put him in a school in Gemerek, and he lived in your great grandfather's house, and shared a room with your grandfather, who was around fourteen. Haig, we're talking about our grandfathers, whom we've never met, sharing a room for a whole year in 1910. Of course, only five years later, their entire world collapsed and disappeared." Carla's voice had turned brittle.

"When did you find out all this?" Haig couldn't get his eyes off the photograph.

"Yesterday. My dad has a large box of old family memorabilia, which he hadn't opened in twenty-five years. I told him about our talk last week with Van about Sepastia, and how you had said that we've lost too much history. He dug through the box. He knew that his ancestors were into wine, but he was not prepared for what he found. Copies of old invoices and receipts, and books full of detailed numbers about harvests and volumes of wine produced. Unfortunately, the invoices are in Ottoman Turkish. They don't appear to have any brand names for the wines—at least none was found in my dad's box. Nor a description of the grapes. But the volumes were substantial—some years around 75,000 liters, or 100,000 of today's bottles. There was also a letter from Hagop Koleyan, your great grandfather, to Garabed Almayan, my great grandfather, telling him how well little Sarkis, my grandfather, had adjusted and was doing great in school."

Haig sat there, stunned, lost for words. Memories of his father weeping while telling him his grandfather's story created a storm in his brain. He had never seen a photo of his grandfather and had always wondered what he might have looked like.

"So you see, Haig, we're not as 'Russian' as you may have thought," said Carla gently, almost in a whisper. "Fate somehow threw my grandfather in Moscow, yours in Lebanon. But that's just the tip of the story of the two families. Everything before that tip is shared history."

Haig's eyes were wet. The fate of that little boy, his grandfather, had haunted him ever since he had first heard the story. He kept staring at his curly, unruly, thick hair, his defiant gaze into the camera, his proud posture against his father's knee. He wiped his eyes with the back of his hand.

"May I make a copy of this photo?"

"Absolutely."

"What a twist of fate that we end up here," he said at last, slowly coming out of his reverie. "And how fitting." Then, as his signature broad smile returned and reclaimed its dominion over his face, he stood up and said:

"What do you say we go dedicate some of the new wines to the memory of Sarkis and Vanés?"

Boyakhani, an indigenous Armenian variety preserved in the ancient vineyards of Vayots Dzor. The bunches are large, dense and cylindrical. The berry is medium round and black. The skin is of medium thickness, covered by a dense layer of bloom. The flesh is juicy, the juice is colored scarlet. Fully ripe berries have moderate sweetness and high acidity. Boyakhani is used to make dark red, tannic table wines.

CHAPTER NINETEEN

Haig arranged for the vast atrium-lobby of the Abovian Hotel to be turned into a banquette hall. The furnishings, comprised of over twenty different cozy sitting sections with soft leather couches and armchairs, were replaced with thirty-six round tables each with an elaborate floral arrangement and white table cloth, with white, upholstered skirted parson's chairs.

The twelve different wine glasses needed to serve the wines on the menu wouldn't fit at each place setting. There wasn't room for the necessary cutlery for the various courses either. So he decided to have two wine glasses at a time, to be changed as quickly as possible by the forty-five waiters and waitresses working that night. The cutlery would be refreshed as each plated course was served. A podium had been set up at one corner. The hotel's two kitchens and staff were commandeered for the evening, and the two restaurants had closed their doors that night with a '*Private Event*' sign.

Kole bubbly would be served as the guests walked in and would continue while the appetizer of duo caviar was served at the table. After that, appropriate wine glasses would be set on the table for the two wines that accompanied each course.

In her dark maroon evening gown, curled, cascading hair, and dazzling diamond earrings, Carla Almayan was beyond glamorous. She was radiant, warm, cheerful, and absolutely stunning as she greeted the incoming guests. Most couldn't keep their eyes off her and turned to take another look long after she had passed on to welcome the next guest. Next to her, Haig felt under dressed in a black suit, white shirt, and black tie, and had only his trademark beaming smile to charm the guests. Of course, he did not mind. He was glad that Carla had gone all the way to look smashing that night. That was not only a good image for the wines of Armenia, but also the right one.

It took almost an hour for all the guests to walk in, be greeted, and finally take their seats. Groups of ten were assigned to a table, but the seating arrangement at each table was left free for the occupants to decide. It had taken Haig, Carla and Isabelle three late nights to reach the initial groupings, and even then they kept revising the composition of the groups until the last hour. At events like this, each table would assume a life of its own, and its ten occupants would create their own social microclimate. It was critical to get the chemistry and dynamics right for optimal social interaction.

Kole bubbly had flowed freely, and there already was a buzz in the hall when everyone was finally seated, and Haig made his way to the podium.

"Dear friends, on behalf of my cohost, Carla Almayan and myself, I'd like to welcome you again to the inaugural Wines of Armenia Harvest Dinner, hosted by the Food and Wine Society of Yerevan." He nodded as the room applauded. "That's a mouthful. We have to find a shorter way to say all that."

There were chuckles around the room, which he surveyed with satisfaction.

"They say you cannot really know a country until you taste its food and drink its wine," he continued. "As you can see from the menus on your table, we'll do our best to give you a flavor of Armenia tonight, both through our food and our wine. But, as the great French writer Alexander Dumas said two centuries ago, 'wine is the intellectual part of the meal.' And that's the part that we'll focus on. The food, though an important part of the culture here, will be an accessory tonight, playing a supporting role.

"Carla and I will take turns introducing each course and the wines that go with it. But before we start, you'll have to endure a few short words from each of us. As a reward, the Kole Brute Extreme will continue to flow while we speak. Let me add that the Kole Brute Extreme is produced from grapes grown in the village of Khachik in Vayots Dzor at 1,750 meters above sea level, the highest altitude ever attempted for producing wine grapes. That's just one uniquely Armenian feature that we intend to introduce to you tonight.

"But I'm afraid it will no longer be served once Carla and I finish our remarks and we move on to the menu. So I won't be surprised if some of you wished we talked longer."

Laughter filled the hall.

"Before I hand the mic to Carla, I'd like to recount a story that came to light about Armenian wines in recent months. Perhaps you've heard of the incredible wine scam that went down in Moscow for well over a year before it was discovered. A group of well-organized fraudsters managed to take a good Armenian wine, mix it with some bulk wines from Areni, and sell it to experienced, but apparently impressionable wine collectors, for $2,500 a bottle. The buyers smelled it and tasted it and were convinced that it was worth that price. Granted, that was a con job. But the swindlers were smart. They knew they could not convince experienced collectors with just any wine. They, none of whom were Armenian by the way, chose an Armenian wine and got away with their fraud not just once or twice, but several times for about a year-and-a-half before they were caught. This says a lot about the quality of the wines we're producing in Armenia today. One last point about that incident: while none of the fraudsters were Armenian, the man who eventually exposed them was. If he had not entered the scene, the scam would have continued undetected for many more years. Isn't that something?"

Haig had wanted to announce that the man was none other than Aram Almayan, but Carla asked him not to. "He's a very private man," she said. "The last thing he'd want is to attract that type of attention."

"Without further ado," continued Haig, "I pass the podium to Carla, my amazing cohost."

As Carla walked to the podium, the hall burst into applause. At some tables, people were on their feet giving her a standing ovation. "Go Carla!" calls were heard throughout the hall.

Haig was waiting for her at the podium, applauding. She went straight to him and gave him a peck on the cheek, at which the entire hall burst into cheers. All of the Armenian guests and a few of the foreign ones knew of the feud between Haig and Carla, so that little peck carried a lot of weight. She had to wait several minutes for the commotion to subside.

"What Haig failed to mention," she began, "is that the wine that the fraudsters used as their base was in fact the Korah, from the Koleyan winery in Vayots Dzor. They were indeed smart—they chose one of the best Armenia has to offer."

The hall erupted in applause again, this time with 'way to go Haig' calls.

"I'm sure everyone here tonight has heard many quotes and anecdotes about wine. Celebrities like Sir Winston Churchill and Ernest Hemingway alone have left us enough wine wisdom to liven up many drunken nights. But one of my favorite quotes on wine is from a less known figure. Eduardo Galeano, a Uruguayan journalist and novelist, said: 'We are all mortal until the first kiss and the second glass of wine.' That's worth a moment's reflection. The first kiss is obvious," she said in such a seductive voice that almost everyone in the audience stirred and smiled. "But 'the second glass of wine'? That was clever on Galeano's part. He knew what he was talking about. He knew that when it comes to wine, the second glass is validation and confirmation of the first. The second glass is not testimony to quantity. No wine lover will reach for a second glass if the first has not already seduced them. The second glass is testimony to how the first glass made us feel. And it is that quality that liberates us and pushes our mortality aside."

The audience applauded. Haig now was ecstatic. He had the audience where he wanted it—just a little drunk, elated, jovial, receptive.

"Thank you. But I'm afraid I'll disappoint all those who've thought I'm too set in my ways to change my mind about anything," continued Carla when the applause subsided, unleashing another round of cheers and laughter in the crowded room. The vast majority of the guests knew Carla and considered her reputation as a strong, often stubborn woman to be justified.

"I have recently changed my mind about something important," she continued when the laughter died down. The room went quiet in anticipation. "I've changed my mind about something that I've repeatedly talked about and believed in for years. Many of you have been to Alma Wines and have heard me talk about the three stages of building a winery: man against nature; man against man; and man against the market. I've explained our experience of each phase to every visitor to Alma Wines. But I've now come to realize that, in all those years, I've looked at the process in the wrong way. The process is the exact opposite. It is: man *with* nature, man *with* man, and man *with* the market.

"As I reflect over the past several years, I realize that we have in fact worked with, not against, nature to build our vineyard; we've worked with man to build our winery; now we're working with the market to get our wines to your tables." Carla paused and looked toward Haig. "And what's even more thrilling," she added while still looking at him, "I'm proud to say that we're all working together toward the same goal."

The hall erupted again—the significance of the last statement was not missed. The applause lasted for several minutes. Haig walked up to the podium and gave Carla a hug, at which point everyone was on their feet again. Haig took the microphone and tried to stop the commotion.

"I know you're all looking forward to dinner," he announced. "In fact, as my dear friend Van Dorian pointed out, what we propose to offer you tonight is not a dinner, but an orgy of the senses."

The room gradually started to quiet down, but it still was too noisy for Haig to make his remarks effectively.

Regardless, he continued: "When you received our invitation, some of you asked me 'What's the occasion?'" He paused to give the audience another chance to settle down. "Normally, I don't need occasions to invite friends to a dinner. Frankly, I don't even like occasions because they dictate a specific style, which I find difficult to conform to. But, ladies and gentlemen, tonight is different. Indeed, tonight, we happen to have an occasion. And I happen to accept the style that it dictates because it is about our senses and about our history."

Now the hall was finally quiet.

"Legend has it," continued Haig, "that Noah's Ark landed on Mount Ararat. When he finally came out to dry land, he began to farm, planted a vineyard, drank the wine, and got so drunk that he was found naked in his tent. Now, you have to admit, that must have been some real badass wine to knock Noah over like that."

Laughter rose through the hall again.

"After all," Haig continued, "he was the one virtuous man God decided to save from the flood, and, with him, also save the entire animal population of earth. The grapes he grew right around here, around the Ararat plateau and in Western Armenia, must have been exceptional. The wine he made must have been even more exceptional because someone like Noah couldn't have gotten that drunk by just one sip or one cup. As Carla so aptly explained, the first cup must have been the seduction. My guess is that the wine was so good that one sip led to another, one cup led to another, one jug led to another, until the giant Noah collapsed in his tent.

"And we all know the syndrome. We know what makes us reach for that second glass, then that second bottle. We don't do that with a mediocre wine. We've all been where Noah was, who knows exactly how many millennia ago? So, one has to ask, what happened to Noah's vines?

"When I first came to Armenia, I couldn't find them; there wasn't a single locally produced wine that any of you would be able to drink."

The audience laughed.

"At some point from the time Noah planted his vines, something went wrong, and the vines went dormant, which brings me to the special occasion for the dinner tonight.

"Ladies and gentlemen, Carla and I and the thirty-eight other vintners of Armenia are here to announce that we're waking Noah's vines. We're breathing new life into a brilliant 8,000-year-old tradition that has gone dormant for too long. Let's raise our glasses to the incredible journey we've embarked on," he raised his glass to the audience at large. "Here's to the amazing mission that we've accepted. Here's to waking Noah's vines!"

EPILOGUE

Van Dorian remembered what Haig had said four years earlier—that the revolution wouldn't come crawling; it would erupt. And indeed, it erupted. It took the capital city, then the country and then the whole nation scattered all over the world by surprise. It was as radical as revolutions get, and as uncompromising on principles and in its refusal to accept compromises with the ruling system it sought to topple. And yet, it was peaceful. Several hundreds of thousands of people, including a huge contingency of young students who had not known the Soviet system, took to the streets in the largest and most incapacitating act of peaceful civil disobedience Armenia had ever known.

Dorian watched, and participated, in the events in total bafflement. "Nothing went wrong," he kept repeating to anyone who'd ask, and often to those who did not bother to ask. "A thousand things could have gone wrong but didn't. At one point, there were more than 400,000 people in the streets, all emotionally charged, and no one did anything rash. Not a single window was broken, not a single store looted, not a single drop of blood spilt. The leader of the movement could have made many mistakes. He did not. The ruling elite could have made mistakes, it did not. The newly elected Prime Minister just resigned when he could have ordered the police to open fire on the demonstrators and disperse them. It wouldn't have been the first time neither in Armenia nor in other countries of the former Soviet Union. The police could have made all types of mistakes, they did not. This was the antithesis of Murphy's Law."

At the end, an entrenched, corrupt and all-powerful ruling elite, modeled along the lines of the political monopoly of the Communist Party that had ruled Armenia not too long ago, was ousted in just a matter of days. Total strangers hugged and kissed each other in the streets. An incredibly festive mood prevailed throughout, with music and dancing in the streets and food being distributed by euphoric supporters of the movement. Even tourists joined the action, some thinking they were in some kind of national carnival that tourist guidebooks had failed to mention, and others in solidarity with the people. The euphoria was so contagious that it found resonance all over the world, wherever there were Armenians watching the events. The shock of seeing a hitherto indestructible ruling system shattered, by nothing other than a unified and unflinching popular will, was transformative.

The revolutionary zeal demanded not just for the old elite to go, but also for the widespread corruption in all aspects of life to go with it; monopolies had to go too and, for once, the average citizen had no desire to emulate them; bribes had to go, whether one was trying to get a birth certificate for a newborn child or clear an imported item from customs, and, again, people wished for an end of the corrupt system, instead of aspiring to be part of it as they had done before the revolution. The hearts and minds of the average citizens were being miraculously transformed.

"There's a clear explanation for all this," said Dorian. He had expanded The Realm by adding a new Asian kitchen and a new dining hall adjacent to the old one. His already formidable wine cellar now boasted a wider variety of new Armenian wines. He and Haig were trying the shrimp spring rolls, a new addition to the menu from the Asian kitchen.

"Van, there cannot be one clear explanation for something of this scale," challenged Haig.

"Even those who were practicing and benefiting from the ills of the old system were tired of it," continued Dorian, without bothering to counter him. "They practiced it out of necessity. It was like joining the Communist party in the old days out of necessity, in order to survive. But as soon as the system collapsed, the pent-up anger rose, and the repulsion was real. Now there is no turning back."

In the past four years, several new wineries had come on line with new releases, and the established wineries, with more mature vines, had started to produce wines that attracted the attention and approval of even the most discriminating tastes in Europe and the U.S. Isabelle's winemaking career at VanDor had taken off. In the fall, they expected to celebrate the first harvest from the new sixteen-hectare vineyard which they had exclusively devoted to Primitivo three years earlier. That would unleash a whole new line of Areni-Primitivo blends, as envisioned in Isabelle's dream and inspired by a wine from a small winery in Fair Play, California.

Dorian was not satisfied that Armenian winemakers and the average Armenian citizen had made much progress in claiming their legitimate historic legacy as the standard bearers of the global wine discourse. Many more years of education and patient coaching would be required to bring that vision to fruition.

But he was gratified with one important development—the hitherto misdirected emotion of disillusionment with justice had finally found its proper definition in peoples' hearts, and Dorian had found a wine to pair with it. Along with the revolution, the first line of the Koleyan-Cobb wines, an Areni reserve, was released, and was an instant hit. It won several international awards and the first 50,000 bottles were sold out within a few weeks. Dorian deemed it worthy of being paired with disillusionment with social justice, which the revolution had managed to articulate correctly. Finally, the wine and the emotion had found each other. And that was certainly worth raising a glass to.

Main Characters

Haig Koleyan. A veteran vintner who, having spent decades making and trading in wine in Lebanon and Italy, moves to Armenia and pioneers the rebirth of the country's wine industry.

Van Dorian. A successful CPA from Los Angeles, who sells everything and moves to Armenia to start a vineyard and winery and opens one of the very first wine bar/restaurants in Yerevan, to test his theories of the link between wine and human emotions.

Henry Cobb. Owner of a major winery in Sonoma, who starts a joint venture with Haig Koleyan in Vayots Dzor, Armenia.

Isabelle Karayan. An aspiring wine maker, who works for several wineries in Armenia, and unknowingly gets involved in an unfolding crime.

Sandro Kashvili. Renowned professor of wine at Enotria wine school in Moscow.

Carla Almayan. The CEO of one of the new wineries in Armenia and a believer in reviving the age-old Armenian wine industry.

Sergei Petyan. Co-founder and head of Ludwig, the largest wine and spirits merchant in Russia.

Stella Fedorov. Wife of the murdered co-founder of Ludwig (Vladimir Fedorov).

Dmitri Markov. One of Stella Fedorov's lawyers.

Armen. Haig Koleyan's wine maker.

Jack Hakobyan. A manager at Ludwig who used to work for Aram Almayan and who is secretly in love with Carla Almayan.
Vitaly. Jack Hakobyan's assistant.

Gaspar Melkonian. Renowned archeologist in Armenia responsible for many archeological discoveries.

Lui Li. A Chinese Ludwig employee who gets embroiled in a wine scam in Moscow.

Joe Connors. US Ambassador in Armenia.

Valerie Lefebvre. The master con artists in a wine scam in Moscow.

Domonique Martin. Seductive mastermind behind the wine scam in Moscow.

Aram Almayan. Carla's father, and an influential Russian Armenian who builds the Alma winery.

Feodor Shulgin. Officer in the criminal investigations division of Moscow police department.

ACKNOWLEDGMENTS

Researching this book was by far the most pleasant homework I've ever done. And my decision to personally test the claims made in the book about various wines and their interaction with human emotions was not only the easiest decision to carry out, but also immensely gratifying. But I couldn't have completed this task without the guidance and coaching of several individuals. I am particularly indebted to Vahe Keushgerian, Victoria Aslanian, Paul Hobbs and Varuzhan Mouradian for opening their wineries and showing me how it all works. The knowledge and experience that resides with these individuals about wine is astounding. I cannot thank them enough for sharing their wisdom and their stories.

Prof. Richard Hovannisian guided me in my research on the two villages in Sepastia, Gemerek and Shar Keshla. Boris Gasparian, one of the busiest archeologists around, went out of his way to educate me on the ancient world of wine. Irina Ghaplanian and Lilia Khachatrian made invaluable contributions to my understanding of wine facts and history. Viken Yacubian helped enrich the plot with unique stories. Special thanks are due to my editor, Tanya Egan Gibson, for salvaging an earlier draft of this manuscript from many violations of the craft of writing. I also want to express my admiration for Bianca Bosker, whose book, *Cork Dork*, provides one of the most thorough and definitive expositions I've read about the intricate relationship between the human senses of smell and taste and wine.

Finally, I am grateful as always to my regular early readers: Jane, Silva, Nora, Patrick, Shahan, Armine, Raffi and Varant. They dutifully put up with the largest amount of errors and inconsistencies. I only hope that the theme of this book inspired them to pop as many corks as I did while writing it, thus compensating for the shortcomings in the narrative.